On Equal Ground

Elizabeth Adams

DEDICATION

For my husband.
I love you more than I can say.

On Equal Ground

ON EQUAL GROUND
BY ELIZABETH ADAMS

On Equal Ground

PROLOGUE

Winter, 1807

"What did you think of Miss Grange?"

"She was as expected."

"And what does that mean?"

"It means she was terribly dull, if I may say so of a lady."

"You may. What of Mrs. Carteret?"

"Calculating eyes."

"Miss Thornton?"

"Too stupid by half."

"Lady Leticia Worthington?"

"Who?"

Alfred sighed and threw his hands up. "Really, Robert, it wouldn't hurt you to be moderately helpful."

"Ah, helpful, what an interesting word. And what exactly am I supposed to be helping with, cousin?" Robert leaned back in his chair and sipped his brandy slowly.

"You know what! You need a wife!"

"I've had a wife. Two, as a matter of fact. I see no need for another."

Alfred looked stricken. "What are you saying?"

"I'm saying I will not marry to please the family. Not again."

"Not marry!" he spluttered. "You need an heir!"

"I have twice married ladies of considerable rank and fortune. I have had three heirs, and they have joined their mothers in the churchyard. No, I have no desire to do it all again."

"Who will inherit if you do not have a child?"

"My sister's son may inherit if it comes to that. He's a fine boy."

"But, but..." his cousin trailed off.

"I am sorry to disappoint you, but I have decided to live life on my own terms. I have been a slave to duty these thirty years and now my life will finally be my own."

His cousin looked at him with suspicion. "You're not going to marry a milkmaid, are you?"

He laughed. "You do say the most ridiculous things! Where would I even meet a milkmaid?" He chuckled again. "At the barn, I suppose," he added thoughtfully.

Alfred looked at him seriously after the laughter died down.

"Just promise me you won't do anything *too* rash," he said.

"Define rash," answered Robert. At Alfred's exasperated expression, he had mercy on his cousin. "I won't do anything disastrous, you have my word."

"No milkmaids?"

"No milkmaids."

CHAPTER 1

February 1809

The Gardiners' carriage was moving nicely along the road when it suddenly began to slow. Mr. Gardiner looked out the window at the grey landscape covered in fog and spitting rain and tapped his cane on the roof.

He spoke quietly to the footman, then turned to the ladies inside the now still carriage.

"Excuse me, my dears, there's another carriage up ahead that seems to have had an accident. I'll just see if they need any help."

After telling him to be careful, his wife and niece watched out the window as he hurried over to a carriage set at a precarious angle on the side of the road.

"May I be of any assistance?" Mr. Gardiner called to the men working to unload the carriage.

A well-dressed man a little older than himself stood from where he had been crouched next to the carriage, assessing the damage.

"Good day, sir. As you can see, we've run into some trouble," he said with good humor. "It appears the axle is broken."

"Oh! Could I offer you a seat in my carriage into the next town? It is about five miles on," Gardiner offered genially.

The man looked to his driver who had been unhitching the horses, apparently planning to ride one of them into the nearest town for assistance. Gardiner could see the man weighing the options and deciding between riding with strangers for half an hour and then being in the comfort of an inn, or staying on the side of the road in the cold and damp and waiting more than twice as long for his man to go to town, hire a carriage, bring it back, and load it.

"Thank you, sir, that would be most kind of you," said the stranger.

Mr. Gardiner nodded and introduced himself as they walked toward his carriage.

"Pleased to meet you, Mr. Gardiner. I am Robert Talbot."

Gardiner popped his head into the carriage and said to his wife, "The gentleman's carriage has broken an axle, and I've offered him a ride into the next town."

Mrs. Gardiner nodded. "Of course, as you should. Was anyone injured?" she asked as he climbed in and sat across from the two ladies.

Gardiner looked to the gentleman climbing in behind him.

"Thankfully not," Mr. Talbot said sincerely.

Gardiner quickly introduced him and then turned to the ladies. "This is my wife, Madeline, and my niece, Elizabeth Bennet of Longbourn in Hertfordshire."

"I am pleased to meet you, ladies, and much obliged for the assistance. You have saved me from a wet afternoon on the side of the road." He smiled and the ladies smiled back charmingly.

"Where are you headed, sir?" asked Gardiner.

"London. And you?"

"The same. We've been on a short visit to Oxford and now our niece will spend the season with us in town."

Mr. Talbot looked toward Elizabeth and smiled kindly. "Is it your first season, Miss Bennet?"

"No, sir, not completely. But it will be my first proper London season," Elizabeth replied.

"I wish you luck on the battlefield," he said seriously.

Elizabeth couldn't help but laugh and respond, "Surely it isn't so dreadful, sir?"

"I will let you find that out on your own," he said with a twinkle in his eye. "Just remember, their barks are worse than their bites. Most of the time."

Elizabeth let out a bubbling laugh and the remainder of the drive was filled with good conversation and easy laughter.

When they arrived at the coaching inn, the ladies settled into a sitting room to have tea while the men settled business. Talbot's driver was seeing to the axle and his man was securing another carriage. The only trouble was that there were no carriages to be had. The proprietor apologized profusely and said one was due to be returned late that evening, but in the meantime, nothing but a wagon could be procured.

Mr. Gardiner offered to convey Mr. Talbot the remainder of the way to town, and after some polite refusing and insisting, it was decided that Mr. Talbot would travel with the Gardiners into London while his man took the wagon to the damaged carriage and collected the luggage and footmen. As the driver saw to the repairs, an express was sent to Talbot's house in Town explaining what happened and asking that another carriage collect him at the Gardiners' residence. Gardiner tried to insist that they could deliver him safely to his home, but Talbot would hear none of it. He said he had inconvenienced them enough and he wouldn't dream of forcing the ladies to spend another hour in the carriage when they could be resting comfortably.

By the time the carriage arrived at the Gardiner home on Gracechurch Street, no one could remember having had a more pleasant journey or with better conversation. The Gardiners and their niece found Mr. Talbot to be pleasant, conversant on a wide variety of topics, unfailingly polite but not so much as to be dull, and the possessor of a

11

wonderful sense of humor that delighted in teasing and being teased.

Mr. Talbot thought the Gardiners were genteel and uncommonly kind—helping a complete stranger as he was—and excellent company besides. Mrs. Gardiner was gentle and intelligent, and he thought he saw wisdom in her grey eyes. Mr. Gardiner was funny, sensible, and discreet—not prying into others' business or asking personal questions as many were wont to do.

Their niece, the young Miss Bennet, he found intriguing. At first he had not paid her much attention. He'd thought she was a child, tucked under rugs in the corner as she was, until she spoke and he could hear the maturity in her voice. She had been a good conversationalist, but he hadn't thought beyond that.

Once at the inn, she'd stood stretching her back outside the carriage and he realized he'd made a grievous error. She was not a young girl thrust into society straight from the school room. She was a lovely young lady, fresh-faced with a fully-formed figure. He felt a bit of a dunce for not noticing her beauty before, but the carriage was dim and outside wasn't much better, so he hadn't really seen her. He wasn't ashamed to admit she was a pleasant inducement in his accepting the Gardiners' offer of conveyance.

His carriage was waiting on Gracechurch Street when they arrived, and he bid the family farewell cheerfully, once again thanking them for their assistance.

The next day, when Elizabeth entered the parlor with her five-year-old cousin Jenny, she was surprised to see a beautiful bouquet of flowers on the table.

"Aunt, wherever did those come from? Did Uncle send them? Is it a special occasion?" she asked eagerly. She walked over to the blooms to smell their exotic fragrance, entranced by the deep colors and the varieties she'd never seen before.

"No, they came from quite another source. Mr. Talbot sent them as thanks for assisting him yesterday. He must be a very kind man. His note was all politeness."

Elizabeth tore her gaze from the bouquet and looked to her aunt. "That was very generous of him. Shall you maintain the acquaintance?"

"I believe so. He also sent a parcel," she looked at Elizabeth shrewdly. "It contained two books. One for Edward and another for you."

"For me?"

"Yes. Apparently, Mr. Talbot remembered you mentioning it in the carriage yesterday and he thought you might like your own copy. It is a very fine edition."

She passed the book to her stunned niece who took it reverently, turning it over in her hands, caressing the fine leather casing and tracing her fingers over the gold embossed letters.

"Oh, Aunt, surely it was very expensive. Should I accept such a gift?" she asked tentatively.

"I believe in this instance it is acceptable. After all, he sent one to your uncle as well and flowers to me. I imagine he did not want to slight any one person, hence the gifts all around. You are free to enjoy your book, dear."

Elizabeth sighed in relief and hugged the book to her. "I'll just put this away upstairs."

Pursing her lips in thought, Mrs. Gardiner wrote out her thanks and an invitation and sent it on its way.

"What did you send, Mama?" asked Jenny.

"Just a little note, Jenny. Nothing exciting."

Jenny looked disappointed and went to play with her doll.

*Nothing exciting **yet**,* thought Mrs. Gardiner.

~

Two days later, Elizabeth and her aunt waited in the drawing room for Mr. Talbot, their dinner guest.

"Will it not be strange with only one guest?" asked Elizabeth.

"Not at all. Intimate perhaps, but that is all the better for getting to know someone. We do not know Mr. Talbot well enough to choose which of our friends would be good dinner companions," said Mrs. Gardiner.

"So you think you will become friends with him?" asked Elizabeth.

"Yes, I believe we will. After all, we are already well on the way." She smiled at her niece just as the maid opened the door and announced their visitor.

"Mr. Talbot, how nice to see you again," said Mrs. Gardiner.

"You as well, Mrs. Gardiner, Miss Bennet." He bowed to the ladies. "I am glad it is under better circumstances than our last meeting," he said with an easy grin. "I make a much better impression when I am dry."

Dinner was just as successful as the carriage ride had been. Conversation flowed easily, laughter was frequent, and everyone seemed well pleased with the company.

Afterward, the ladies left for the drawing room while the men enjoyed their port. Elizabeth was at the pianoforte playing a simple favorite of her aunt's when the gentlemen rejoined them.

"That is lovely, Miss Bennet," complimented Mr. Talbot.

"Thank you, sir. I'm afraid I do not practice as often as I should," she said with a contrite look in her aunt's direction.

"We are considering engaging a master while Elizabeth is in Town," added Mrs. Gardiner.

"If we can find someone patient enough," quipped Elizabeth.

The men chuckled and Mrs. Gardiner replied,
"You've a very good notion of fingering. It's finding a
master free to take you on that is difficult."

"Have you had trouble in that regard?" asked Talbot
curiously.

"I have made a few enquiries, and the instructor I
most wanted is not available, and those that are leave
much to be desired."

"I see," said Mr. Talbot. "Are you looking forward to
formal instruction, Miss Bennet?"

"Yes, I am. I realize you do not know me well enough
to know I am teasing more often than not, but I would
enjoy being more skilled at the instrument." She smiled
and he nodded cordially.

"My cousin engages a young man for her daughters. I
shall ask her the name of the fellow and if she
recommends him I'll pass the information along," he said
decisively.

Mrs. Gardiner and Elizabeth both thanked him
heartily and he was soon on his way.

"Well, that was an enjoyable evening," said Mr.
Gardiner after seeing their guest out.

"Yes, he is a very pleasant guest. Did you not think
so, Elizabeth?" asked Mrs. Gardiner.

"Yes, he has excellent conversation and a wonderful
sense of humor. I think Papa would like him."

"I imagine he would," said Mr. Gardiner thoughtfully.
"At the risk of upsetting such an agreeable evening, I must
give you some surprising information."

His wife and niece looked to him expectantly.

"Mr. Talbot is not who he appears to be," said Mr.
Gardiner.

"What?" cried Mrs. Gardiner. "What do you mean?"

"I mean," he said, walking toward them and dropping
a card on the small table between their chairs, "that he is
Robert Talbot, Earl of Asheland."

The ladies gasped and Elizabeth put her hand to her mouth.

"He asked me to tell you after he left, he didn't want to upset you," said Mr. Gardiner. "Apparently, when meeting strangers on the road, he does not reveal his true identity for fear of theft or worse."

"What would be worse?" asked Elizabeth. She tilted her head thoughtfully. "I suppose ransom."

"I imagine that would be an extreme case, but he is right to be cautious. One never knows who is behind a friendly smile," said Mr. Gardiner. "In any event, he is determined to maintain the acquaintance and wants us to know who he really is. I am inclined to accept the offer of friendship."

He looked to Mrs. Gardiner and she nodded. "Of course. He has been nothing but kind. It may be a little eccentric to keep the title to himself, but I can understand his reasons and he did tell us his name."

"I suppose it serves us right for not studying Debrett's," teased Elizabeth.

~

Two days later, a note arrived from their new friend listing the name of a pianoforte master and his willingness to meet Elizabeth on Tuesday and assess if she would make a good pupil. It also included an invitation to the opera Friday evening and dinner after at the Asheland townhouse.

Both were accepted with alacrity and Elizabeth and Mrs. Gardiner scrambled to put together dresses and gloves and slippers for the opera that would do the box of an earl justice. Naturally, an urgent trip to the dressmaker was in order.

By Tuesday, Elizabeth had had the first fitting for her new theatre gown, placed orders for five more gowns at her aunt's insistence (five!), and had practiced for hours in preparation for meeting the music master.

He arrived promptly and asked Elizabeth to play him something. She knew the piece he requested and thought she acquitted herself well, though his expression revealed nothing. Then he asked her if she sang at all and she told him she did, followed by another song. She wondered what he was thinking behind his thick blond brows and harsh expression, but he gave nothing away.

Finally, though the suspense was excruciating, he told her he would see her every Monday morning at precisely eleven o'clock, and that he expected her to practice diligently between her lessons. He would occasionally see her twice a week if she was in particular need of instruction.

Elizabeth thanked him and showed him to the door, feeling a bit like she had just been insulted, and shared the news with her aunt.

"We shall have to thank Lord Asheland for the recommendation," she said.

"Yes, though I may reserve my thanks until after the first fortnight of lessons," replied Elizabeth dryly.

~

The theatre was resplendent and Elizabeth had never looked forward to a show more. It would be her first time sitting in a private box and wearing such an expensive dress; she was especially excited to see the performance of which she had heard wonderful things.

Lord Asheland met them in front of the theatre and took Mrs. Gardiner's arm to lead them to his box. Elizabeth held her uncle's arm tightly, trying to contain her enthusiasm. He patted her hand and smiled at her kindly.

The box was large and their party small, so all four were able to sit across the front row. The ladies sat in the middle, Lord Asheland on Elizabeth's right and Mr. Gardiner on his wife's left. Elizabeth leaned forward in anticipation as the lights dimmed, scooting almost to the end of her seat. She ignored her uncle's amused chuckle.

The party had one libretto and Mr. and Mrs. Gardiner were using it at Lord Asheland's insistence. Unfortunately, Elizabeth found herself mildly confused in the middle of the second act.

She leaned slightly toward Lord Ashland and whispered, "Is she more angry at her brother or her lover? She appears to be yelling at both of them."

He leaned toward her and whispered back, "Her brother. Without her knowledge, he has promised her to Count Rossi."

Elizabeth gasped and glared at the stage. Lord Asheland hid his grin.

"Now she is telling him that she loves Basilio and will marry none but him. Her brother threatens to disown her."

Elizabeth shook her head and raised a hand to her mouth, moved by the swelling music and the beautiful voices on the stage, their costumes shimmering in the lights as their faces contorted in emotion.

Without prompting, Lord Asheland continued translating for her, whispering softly to her as she leaned into his side, so engrossed in the opera that his breath on her ear became a part of the story, the darkness and intimacy of the situation only heightening the drama on stage.

Her hair tickled his cheek and the light dancing off her eyes was enchanting. Suddenly, Robert Talbot, Sixth Earl of Asheland, thought he might be in a bit of trouble.

CHAPTER 2

"**I** thought we might host a small dinner for your birthday. What do you think, my dear?" asked Mrs. Gardiner one morning as the ladies sat in the sitting room.

Elizabeth looked up from her needle work and answered, "That sounds lovely. Who would we invite?"

"I had thought the Brigsbys, of course, and the Barings—I know you get on with their daughter. Would you also like the Hutton family? Their son is in town," she added slyly.

Elizabeth made a face. "No, thank you. Let's invite the Swansons instead."

Mrs. Gardiner laughed. "Understood. And Lord Asheland?"

"Of course! We couldn't possibly leave him out," said Elizabeth matter-of-factly as she went back to her sewing.

Mrs. Gardiner raised a brow but said nothing as she added another name to her list.

~

Eight weeks after her arrival in town, and her introduction to Lord Asheland, Elizabeth helped her aunt welcome a small gathering of friends to celebrate her birthday. She was wished well by all and received many kisses to her cheek.

The dinner was filled with laughter and good company. Each guest was dear to the Gardiners or Elizabeth, and each came prepared to please and be pleased. When it was all over and she had bid goodnight to the last guest, her uncle called her into his study.

"Have you had a pleasant birthday, my dear?" he asked her kindly.

"Yes, I have," she said before releasing a large yawn. "Though I am rather tired!"

He smiled. "I imagine you are. Before you go to bed, I want to speak with you about something. Lord Asheland left a gift for you."

He held out a small parcel to her and she took it curiously. "Why did he not give it to me himself?"

"He wanted to ask my permission before giving it to you. I believe it is quite valuable. And I don't think he's the kind of man who wants to be liked for the gifts he gives," said Mr. Gardiner.

She opened the package gingerly and removed a small carved box. She set aside the paper and lifted the lid before gasping aloud. "Oh! It is beautiful!"

She held up a small brooch covered in amethyst and opal stones in the design of a delicate flower.

"There should be a note there somewhere," said her uncle.

She found a piece of paper in the bottom of the box and read,

Miss Bennet,
I picked this up on my tour of the continent several years ago. I believe at the time I thought I would give it to my sister or some other female relation, but truly it was too beautiful to leave behind. When it came time to hand out gifts, it didn't suit my sister or any of my cousins. I think it has been waiting for you. Happy birthday.
Your friend,
R. Asheland

"Oh! How kind of him! And what a lovely gift. It is almost too nice to accept, but I don't want to injure him by refusing."

She looked at her uncle with a question in her eyes and he answered, "I believe it is all right to accept it. It is your birthday, and you did receive various gifts today, though of course none as valuable as this. He asked my permission first and has been a good friend to the family, so I think you may accept if you are comfortable doing so. But Elizabeth," he said, his voicing dropping seriously, "I must caution you about Lord Asheland."

"Caution me?" she asked in surprise.

"Perhaps that is too strong a word. Let us say 'discuss.' I think he may have tender feelings for you."

Elizabeth stiffened in surprise and her eyes widened.

"He has said nothing to me formally, but I have seen the way his eyes watch you, and I don't think he calls here twice a week to see my pretty face," he said with humor.

She laughed. "But uncle, he looks on me as a younger sister or a niece. He has compared me to his sister more than once."

"His sister was only five years his junior, and the comparisons I have heard have all been favorable. His gift is further evidence of his regard. I am not trying to alarm you, but in the event Lord Asheland makes his addresses to you, I want you to be prepared. You must decide if you want to live life beside a man so much older than yourself, though that is not so very unusual, and if you would like to live in his society."

"You really believe he may offer for me?" she asked.

"I do not know. I don't believe I am raising your hopes as I knew you to be ignorant of his feelings until now, but neither do I want him to feel humiliated if you are completely taken aback at his overture. If you cannot like him as a man, if you cannot imagine life as his wife, it would be kind to withdraw."

"Do you believe I have encouraged him?" asked Elizabeth in disbelief.

"No, I do not think you have. But you are a naturally vivacious lady and certain men find that very attractive. It would be a kindness to avoid him if he does have tender feelings you cannot reciprocate."

She looked down at the brooch still in her lap. "I see. You've given me much to think on."

~

Elizabeth went to bed with a troubled mind. She remembered the conversation she had had with Lord Asheland earlier that week when he had asked to join her on a walk with her eldest nephews. He had asked her if she would obtain her majority on her upcoming birthday and she had laughed and said that was a few years off; she would be eighteen this birthday.

Asheland had stared at her in shock for a full minute before spluttering his surprise, much to Elizabeth's amusement.

There was always laughter and easiness between them. That was one of the things she loved about spending time with him. While they shared a similar sense of humor, there were differences enough to provide the occasional surprise.

She supposed it was silly of her not to realize by now that asking to walk with her, several times, in fact, should have been a sign of his interest. But she had never thought of him in that way before.

She made herself stop fretting and think rationally. Was he really so much older than she? She wasn't sure of his exact age, but he seemed near her uncle's age or thereabouts. Her own father was eight years older than her mother, and her uncle was nearly ten years older than Aunt

Madeline. He had been building his business and not married until he was over thirty.

But twenty years was more than ten. *Twice as many*, she thought acerbically. With a man that much older than herself, she would most assuredly end up a widow, and possibly at a young age. Did she want to live her later years on her own? Of course, there was no guarantee that she wouldn't be widowed if she married a young man, or that she might not die and leave him alone.

Mr. Pratt, an elderly man in Meryton, had been married three times, and widowed three times. His most recent wife had been scandalously younger than himself, and yet she had been the one to die from a fever, not him.

Did she want to be like the young Mrs. Pratt? Gossiped about and laughed at for marrying an old man? Of course, Lord Asheland was hardly old! He was still quite attractive and his hair hadn't even begun to gray yet. It wouldn't appear she was walking with her grandfather! And there was the matter of his being an earl. It was a very advantageous match for her, everyone would say so. They would all ignore his age for the sake of his eligibility. But she did dread people saying she had married him for his money. After seeing his townhouse and riding in his carriage, she was sure his income was far above what she was accustomed to.

But she could never choose a husband on security alone. There must be something more between them. She was romantic enough to want respect, esteem, and affection in her marriage, but practical enough to realize that the love described in fairy tales was not easily attainable and may not even exist. Who fell in love with someone the moment they saw them? Who felt a burning passion on such a short acquaintance and how would it last throughout time?

She desired a marriage like her aunt and uncle's. They respected each other, clearly admired one another, each liked the other and enjoyed their company. They were good friends and she could tell by the soft look in her aunt's eyes when she gazed on Mr. Gardiner that the lady held him in affection. Likewise, his attraction was clear. Beyond that, she did not want to imagine, but theirs was a relationship she thought realistic to emulate.

Could she have that with Lord Asheland? *Silly girl! He isn't even courting you yet*, she thought. *No, he comes to Cheapside twice a week and accompanies you on walks with the children because he simply has nothing better to do*, she answered herself dryly.

She laughed at herself and rolled over fitfully. She liked him. She respected him. She enjoyed his company. If anything were to grow from there, she thought that a good basis for it.

~

A month passed and nothing was declared. Lord Asheland continued to call at least once a week, and he often invited them to dinner or to see an art exhibition or to take a walk in the park. It was clear Elizabeth was his main object. Or at least it was to her aunt and uncle. Elizabeth wasn't entirely sure, as the gentleman never made any advances and didn't appear to be flirting with her, though she was the first to admit she had little experience in that arena.

She wondered that her uncle was continuing to allow him to call without declaring himself, and this, above anything else, convinced her that he was only interested in friendship. She could not know that her uncle had questioned the earl on the subject of excess attention given to his niece and received every assurance that Asheland's intentions were honorable, and that he wished to take things slowly with Elizabeth in deference to her age and the years between them.

One day in mid-May, Elizabeth was walking in the park on the arm of Lord Asheland while her aunt sat on a bench nearby watching the children play with their nurse. Elizabeth had been laughing at some story he had told her about his cousin Alfred when she looked at him and saw something in his eyes that made her stop and blush, then look down with uncommon silence.

Asheland took this as encouragement and decided to speak. "Miss Bennet, might I share something with you?" he said quietly.

"Yes, of course," she answered, slightly unnerved. Was it her imagination or was he holding her arm closer than he usually did?

"I'm sure you've noticed my attention toward you these last weeks."

She looked down and gave a tiny nod.

"Do you consider me a friend, Miss Bennet?" he asked.

Her head shot up. "Of course!"

"Do you think me an old man?" he asked again.

She noticed a tiny twitch in his jaw and thought it a sign that he was uncomfortable. "No sir, I do not. My grandfather was an old man, and you do not resemble him in the slightest."

He laughed at her tease and patted her hand on his arm. "My dear, you are a wonder. If I may, I would like to share some of my history with you." He knew he was muddling this up something terrible, but she did make it hard to think clearly sometimes.

"I will listen to anything you have to say to me," she said with more calmness than she felt.

"Thank you. When I was five and twenty, I wed Lady Beatrice Alsop, the eldest daughter of Lord Langley. She was a typical woman of fashion; she shopped, hosted parties, and attended salons. She managed my homes well and less than two years after we were married, she bore me a son, Edmund."

Elizabeth was about to say that she had not known he had a son when she noticed his pinched lips and lowered brow.

"He was a good, sweet-natured boy. Beatrice and I were not particularly close—our marriage was little more than an arrangement by our parents—and we barely knew each other when we wed, but we were kind to each other and had a measure of friendship between us. We were always respectful of one another, which is more than many can say about their unions."

Elizabeth nodded and squeezed his arm where her hand rested on it.

He continued, "Shortly before Edmund's second birthday, he contracted a fever. Many in the household became ill, including the butler who had been with us since my infancy. In the end, Edmund and Beatrice both succumbed to the disease. I was away on business and was spared."

"I am so sorry, my lord. That must have been a difficult time," she said.

"Yes, it was." He tried to smile at her and continued walking around the small pond the children were playing near. They were on their second loop now and Mrs. Gardiner could be seen watching them from across the water.

"After two years of mourning, my family began to insist I marry again. The earldom needed an heir. I had a younger brother and several cousins, so I did not exactly agree with them, but I bowed to family duty and wed Sarah Wainwright, an old family friend. She was seven and twenty at the time and her family dearly wished her to marry. She had turned down numerous suitors and only agreed to marry me because she had known me since childhood."

26

Elizabeth wanted to ask if he had been happy with her, but thought it too intrusive a question.

"She was an intelligent woman and we got on well enough. We had two children together, Mary and Jenny." He did not tell her that his wife had had a strong aversion to men and that she had barely tolerated his person, making the begetting of children uncomfortable in the extreme. He had offered a cessation of the activity, but she wished for more children, so the awkwardness continued. She became particularly shrewish after a few years, making her presence more of a duty than a joy, but he would not speak ill of the dead.

"Sarah took the girls to visit her brother's family and there was an accident. The roads were icy and the horses lost their footing. The carriage slid down an embankment into a river and all were lost, including my daughters. Jenny was not yet a year old."

"Oh, Lord Asheland, I am sorry. How incredibly dreadful for you!" she said with feeling.

He looked at her with sad eyes and was somewhat surprised to feel the tightness in his chest lifting a little with her obvious concern.

"Yes, well." He cleared his throat. "That was six years ago now."

"My lord," Elizabeth started but then stopped herself.

"Go ahead, you may ask me whatever is on your mind," he said.

"Thank you. It is just, I wonder, why are you telling me all of this?"

"Miss Bennet, I tell you because I wish you to know that I understand what marriage is, what it entails and requires, that I am no stubborn bachelor. But mostly because I want you to know *me*."

She looked at him with some disbelief but said nothing.

"My marriages had their good and bad, seasons of warmth and of reserve, but I never felt I had a true partner, a companion. I never felt that my wife considered me her peer." At her confused look, he elaborated. "I know I sound revolutionary, but I mean to say that there was always a distance between us, a chasm I could never cross, even had I wished it. Neither of them wanted to know me intimately and did not wish for me to know them as such. They were content with a cordial friendship, but I wanted more. I wasn't sure what that more was until I met you, Miss Bennet."

"Me?" she squeaked.

"Yes, you. You who have never cared about the size of my house in town or the number of carriages I keep. You who want to discuss books and will take the opposite opinion of the one you hold just for the sake of a good argument. You who make me laugh more than I have ever laughed with a lady. You have awakened something in me that has long lain dormant, and I have come to admire you fiercely."

Her jaw dropped and left her mouth hanging open in a rather unladylike fashion as he turned to stand in front of her and took her hands in his own.

"Miss Bennet, Elizabeth, I believe we could be wildly happy together, if you could find your way to learning to care for me."

She stared at him, mouth agape, for some minutes before she finally spoke. "Me? Truly? Are you certain?" she asked, clearly in shock. "What do you see in me?" It was not that she thought herself undesirable, but rather she thought him a man of the world with infinite options. She simply thought herself an odd choice for one such as he.

He chuckled. "Don't you see, darling girl? In you, I see a future of warm talks and passion-filled discussions. Long walks and lively dinners. Companionship.

Friendship. Love. Joy. A beautiful life, that's what I see in you."

"Oh!" she was breathless all at once, and all she could do was look into his eyes, trying to decipher what she saw there.

"Don't answer now, just promise me you will think about it," he said softly.

"Yes, of course. I'll think about it." Before he had offered his arm again, her tendency to tease came to the fore and she said, "Just what am I supposed to be considering exactly, my lord?"

He laughed. "This is what I love about you. You are not afraid of me."

"Should I be afraid of you?" she asked, genuinely perplexed.

"No, my dear, I believe *I* should be afraid of *you*," he said with a certain look she could not comprehend.

She huffed. "What a silly thing to say!"

"If you agree to become my wife, you can tell me how silly I am every day," he said simply.

She instantly flushed and looked to the ground. "I will consider it carefully, sir."

"As you should," he answered.

They made their way back to her aunt in silence, both too filled with thoughts of the future to speak.

~

That night, Elizabeth and her aunt sat on Elizabeth's bed discussing the earl's proposal. After nearly an hour of discussion, in which Elizabeth told Mrs. Gardiner everything he had said and how he had looked when he said it, they had still not made a decision.

"What you must consider, of course, is where you will be in twenty years' time," stated Mrs. Gardiner. "If you were to marry a younger man, there is a good chance he would still be alive and you could grow old together. If you marry Lord Asheland, he may have died by then or be quite infirm."

"How old is he exactly?" asked Elizabeth.

"I think he is forty-two, but I am not certain."

Elizabeth blanched. "That's only four years younger than Papa!"

"And four years older than your mother," Mrs. Gardiner murmured.

Elizabeth put her head in her hands. "Why is this so complicated!" she cried. "If he were younger, or not so very important, I would not hesitate. He is a kind man, amiable, generous, intelligent. I have never enjoyed a man's company more!"

"And yet?"

"And yet, I do not want to be a widow in five years' time!"

"I doubt that would happen. He is very healthy and hardly an old man!" interjected Mrs. Gardiner.

"And I do not know if I want to be scrutinized and judged by everyone I meet. They will think me a fortune hunter and unworthy of him. I will be the penniless girl from the country who somehow turned the old earl's head. I do not want to live my life under a cloud."

"It sounds like you have made your decision, then," said her aunt steadily.

Elizabeth nodded and looked at the coverlet she was plucking at with nervous movements. "But I cannot imagine not seeing him again. Surely, if I refuse him, he will cease calling. I cannot expect to receive his attentions after such a rejection."

"No, you are right, you cannot," agreed Mrs. Gardiner.

"What will I do without him? He has become a very dear friend!"

"Elizabeth," Mrs. Gardiner began carefully, "do you think your happiness may depend on Lord Asheland?"

Elizabeth sat up straighter and looked surprised. "I do not know. I haven't given it much thought."

"Let us change our direction somewhat. If you do not think of anything else, not his title or money or society, and not his age, can you see yourself living happily with him? Can you picture being on his arm and attending the theater? Dinners together, walks in the park?"

Elizabeth closed her eyes and imagined her life with Lord Asheland. As she pictured the scenes her aunt had mentioned, a slow smile worked its way onto her face.

"Yes, yes I can. It's lovely," she said softly.

"And can you picture having children together?"

Elizabeth imagined taking a walk with a young girl like herself, and beaming proudly at a boy who had learned to ride a horse on his own.

"Yes, I can," she said simply, looking at her aunt with bright eyes.

"Good. Now, I know it is awkward, but we have talked before about what happens between a man and a woman." Elizabeth nodded with trepidation and her aunt continued. "Can you perceive being intimate with Lord Asheland? Could you be comfortable with him kissing you, touching you, caressing you? Sharing a bed with you?"

Elizabeth's cheeks flushed brightly and she looked down.

"You are young, and very pretty. Lord Asheland is clearly attracted to you. He will likely be a frequent visitor to your chambers. If you cannot imagine welcoming him with equanimity, and even with joy, you should not accept him. The marriage bed is a large part of your relationship and must be considered seriously before you make any decisions."

31

Elizabeth nodded. "I understand, Aunt. I will think on all of this carefully."

~

Elizabeth spent the next few days deep in thought. Lord Asheland showed his good breeding and stayed away to allow her to reflect without interruption. After five days had passed, he sent a note asking if he could call the following day. Elizabeth was the only one home when the note arrived, so she quickly penned an answer to send with his servant. She would receive him at one the following day and was looking forward to taking a walk if he would be so kind as to accompany her.

~

Lord Asheland arrived promptly and Elizabeth was already wearing her bonnet and gloves where she awaited him in the entrance hall. He offered her his arm and she took it with quiet thanks; neither said anything until they reached the park and began strolling slowly around the pond.

"I suppose you must be wondering about my answer to your question," she said, sounding more mature than he had ever heard her.

"Yes, I will admit to an inordinate amount of curiosity," he said.

"As much as I hate to disappoint you," she said quietly as he stiffened beside her, "I must ask you some questions before I can answer you properly."

"Questions?"

"Yes."

"Oh, my dear! I thought you were refusing me!" he said. He released a long breath and his shoulders relaxed. "Please, ask what you will."

"Thank you. Firstly, how old are you?"

He chuckled softly and answered, "One and forty, though some days I feel much older."

She nodded, relieved to find it was not more than she had expected. "And do you have any children living?"

"No, none of my children survived beyond the age of three."

She squeezed his arm. "I am sorry, my lord."

He nodded and they walked on quietly for some minutes.

"Do you spend more time in town or in the country?"

He smiled and answered, pleased that she was thinking about the future—it meant she was considering accepting him. "I prefer the country to town in the warmer months, of course, and for the deep winter, but spring is nice in town, though it comes with the unfortunate accompaniment of the season."

"Should I take from your answer that you are not fond of society?" she asked.

"Not at all, I simply dislike people who constantly try to manipulate me into doing what they want, in parliament and in drawing rooms. I find it exhausting."

She smiled. "I understand you perfectly. Do you limit your acquaintance accordingly?"

"Do you mean do I avoid those whose company I don't actually enjoy? As much as possible, though the occasional meeting cannot be avoided."

She nodded reflectively and he continued.

"If you are wondering if I associate with those who would be rude to you, or treat you meanly in any way, I do not. Of course, we cannot control others' guest lists and I am sure we will have to spend some time with the old guard, especially in the beginning when we are deciding who we like and who we do not, but the name Talbot is old and respected, and the Asheland title is noble and more importantly, wealthy. They may be unkind for a moment, but give them time, and they will all be crawling to you with their tails between their legs and their hands outstretched."

She laughed at the image he presented and the twinkle in his eye as he said it. "Are you so terribly rich, then?" she teased.

"Oh, quite terribly! You will have more frocks than days to wear them and the ladies will be clamoring for your favor."

She laughed. "I have only one other question."

"Go ahead."

"I would ask you to answer me honestly. It goes without saying that anything you say will be kept in strict confidence."

"This sounds serious. What do you wish to ask?" He stopped and took both her hands in his, pulling her off the path to stand in the shade of a large tree.

"Are you in good health? I mean, are you suffering from any malady that might shorten your life? Do you expect to grow to an old age?" she asked worriedly, biting her lip.

"Oh, my poor dear girl. I should not have worried you so. Forgive me for not discussing this when I first proposed. I am in perfect health. Not a thing is wrong with me except for the odd headache when I've been up too late or in the sun too long. Nothing to worry about." He patted her hand and she exhaled in relief. "I will be honest with you, though." She tensed again. "My father died at one and sixty—an ailment with his heart. And my younger brother has also passed on, but his disease was believed to be brought on by his dissolute lifestyle more than anything else."

She raised her brows but did not ask for further details.

"Is there anything else you wish to ask me?" he asked kindly.

"No, I believe that is all. I imagine you would like to hear my answer now, though I still maintain that you never truly asked me a question," she said with an impish grin.

"Allow me to rectify the situation. Darling Elizabeth, you are the brightest, sweetest, most enjoyable woman of my acquaintance. I want to spend every day listening to your laugh, looking into your eyes, and kissing your beautiful mouth. Please, do me the very great honor of becoming my wife and I will do everything in my power to make you deliriously happy."

She stood staring at him, speechless, for some time before she finally smiled at him and he wrapped her in his arms, pulling her further into the shadows along the path. She laughed at his exuberance and felt herself filled with all the joy of knowing she was making the right decision.

"Now, you have taken me to task for not asking properly, I must insist that you answer properly," he said as he released her.

"Yes!" she cried, all urge to tease gone. "Yes, yes, yes!"

He laughed and embraced her again, lifting her feet off the ground and twirling in a circle. "My darling girl," he whispered in her ear.

CHAPTER 3

M̲r. Gardiner was quickly applied to and his consent given, as everyone knew would happen. Lord Asheland made plans to go to Hertfordshire and speak with Mr. Bennet in person at the end of the week when the settlement papers had been drawn up. He wanted everything completed as soon as possible. He had waited years for someone like Elizabeth and he did not want her to slip away.

Lord Asheland arrived at Longbourn on horseback by noon that Friday. He had sent a letter asking for an audience and had the settlement in his pocket. He had chosen to not take his carriage, both for the purpose of speed and because Elizabeth had warned him of her mother's exuberance when confronted with wealth such as his. He was less conspicuous on horseback.

He was admitted discreetly into Mr. Bennet's library and assessed Elizabeth's father carefully. Mr. Bennet was a little older than himself and his hair was fully grey, though it was still thick upon his head. The thought tickled in the back of Asheland's mind that between his and Elizabeth's family propensities, their children would have marvelous hair. He almost chuckled at his wayward thoughts and extended his hand in greeting.

The meeting proceeded without difficulty. He laid out his friendship with and affection for Elizabeth, and his own financial solvency. Mr. Bennet was duly impressed with the size of the gentleman's fortune and his apparent respect for his daughter, though he expressed concern for the difference in their ages and wished to ascertain if the gentleman's affections were deeper than an infatuation with a pretty face.

"I would not wish to see my daughter resented by her husband when time takes its natural course and she is no longer the youthful beauty she is today," Mr. Bennet said seriously.

"I understand you perfectly. Be assured that I am no fickle youth or an old man simply wishing to appease his baser instincts. Mr. Bennet, I do not wish to be offensive, but you know I have no need of marriage if all I want is the company of a pretty young woman. In your daughter, I have found something I have never before encountered, and I have lived long enough to know that chances like these do not come very often. I care for her very deeply, and she will have my respect and affection all my days. Do not worry yourself on that account."

Mr. Bennet looked out the window for a moment, sighed, and reached his hand across the desk. "I see everything is as it should be, and I would be remiss in denying my consent. Do you know when you would wish to marry?" asked Mr. Bennet.

"Thank you, sir, I appreciate your trust in me." Asheland tried to hold back the smile attempting to take over half his face. "I would like to marry in two months' time, if that is agreeable to you. It would give Miss Elizabeth time to prepare herself and my staff to make my homes ready, as well as allow sufficient time for the preparations. What say you?"

"I think that is a fine idea. I will inform Mrs. Bennet. Will you marry here at Longbourn or in London?"

"I think here would be best. Miss Elizabeth would like to marry from her home and I would not wish to deny your wife her due," Lord Asheland said respectfully.

"That is good of you, my lord," said Mr. Bennet in some surprise.

"Not at all, it is a woman's prerogative to marry from her home. And please, call me Asheland," he said warmly.

"Very well, but you must call me Bennet."

They smiled and nodded and before the pause could become awkward, Asheland indicated he had brought the marriage settlement with him if Bennet would care to peruse it. Asheland was introduced to Mrs. Bennet as a friend of the Gardiners—Mr. Bennet would announce the engagement once he had agreed to the settlement—and the earl sat in her best drawing room and listened to her complain of her nerves while Mr. Bennet examined the marriage articles.

Asheland was an old hand at steering conversations and before long, Mrs. Bennet was telling him about Elizabeth as a child and even showing him a painting done of the family when Elizbeth was six years old. As he had suspected, Elizabeth had been a beautiful child with bright, dancing eyes and chocolate curls.

Soon enough, Mr. Bennet called him back to the library and signed the articles, seeing no need to change the already generous settlement, and with very little trouble, Lord Asheland was on his way back to London.

~

Lord Asheland arrived in London too late to call on Elizabeth, which he regretted, but he took great pleasure in penning her a letter and sending it to Gracechurch Street. It arrived as she was preparing for bed and was brought up by a maid. She smiled and opened it eagerly, knowing that if he was writing her so openly, her father must have consented and they were now officially engaged.

My Dearest Elizabeth,

It is with great joy and the utmost humility that I inform you of my conference with your father. He has consented. We are to be married in two months' time. I can hardly wait to bring you home, my love. We will be the happiest couple in England, I am sure of it.

I know you must be wild with curiosity and long to know each word exchanged between us, so I will wait on you tomorrow at the earliest possible moment and tell you everything.

Sleep well, my sweet.

Yours,
Robert

Elizabeth sighed happily and hugged the letter to her. She was to be married! And to such a man! She knew she would be wildly happy. She was so excited about the prospect of her new life, and imagining all the adventures they would have together, that she could not fall asleep for nearly two hours.

~

As soon as Lord Asheland entered the sitting room, Elizabeth rushed to him and took his hand, practically dragging him to the sofa.

He laughed. "What is all this excitement about?" he asked through his chuckles.

"You know exactly, sir. Now, tell me everything that occurred between you and my father," she said as they sat, her hand holding his firmly in her lap.

"Very well, but it isn't half so thrilling as you believe it is."

"I will be the judge of that, sir," she said.

"Dearest, would you call me Robert? I do tire of this 'sir' business."

"Of course, if you wish it. You do not want me to call you Asheland?"

"No, I hear it enough from everyone else that I tire of it. I would like to be Robert to you, if I may."

Her face softened and she smiled gently, "Very well, Robert. You will not be a title to me, but a man. *My* man."

He stared in disbelief at her perception and stroked her cheek softly with his free hand. "How well you know me, Elizabeth."

She smiled and leaned into his palm, a soft blush warming her cheek. Before anything else could be said, they heard footsteps in the hall and broke apart just before her aunt entered the room.

Lord Asheland stood to greet her and Elizabeth smiled and said, "You are just in time, Aunt. Robert was about to tell me of his visit with my father."

"I assume by your expressions that all went as expected and your betrothal has been sanctioned by Mr. Bennet," said Mrs. Gardiner with a warm smile for both of them.

"Yes, it went very well. You are now looking at the future Countess of Asheland," he said with obvious pride.

Elizabeth started a bit at the announcement. She, a countess! How very extraordinary!

~

A fortnight later, Elizabeth sat in her uncle's study going over her marriage settlement. After much conversation, Lord Asheland had persuaded her to discuss it in detail with her uncle. He insisted that a woman be familiar with her own situation and strongly believed that ignorance could not make one secure.

Her uncle had agreed and so they sat, reviewing papers and articles and copies of wills.

"Well, Lizzy, you shall be very well looked after," said her uncle.

"I expected no less, Uncle. Robert says I must know the details or I will be at the mercy of unsavory characters, though I cannot know what he means by that in relation to my settlement."

"I believe he means that if he were to die, he wants you to know exactly what is your due so that others cannot cheat you," stated her uncle seriously.

Elizabeth gasped. "Surely he doesn't think that will be necessary? Does he have unscrupulous family members he is worried about? And he is far from being an old man!"

"True, he is not an old man, but he is significantly older than you and is wise to prepare for your eventual widowhood. I would want no less for you, even from a young man. It is a reality we must face in this world, my dear, as much as I wish it were not. I have prepared similarly for my wife."

Elizabeth nodded. "Very well. I suppose you should tell me everything, then."

"I wish I could say it was all very simple, but there are quite a lot of conditions. Let us begin with the assets. There is, of course, the country seat in Nottinghamshire. The estate itself is quite large and is attached to the title. The majority of the lands and the main house are entailed on heirs of the body, meaning your daughter could inherit if there were no sons and hold the title for her firstborn son. There is additional property attached to the estate and generally considered to be part of the whole. There are several smaller estates, six in total, ranging in size and profitability."

"Six!" she exclaimed.

"Yes, the largest had been his brother's, and when he died unexpectedly, it reverted back to the earl. He had never married and had no children."

She nodded. "You say the largest. How large is it?"

Mr. Gardiner looked at the paper carefully. "According to this, it has a good-size house, though I am not sure what their definition of good-size is, multiple tenant farms, and an income of seven-thousand a year."

Elizabeth gasped and fell back in her chair, astonished beyond speech.

"It is designated for your second son, should you have one. If you do not, it will go to your eldest daughter as part of her dowry, or in the absence of sons, your second daughter."

Elizabeth shook her head in wonder. How had all of this come about?

"Are you well, Lizzy?" her uncle asked softly.

"Yes, yes, I am well. Just astonished. Did you know he was so *very* rich? I confess I did not!" she said, somewhat hysterically.

"Perhaps we should continue this tomorrow," Mr. Gardiner said carefully.

"No, no, I am well. Just surprised. I am quite recovered now," she said, sitting up. "Please, do go on."

Gardiner nodded, though he looked at her warily. "Two of the other estates bring in roughly six-thousand a year, one more five-thousand, and the other two bring in four and three-thousand respectively."

"Finally, some numbers I am accustomed to. I imagine their dispensation follows the ages of the children? The eldest son gets the earldom, the second the largest estate, the third the next largest estate, and so on?"

He nodded.

"And daughters take their places accordingly if we do not have sons?"

Again, her uncle nodded and she laughed nervously. "It is funny, don't you think? When you collected me in January to visit Great Aunt Seymour, I never imagined that the following summer I would be engaged to an earl and making plans for my seven children!"

"Elizabeth, is this all too much for you? Are you having second thoughts about marrying Lord Asheland?" he asked.

"No!" she cried. "I very much want to marry him! It is just, this is all, all so…"

"Sudden and overwhelming?"

"Yes," she exhaled loudly. "Exactly. Thank you, Uncle. All will be well, I will be well, I know it. I just need time to adjust to so many changes and so much money! I'm sure there are many women who always hoped to marry a wealthy man, but I confess I never truly thought I would. I thought Jane might, but I never expected to be more than comfortable."

"It is a good surprise though, yes?" he said with some humor.

"Yes! If I must choose, I'd rather be wealthy than poor," she teased. "Now, tell me how many grand carriages I am to have."

Her uncle laughed and continued detailing the three houses in town—one accompanying the title, Asheland House, one inherited from an uncle, Talbot House, and another from his mother's family. Two were let and one was currently in use. There was a good amount of money in the funds and in the bank, amounts which were not specified, but clearly there was enough for him to settle forty-thousand pounds on her without strain. When her uncle told her this, her eyes bulged and he had to call for tea before they could proceed.

Her pin money was more than she could ever imagine spending and the dowries set aside for their daughters were, to her mind, inconceivable, but of course the amount would be lowered if she delivered more than three Miss Talbots.

Upon her husband's death, she would be an incredibly wealthy woman in her own right. Apart from the money settled on her, she would have an annuity and her choice of one of the five unclaimed estates plus lifetime rights to Talbot House in town. She would also live on the main estate, Cressingdon, until her son came of age. Obviously, she and her son may choose for her to live there longer, and if they did not wish to reside together, there was always the dower house.

It was all so very grand, so extravagant, so *much*, that she felt herself alternately giddy and grave, lightheaded and slightly terrified. They finished the meeting without many more interruptions and Elizabeth went to bed that night wondering if she knew what she was about.

When Lord Asheland called the next day, all her doubts flitted away. He was so kind, so intelligent, able to make conversation on so very many topics and always willing to please. He was obviously in love with her and falling more under her power every day, something she could not quite understand the workings of but enjoyed the results nonetheless.

She toured his London home and met with various craftsmen to discuss the changes to her chambers and personal study. She was introduced to his cousin, Alfred Downing, at a private dinner and found him vastly entertaining. He was roughly five years older than Lord Asheland and reminded her of her own father, only more voluble. His wife Sylvia decided to take Elizabeth under her wing and had made shopping arrangements and plans for a ladies' tea to introduce her to her friends before the second course. Their son John was only a few years older than Elizabeth and particularly close to her betrothed. To no one's surprise, they quickly struck up a sibling-like relationship and Robert was pleased to see her assimilating into the family so easily.

She also met Robert's brother-in-law, Stephen Carew, who had been married to his sister Violet. The siblings had been close and Lord Asheland was devastated when she died in childbirth seven years ago.

Elizabeth marveled at the losses Robert had endured. One expects to lose parents, it is the natural order of things, but to lose both his siblings, both his wives, and all of his children—it was positively Biblical! She had held him tightly when he told her of his son Edmund, of the silly words he would say and how he was utterly fascinated with horses and always wanting to visit the stables, and how little Mary had loved her blocks best, always building large colorful towers and crying if anyone knocked them down.

She did not know it, but her compassion in hearing and comforting him only confirmed to Asheland that he was making the right choice of bride. He rewarded her kindness with a gentle kiss to her pink lips and she stared at him with wide eyes for a moment before asking him to do it again, for she had not been expecting that one and had not savored it as she ought.

He laughed. Elizabeth was always making him laugh. He had never been happier than he was with her. She was quickly becoming essential to his existence and he found himself wondering how he had ever lived without her. He finally understood what men meant when they said they wanted to make their wives as happy as the ladies made them. Now he knew. If he could make Elizabeth even half as happy as she made him, then she would be happy indeed.

~

Lord Asheland went to Hertfordshire a fortnight before the wedding. As expected, Mrs. Bennet was all aflutter at having an earl for a son-in-law, never mind that he was older than herself. She fawned and flirted and made a general fool of herself while Elizabeth sat by silently, her cheeks aflame.

Mr. Bennet was no help, only watching with amused eyes as his wife make their guest uncomfortable. Elizabeth was grateful that Kitty and Lydia were not yet out—though Kitty would be next spring—and thus were spared their incessant giggling. It was embarrassing enough listening to Mary play so very badly while demanding an attentive audience. Only Jane was perfectly behaved and tried to direct their mother's attention elsewhere.

Eventually, Elizabeth took Lord Asheland for a walk in the gardens, more out of a need to get away than to actually show him anything.

"I must apologize for my family, sir," Elizabeth said quietly.

He patted her hand where it rested on his arm and pulled her a little closer. "Do not, it is not your fault."

She nodded and looked down, shame washing over her. He had not said it was unnecessary or that they had not been that bad. No, he had simply said their bad behavior was not her fault. She couldn't look at him; he with the title and the grand estates and the well-behaved family.

"Dearest, do not let them worry you. I am not bothered, truly. Surely every family has some manner of..."

He searched for a word and she supplied it for him. "The ridiculous?" He inclined his head and she continued, "But surely not quite so many in one room at the same time?"

"I don't know. The Shrewsburys can be quite taxing. But one never corrects an earl, unless one is a duke, and there aren't many of those."

She relaxed and laid her head on his shoulder with a faint laugh. "You are so very good at cheering me, my love," she said.

He beamed with pride and they walked on quietly.

~

Lord Asheland was a perfect (and patient) gentleman. He allowed Mrs. Bennet to host multiple teas and dinners in his (and Elizabeth's) honor and drag him all about the neighborhood to call on all her friends and enemies to crow about her daughter's great conquest. Through it all, he was polite and well-mannered and never lost his temper or composure, though Elizabeth came close to it on more than one occasion.

After one particularly trying episode involving her mother and Sir William and Lady Lucas, Elizabeth was pacing in the garden, trying to calm her frayed nerves and feeling as though she had just found her wits' end, when she was approached by her betrothed.

"Dearest, what troubles you?" he asked, pulling her into his arms.

She rested her head just below his chin and wrapped her arms tightly around him. "My mother. My father. Mary. Our neighbors. Need I go on?"

He chuckled. "No, I understand perfectly."

She sighed. "I feel so terrible for leaving Jane here all alone with them. What will she do? What will become of her?" They were silent for a moment, then she spoke tentatively. "Robert, what do you think of Jane coming to stay with us? Perhaps just for the Season? Or maybe for the autumn?"

"I think it a fine idea."

She pulled back abruptly and looked at him. "You do?"

"Of course. She is your sister and you will miss her. And she is old enough to marry and not likely to meet many gentlemen here. She should spend the winter with us at Cressingdon and then travel to London. We must be there for the entire Season, unfortunately, but that will give you more time to shop."

"Very funny, my lord. Is that all I am expected to do while you sit in Parliament and shape the nation?"

"No, you will also plan menus and visit friends and receive some truly ghastly callers."

She laughed and snuggled into him again. "You are the best of men. I am very pleased to be marrying you."

He squeezed her to him. "No more pleased than I am to be marrying you, my love."

~

That evening, after the ladies had retired upstairs, Lord Asheland knocked on the door to Mr. Bennet's bookroom. After being invited in, he stepped into the cozy space and wondered at its owner. How could a man so conscientious about his books be so neglectful of his family?

"What can I do for you, Asheland?" asked Mr. Bennet.

"I wanted to speak with you about Miss Bennet."

"She will be your wife in two days," he began.

"No, not Miss Elizabeth, Miss Jane Bennet."

"Oh?"

"Elizabeth would like her to come and stay with us for some time this winter. We would also like her to accompany us to Town for the Season."

"Ah, I see. I am not surprised. They have always been close. My permission is granted, if that is what you are after."

"Partly, yes, and I thank you. There is more," he stated matter-of-factly.

Bennet looked at him with curiosity and raised one brow in question.

"Miss Mary. What do you think of sending her to a seminary? There is one in
Town that specializes in music—my cousin sent his

48

daughter there last year. There is also another in Nottinghamshire that would be suitable. It is near Cressingdon, so we could keep an eye on her."

Mr. Bennet's brows were nearly to his hairline. "Are you attempting to educate my children, Lord Asheland?"

"Someone should," he said simply.

Mr. Bennet's eyes widened and his face flushed. Asheland looked perturbingly calm.

"Did Elizabeth ever mention to you that I was married before?"

Bennet looked surprised at the turn in conversation and said, "She told me you were a widower."

"Yes, twice over." Mr. Bennet's eyes widened again and Asheland continued. "Did she tell you about my children?"

"You have children?" Mr. Bennet asked, shocked and slightly angry.

"Yes, I did. Odd that you never asked me that, knowing I had been married before and that I was nearly of an age with yourself."

Mr. Bennet flushed, feeling the weight of the insult.

"I had a son, Edmund. He is unfortunately no longer living, but I had great plans for him. I would teach him to love our estate, our land, the Asheland legacy. I would teach him to ride and to hunt. He would be a credit to the Talbot name. When he was old enough, he would go to Eton, though my wife argued for Harrow, and then on to Cambridge or Oxford. He would take my seat in the House of Lords and marry a kind woman, one nice to share a house with. His children would be well-loved and spoiled by their grandparents.

"He died just before his second birthday, along with his mother, and none of my plans for him will ever come to pass." He walked around the room quietly, looking at books, pacing the rug, staring out the dark window as he talked.

"Does Elizabeth know all this?" asked Mr. Bennet quietly.

"Yes, she does, and more. I told her before I asked for her hand. I wanted her fully informed before she made her choice." He picked up a small ornament on the bookshelf and replaced it before continuing. "I also had two daughters with my second wife. They had a nurse, naturally, and I had already engaged a governess for my eldest. Their dowries were set aside, as are the dowries for Elizabeth's daughters. I considered sending them abroad for a year to be finished, but that was something to be decided at a later date. Those dreams were also ill-fated."

Bennet nodded and leaned back, his eyes calculating. "Are you telling me this to shame me into planning better for my own children? Since I am so blessed to have them?" His tone was more biting than he had intended and he winced a little as he heard it.

"Your feelings are your own, Bennet," snapped Lord Asheland quickly. His voice was immediately smooth again. "Elizabeth is a caring woman, and she loves you. I gather she is your favorite daughter." He looked questioningly at Mr. Bennet.

Bennet nodded.

"She is greatly distressed by her sisters' lack of prospects," said Asheland.

Mr. Bennet looked surprised at this and raised one hand to his chin.

"I do not like to see her upset," said Lord Asheland quietly.

Bennet straightened in his seat and said, "What would you suggest?"

"Miss Bennet coming to stay with us is a start. I imagine Elizabeth will suggest she move in with us eventually."

"And what would you say to that?" asked Bennet suspiciously. He did not want to lose his most sensible daughter on the heels of his favorite one.

"As I said, I want my wife to be happy. If providing for her sister, either in our home or her own establishment accomplishes that, I will happily give that to her. She is my first priority."

Bennet nodded and wondered at the prickling sensation he felt on the back of his neck.

"Miss Mary is old enough for seminary, as we have already discussed, and Miss Kitty and Lydia would benefit greatly from a governess, then school when they are a little older and more mature."

Bennet snorted. "So that is your plan. To completely take over the running of my family, just because you're marrying into it?" He tried not to sound as threatened as he felt but his tone sounded defensive and belligerent.

Asheland shrugged. "As I said, I do not like to see Elizabeth distressed. I'm surprised you do." He turned and walked to the door as Mr. Bennet stared at him with his mouth slightly open.

Bennet tried to regain some of his earlier flippancy. "I assure you, an education would be completely wasted on Mary. She cares for nothing but Fordyce and sermons. And Lydia is quite untamable, I assure you."

Asheland was halfway through the door and merely looked over his shoulder and said, "Nevertheless."

CHAPTER 4

The wedding was simple and beautiful and before she knew what had happened, Elizabeth signed the name Bennet for the last time and was off to London with her husband. They spent a few days in Town before heading on to the sea where he had taken a house for six weeks and they both declared it the most idyllic time of their lives.

Elizabeth had never felt so cared for, so thoroughly loved, and Asheland was sure he had never been so content, nor so utterly enchanted as he was with his young wife.

They removed to Cressingdon in Nottinghamshire in time for the harvest and Elizabeth eagerly stepped into her role as mistress. She saw to tenants' families, met with the housekeeper, and redecorated her rooms and the most commonly used drawing room. Being mistress of such a large estate was daunting at first, but she eventually became proficient, though there were some notable bumps in the road. She preferred not to think about how she had lost her composure and cried in front of her new lady's maid, or how she had asked the housekeeper so many questions she was sure the woman had considered poisoning her soup.

She and Lord Asheland got along famously most of the time. He was patient with her and made allowances for her relative inexperience. His faith in her abilities was steadfast and she drew strength from his belief in her. They did quarrel on occasion, but nothing overly heated, and they both found the act of resolution quite worth the trouble of arguing.

After being married twice before, Lord Asheland had learned how to pick his battles and to value keeping his wife happy over being right. No matter how many mistakes she made, and truly they were small and infrequent, nothing could detract from the joy she brought him. He daily thanked heaven that his carriage had hit a rut that wet February day.

Neither Elizabeth nor Lord Asheland had any complaints about their intimate relationship and Elizabeth found that, to her surprise, it was incredibly enjoyable and something she looked forward to. Lord Asheland, of course, was beyond pleased at his wife's response, especially after his previous experience, and hardly a night passed that he did not sleep in her bed.

His friends and neighbors saw how happy he was and were not foolish enough to say anything about the country nobody he had married. They may have *thought* she was a gold-digging child barely out of the schoolroom, but they feared and respected his power too much to say so. Most were polite to Elizabeth, several going so far as to attempt to curry her favor, and eventually they became genuinely fond of her, as Asheland had known they would. No one could truly know Elizabeth and not love her.

Lord Asheland arranged for Mary to attend a seminary in London and Mr. and Mrs. Gardiner promised to keep an eye on her there. Mary herself was beyond pleased to be going, for the education as well as the opportunity to be away from her family.

A governess was engaged for Kitty and Lydia, and Mr. Bennet was prevailed on to postpone Kitty's coming out until she was seventeen, perhaps eighteen. Mrs. Bennet was not pleased at the idea, but Lord Asheland penned her a very flowery letter saying how happy he would be to take Kitty to Town for a season, but that she was much too young to be considered out by Town standards, and he would hate for the Bennet family to be viewed as country or backward in any way. Mrs. Bennet immediately agreed and the governess set to work making the girls into presentable ladies.

Jane joined them in December and Elizabeth's happiness was complete, especially since she suspected she was with child and desperately wanted a woman to speak to about it. They travelled to London in January for the opening of Parliament, and shortly afterwards Elizabeth felt the first fluttering of her child in her womb. Lord Asheland was beside himself with excitement and Elizabeth was so happy, so luminescent, that she was an instant sensation in town. Asheland teased her that she had them eating out of her hand, to which she said it wasn't her but the title they were responding to. In part she was right, but she never would have been so successful, nor on a first name basis with Lady Alice Montgomery *and* Lady Julia Sheffield, had she not been truly likeable.

They removed to the country in her eighth month, a truly horrendous journey for Elizabeth, and eleven months after she wed, she was delivered of a boy. The labor was mercifully quick and despite not being wed herself, sweet Jane stayed by her side throughout, except for when she went into the hall to give word to Lord Asheland who was pacing in helpless anticipation.

Their son, Robert John Thomas Talbot, Viscount Lisle, named for his father and grandfathers, was healthy and happy and utterly doted on by his parents and aunt. Elizabeth was thankful it was summer and they were at their leisure in the country and not required to entertain or attend parties as they did in London. The Season had been enjoyable, but she knew it was one of those things best savored in small doses.

Jane went home to Longbourn at their mother's request after nine months spent with her sister. Mrs.

Bennet wasted no time in berating Jane for not yet being engaged and Elizabeth for not finding her sister a husband. But since Elizabeth had just produced her first grandchild and the heir to the earldom, she wasn't too vehement in her reproofs.

They went to Town briefly for the Little Season, visited Longbourn, and returned to the country where they were happiest. By the time they traveled to London at the end of winter, Elizabeth was again increasing and expecting a baby in mid-summer. She was surprised at the speed of it, but her aunt told her that her youth increased the likelihood of conception, as did the fact that she had not nursed her son herself.

Jane rejoined them in Town in late April, they were on the way to Nottinghamshire in June, and in mid-July Elizabeth's pains began. The labor was significantly longer than her first had been—the babe did not want to descend and Elizabeth grew exhausted after a day and a half of much pain and very little progress. Finally, Lord Asheland had had enough of pacing in the hall and barged into her room. He was an earl after all, and this was his beloved wife, birthing his child in his home. He had, in his estimation, more right to be there than anyone.

Elizabeth took one look at him and could see the terror in his eyes. She immediately reached out a hand for him and he climbed onto the bed next to her and began rubbing her back as he had seen Jane doing. Both he and Jane shushed the midwife when she protested and the two shared a look of solidarity over the prone Elizabeth, making of them true siblings.

He supported his wife as she tried to walk around the room, and when she sat on the birthing chair he stood behind her, rubbing her shoulders. He had never been so frightened in his life. Elizabeth was pale and drenched with sweat, and he could tell by the lines in her face and the soft whimpers in her throat that she was in incredible pain.

The position in the chair wasn't right and the midwife moved her onto all fours for a time, then to stand near the bed and clutch the post, her husband helping to hold her up. The next thing he knew, a squalling pink babe was being placed in his arms and Jane was helping Elizabeth to lie in the bed while the maid rushed around cleaning up the blood. He took the baby to the bedside and climbed up next to his exhausted wife where she lay on her side and set the baby carefully in her arms. The tiny pink mouth instantly began rooting around and he watched in fascination as Elizabeth brought the babe to her breast and closed her eyes, then drifted into a light slumber.

It was the single most momentous occasion of his life, and he hadn't even been told the baby's sex yet.

~

After the birth, Elizabeth and Lord Asheland were closer than ever. She had decided to nurse the baby herself, a beautiful girl they named Violet Jane Augusta. He had wanted to name the baby after her, but she said they could name their next daughter Elizabeth; this one would be christened after his late sister.

He was touched and awed at his wife's kindness. So was his brother, Mr. Carew, when he was asked to stand godfather. He performed the office with gravity and honor, and if he dabbed a handkerchief at his face afterward, no one said a thing.

Elizabeth continued to nurse her daughter, hoping to lengthen the time until her next confinement, and found that it created a bond between her and the baby that she never could have imagined. Lord Asheland found the practice odd at first, but he would give Elizabeth anything she wanted, and after seeing what she had gone through in her last delivery, he was not eager to put her in that position again. They eventually brought in a wet nurse and the two women split the duties between them, Elizabeth feeding Violet in the mornings and evenings, and once or twice during the day, and the nurse taking care of her at night and when Elizabeth was otherwise occupied.

They carried on, comfortable in their routine, until October, when a letter came from Longbourn requesting Jane's presence back at home and a visit from Elizabeth and the children. Mrs. Bennet wanted Jane to meet the new neighbor, who by all accounts was very amiable as well as young and rich, and quite fortuitously, he had brought rich friends with him. And of course, Mrs. Bennet could not wait to see if the babe had inherited her looks. Elizabeth was too happy to argue with her silly mother.

The day before they were to set out, Lord Asheland received a letter from his estate in Northamptonshire requesting his presence; there had been a fire and the steward would like his assistance. The carriage would leave him there with his horse and he would join them in Hertfordshire when he was able to get away. It was the first lengthy separation of their marriage—he had only ever left her for a few nights before, and only when absolutely necessary—and their parting was all that could be expected between two people who loved and respected each other as much as they did.

Lord Asheland made Elizabeth promise to keep Violet with her in one coach, and young Robert John in the other with his nurse. Elizabeth understood the fear behind his commands and promised she would keep the children in separate carriages until they were safely at Longbourn, and that they would not go out at all if conditions looked even slightly dangerous. He was much relieved by her promise and kissed her goodbye.

~

Mrs. Bennet was beside herself. She was to host an earl, a countess, and their two children. The fact that the countess was her daughter only made it sweeter. In the two years since Elizabeth had married, Mrs. Bennet had taken to referring to her as the countess in company, and eventually amongst her own family as well. She had begun with Lady Asheland, but she thought 'the Countess' had a better ring to it.

When the carriages arrived, she was all aflutter. Everyone was quickly rushed inside where Mrs. Bennet held Violet and cooed over her, claiming she had her own mouth and that she had always known her grandchildren would be beautiful. Mr. Bennet immediately claimed Robert John, whom everyone was beginning to simply call Robbie, despite his mother's request that they not. Bennet held him close and took him off to the library with barely a word to anyone, making Jane and Elizabeth laugh and shake their heads.

"Oh, Jane, you must show me all your new gowns! How generous of Lord Asheland to buy them for you," Mrs. Bennet tittered as she followed Jane upstairs to unpack.

Elizabeth immediately went in search of Mary, who had left school at the start of summer and was now practicing in the music room. Mary would be presented in the spring and Elizabeth was giving her a season in Town to celebrate.

"How are you, dear sister?" asked Elizabeth as she sat on the bench next to Mary.

"Lizzy!" She embraced her sister as Elizabeth laughed. "I was so absorbed in my music I didn't hear you come in. How was your journey?"

"It was perfectly uneventful. Have you enjoyed your summer at home?"

"Yes, though I'll admit I was a bit surprised to feel so. But I thought it might be my last chance to be with Kitty as girls. What if I marry this year and we never live together again?" Mary said with wide eyes.

Elizabeth laughed lightly. "Dearest, I'm sure you would see her again. Look how often I see Jane?"

"How is Jane?" asked Mary with a serious look. "Has she shown interest in anyone yet? Mama is saying she must marry soon and is making all sorts of dreadful plans."

"Oh dear! That sounds serious! She met a great many gentlemen in Town when we took her for the Season, but none she seemed particularly interested in. I'm afraid we were a very confined party over the summer."

"I can't wait to see the baby! Is she very like you?"

"I suppose she is a little, but I think she will not truly resemble anyone for some time yet. Have you heard from Kitty?" asked Elizabeth.

Kitty was enrolled in a girls' seminary near London. Elizabeth hoped it would bring about as great a change in her as it had in Mary. Her next youngest sister hardly resembled the pedantic, somber girl she had been before going to school. All her serious focus was now on her music instead of religious texts, and the entire family was grateful for it. Being surrounded by other girls that weren't her sisters had brought out a cheerfulness in her character that no one had known was there. Elizabeth told herself to thank her husband profusely when she saw him again.

"She is doing well. She has made friends with a few of the other girls and likes most of her teachers."

"I am delighted to hear it. We shall have to visit her soon," said Elizabeth.

Before she could say more, Lydia burst into the room. "Lizzy!" She kissed her sister's cheek and sat down near the instrument. "I'm sorry I missed your arrival. I was riding and lost all sense of time. How was your journey?"

"Uneventful. How was your ride?" she asked indulgently.

Lydia was a boisterous, fun-loving girl of fifteen whom Elizabeth would have been greatly concerned for had it not been for the firm governess her husband employed for the Bennet girls. Mrs. Standish, a staid widow who had fallen on hard times, was just the right sort of person to take Lydia in hand. She ensured Lydia had at least some solid accomplishments and kept her in line with propriety, even when Mrs. Bennet was actively encouraging her away from it.

Last year, Mrs. Standish had written to Lord Asheland that she believed Lydia needed some activity to occupy her considerable energies or she would be in danger of becoming quite wild and rebellious. Lord Asheland had bought Lydia a horse for her fourteenth birthday and her father, knowing of the gift, had purchased her a beautiful new saddle. No one had known what they were starting, but soon enough Lydia spent hours a day on horseback, and only a few months ago, she had organized a children's mock-derby in her father's back pasture.

Elizabeth smiled as she looked at Lydia in her stylish blue riding habit and wondered when her baby sister had grown up.

"You look very smart, Lydia."

"Thank you, Lizzy! That gown is lovely." Elizabeth turned toward her so Lydia could see the lace on the front and Lydia exclaimed, "My lord, Lizzy! Your bosom is enormous!"

Lydia seemed to realize a moment too late that she was speaking out of turn and clapped a hand over her mouth. Elizabeth was shocked silent for a moment, then spluttered that she was nursing a baby, but it was lost in her giggles, which quickly became laughter as she saw her sister's chagrined face, and before she could stop herself, she was lost to her mirth and gasping for breath, finally joined by Mary and Lydia, all three of them lost to their giggles.

When she could catch her breath she said, "Now, come upstairs and see the baby! And we must rescue Jane from Mama!"

~

A few days later the house was in uproar as Mrs. Bennet ran around, preparing each daughter in turn for the assembly. Their new neighbor, Mr. Bingley, was to be there, and he would be bringing his party, which was rumored to be quite large. She was convinced there would be a man among them for Jane, and perhaps even for Mary. She made sure each of the girls was in her best gown and commandeered Elizabeth's maid to help prepare.

"You look positively radiant, dearest," said Elizabeth as she looked at Jane putting flowers in her hair.

"It is the very nice dress you gave me, Elizabeth," returned her sister.

"Nonsense. You are five times as pretty as every woman in Meryton and if Mr. Bingley and the gentlemen in his party aren't fighting over you by the end of the night, I will be terribly disappointed."

"And I shall be terribly relieved."

"Impertinent sister!" teased Elizabeth.

Finally, they were ready to depart, and the three eldest sisters and their parents piled into Elizabeth's coach, which Mrs. Bennet insisted on using when her daughter was visiting. It wouldn't due for the Countess to arrive in anything less than a well-sprung, late-model carriage with the Asheland crest proudly emblazoned on the side.

The assembly was a crush, and Elizabeth enjoyed renewing her acquaintance with neighbors she had not seen in many months. She did not feel much changed from the girl who had left Hertfordshire two years ago—a little wiser, more mature certainly, but that was to be expected as one aged. She was more capable, but in essentials, still the same person.

Her neighbors thought otherwise. Everyone spoke of her regal bearing, how she held her head, how she seemed to have a sense of importance about her. Her gown was remarked upon, her elegant taste and knack for flattering her own coloring and figure; her laugh was cheerful but not boisterous, her conversation interesting but never offensive, and unlike some of their acquaintance, she was not constantly going on about whom she saw in Town and where she saw them. In short, she was their very own success story, a homegrown countess, and they could not have been prouder of her.

At a pause in the music, when Elizabeth was dancing a quadrille with one of the Goulding sons, there was a commotion near the door and everyone began to whisper in excitement. For even in a town with its very own countess, newcomers were still rare—and eligible young men even rarer. The music recommenced and Elizabeth caught a glimpse of the gentlemen between the other dancers.

"Do you know who they are?" she asked her partner.

"I know the light-haired one is Mr. Bingley and the two women are his sisters. I don't know about the other two men."

Elizabeth nodded and, when the dance ended, sought out her friend Charlotte who always knew everything there was to know about Meryton.

"The portly man is Mr. Hurst, he is married to the shorter of the two women. The taller woman is Miss Bingley and is to keep house for her brother. The dark-haired man is Mr. Darcy, of Derbyshire. Perhaps he is known to your husband?"

"Darcy, Darcy, I don't think I know the name," said Elizabeth thoughtfully. "But Robert may very well know him. I expect him within a fortnight and shall ask him then."

"The ladies look very elegant," Charlotte said.

"And very bored. They clearly think highly of themselves. Look at Miss Bingley's nose! I can practically see the back of her skull, she holds it so high."

Charlotte laughed and elbowed her friend gently. "You don't think she shall be your next bosom friend?" she asked teasingly.

"Oh, dear! Perish the thought! I shall like having a little fun with them, though. It can be so tiresome in the country, you know." She said the last in a haughty accent that had Charlotte shaking with laughter.

"Come, I will introduce you," she said as she pulled Elizabeth behind her.

Charlotte dragged her near the ladies where they were standing with Mr. Hurst. "Mrs. Hurst, Mr. Hurst, Miss Bingley, how nice to see you again," greeted Charlotte kindly.

Miss Bingley only gave a bare nod to Charlotte's curtsey, Mr. Hurst grunted something unintelligible, and Mrs. Hurst favored them with a slight dip of the knees.

Elizabeth bristled but held her tongue. She hated that she already disliked this Bingley woman. It was terribly inconvenient.

"May I introduce you?" Charlotte asked. She was asking Elizabeth, who held the highest rank in the grouping, but Miss Bingley assumed the question was directed at her and answered.

"Of course."

Charlotte rattled off the newcomers' names while each nodded and then turned to Elizabeth. "This is—"

"Mrs. Talbot," Elizabeth interrupted with a smile.

Miss Bingley examined her gown with an appraising eye and apparently deemed her worthy of a shallow curtsey. Elizabeth nodded condescendingly and was pleased to see the other woman purse her lips in displeasure.

She told them how nice it was to meet them and excused herself. She saw Mr. Bingley and Mr. Darcy were currently being introduced to her mother and sisters. Mrs. Bennet was loud enough she could hear her perfectly from her position several feet away. She could not see the gentlemen's faces, but she thought them terribly patient for listening to her mother speak at such length on topics that couldn't possibly interest them.

"Have you met the Countess?" Mrs. Bennet was asking in her over-loud voice.

"Not yet, madam," said Bingley jovially.

"I shall introduce you later," said Mrs. Bennet. She then referred to the dancing in such a way Mr. Bingley felt obliged to ask one of her daughters to dance. Elizabeth shook her head as he led Jane to the floor and Mr. Darcy bowed slightly before walking away without requesting Mary for a partner.

She went toward the punch bowl and Charlotte rejoined her.

"What was that about, Mrs. Talbot?" she asked with a sly grin.

"It was not an untruth."

"No, but neither was it the whole truth."

"I owe nothing to Miss Bingley or her family. My identity is my own to do with as I please."

Charlotte shook her head. "Sometimes I think that husband of yours is a bad influence."

"You only say that because you have yet to come and stay with me. But I have come tonight to issue an invitation to spend six weeks with us in Town this spring and accompany us to Nottinghamshire for the summer. But of course, if you think the earl such a bad influence, perhaps you should refuse."

Charlotte looked increasingly excited as Elizabeth spoke. "Refuse! Whatever can you mean? I shall accept with alacrity."

The two friends smiled at each other and Elizabeth linked their arms. "Let us find me another partner. I must be going home after two more sets."

~

An hour later, Elizabeth was near the door, waiting for her carriage to be readied. She had a most pressing need to feed her daughter and after dancing the last jig, she was a trifle sore. Her partner was tired and a touch in his cups and when she turned under his arm, her coiffure caught in one of the buttons on his coat sleeve. They proceeded to untangle it amidst much laughter and silliness, but it left Elizabeth looking rather bedraggled. She only wished Robert had been there to see it. He would have found it most amusing.

She looked out at the empty street, searching for her carriage when she heard her sister's name. Something or other about Jane being an angel. As if that were a novel term for her! Elizabeth shook her head at the lack of creativity and would have walked away had she not heard a snide voice responding to the jovial Mr. Bingley.

Of course, he would say Jane was the prettiest girl in the room! She was the prettiest girl in most rooms. Now Bingley was suggesting the snide man dance with *herself*. As if she were searching for a partner! She looked up just in time to catch the fleeting gaze of Mr. Darcy and heard him say, "The disheveled woman by the door? She is tolerable, I suppose, but not handsome enough to tempt me. She cannot even keep her dress clean! I am not that desperate, Bingley."

Elizabeth looked down and saw, to her embarrassment, that her shawl had slipped and she was rapidly leaking milk onto her silk gown. She had known that last jig was too active to escape unscathed. Fighting the urge to laugh, she finally saw her carriage pulling up to the door and waved to her sister before leaving the building.

She entered Longbourn to the sound of Violet's wails and immediately made her way to the nursery.

"Lord, but she's loud, Lizzy!" cried Lydia as Elizabeth passed her sister in the hall.

"She's hungry," she stated simply and entered the nursery.

"Help me with these buttons, Polly," she said to the nursery maid.

In less than a minute, Elizabeth had pulled her dress down below her bosom and sat in the rocking chair, partially covered by her chemise, nursing her daughter.

"There, there. I'm sorry, love. Mother was away too long," she cooed to the baby.

"Sorry, m'lady. I almost fed her meself, but I thought how you'd be hurtin' if you didna' do it, so I waited," said the wet nurse.

"You did the right thing, Martha, don't worry. I was simply a little late getting back. Would you please fetch Watson?"

The wet nurse left to find the lady's maid and Elizabeth rocked contentedly, humming softly to Violet.

As expected, Watson was not happy with the state of her lady's hair and especially not her stained dress, but she promised she would do all she could to clean it. She left Elizabeth in the nursery wearing a robe and took the soiled dress to the laundry, tutting all the way.

Elizabeth missed Robert mightily in that moment. How he would have laughed with her and soothed her! She had it on the best authority that he found her incredibly tempting. The haughty Mr. Darcy was clearly an ill-

tempered sort of man. She suppressed a sigh and laid
Violet down in her cot, stroking her soft cheek gently.
"Goodnight, Lady Violet. Sleep well."

CHAPTER 5

The Lucases hosted a small party a few days after the assembly and Sir William was terribly disappointed that Lord Asheland had been detained. He was so looking forward to telling everyone he had entertained an earl.

Sir William could not even be consoled with Elizabeth's presence, for young Robert John had a cold and was all sniffles and coughs. He wanted nothing but to be held by his mother and Elizabeth saw no reason not to oblige him. She sent her sincere regrets and promised that she would bring the earl to call when he arrived, which went some way to mollifying Sir William.

As soon as the Bennet family arrived at the party, Mr. Bingley attached himself to Jane. Miss Bingley and Mrs. Hurst stood to the side for some time and eventually permitted Charlotte to introduce them to the least offensive guests present. Caroline paid little attention to what others said—they were so obviously beneath her—until she heard the word countess.

"I beg your pardon?" she asked, pretending she hadn't heard due to the noise in the room.

"Oh, I was only asking Charlotte if the Countess was coming later," said Mrs. Long, an elderly neighbor. Mrs. Bennet's manner of referring to her daughter had been adopted throughout the neighborhood.

"I'm afraid Robert John isn't well tonight, but I'm sure we shall see her soon," said Charlotte.

"She was looking so well at the assembly," said Mrs. Long. "I'm so glad she's recovered from her ordeal."

Charlotte nodded at the reference to Violet's birth three months previously and asked after Mrs. Long's nieces.

At that point, Caroline stopped listening, for she was not interested in this nobody's family. She had almost asked about the countess, but was prevented by Mrs. Long speaking before her. Caroline knew she had not been introduced to any countess at the assembly and she was quite sure she had met everyone worth meeting. She deduced from this that the countess must be some impoverished aristocrat, in all likelihood an old woman like Mrs. Long, who warranted no notice. Especially if she had recently been ill. Caroline hated sick people. It was all so terribly untidy!

Charlotte observed Caroline's absent look from the corner of her eye and saw the wisdom in Elizabeth's little game. Miss Bingley had entirely too high an opinion of herself and a rather low one of everybody else. She would have been insufferable had she known who Elizabeth really was. Her friend's quick thinking had likely spared them all many unpleasant scenes.

~

After less than a sennight, Jane received an invitation to dine with Miss Bingley and Mrs. Hurst while the gentlemen were dining out. Mrs. Bennet tried to engineer a way for Jane to spend the night by refusing the carriage and insisting she go on horseback, but Elizabeth thwarted her plans by offering her own carriage. Much negotiation followed and somehow, it was decided that Elizabeth, Jane, and Lydia would all ride out together, Elizabeth's groom following. Lydia wanted to call on Maria Lucas and turned off when they reached the lane. Jane and Elizbeth arrived at Netherfield just as a storm broke out. Elizabeth had intended to ride home after seeing her sister to the door, but the rain prevented her.

They entered the drawing room together and Jane looked surprised when Miss Bingley greeted Elizabeth as Mrs. Talbot, but Elizabeth shook her head discreetly at her sister and Jane said nothing about it.

Two and a half hours later, the storm had not abated, despite Elizabeth's fervent hopes, and seemed to be growing stronger. She was on the verge of sending her groom to Longbourn for the carriage when the gentlemen arrived.

"Hello!" cried Mr. Bingley. He quickly walked to Jane and bowed over her hand.

Elizabeth stifled a smile at the way they both blushed and stared at each other, but she was truly delighted for Jane. Her sister's heart had gone untouched for too long. Elizabeth sincerely hoped it would grow into true affection and not be a disappointment that would only make shy Jane more reticent.

"I was just about to send for the carriage," she said, foregoing introductions. They were, after all, acquainted. Almost.

"I do not think it possible. The road is almost impassable now, and the water under the bridge is rising rapidly," said Mr. Darcy seriously.

She noticed then that the men were slightly damp and their breeches had a few splatters of mud just above their boots.

"You're welcome to stay the night, of course. I'm sure Caroline would like that," said Bingley jovially.

He looked to his sister with a smile and completely missed her look of distaste. However, it was not lost on Elizabeth or Mr. Darcy.

Jane smiled and said it was kind of them, and Elizabeth immediately excused herself. She made her way to the hall and had a footman send for the groom who had accompanied them from Longbourn. He had been awaiting her in the kitchens and met her in the hall a minute later.

"James, I must return to Longbourn immediately. The children cannot be without me so long."

He nodded in understanding. "I'll ready the horses, m'lady."

"Thank you. I shall meet you at the door in ten minutes."

She re-entered the drawing room unnoticed and sat next to Jane. She whispered a few words in her sister's ear, to which Jane nodded with a furrowed brow, and then Elizabeth stood at the window looking out at the storm. It was very heavy and she would be drenched through by the time she got home, but she simply could not be away from her children all night. Since Robert John's birth less than eighteen months ago, she had never slept away from him and she was not about to begin now, without her husband in this unwelcoming house.

Not to mention that within an hour, her breasts would swell and ache and Violet would be screaming for her dinner. The wet nurse would not have enough milk to get her through the evening, the night, and the following morning, not to mention Elizabeth's own discomfort. Just thinking about her baby, hungry and crying, filled her with resolve. She saw James heading towards the door with her horse and immediately turned to Miss Bingley.

"Thank you for the hospitality, Miss Bingley. I'll be going now. Goodbye, Jane." She pressed her sister's hand, gave the slightest curtsey to the room, and was gone before anyone realized what had happened.

Elizabeth took her cloak from the footman and wrapped it around her before bursting out the door and mounting her mare. She and James quickly headed across the highest field towards Longbourn.

Just as they reached the fence separating the park from the pastures, Elizabeth heard a stern voice yelling, "Madam!" over the rain.

Turning, she saw Mr. Darcy riding towards her on a great brown beast.

"Mr. Darcy?" she called in question.

"Madam, I must insist you come back to the house. It is raining much too hard to be out of doors."

"You are out of doors, sir," she said.

"I came to fetch you. The ladies are very worried. Please, accompany me to the house," he said as he brought his horse up next to hers.

"As worried as I am sure the ladies are, Jane will reassure them. She knows I have ridden through worse and she knows I cannot stay," she stated simply, her voice raised above the rain. She looked to where James was opening the gate.

Darcy stared at her in shock. Why was she being so unreasonable? "Madam, I must insist. This is madness!"

"No, Mr. Darcy, I believe madness is following a near stranger out into the rain and trying to convince her to return with you to a house of more strangers while leaving her poor groom to be soaked in the rain as he listened to two strangers argue."

He breathed deeply. "I take your point, madam, but surely you do not consider your own sister a stranger?" he asked, his voice softening cajolingly.

Elizabeth gave him a pitying smile. She hated being patronized. "I see what you are about, Mr. Darcy, and it shan't work. Good day." She turned and began to direct her horse through the now open gate.

He brought his horse up in front of hers to block the opening and looked at her in shock. Was she *arguing* with him?

"What? You can't truly mean to ride through this muck? And what do you mean by saying you know what I am about? I am merely trying to see you to safety, which appears an impossible task since you are clearly bent on foolishness!" he cried in exasperation, water beginning to drip off his nose.

Elizabeth pulled her shoulders back and lifted her chin. "Mr. Darcy, I am not a fragile flower who needs your protection, neither would you be in any position to give it if I were. Your attempts to manipulate me will not work. Good day to you, sir."

He did not move out of her way and she glared at him stubbornly.

"Please remove your horse, Mr. Darcy," she said through gritted teeth.

"Mrs. Talbot, surely there is nothing so pressing at Longbourn that cannot wait until morning. Your parents will realize you've remained at Netherfield because of the rain. You can send your man on if you are concerned they will worry." His words would have been kind, or at least neutral, coming from someone else, but coming from him they sounded superior and condescending, as if he were explaining something complex to a very small child.

Elizabeth took a deep breath, then looked up at him with fire in her eyes. "My *children* need me, Mr. Darcy. Not that I owe you an explanation."

He looked taken aback for a moment. Clearly, he had not known she had children and Elizabeth felt a moment of triumph.

But then his face returned to stone and he said, "Surely their nurse can look after them, or your sister."

Elizabeth felt something snap inside of her. Who was this man and why was he involving himself with her concerns? James had been watching it all with a sharp eye and seeing Lady Asheland's frustration, he moved forward.

"My daughter needs me because I am her source of food, Mr. Darcy. Now let me pass!"

Mr. Darcy looked confused for a moment, then his eyes bulged as he glanced toward her bosom, remembering the marks he had seen on her dress at the assembly and how she had left early. He flushed a bright crimson and when her groom edged his own horse nearer and gave him a hard look, he moved away from the gate and watched her go through it with her head held high.

Elizabeth turned and set off through the field, leaving Darcy on the other side of the fence, silently fuming.

Of all the insolent, ridiculous, foolhardy women!

~

When Darcy returned to the house, it was to find it in uproar. No one could clearly tell him what had happened, but it was something to do with Miss Bennet's skirt, which Bingley may or may not have tripped on, or perhaps he tripped on a chair leg, and the lady tried to jump out of the way, or perhaps to assist him, when she herself had fallen. Regardless of what truly occurred, Bingley was left apologizing profusely while Miss Bennet was left with a swollen ankle and a rather impressive bump on her head.

Soon enough she was sent off to bed with some tea for the pain and ice for her head. Darcy shook his head at Bingley for his clumsiness and the sisters experienced a moment of regret at not having the opportunity to canvas Jane on all her connections, but as they were doubtlessly poor and unimportant, they did not concern themselves overmuch.

"She did mention an aunt and uncle in London," said Louisa.

"Yes, near Cheapside," sneered Miss Bingley before the two of them giggled unkindly.

"And the other uncle is an attorney, you know."

"Yes, right here in Meryton! I'm sure he can help with drawing up a lease if one is required." More sniggering and snide looks followed.

Bingley sighed and looked away, annoyed at them for being themselves, and Darcy went to the window where he proceeded to watch the rain as it fell in steady sheets.

At a rather late supper, Bingley looked terribly guilty and forlorn and his sisters seemed annoyed, though that was not so very unusual.

"There is no society, no fashion. Really, Charles, you would do much better to give up the lease and find an estate in Derbyshire," Caroline was saying.

Bingley only looked at her blankly and Darcy was left to answer.

"Miss Bingley, your brother has only just taken the lease. It would be impossible to be rid of it so soon," said Darcy rationally. He was tired of dealing with Caroline's inane requests such as this one and wished for nothing but the fire in his room, a good book, and a glass of port.

"But who are we to visit? What are we to do?" she whined.

"This is life on an estate, Caroline. What did you expect? Weekly balls and nightly dinners?" asked Charles, finally joining the conversation.

"Surely not every neighborhood is so," she hesitated to find the right word, "barbaric."

"Barbaric? You don't think that's a bit strong?" cried her brother. "You've been here less than a month!"

"It's time enough," she sniffed. "Why, just look at that Mrs. Talbot, Miss Bennet's sister. She wasn't even invited and yet she arrived here for dinner—"

"She was escorting her sister. She stayed because of the rain," interrupted Charles.

Caroline ignored him and continued, "— and then she ran off without even saying goodbye! On horseback!"

"As I recall, she did say goodbye, I heard her myself, and how can you be angry she left if you didn't want her here in the first place?" asked her brother, now perturbed himself. He really must marry her off. This was becoming tiresome.

"You must admit it was rather odd, Charles," said Mr. Darcy quietly. He was still smarting from Elizabeth's dismissal of his offer of assistance.

"Talbot... Is she connected to the Asheland Talbots?" asked Mr. Hurst, finally looking up from his plate.

Caroline sniffed. "I doubt it. Can you imagine, the relation of an earl scampering about the countryside dripping wet like that." Caroline sniggered at her own joke and Louisa joined her in sheep-like fashion.

Bingley rolled his eyes and stabbed at his meat. It really was ridiculous how they went on about nothing, but he knew saying more would only make them continue. Silence was the quickest way of changing the subject.

~

The next day, the sun was shining and, thankfully, much of the mud had dried up. Elizabeth fed the baby and went down to breakfast, surprised to see her mother up and in a very good mood.

"Perhaps she'll stay the entire week," she was saying.

"Mama, what are you talking of?"

"Jane being at Netherfield, of course," she said, waving a letter gleefully.

Elizabeth snatched the letter from her mother's hands and read it herself.

"Oh, poor Jane! I must go to her at once!"

She left the room and immediately asked for her carriage to be readied. She turned in the narrow hall and nearly ran into her mother, who had followed her out, flapping like a goose.

Elizabeth Adams

"Now Lizzy, what are you doing?"

"Going to see Jane, Mama, what do you think?" she said impatiently.

"You mustn't!"

"Mama! Jane must be mortified! Mr. Bingley's sisters haven't an ounce of tenderness between them. She will be all alone in her bedchamber, with no one to look after her and nothing for distraction. She will find herself the greatest imposition and will fret ceaselessly, you know she will."

Mrs. Bennet sighed. "Very well, but you must leave her there!"

"What? No, I cannot!"

"How is she supposed to catch Mr. Bingley or his rich friend if she never sees them?"

"How will she see them if she is resting in one of the bedchambers? It isn't as if Mr. Bingley can nurse her himself. And I'm not sure you want his friend," she added.

Mrs. Bennet looked thoughtful at that.

"Mama, proper young ladies do not throw themselves into the paths of young men. Proper ladies make themselves more attractive, through accomplishments and deeds and education, and let the good men come to them, remember?" she said with great patience, as if they had had this conversation multiple times before.

Mrs. Bennet's shoulders slumped and she sighed in defeat. "Very well, but he could at least carry her to the carriage!"

Elizabeth shook her head and went upstairs to change. Lord love her, but her mother would never change.

Less than an hour later, Elizabeth's carriage was pulling up in front of Netherfield. She had decided that enough was enough and she was leaving with Jane and no arguments. If she had to use her position to accomplish that, she would and gladly. And she was looking forward

77

to seeing the shock on Miss Bingley's face. The woman could sorely use a set down.

She entered Netherfield in her best day dress, for the collective benefits of Miss Bingley and Mr. Darcy, gave the butler her card, and waited to be announced. When she heard him say, "The Countess of Asheland," she almost laughed at the sound of chairs scraping backwards and boots hitting the floor.

She walked in gracefully, head held high, and tried not to smirk at Caroline's open mouth or Darcy's narrowed eyes.

"Forgive me for disturbing your breakfast. I've come to see my sister," she said smoothly, as if she visited lame sisters at her neighbors' homes every day.

She tried not to notice the ticking of the clock as she waited for a response. "Of course," said Bingley. "I'll take you to her."

He quickly ushered her out of the room before anything else could be said and she merely nodded to Mr. Darcy and Miss Bingley as she left.

Mr. Bingley babbled on about nothing until they reached Jane's room and she gently told him she would like to be alone with her sister. Jane was feeling much better, though terribly embarrassed, as expected, and with a mild headache. It was quickly decided that the largest footman would carry her down the stairs and they would drive home very slowly to avoid jostling her.

Elizabeth went downstairs to inform their hosts and fetch the footman while Jane dressed with the help of the maid. Elizabeth reached the drawing room and paused outside the door for a moment when she heard Miss Bingley's voice.

"You don't really believe her, do you?" the woman hissed.

Not wanting to eavesdrop, and not caring enough about what they were saying to investigate further,

Elizabeth entered the room. Miss Bingley and Mrs. Hurst looked up from the sofa they were sharing, and Mr. Bingley and Mr. Darcy leapt to their feet.

"Lady Asheland, how is your sister this morning?" Bingley asked, leading her to a chair far away from his sisters.

"Much recovered, I thank you. I shall be taking her home with me. We thank you for the hospitality," she said evenly.

"Oh, but, is she well enough to travel?" asked Mr. Bingley anxiously. "How will she traverse the stairs?"

"My footman will do the job." At his incredulous look, she said, "He is very large and Jane quite light. I'm sure he shall manage." She gave him a sweet smile to ease his disappointment; she really thought he was a decent enough man, if encumbered with a truly awful sister. She almost suggested her mother's idea of having him carry her down, just to make him feel better, but she knew it would mortify Jane and was entirely improper. She was fond of a friendly joke here and there, but she did have *some* limits.

"Mrs. Talbot," called Miss Bingley as she rose from her seat across the room.

"Yes?"

"You are familiar with Lord Asheland?" she asked, clearly doubting the veracity of Elizabeth's identity.

Hurst walked into the room at that moment and, hearing Caroline's question, turned to Elizabeth and said curiously, "Are you a cousin of Lord Asheland?"

"No," she said with a smirk. "I'm the wife of Lord Asheland." Her lips twitched in amusement as she watched the surprise register on the faces of Mr. and Mrs. Hurst.

"Of course," said Miss Bingley, clearly not believing a word. "And is he here with you in Hertfordshire?"

"Not as yet. He was needed at his estate in Northamptonshire. I expect him shortly."

Caroline nodded. "I thought the Asheland estate was in Nottinghamshire, but I suppose it must be easy to confuse them."

"Caroline," said Mr. Bingley quietly.

"How funny, Miss Bingley. I cannot imagine ever confusing two such counties, but then we do not all have a talent for geography." She smiled as Bingley hiccupped rather loudly. "Cressingdon is in Nottinghamshire, but my husband has additional holdings in Northamptonshire. And in Yorkshire, Somerset, and Hertfordshire, but we mustn't bother with the details." She smiled and brushed her skirt. "Excuse me, I will see to my sister."

She walked out the door leaving a furious Caroline and an amused Mr. Bingley. Even Mr. Darcy appeared entertained.

"That scheming little—"

"Caroline," Bingley warned again. Really, he must find someone to marry her, and soon.

Before anything else could be said, there was rather a lot of noise in the entrance hall and Bingley and Mr. Darcy stepped out to see what was going on.

There was Elizabeth Talbot, in the arms of a man neither of them had ever seen before, laughing and clutching him to her in a most inappropriate way. He was hardly better, hugging her so tightly her feet were off the ground. Lending the entire scene a modicum of propriety was Mr. Bennet, standing a few feet away and laughing quietly at the couple.

"Put her down now, Asheland, before you shock Mr. Darcy," said Mr. Bennet jovially.

Darcy stiffened and tried to wipe whatever expression he had been wearing off his face.

"Forgive me, I am simply overjoyed to see my wife." Asheland held Elizabeth's hand tightly and beamed at his father-in-law.

"Mr. Bingley, Mr. Darcy, may I present the Earl of Asheland, my daughter's husband. He insisted on coming straight over when he heard Elizabeth was here and Jane was injured," said Mr. Bennet with a twinkle in his eye.

For the life of him, Darcy couldn't see what was so funny. The gentlemen bowed, Asheland gave a nod, and soon enough it was explained what the plan was, and before any objections could be made, Lord Asheland had gone with Elizabeth upstairs and had Jane in his arms, carrying her down to the carriage.

Bingley followed after them, knowing he was useless but not wanting to leave Jane alone. She smiled at him shyly and Elizabeth sighed, knowing she would now have to be nice to Miss Bingley, if only for Jane's sake. Well, *mostly* nice.

Once Jane was comfortably settled in the carriage, the uninjured guests turned and faced the Bingley party.

"Thank you for looking after Jane," said Mr. Bennet.

"Of course, it was our pleasure," replied Mr. Bingley.

Caroline Bingley chose this moment to come outside, belatedly realizing it was incredibly rude not to have greeted their recently arrived visitors.

"Dearest, let me introduce you to Miss Bingley, Mr. Bingley's sister," said Elizabeth sweetly. "Miss Bingley, this is Lord Asheland, my husband."

Miss Bingley appeared somewhat pale as she looked from the finely clothed man in front of her to the liveried footmen near the expensive carriage emblazoned with the Asheland crest.

She curtsied deeply, her knees nearly reaching the floor, and smiled her best smile. "It is a pleasure to make your acquaintance, my lord."

Asheland smiled in response, thanked Bingley for looking after his sister, and allowed Mr. Bennet to ride with Jane in their carriage while he and Elizabeth took the Bennet coach that the men had arrived in. Caroline could not understand why they did not all ride in the nicer equipage; even with Jane's leg on the seat, there would surely have been enough room.

"Of course, Caroline. Why would a healthy man reuniting with his pretty wife after a long separation possibly want to be alone in an inferior carriage?" teased Charles.

He and Darcy chuckled and walked inside, and Caroline shook her head, not understanding what they meant but feeling herself blush nonetheless.

~

"You've done it this time, Caroline!" cried Bingley with a wide smile as he joined his sister in the blue parlor.

"Done what?" she asked testily.

"Done what? Do you truly not know?" he asked, a look of amused disbelief on his face.

"What has she done?" Louisa asked as she entered the room, one hand playing with her bracelets.

"Caroline has insulted a countess, that's all," said Bingley smugly, as only a brother could do.

"I did no such thing!" cried Caroline, though her face was flushed.

Bingley guffawed and flopped onto the sofa.

"Surely you didn't!" cried Louisa.

"You were there!" said Bingley. "Do either of you truly believe she didn't see the looks you gave her, or hear you when she was just outside the door? You made no effort to lower your voices. And of course there was the scene this morning where you practically accused her of lying."

Louisa looked worried and turned to Caroline.

"It wasn't so bad, not really," said Caroline, not truly believing it.

"Do you think yourself so clever that she didn't realize what you were about? I think she's rather better at that particular skill," said Charles.

"What do you mean?" asked Caroline suspiciously.

"Come, Caroline, do you truly not see?" His sister continued to look at him in confusion and he sighed in exasperation. "She does not like us. She may dislike me less than the two of you, but I am sure she holds none of us in any kind of favor."

"What? How can you say such a thing?" cried Caroline. She and Louisa expounded for some minutes on how likeable they were, how kind they had been to the countess (Bingley rolled his eyes), and how they were sure they could be friends in the future.

"Believe what you will, but you are deceiving yourselves if you think you don't have much ground to make up." With that final statement, he left the room, leaving two fretful sisters behind him.

~

Elizabeth's reunion with her husband was all that either had hoped it would be. As soon as they returned to Longbourn, they went upstairs to see the children. Robert sat with Robert John in his lap, reading his son a story, while Elizabeth quietly hummed to Violet as she nursed her. Eventually, Robert's voice tapered off into a whisper and finally stopped, and Elizabeth looked up to see that her son had fallen asleep on his father's chest. She smiled at the picture they presented and Robert carried their son to bed.

"I have missed you all so dearly," he said as he sat back down in a chair near her.

"We have missed you. Is everything all right? Was there much damage from the fire?" she asked.

"Yes and no. The fire did not reach far, but what it did touch it burned to the ground. The entire kitchen must be rebuilt and one of the smaller outbuildings. Thankfully, there was no loss of life and only a few minor injuries."

She nodded and placed the now sleeping Violet in her cradle before rejoining her husband and leading him away for a nap in Longbourn's best guest room. Mrs. Bennet allowed nothing less for an earl and countess.

"I hope we never have such a separation again," she said as she slipped into his arms as soon as the door closed.

"I couldn't agree with you more, my love. I've slept very ill without you." He kissed her upturned face and pulled back to loosen his cravat and coat. "But surely you've had *some* entertainment."

"Of course," she answered as she turned her back to him to receive help with her buttons. "I have enjoyed seeing Charlotte—she accepts our invitation, by the way. I do hope she and Mr. Rippen get on. I want her to be well situated and it would be lovely to have her so close."

"All we can do is introduce them, darling. The rest is up to Providence."

"I know, but it doesn't stop me from hoping." He smiled and she continued, "It would seem that Jane has taken a liking to Mr. Bingley."

"Has she?" he asked, interested. "What do we know of him?"

"Not much. He has a perfectly horrid sister and another perfectly dull one who follows wherever the horrid one goes."

He chuckled.

"His taste in friends is suspect," she said. "Mr. Darcy seems perpetually dissatisfied with life."

"Darcy," her husband repeated thoughtfully. "The Darcys of Derbyshire?"

"I believe so," she answered.

"If it is the family I'm thinking of, I knew the elder Mr. Darcy and visited his estate once. I was very young and accompanying my cousin Alfred; they were friends. I barely knew him, but I recall that he was a nice chap and the estate was beautiful and well cared for. You would have loved the grounds. Pemberton? Pembrook?"

"Pemberley?"

"Yes, I think that's it."

"Miss Bingley mentioned it yesterday, but I had no idea what she was referring to. She said it as if everyone should know what it was." She made a face and imitated Miss Bingley. "You must visit, Paris, Rome, and Pemberley. No education is complete without it."

Robert laughed and she climbed onto the bed.

"I was introduced to Miss Bingley as Mrs. Talbot," she confessed while sliding under the covers.

"That old trick! It never ceases to be useful, does it?" He joined her under the blankets and pulled her close.

"She has been perfectly insufferable. I wonder how her behavior will change now."

"She'll likely fawn over you or pretend to a friendship. Try to let her down gently, my love," he said with a kiss to her neck where it lay so temptingly close.

She sighed. "I suppose I should, but she doesn't deserve it. You should have seen how rude they were to poor Jane! As if she were merely there for their entertainment. They kept hinting at how unsuitable a match would be between her and their brother. I wanted to bang their heads together."

He laughed. "You would do no such thing!"

"No, I would not, but that does not stop me from wishing I could."

He laughed again and she felt the rumble of his broad chest all along her back and sighed happily, snuggling deeper into him.

"I have missed you. I sleep terribly when you're gone. Promise you won't go away again soon." She knew she sounded petulant, but she really did hate it when he was gone, and she was finding it difficult to be stoic about it at the moment.

"Wild horses couldn't drag me from you," he said softly and kissed her hair.

CHAPTER 6

To no one's surprise, an invitation arrived the next day addressed to Lord and Lady Asheland and the Bennet Family, inviting them to dinner in three days. Elizabeth was of a mind to refuse; she truly did not like Caroline Bingley and if being married to an earl had taught her anything, it was not to waste time on people who brought neither pleasure nor gain. But she saw Jane's hopeful smile and they both knew the invitation had been issued because of the earl's arrival. If the Bennets arrived without him, Miss Bingley would be terribly put out.

Elizabeth sighed and did her sisterly duty, quickly sending a reply in her elegant hand as Jane stood happily beside her.

The day of the dinner, Elizabeth fed Violet before they left to be sure to avoid an unfortunate accident as had happened at the assembly, and she wore one of her better gowns, assuming correctly that Caroline Bingley would take the opportunity to wear something ostentatious and inappropriate for the occasion.

They were welcomed with an almost embarrassing amount of civility. The difference in the Bingley sisters' behavior was impossible to miss. Mr. Bingley behaved much as he ever had, though perhaps slightly less voluble. Elizabeth could not but respect his genuineness. Mr. Darcy also behaved as he ever had, but since his usual behavior involved insulting her and attempting to command her, she was less happy to note his constancy.

Elizabeth was placed on Mr. Bingley's right and Jane across from her on his left. Lord Asheland was on Miss Bingley's right and Mr. Darcy on her other side. The Hursts, Mr. and Mrs. Bennet, and Mary filled the center seats. Elizabeth smirked at seeing Miss Bingley's delight in having Mr. Darcy trapped so near to her with an earl on her other side. Elizabeth didn't know how the woman had failed to see the man's indifference towards her, but hope springs eternal and Miss Bingley was clinging to her illusions like ivy to a stone cottage.

For herself, Elizabeth failed to see why Mr. Darcy provoked such interest. He was handsome, to be sure, but so was Mr. Bingley, and significantly easier to get along with. She looked at her own husband and admired his straight nose and firm jaw. Yes, he was handsome as well, though in a completely different way. His hair was chestnut brown, where Mr. Bingley's was pale blond and Darcy's was nearly black. Robert's eyes were warm amber, the color of toffee, and his skin light but always darker in the summer. Mr. Bingley had light skin that she suspected would turn pink in the sun and gray-green eyes. Mr. Darcy's eyes were a bright blue, almost cold, and his skin almost looked tanned, more so than hers, which her mother had always lamented, and she thought he would get even darker than she did in the summer months. Three more different men could not have been found in a dining room together, she was sure of that.

Robert and Mr. Bingley were both amiable, but Mr. Bingley seemed eager, and not very steady to his purpose, though she could admit that she did not know him well as yet. Robert was just as good company, but he was confident, reliable, and wise. She suspected Mr. Darcy might be confident and reliable, but he was certainly not amiable. Time would tell if there was wisdom behind those stormy eyes.

Beginning to be bored with her character studies and alternately watching Jane and Bingley flirt, Elizabeth was relieved when Caroline stood and requested the ladies follow her to the drawing room. Elizabeth fleetingly touched Robert's arm as she passed and he reached up and grabbed her hand for a moment before letting her go. Neither of them noticed Mr. Darcy following the motion of her hand and her retreat from the room.

When the gentlemen rejoined the ladies, Mary was playing on the pianoforte and Caroline was attempting to talk to Elizabeth. Lord Asheland nearly laughed when he saw the look on his wife's face, then moved to sit beside her.

"Oh, Lord Asheland!" cried Caroline too loudly. "How are you enjoying Hertfordshire?" Before he could answer, she continued, "Of course it is nothing to Town, but the country is so much more pleasant in the autumn, don't you think?"

"Yes, the country is more pleasant at most times of year, I think. And I find Hertfordshire lovely." He smiled at Elizabeth and she bit her cheek to keep from laughing at the sheer ridiculousness of it all. "How do you find the countryside, Miss Bingley?"

"Oh, it is lovely, my lord."

And so it went, inane question followed by dull response until Lord Asheland lost count of how many times she had called him my lord.

~

"That was one of the most painful dinners I've ever had to sit through," said Robert as they entered their room at Longbourn.

"Does Miss Bingley actually think she will gain your favor by boring you to death?" asked Elizabeth with a groan as she bent to remove her shoes.

89

Robert chuckled as he tugged off his coat. "I could almost feel sorry for her if she wasn't so difficult."

"Difficult?" said Elizabeth with raised brows. "Horses are difficult. That woman is a harridan."

He laughed again. "I saw your expression when she suggested you call her Caroline."

"What on earth was the woman thinking? Not four days ago she was behaving like a spiteful cat and accusing me of lying about my own husband. Now she thinks I will want to be her friend? Is she mad?"

"You are right, dear, of course, but it is amusing." His eyes twinkled as he smiled at her and she shook her head at him. "At least you put her in her place, love. I doubt she will soon ask again."

"It was ridiculous of her to ask the first time," she grumbled again. "Poor Jane. She seems to sincerely like Mr. Bingley, and he seems like a good sort of man, but those sisters! However is she going to manage them? Had I never met you, I doubt I could have done it, and I'm more forceful than she."

"Don't worry, darling. I'll look into Bingley's situation, and if all is as it should be, perhaps a subtle word about distancing himself from his sisters would be helpful."

"Perhaps. But what if he likes them? I don't want him to give them up for our sakes."

"Dearest, you did not hear the conversation when the men were alone. Trust me, he will be thrilled when Caroline is removed from his home."

She looked at him in surprise.

"Marriage would be best for her, but if she becomes a nuisance or disrupts his marriage, he'll send her off," he added.

"Would he set her up in her own establishment? Would that not look odd? If Jane is serious about him, I would hate for her to be touched by scandal."

"He is not without options. She could have her own establishment with a companion. It is not too strange. She could continue to live with her sister; they seem to get on, or he could send her to another relative. He mentioned family in Scarborough."

"What you men talk about when the ladies withdraw!" He laughed and she continued, "I don't know how you always manage to find out so much in so little time, but I am grateful for it. For Jane's sake, we should know as much as possible."

She turned her back to him and he undid her buttons. She chuckled quietly and he asked what was so funny.

"I was just remembering Miss Bingley and her incessant fawning. 'My lord, would you like more tea? My lord, can I bring you a cake? Do you prefer Town, my lord, or country, my lord?'" she teased in a high-pitched imitation of Miss Bingley.

He laughed and removed his waistcoat and draped it on the back of the chair. Elizabeth reached up to untie his cravat and continued with her joke.

"How tall you are, my lord. I can hardly reach your neck, my lord."

"Dear, stop before you give me indigestion," he said, clutching his stomach.

"Shall I bring you a tonic, my lord?"

He laughed louder, his shoulders shaking. "You little minx. What am I to do with you?"

"I haven't the slightest idea, my lord." She looked at him through her lashes and suddenly he felt less like laughing and more like kissing his wife.

She turned away and removed the last of her petticoats, sliding into the bed in her chemise. He looked at her with warm eyes until she patted the place next to her.

"Coming to bed, my lord?"

He shook his head. "How long will you keep that up?"

"Keep what up, my lord?" she asked innocently.

He slid into bed beside her and gathered her close. "Elizabeth, you are the greatest joy of my life."

"Thank you, my lord," she whispered.

He kissed her neck. "Do you intend to do that all night?" he asked as he nibbled her ear.

"On occasion it is immensely appropriate. My lord," she said with a wicked grin.

"Hmm," he nearly growled as he kissed her neck and ran his fingers through her hair.

"Oh, lord," she breathed.

~

Caroline Bingley was exceedingly pleased with herself. She had just hosted an earl—for the first time—at her country estate. Well, her brother's estate, and it was leased, not owned, but she didn't allow those details to bother her. The evening had been a triumph. The earl had been very attentive to her and she thought they would all become good friends. Oh, how grand it would be to sit in the Asheland box at the theatre! And he was cousin to Alfred Downing, whom everyone knew was the heir of the Marquess of Devonshire. By all accounts, the two were very close. Oh! How grand they would all be.

She entered the breakfast room with a smile on her face and a spring in her step.

"What has you so cheerful this morning, Caroline?" asked Bingley from his place at the table.

"I am just pleased with our time in the country, brother," she said lightly as she began to fill her plate.

"I suppose you refer to dining with Lord and Lady Asheland last evening?"

"Wasn't it lovely?" she sighed and sat down, filling her cup with tea.

"Yes, it was a pleasant evening," he answered, his thoughts filled with Jane Bennet.

Darcy entered the room to the sight of two Bingley siblings staring dreamily off into nowhere, silly smiles on their faces.

"Good morning," he said carefully, suspicious of their attitudes.

"Good morning, Mr. Darcy. I plan to call on Longbourn today. Would you care to accompany me?" asked Caroline.

"As a matter of fact, I would. I planned to speak to Lord Asheland today on some business."

"I can depend on you to turn a hunting party into a business meeting, Darcy!" said Bingley.

Darcy ignored him and ate his breakfast.

~

The Bingleys and Mr. Darcy were shown into the sitting room at Longbourn. Clearly, the Bennets had not been expecting visitors. Mrs. Bennet sat by the window holding a small bundle and humming softly. A girl the Netherfield party didn't recognize and Jane Bennet sat on the floor with a tiny boy and a pile of blocks, and Lady Asheland sat at the writing desk composing a letter. Soft music was coming from another room.

"Mr. Darcy, Mr. Bingley, and Miss Bingley," announced the butler in dry tones. Everyone but Mrs. Bennet rose. She looked at the party with wide eyes, then signaled everyone to be quiet.

"Forgive us, Mr. Bingley, Miss Bingley, Mr. Darcy," said Lady Asheland. "We weren't expecting company and Lady Violet has fallen asleep in her grandmama's arms. If you'll excuse me for a moment." She smiled at the party, then took the sleeping babe from her mother and left the room.

"We apologize if we've come at an inconvenient time," said Mr. Bingley.

"Not at all, we are just a family party here. Neighbors are always welcome," said Mrs. Bennet. She gestured for them to be seated. "This is my youngest daughter, Lydia." Lydia curtsied and smiled at the strangers. "And my grandson Lord Lisle, the viscount." She gestured to a chubby cheeked boy with golden hair and large, caramel eyes who was regarding them all seriously. "Lydia, please take Robbie to the nursery."

"Yes, Mama." Lydia curtsied to the group, scooped up the toddler, and left the room.

Jane and Mrs. Bennet sat across from the three visitors, for a moment not knowing what to say.

"I heard a rumor you were considering a ball, Mr. Bingley," said Mrs. Bennet finally. "Have you decided yet?"

"Oh, not as yet, though we are considering it." He looked around quietly for a moment, then spoke to Jane. "Miss Bennet, I hope your ankle is fully recovered?"

"Yes, it's quite well, thank you," she said, her cheeks blushing softly.

"Is Lord Asheland available this morning? I had hoped to speak to him," said Mr. Darcy.

"He is in the book room with Mr. Bennet," said Mrs. Bennet.

"I will show him, Mama," said Elizabeth as she reentered the room.

Darcy nodded to the ladies and followed Elizabeth. She led him through the hall and down another corridor in silence before knocking on a door on her right and opening it before there was an answer.

"Papa, *my lord*, Mr. Darcy is looking for you," she said brightly with a saucy smile for her husband.

Lord Asheland stifled a chuckle as she entered the room with Mr. Darcy on her heels. Her husband and father looked up and smiled at her happily.

"Thank you, my dear. Would you ask Hill for some tea and those biscuits I like?" asked Mr. Bennet with a wink.

"Yes, Papa." She gave the men another smile and was gone.

Darcy couldn't explain it, but he felt something odd in her manner toward him. It was almost like hostility, but not quite. He shook off the feeling. Women were strange creatures; it was best not to try to understand them.

"Lord Asheland, may I have a word?" he asked.

"Of course," he answered.

Mr. Bennet considerately busied himself at his desk while the two men sat near the fire.

"Lord Asheland, I'm afraid I owe you an apology."

The earl's brows raised. "Oh? Whatever for?"

"I spoke rather strongly to your wife as she was trying to leave Netherfield last week. It was raining, and I wanted her to return to the house. She insisted on riding on to Longbourn and we exchanged some harsh words. You have my apologies, my lord."

Lord Asheland looked at him silently for several moments until Darcy began to feel uncomfortable under the scrutiny.

"You exchanged words with my wife?"

"Yes, sir."

"Because she wanted to go home?"

"Yes, sir."

"But you did not want her to?"

"It was raining very heavily, sir."

Lord Asheland nodded. "Mr. Darcy, I accept your apology to the extent that I am able, but I believe the one you really should be offering it to is my wife."

Darcy looked thoughtful for a moment, then nodded. "Of course, my lord. I will see to it."

"A word of advice, if I may, Mr. Darcy."

The younger man looked to him quizzically.

"In future, you might consider *not* commanding the movements of ladies wholly unrelated to you, and perhaps those related to you as well."

Darcy flushed as the earl managed to look both wise and amused at the same time.

"Intelligent women do not appreciate being ordered about like children," said the earl.

He smiled and stood, rejoining his father-in-law while Darcy stared into the fire, a thoughtful look on his face.

In the sitting room, Caroline left her seat next to Jane and walked over to where Elizabeth was writing a letter at the desk by the window.

"How quickly you write, Lady Asheland," she exclaimed, as if Elizabeth had completed some great feat.

"On the contrary, I write rather slowly."

"You must have so many family members to keep up with, and the housekeepers of your estates as well, I assume."

"Yes."

Caroline walked closer, glancing over her shoulder. "To whom do you write, Lady Asheland?" she asked in a voice overly sweetened with false sincerity.

"A friend in Town, Miss Bingley," she answered succinctly.

"Who is in Town this time of year?" asked Caroline curiously, leaning over Elizabeth's shoulder further.

Realizing she would not be able to continue, Elizabeth turned in her chair, blocking Miss Bingley's view of her letter, and answered, "Lady Montgomery is currently in Town, attending her sister's lying-in."

Caroline searched her mind for the name of Lady Montgomery's sister. Who was she?

"Surely you know Mrs. Carlisle?" Elizabeth asked. She knew she was sporting with Miss Bingley and that it was beneath her and quite possibly rude, but she couldn't resist. The woman was incredibly irritating!

"Oh, yes! Mrs. Carlisle! This is her first babe, is it not?"

"Her third."

Caroline cleared her throat uncomfortably. "Well, then I'm sure she will come through it admirably."

She turned to rejoin her brother and Elizabeth grinned to herself as she returned to her letter, feeling slightly wicked.

~

A week later, Lord and Lady Asheland were set to leave for London. At the Bennets' request, they planned to leave their son, along with his nurse, with his grandparents since they would only be gone for a few days and take Lady Violet and her wet nurse to Town with them.

Elizabeth and Jane paid a farewell call to Netherfield the morning they were to depart.

"How long will you be away?" asked Miss Bingley, clearly distressed.

"Only a few days. I need to order some clothes for the winter and Lord Asheland has some business to attend to."

"Are you accompanying your sister, Miss Bennet?"

"No, I will be staying here. Our sister Mary will accompany Lady Asheland."

"I'm taking her with me to Town for the season and I want to begin ordering her clothes," said Elizabeth happily. She was truly excited about Mary's upcoming season and couldn't help but show her enthusiasm.

"Will she be presented this year?" asked Miss Bingley.

"Yes, and we will host a ball in her honor. I am looking forward to it. Alice, that is, Lady Montgomery, has agreed to help me with the preparations. It will be delightful."

Caroline's eyes lit with interest and Elizabeth barely managed to hold in her grin. Really, it was almost too easy; there was hardly any sport in it.

"I assume you are sponsoring your sister?"

"Yes, of course."

"May I ask, who sponsored you, Lady Asheland? I don't mean to be impertinent, I am merely curious."

For the first time, Elizabeth thought Caroline might actually mean what she said and answered accordingly. "Lady Devonshire, the Marchioness, sponsored both me and Jane. She is a cousin of my husband and my son's godmother."

Caroline made a small squeaking sound in the back of her throat and her stomach filled with butterflies.

"And will you accompany your sisters for the season, Miss Bennet?" asked Caroline with an ingratiating smile.

"Yes, I will be there. I wouldn't dream of missing Mary's debut," said Jane sweetly.

Caroline nodded. This was all very good news.

Elizabeth rose and smiled at Miss Bingley. "Thank you for the tea. We must be going. My husband wishes to be on the road by midday."

"Thank you for the call. I do hope you will return in time for the ball," Caroline said as she followed them to the door. "I was going to send out invitations soon."

"When is it?" asked Elizabeth.

"The twenty-sixth of November."

"I believe we will be back in time. If we are not, you have my best wishes for a successful affair. Good day," said Elizabeth kindly.

"Good day, Lady Asheland, Miss Bennet."

98

Elizabeth Adams

In the carriage on the way back to Longbourn, Elizabeth turned to Jane with a concerned expression.

"Jane, you must tell me the truth. Are you serious about Mr. Bingley?"

Jane flushed. "Have you known me to flirt with men I am not serious about, sister?"

"No, but he is a flirt himself; I want to make sure you are not merely responding in kind."

"Of course I am not!" Jane cried. "You know me better than that!"

"I do, I am sorry. I just want to know how you really feel about him." She gave her sister a conciliatory smile. "So you think you would like to see more of him?"

"Oh, Lizzy. He is everything a young man ought to be. Kind, amiable, handsome."

"Conveniently rich," interrupted Elizabeth.

Jane nudged her sister with her shoulder and gave her a mock-glare. "You know, I think I might like him even if her weren't wealthy, or handsome."

"That is always a good sign. Shall I invite him to Mary's ball in the spring? Or do you think he will have come to the point by then?"

Jane was impossibly red now, but she knew Elizabeth was teasing her. "I think perhaps we will have an *understanding* by then, but I cannot be sure. It is possible he feels only friendship for me."

"Jane, surely you aren't serious? If every man who felt friendship for a woman looked at her the way Mr. Bingley looks at you, there would be a lot more duels at dawn, I can promise you that."

Jane just laughed and rolled her eyes at her sister.

~

"Well, Lizzy, be safe and take care. We will watch over Robbie until you return," said Mr. Bennet as he bid his daughter farewell.

"Must you call him that?" she asked with a kiss to her son's full cheek. "Oh, I shall miss him so! Perhaps I should stay..."

"And send Mary shopping with Asheland? I think not. It is only a sennight, and if you miss us too badly, you can come home early."

"All will be well, Lizzy, stop fussing. I did raise five children, you know," clucked Mrs. Bennet as she bustled over to them and took her grandson from Mr. Bennet's arms. "Between your sisters and your father, he will be well entertained. Now off you go. You don't want to arrive in the night."

Elizabeth gave her son one last squeeze and walked outside on her father's arm. "What did you decide to do about that cousin of yours?" she asked.

Her father stopped beside the carriage and answered, "I have told Mr. Collins that we are full of houseguests and couldn't possibly accommodate him until February. I'm sure his noble patroness will assuage his disappointment."

"Thank you for sparing us, Papa," she said wryly.

He handed her into the carriage where Violet was waiting in the arms of her wet nurse, and Robert quickly followed, shaking hands with Mr. Bennet and extracting a promise to look after his son.

As the carriage pulled away, Mr. Bennet shook his head, wondering how such a fine daughter had come from two such flawed people as himself and Mrs. Bennet. And then she had gone on to marry such a fine man! Asheland was a better man than Bennet had ever been, he could admit that, but through the earl's example, Bennet was improving, bit by tiny bit.

In a nod to his improved self, he asked for his horse to be saddled so that he might ride over the eastern fields and check on the tenants there, when what he really wanted to do was return to his book and the warm fire in his book room. Damn if he didn't resent Asheland for making a more productive man of him, though he knew it was for the best in the end.

Shortly after their marriage, Elizabeth had expressed to Lord Asheland her worry for her sisters. They each had a small dowry of one-thousand pounds, payable only on their mother's death. Mrs. Bennet was hearty and hale, and not of advanced years, and the girls were quickly reaching marriageable age, and thus were essentially dowerless. Not wanting to see his wife upset, but also not willing to enable his father-in-law's indolence, Lord Asheland struck a deal with Mr. Bennet.

He would buy a large parcel of land adjacent to Longbourn. It belonged to Netherfield Park, but the owner was looking to sell that property and had no qualms breaking it up. Lord Asheland purchased the land and made repairs to the farms therein, with the agreement that Mr. Bennet would manage it and all the proceeds would go directly to dowries for Elizabeth's sisters. The first eighteen months' income was allocated to Jane, in respect to her age, thereafter split between her and Mary, until Jane's was large enough it needed no addition and Kitty was in need of it. Asheland's reasons were not entirely altruistic; he didn't want his own son to be saddled with a bevy of poor relations to support.

Mr. Bennet was surprised at the feelings this action engendered in him. He had always been an idle sort of man, one who preferred to let things happen around him instead of making them happen himself. His son-in-law's actions (and really the man was only a few years younger than himself) were exactly calculated to show him how lax he had been. Yes, he had thought they would have a son, but surely he could have set something aside, just a little something, for his girls? It would have made a great difference to their peace of mind and to his wife's. It was a humiliating thing to see a man who barely knew his family taking better care of them than he himself had.

When she was made aware of the arrangement, Mrs. Bennet was much relieved. With such good connections, and improved dowries, though still not impressive, she thought her girls stood a chance of making good matches. It motivated both her and Mr. Bennet to put aside a little of Longbourn's income to the same endeavor.

Longbourn had once been a more profitable estate but, three generations ago, hard times had come, as they are wont to do. Unfortunately, the owner at the time had recently made some unwise investments, leaving the coffers low and the estate unable to weather the difficult season. He had sold off a portion of his lands to keep the estate solvent. It was divided amongst the neighboring estates, some going to Netherfield Park—in fact, the same parcel which had recently been purchased by Lord Asheland. Not wanting it to happen again, the entail with its existing restrictions was put into place by the then owner, leaving the current Mr. Bennet in a precarious position.

Since he owned the land surrounding it, Lord Asheland eventually decided to purchase Netherfield Park. He installed a steward and maintained the majority of land surrounding the house and let the house and park out, firstly to a family that had not kept it above a twelve-month, and now to Mr. Bingley, though the latter did not realize the identity of the owner as everything had been done through solicitors.

Lord Asheland intended to allow Mrs. Bennet and any unmarried daughters to live in Netherfield for their lifetimes, though he thought it likely all the girls would marry. Then he would have another estate to pass down to a child or to strengthen the family's wealth. He could admit to a little trepidation about the number of children he and Elizabeth would have. Mrs. Bennet had had five children in less than eight years, and had Lydia's birth not been preceded by an accident that caused some difficulties, she might have gone on to have even more. Elizabeth was young when they married and young still. She was proving as fecund as her mother, perhaps more so, and he wondered how many children they would have all told.

In truth, though he would give Elizabeth anything she sincerely wanted, he had not fought her on nursing their daughter because of her assertion that it would lengthen the time between babes. He couldn't realistically imagine removing himself from her chambers, and this seemed a logical solution.

In the meantime, he was setting aside Netherfield's income for his sisters' dowries. Once they were all married, it would make a nice addition to the family properties.

~

The Ashelands' time in Town passed quickly. More than a dozen dresses were ordered for Mary, who was agog at all the fabrics and trims available to her. She was fitted for her presentation gown, and Elizabeth took the opportunity to introduce her to what friends were in Town at the moment.

Lady Asheland did quite a bit of shopping for herself, ordering several dresses to accommodate her new figure and many day dresses with buttons down the front for easy nursing. The modiste and her assistant seemed surprised when she requested them, but she winked and told them how much her husband enjoyed her enhanced figure, and they just giggled and went on with their business, any questions they may have had now answered.

Lord Asheland adjusted his will for the third time in as many years, now to provide for young Lady Violet. Unless another son was born, she would inherit the largest of his supplementary estates in addition to her sixty-thousand pound dowry. He decided that with only two children, he could be generous with his daughter—it would allow her more choices in the future.

He insisted Elizabeth be involved in all the legal transactions, sharing documents with her when he returned home. He also recounted various meetings with other members of Parliament. He was remarkably good at impressions, and the more his wife laughed, the more he threw himself into the renditions of his fellow peers.

After a week, their business was completed and they made their way back to Hertfordshire. Elizabeth's reunion with her son was happy and somewhat tearful on Elizabeth's part. She'd had no idea motherhood would make her so weepy! To her surprise, her father had taught him a new word and he proudly repeated it to his mother until she laughed in delight.

"Papa, must you teach him such words?" she asked in fond exasperation.

"Oh, come now! It does the boy no harm. He will have to learn them soon enough, anyhow."

"But hedgerows? You couldn't think of a better word?"

"It's really just 'rows; hedgerows is a bit much for the boy."

Elizabeth just shook her head and held her boy close.

CHAPTER 7

The day of the Netherfield ball, Longbourn was once again thrown into turmoil as the women curled and pinned and pulled themselves into the latest fashions. After much waiting in the hall, the men were joined by four very fashionable women.

In the midst of the compliments, Lydia said, "You must tell me everything. I want to know all about Miss Bingley's dress and whether she has any luck with Mr. Darcy. And see if Maria is wearing that ridiculous gown again. I've told her it doesn't suit her, but she doesn't listen to me!"

Her sisters promised they would faithfully relay all that occurred and were out the door, into the carriage, and pulling onto Netherfield's drive in short order. The house was aglow with candles and the moonlight illuminated the path beautifully.

"Lovely night for a ball, is it not?" said Lord Asheland quietly to his wife.

"Yes, the moonlight is perfect. I suppose I should commend Miss Bingley on her choice of date," said Elizabeth reluctantly.

Lord Asheland laughed at her and led her into the house.

"Mr. Bennet, Mrs. Bennet!" cried Mr. Bingley. He proceeded to greet Jane and Mary, then finally Lord and Lady Asheland. They greeted Mr. Bingley and walked on to his sister.

"Lord and Lady Asheland! We are so pleased you returned in time for our little ball," said Miss Bingley in a voice that made Elizabeth want to poke her with a hat pin. "Was your trip pleasant?"

"Quite. I must commend you on choosing the perfect night for a ball, Miss Bingley. The moonlight is splendid," Lord Asheland spoke charmingly, causing Miss Bingley to blush at his smile.

"Thank you, my lord. A good hostess must always pay attention to these things," she said.

"May I take the opportunity to request a dance?"

Caroline tittered and blushed more and it was decided he would dance the fifth with her, for the first three were taken by his wife and sisters, and the fourth by Miss Lucas.

Caroline waited anxiously for their dance. She would have the uninterrupted attention of an earl for half an hour! She had danced with a handful of viscounts and a baron or two in London, and there was an older earl that always danced with the young single women, but it wasn't an everyday occurrence and she had never had the company of one quite so high as Lord Asheland.

When he finally led her to the floor, she couldn't contain the self-satisfied smile that overtook her face. Asheland refrained from grimacing, but it was a near thing.

Miss Bingley prattled on with small talk until halfway through the dance when she began speaking of Elizabeth.

"What was that, Miss Bingley?" said Lord Asheland as her rejoined her after a turn.

"I was saying that when I first met Lady Asheland, I had no notion she was a countess. She said her name was Mrs. Talbot."

"She is Mrs. Talbot," he replied with a straight face.

"Of course," Caroline said quickly. "I just wondered at her not using her title more regularly, that is all." She pinched her mouth shut, hoping she hadn't offended him.

He shrugged slightly. "Most everyone in Meryton is known to my wife and knows her title. We introduce ourselves as Talbots when we are unsure of a new acquaintance." He smiled politely and she could only return it with a bemused smile of her own, her face slightly flushed.

She wasn't entirely sure what he meant by his statement, but she felt the sting of an insult nonetheless. In an effort to turn the conversation back to her good qualities, she said, "I am thinking of redoing the ballroom. A new crystal chandelier would give it a sense of grandeur, don't you think?"

He looked up at the current chandelier and back to his dance partner. "My wife is fond of this one, but I shall ask her what she thinks of another."

"My lord?" said Caroline, confused.

"She chose it last year, but she may have changed her mind. One never knows when it comes to fashion. One moment an item is beloved, and a few months later it is being replaced," he said with good humor.

Caroline's face was growing pale. "Are you saying, do I understand you correctly, that you *own* Netherfield Park, my lord?"

He looked at her innocently. "Forgive me madam, I thought you knew. Yes, I purchased it shortly after my marriage. With my wife's family being so close, it seemed an ideal investment. Wouldn't you agree?"

She made a sort of squeaking sound and turned away in the dance. Thankfully, the movement kept her occupied and away from Lord Asheland for a few moments. She wasn't sure how she felt about this information. It wasn't all bad, of course. She had known Charles was renting the estate and it must belong to someone. But in her mind, that someone had been an impoverished peer, or a gentleman who'd lost his money gambling or on a bad investment. Charles would then be in a good position to buy the estate, and while she did not love the immediate neighborhood, it was very close to London and boasted a mild winter. The recent addition of the Ashelands to the neighborhood was also in its favor.

But now, knowing the house and all its furnishings were nothing but a matter of investment for one of the richest earls in the kingdom, that she and her family were merely viewed as renters to provide a little income for them until they found need of the estate, she felt quite disheartened. Her image of herself as benevolent landowner was cut to pieces. She was not rescuing a sad property and would not be welcomed by the neighborhood as a savior of gentility. She was merely a renter. Expendable. And utterly unimportant—not even able to choose her own chandelier without consulting with the current owners.

It was very disheartening, indeed.

~

Much to Elizabeth's surprise and chagrin, Mr. Darcy asked her to dance. She said yes before she could think of a plausible excuse for refusing and when he led her onto the floor, she gave him a tight smile and reminded herself to mind her manners.

After several minutes spent dancing in silence, Mr. Darcy spoke. "Lady Asheland, I apologize for speaking to you so harshly before."

She took in his stiff demeanor and his solemn features, his expression showing all his distaste for the current conversation.

"Before you knew I was a countess, you mean?" she said as she turned away from him to dance with the other ladies.

When she returned, he said, "No, I simply meant before as in earlier, though I suspect you knew that and are willfully misunderstanding me."

She tilted her head and looked at him with one eyebrow arched. "Am I?"

It was his turn to turn away from her and she waited patiently, wondering what he was about.

"Nevertheless, I apologize for speaking harshly and inserting myself into your business. It was none of my affair."

She looked at him in surprise and said, "Apology accepted, Mr. Darcy."

He nodded and she noticed his ears were red at the tips and his jaw was flexing. *Not used to apologizing, are you?* she thought.

They moved through the remainder of the dance in silence and when it was over, Elizabeth gladly took her husband's arm and hoped the pairing would never be repeated.

~

Shortly after the ball, Mr. Darcy attended a hunting party with Lord Asheland and only found more to respect in the older man. Lord Asheland was fair, patient, kind, generous, and amiable. He watched the earl with his wife, unable to explain his curiosity. There was something between the two of them, something almost palpable, that he couldn't quite understand but was drawn to nonetheless.

He had heard stories of the earl. A wealthy man does not lose two wives and three children in such tragic circumstances without society speaking of it. He understood that the ton considered him an eccentric for choosing his young wife, but then the wealthy could afford to be so and after all he had been through, could anyone blame him?

He had heard of Lady Asheland, as well. No one could decide if she was a country upstart who had manipulated the earl into marriage or a young goddess who was positively enchanting. He agreed there was something bewitching about her. Her husband was certainly besotted, anyone could see that. But it wasn't only that she had inspired the devotion of a great man, though that in itself was an impressive feat, but that she was beguiling, witty, charming, quick to laugh and entirely devoted to her husband and children. In short, it was clear how she had drawn the notice of Lord Asheland, and why he would refuse a well-connected and dowered bride in favor of a vivacious country beauty.

Darcy couldn't help but see all these things, observant as he was, and as the time approached for him to leave for London to spend Christmas with his sister and Fitzwilliam family, he found himself wishing he might have a marriage such as the Ashelands. Alas, he didn't truly think he would be so lucky. Darcy was rich, to be sure, but Asheland was fabulously wealthy. He would have to make up for Georgiana's dowry when she married, and though he thought he could weather that without too much trouble, he knew his family expected him to marry a well-connected bride to strengthen their place in society.

He wouldn't be able to do as Asheland had done and marry a penniless girl from the country. He would never hear the end of it.

~

Though they missed being at home, it seemed a bit silly to return to Nottinghamshire for the festive season, especially considering the icy weather and the long journey with two small children, only to turn around and travel to London in February. Elizabeth dearly wished to see the Gardiners and her sister Kitty, as did her husband, and their London family generally spent Christmas and New Year in Hertfordshire, so the Ashelands decided to stay on at Longbourn until it was time to go to London.

The Netherfield party were frequent callers, though Elizabeth was often out riding with her youngest sister or in the nursery with her children. Mr. Bingley continued to tease his sisters on how bad a blunder they had made with Lady Asheland and the two made every effort to ingratiate themselves with her, despite her clear desire to be left alone to visit her family in peace.

All her patience was worth it in the end when Jane became engaged to Mr. Bingley on Christmas Day. Mr. Bennet made the announcement to a drawing room filled with expectant women and a red-faced Mr. Bingley by his side. Congratulations were heard all around and an impromptu dinner party filled with toasts and good wishes commenced.

It was decided that the wedding would take place at Longbourn in mid-March, that Mr. Darcy would stand up with Charles, and that Mary would stand up with Jane. Lord and Lady Asheland were truly pleased for Jane, and Elizabeth promised to host a party for them in spring to celebrate the occasion. Jane was happier than anyone had ever seen her, and Lord Asheland felt a true brother's pride in seeing her so well settled.

~

In February, the Ashelands left for London accompanied by Jane, Mary, and Mrs. Bennet. The ladies shopped for Jane's wedding clothes and prepared for Mary's presentation.

Mr. Bennet entertained a visitor at Longbourn, his cousin Mr. Collins, the heir to his estate. Bennet found him amusing at first, but that quickly turned to annoyance and within a week, Collins was in a hired carriage on his way back to Kent, thinking it very odd that neither the mistress of the estate nor any of his fair cousins had been there to meet him. Only the youngest daughter was about and she was constantly attended by her governess and not yet out. Though, she was a pretty young thing. Perhaps in a year or two, she might make a good wife to a humble parson such as himself.

~

After three weeks of visiting every warehouse, milliner, and bootmaker in London, Mrs. Bennet returned home to prepare for the wedding and Jane enjoyed her first free morning since becoming betrothed.

"You look exhausted!" declared Elizabeth as she joined her sister in the family sitting room.

"I feel exhausted. I know Mama means well, but I do not enjoy shopping quite as much as she does," said Jane.

"Jane, no one enjoys shopping as much as Mama does."

Jane laughed and Elizabeth called for tea.

"I'm glad we are alone, for there is something I wished to speak with you about." Jane sat forward, interested, and Elizabeth continued. "I didn't mention it while Mama was here because I didn't want to embarrass you, but I wanted to give you a selection of night gowns as a wedding gift. One of Madame DuPont's seamstresses has a knack for getting the fabric to hang just right, and it will make you feel even more beautiful, if that's possible."

Jane flushed and looked down. "That's very thoughtful of you, Lizzy. Thank you. And for your discretion."

Elizabeth nodded.

"I was hoping you would be willing to speak to me—about marriage—if you were willing," said Jane nervously.

"Of course, dearest. Ask me anything and I promise to tell you the truth. Did you want to talk today?"

"No!" Jane exclaimed. "I don't think I'm quite ready for that conversation, but soon."

"Of course," said Elizabeth kindly. "I know Aunt Gardiner spoke to us long ago, but it was not so very detailed. Whenever you are ready, I shall tell you all you wish to know."

"Thank you, Lizzy."

~

The next day, Jane mustered up what courage she could find and knocked on her sister's door. Elizabeth had been expecting her and led her sister to her private parlor where they could speak undisturbed.

Jane began with a series of simple questions and once it was confirmed that she correctly understood the mechanics, she asked more personal questions.

"Is it very strange? Having a man so… near you?" Jane asked.

"I'll admit it was odd at first, but not unpleasant. Men are so very different from women. I was quite fascinated with Robert's body when we first wed." Jane flushed at the casual way her sister spoke. "He teased me about it for ages. But I was honestly curious!"

"Are they very hairy?" Jane asked quietly, her eyes on her lap.

"They are not all the same. Your Mr. Bingley is very fair, so I imagine he is not very hairy. Robert is slightly darker, but I don't think he's very hairy either. My friend has a dark husband and she says he is quite furry!"

"Lizzy!"

"It is just us, Jane. We may be honest here if we like."

Jane nodded. "What do you do... after? Should I ask him to sleep with me? Should I ask him to leave?"

"I think it is nice to share a bed. I can't imagine sleeping without Robert now that I have shared a bed with him for so long. But you must decide what you like yourself. The marriage bed is a very intimate place, Jane. It will do you no favors to ignore your own desires. If you wish for him to stay, simply ask him. He cannot read your mind and may not know you want him there unless you say something."

Jane flushed again, but bravely continued. "Do men like that—when you express your desires?"

"I suspect men who truly care for their wives do, yes. I cannot speak for all men, but I have never heard of one becoming upset because his wife asked him to sleep with her or to do something she particularly likes."

"Like what?"

Elizabeth flushed. "Every woman has her own... preferences. You will like certain touches and kisses more than others. It is wise to tell him, or he may not know and will do something else you do not like as much."

Jane nodded. "Is it truly pleasant? Or are you just trying to assuage my fears?"

"It can be very pleasant. Though I will not lie that it can be painful at first and rather awkward until you understand what to do. But then, ah," she sighed, "*then*, it can quickly become your favorite leisure activity."

"Lizzy!"

"It is no time to be missish, Jane!"

Her sister looked down and fidgeted with her shawl. "Did you say do?" Jane looked at her with confusion. "I thought he would know what to do."

Elizabeth looked around the room as if the answers to this conversation could be found hiding behind the draperies. "He probably does, but you should not hold to

114.

mama's notion of lying still and hoping it will be over quickly. You should be an active participant. Aunt Gardiner gave me that advice and it has served me very well."

"She told you to participate?"

"Yes."

"And to voice your desires?"

"Once I knew them, yes."

Jane took a deep breath. "I think I can do that."

"You can. Charles cares for you very much and will be patient with you, I'm sure of it."

"Thank you, Lizzy. You've eased my mind."

~

Since they were all in Town, and her mother was far away in Hertfordshire, Elizabeth decided to host a congratulatory dinner for Jane and Mr. Bingley. It was impossible to exclude Miss Bingley and the Hursts, and since she could not make such a public dismissal without hurting Jane, she decided to use the occasion to show Miss Bingley what she, and by extension Jane, was made of.

Elizabeth was under no illusions that Miss Bingley would smoothly relinquish power to her sister. She thought it likely that Jane would face a series of small struggles: from whom to invite, to how to decorate, to which place settings to use. Caroline would insert herself into the smallest decisions until she had worn Jane down and was mistress of the house in all but name.

Robert was right—it was best for everyone involved if she married soon, and barring that, she should move in with her sister, Mrs. Hurst. Robert would talk to Charles Bingley, Elizabeth would handle Caroline.

The date was settled and the invitations sent and accepted. Jane's sweet nature had endeared her to many of Elizabeth's friends, and more than one man was disappointed that she had chosen Bingley. After all, Jane was easily the handsomest woman a man was ever likely to see and had a sweet temperament besides. A man would forego much to have such beauty for his own. And she had excellent connections. Everyone knew she was the favorite sister to Lord Asheland. Who knew what favors he might bestow on her lucky husband?

Alas, she was taken. The ladies were glad she was removed from the competition (Jane really was terribly pretty) and the men held hopes for the next sister; rumor had it that she was spending the season with the earl and countess. Could she be as pretty as her sisters?

~

Unfortunately for Mary, or fortunately, depending on one's point of view, she was not as pretty as her pulchritudinous sister Jane, nor as enchanting as her vivacious sister Elizabeth. It was wondered if the sisters decreased in beauty along with age, but a loyal Charles Bingley assured them that Miss Kitty was a delicate beauty and that Lydia was just as robust and playful as Elizabeth, while insisting that Mary was pretty in her way, of course.

Mary Bennet was the kind of girl that becomes more attractive on further acquaintance. One's first impression was that she was serious and boring, but once one took the time to know her, one realized her seriousness was dedication, and she was not boring, merely observant, and to observe properly, she must not be constantly prattling on. Of course, when the topic was of interest to her, she could speak without ceasing.

Mary did not like being the focus of attention for a large group of people. Elizabeth had planned to host a proper coming out ball for her, but Mary dreaded the idea and asked for a dinner instead. It was a relatively small affair, held the evening of her presentation. The Gardiners were there, Lord Asheland's cousin Alfred Downing and his wife Sylvia, Lord and Lady Montgomery (Elizabeth's particular friend), Lord and Lady Sheffield, and a few of Mary's friends from her seminary and their families.

It was nothing to the lavish dinner and entertainment she was planning to celebrate Jane's engagement, but it was perfectly suited to Mary. After dinner, Mary and her friends entertained the room with music on various instruments and the evening ended with a contented sister and a proud Lord and Lady Asheland.

A week later, Elizabeth stood in the drawing room in her best evening gown, entertaining guests at Jane's engagement dinner. In two days' time they would leave for Hertfordshire to attend to the final wedding preparations, and a week after that Jane would be married. Tonight was the earl and countess's way of showing they approved of Jane's match and an opportunity to introduce Mr. Bingley to the family.

The Talbot family was there en masse. There were a handful of untitled cousins and their usual friends in Town, plus two of Robert's friends from the House of Lords. The Downings were present, of course, along with their son John and daughter Marianne, now Lady Rockingham, and the Marquess and Marchioness of Devonshire, second cousins to Robert and to whom Alfred was the heir. Robert's maternal uncle, Lord Sedbury, was there as well. Even with a cane and advanced years, he was one of the most interesting conversationalists in the room and a favorite of Elizabeth's. Looking around with a smile, Elizabeth noted that she was very fond of nearly all her guests. It was shaping up to be a delightful dinner.

A solid half hour after everyone else had arrived, Caroline Bingley and the Hursts entered the room. Elizabeth went to greet them, as a good hostess does, and introduced them to two of her untitled cousins before being called away.

Caroline was besieged by so many emotions she didn't know which to pay attention to first. She counted no fewer than six earls in the room and a marquess! Was that Percy Seymour in the corner, Viscount Hyde? Oh! What a grand party! She was glad she had worn her best dress, a shimmering blue concoction that made her look like a goddess. She was determined to make a good impression tonight.

Before she could meet anyone in the peerage, dinner was announced. She was seated in the center of the table, near the untitled cousins and two seats away from Mr. Darcy. He was next to Amelia Herbert, a pretty woman with good connections and a healthy dowry. Why did *she* not sit there? Instead she was seated by Mr. Talbot, one of several in the room, a perfectly decent man made undesirable by his marriage to Mrs. Talbot, the cheerful blonde a few seats away.

Miss Bingley had a few pleasant conversations, and she was introduced to many prestigious people, but the party was so large, and the company so well known to each other, that they spent all their time discussing places and people she knew nothing of and made no effort to include her in the conversation. Everyone was cordial, and no one slighted her in the least, but she nevertheless felt her own unimportance. She had no bit of gossip to entertain them with—they weren't interested in her friends and didn't seem to enjoy that sort of conversation anyway—and she had no idea of the children they spoke of, or the trips they described, or the homes they were making changes to.

She was utterly superfluous and she finished the evening feeling quite dejected, until she remembered that she would be able to boast of all the impressive people she had dined with to her less significant friends. That thought cheered her considerably.

~

When the men joined the ladies in the drawing room, merry with port and good company, Elizabeth was taking her turn at the instrument. Darcy found a place convenient to watch her and let himself relax into the spell she was casting over the room. When she began to sing, he let the tiniest smile escape his lips.

Once again he was reminded of how very good a wife she was. She had eyes only for her husband as she sang the ballad. The looks passed between them would have been indecorous had they not been surrounded by family and close friends. Somehow, and quite without his permission, she had become the standard by which he measured other women. Each time a female acquaintance mindlessly agreed with whatever careless comment he or another man made, he remembered her passionate refusal to concede to him and her dedication to her family's welfare. Each time they simpered and sneered, he remembered her genuine laughter and bright smile.

She was a fine mother, that much was clear, though she was going about it in a strange way. He had not given it much thought before, other than knowing his wife would need to be healthy and able to bear an heir, but suddenly a lady's aptitude for motherhood was something he thought should have more bearing in his choice than he had previously given it.

Yes, Lady Asheland was a fine wife. He should seek someone like her.

~

The next day, Charles called on Jane and Darcy accompanied him. Elizabeth couldn't imagine why the haughty man bothered; he clearly found no enjoyment there. Each time he and Elizabeth had a conversation, generally about books but occasionally about politics, they ended in an argument of some kind. Lord Asheland was often out—Parliament was in session, after all—and she could hardly leave Jane alone with two gentlemen, so Elizabeth was left entertaining Mr. Darcy while Jane and Charles whispered to each other on the settee.

She was grateful for all her serious conversations with Robert about the state of the kingdom that allowed her to hold her own in debate with Mr. Darcy, but really, she wished he would simply cease calling. Why did Charles bring him so frequently?

She thought at first it was for the connection. Asheland was a powerful title, after all, and the Talbot family was well-known and respected. But Darcy was connected to the Fitzwilliam family, one not dissimilar to the Talbots in influence, so he could have little need for noble connections. He wasn't interested in Mary; the two rarely said more than two words to each other and Mary often found a way to avoid the call altogether. If she couldn't, she would play the pianoforte or the harp quietly in the background while the others conversed.

Elizabeth stifled her sigh when the men were announced. Mary was playing in the music room and the peaceful notes floated down the hall, soothing Elizabeth's irritation. Darcy was Bingley's closest friend, and Bingley was to be her brother. She should try to get along with the man. Steeling herself, she greeted the men kindly and called for tea.

As expected, Charles and Jane sequestered themselves on the sofa a slight distance away from the chairs she and Darcy sat in. She asked Darcy how he wanted his tea that day—she had noticed that he took it with sugar when he was drinking it on its own, but with milk when he drank it with cake. When he asked for milk, no sugar, she smiled and handed him the prepared tea and a plate of cakes before he could ask for them.

120

He thanked her and deigned to give her a smile of appreciation for anticipating his needs, which he somehow managed to do as smugly as he did everything else. *Insufferable man!*

"You are a supporter of the Harrington Orphanage, are you not, Lady Asheland?" Darcy asked after some time of idle chatter.

"Yes, I am. Why do you ask?"

"My aunt is as well."

"Yes, I am acquainted with Lady Matlock."

"She was telling me recently about a new initiative some of the board have suggested." He plucked another sweet cake from the tray before them and continued, "It seems they want to start a school of sorts."

"That isn't so unusual, Mr. Darcy. Surely educating orphans to support themselves has been going on for some time," she said patiently.

"Yes, but generally they are trained to be servants or seamstresses, or in the case of the boys, craftsmen of some sort. Higher learning has always been thought to be wasted on them."

"Define 'higher learning,' sir," she said crisply.

He leaned back comfortably and crossed one leg over the other. "I define it as everyone defines it. Foreign languages, music, debate, classical studies. What use would they have for such things?"

"Is your objection then that they would learn useless topics?" she asked.

"I wouldn't call it an objection. I do wonder if it is a worthwhile endeavor. What will they do with such knowledge once they have it? Would their time not be better spent learning something of use?"

"Like how to iron a shirt or shoe a horse?" she quipped.

"Precisely." He flashed his smug smile again before he took a sip of tea and she had a strong urge to dash the cup from his hand and let the tea stain his silk waistcoat.

"Tell me, sir, how often do you speak Latin with your friends?"

"Excuse me?"

"You were at Cambridge and I assume some sort of school before that. Perhaps your parents brought in tutors for you at home."

He nodded, a suspicious look on his face.

"So you must have learned Latin, like most gentlemen. Tell me, do you speak it together at the clubs? Do you have secret conversations in full view of the servants, knowing they can't understand you?"

"Of course not!"

"Then what was the purpose of learning it? Would you not have been better served learning something useful?"

He smiled again at her. "And what would you propose young gentlemen learn in place of Latin, my lady?"

"Oh, I don't know—there are many useful things a man should know how to do. How to mend a carriage for instance." She almost laughed at the comical look on his face. "Carriages are constantly sitting lame on the side of the road while the owners pace behind them, uselessly. Surely it would be better to know at least a *little* of their construction."

He nodded skeptically, his eyes narrow. "I concede some general knowledge of the workings of a carriage would be useful."

"It would also be helpful if gentlemen were more useful about the house. Some gardening skills, laying a fire. Most can't even design a basic menu, let alone prepare any of the food that goes in it!"

"Surely you jest, Lady Asheland," he said with a knowing look, certain now that she was teasing him.

"And men know so little about children!" she
continued. "One is constantly hearing sad tales about how
a mother died in tragic circumstances and the children
were sent to live with an aunt or cousin or near stranger
because their own father couldn't care for them. Would it
not be better for them to grow up with their own parent in
their own home?"

He spluttered.

"You see, Mr. Darcy, people do not learn what is
useful for them to know, but what is *appropriate* for their
position in life." She sat back, her excitement spent.

He took a breath and re-entered the fray. "All the
more reason to teach them trade skills for that is the
position they are born to."

She made a doubtful noise and tilted her head. "I do
not know. Most pity the orphans, and I will agree that
being without home or family is a terrible thing, but there
is something liberating in having no set path. If they are
able to determine their own futures in more meaningful
directions, who are we to say they shouldn't?"

"You are quite revolutionary, Lady Asheland."

"Not revolutionary, Mr. Darcy, merely fair-minded."

He nodded in acknowledgement of her point as
Bingley stood and asked Darcy if he was ready to leave.
Jane and Elizabeth accompanied the gentlemen to the
entrance hall and Elizabeth led Darcy to the door to give
Jane and Bingley a private farewell.

"Thank you for the stimulating conversation, Lady
Asheland," said Darcy as he pulled on his gloves.

"And you, sir. I trust your sensibilities will recover
soon," she said impertinently.

"You may depend upon it. I look forward to our next
debate."

"As do I," she said politely.

He gave her that patronizingly self-satisfied smile
again, the one that always gave her the urge to pinch him

and stick out her tongue. She gritted her teeth and stepped away from the door, allowing him to pass by.

He stepped through the doorway and turned to look at her. "Until we meet again, upon the field of battle."

"Sir, I shall show you no mercy," she said with a sly smile.

"Madam," he smiled and put his hat on his head, "I look forward to it." He nodded and was gone.

Darcy whistled on his walk home. He couldn't remember when he'd had more fun in a drawing room.

~

The wedding was beautiful. Jane was radiant, as always, and Charles was even more ebullient than usual. Mary was quite pretty and Darcy expectedly smug.

Elizabeth's family returned to Town the following day to enjoy the remainder of the Season, this time with Charlotte Lucas in tow. Mary had elected to remain in Hertfordshire. She was enjoying being out in familiar society and London had been a little too much for her. Elizabeth suspected the musical (and handsome) cousin visiting the Gouldings had something to do with her decision as well.

Summer was spent at Cressingdon and Elizabeth tried her hand at matchmaking, inviting Mr. Rippen, the owner of a small estate a few miles away, to dinner to meet Charlotte Lucas. The two had much to talk about, as Elizabeth had thought they would, and to no one's surprise, Mr. Rippen proposed by the end of summer and they were married by Michaelmas. He found Charlotte to be sensible and attractive and kind, and he had long wanted a closer relationship with Lord Asheland. Marrying the close friend of the earl's beloved wife seemed an excellent way to achieve it. The fact that Miss Lucas made him stammer when he would otherwise be

articulate and flush when the room was cool was but a
happy coincidence.

CHAPTER 8

Jane and Charles went to Ireland on their wedding tour and, on the way back to Hertfordshire in October, they stopped at Cressingdon to visit the Asheland family. To Jane's great surprise, she was met with a rather rotund Elizabeth.

"Lizzy! Why didn't you tell me you were increasing again!" she cried, placing her hands on her sister's swollen belly.

"I didn't want you racing back from your tour," she said.

"When will the babe come?"

"Not for two more months at least, perhaps three."

Jane's eyes widened. "So you think sometime in January then?"

"Most likely, perhaps December. He will come when he is ready. I am not overly worried about it," she said simply.

"So you think it is a boy?"

"I have a feeling," said Elizabeth with a secret smile.

Hoping she would soon have similar news to share, Jane squeezed her hand and followed her sister to rejoin their husbands.

~

Jane and Charles spent only a fortnight at Cressingdon with their brother and sister, then went on to Hertfordshire to see the Bennet family. Jane wanted to return for her sister's lying in and her mother would never forgive her if they stayed away for months without a visit. She also knew Elizabeth would have her head if Mrs. Bennet came to Cressingdon to see them. Their mother's nerves were not good companions for a lying in.

By Christmas, Jane and Charles were back in residence at Cressingdon and had looked at two estates available for purchase. The first was in Leicestershire to the south, which was a nice house but not to Jane's personal tastes, and the other was on the border of Nottinghamshire and Derbyshire, less than thirty miles from Mr. Bingley's closest friend, Mr. Darcy, and only twenty miles north of Cressingdon.

The second estate was agreed upon and the sisters were beside themselves with excitement and spent hours making plans for the house, the gardens, and the nursery. Jane felt the first fluttering of her babe during the festive season and the entire family erupted in joyful congratulations at the announcement.

Lord Asheland's extended family was also in residence for the holiday, including his cousin and close friend, Alfred Downing, who had recently inherited the title of Marquess of Devonshire, and his wife and children, who were Elizabeth's age, and their cousin, the dowager marchioness. Elizabeth couldn't keep herself from making the observation to Jane that Caroline Bingley would have swooned at all the titles in the room. It was a pity she hadn't been a more pleasant person, or she might have been invited. Jane tried to chastise her sister, but couldn't hold her laugh in well enough to do it properly.

By mid-January, all their guests but the Bingleys had left. Jane had a small but noticeable bulge under her dress, and Elizabeth was so heavy with child she could hardly move. When she woke one morning with excess energy and a strong desire to clean and sew and cook things (even though she hated sewing and didn't even know how to cook), she knew it was a sign the babe was near. The same had happened a few days before the births of both Robbie and Violet.

After organizing the baby's layette for the third time and triple checking all the supplies in the nursery, she felt the need for fresh air. She found her sister Jane and the two of them took to the gardens, kept warm by their fur coats and burgeoning middles.

"Did you ever think we would be walking in a garden together, both with child at the same time?" asked Elizabeth in amusement.

"Yes," answered Jane simply.

"You did?"

"Of course. With our mother, I knew it was likely we would both conceive easily." She nodded to her sister who returned the gesture. "And you were the one who thought you would never marry. I always knew some lucky man would see your worth and offer for you. It's only natural that we should eventually fall with child at the same time."

"I suppose you're right. It does take nine months."

Jane chuckled. "Yes. Now, if we were both to deliver on the same day, that would really be something."

Elizabeth laughed outright and the two continued walking another quarter of an hour until suddenly Elizabeth reached out and clutched her sister's arm.

"What is it, Lizzy?" asked Jane, worried at the expression on her sister's face.

"We must return to the house," said Elizabeth.

She turned and began walking swiftly up the path that led to the house, nearly half a mile away.

"What is it?" asked Jane, concern in her voice.

"My waters have broken," said Elizabeth simply.

Jane looked down to the ground, then at her sister's dress, and finally behind them, where she could see the faint trace of a water trail following Elizabeth.

"Oh!" she cried.

Elizabeth stopped to take a deep breath and hold her stomach for a minute, then was moving swiftly again.

"How close are you?" asked Jane.

"I do not know. With the first two, I was well into labor before my waters broke, but once they did..." she trailed off and Jane looked at her seriously, remembering the labors and how within an hour of her waters breaking she was holding little Robbie.

"Come, we must hurry," she said as she took her sister's arm and propelled her forward.

They stopped more and more frequently as they went along, rushing up the path between Elizabeth's pains, desperate to get to the house while she was still able to transport herself.

Finally, after what felt like an age but had actually been less than an hour, the house was in sight. Jane saw an estate worker of some sort, she knew not who and neither did she care, and called out for him to fetch the master and Mr. Bingley and tell someone to call the midwife.

Seeing the situation for himself, the young gardener ran to the stables to send a rider for the midwife and another for the master, who was out with his steward on the east side of the estate. He yelled to a laundry maid hanging out clothes as he ran by, asking her to fetch the housekeeper and Mr. Bingley.

With the house in an uproar, Jane and Elizabeth, the latter now sweating and breathing heavily, made their way up the front steps of the house. Just as they reached the front door, it burst open and the housekeeper stepped out.

"Oh, my lady! It's your time! The midwife has been sent for and the master, too. Let's get you to your rooms."

She took Elizabeth's arm and guided her into the foyer, where Elizabeth was again forced to stop and double over in pain. She stepped forward, and to her embarrassment, and the worry of her housekeeper and sister, Elizabeth left a pale pink pool behind her on the polished marble.

"Good God!" cried Charles Bingley as he ran into the room. "Lady Asheland, allow me."

Before anyone could answer or protest, he swooped Elizabeth up into his arms and headed straight for the stairs. She held to his neck with one arm and to her belly with the other, trying not to scream and frightened out of her mind.

"Robert!" she cried. "Where is Robert?"

"He is on the way, my lady," assured the housekeeper.

"Send him," Elizabeth panted, "straight," pant, pant, "to me," pant, "baby," pant "coming!"

"Yes, my lady," said the housekeeper.

She opened the door and Charles rushed into her chamber. Elizabeth's maid, Watson, had just removed the coverlet and was placing a clean white sheet on the bed.

"Put her here," she said.

Charles deposited her gently on the bed and Elizabeth grasped his arm tightly.

"Thank you, brother," she whispered.

He nodded, the gravity of the situation striking him full force. Jane pushed him into the hall and told him to bring Lord Asheland to them as soon as he was seen. She then disappeared back into the room to attend her sister.

"Send for Prue Cleary in the kitchen," barked the housekeeper.

"What?" asked Watson. "I don't think anyone will be needing a snack!"

"Her mother was the midwife and she used to assist. She'll know what to do."

Watson nodded and gave the orders to a maid outside the hall, then returned to her mistress where she began removing Elizabeth's walking dress. Jane bathed her sister's forehead with a cloth and rubbed her shoulders trying to offer comfort.

Elizabeth was insensible to all around her. She could only moan and cry out for Robert.

"Where is he? I need him!" she cried.

"He will be here soon, sister. Hold my hand. He'll be here soon. Shh," cooed Jane.

Elizabeth whimpered, sweat pouring off her head, her body racked with painful shudders. She could only cling pathetically to Jane and pray for Robert to get there soon.

Suddenly, strong arms wrapped around her and she felt herself lifted off the bed and onto her feet.

"I know it hurts love, but you must move," her husband's voice whispered in her ear.

"Robert!" she cried as loud as she could, which was barely more than a whisper. "You came!"

"Of course, love. I always come when you call for me, you know that." He smiled at her with that familiar twinkle in his eyes and she felt herself buoyed. She nodded and looked to Mrs. Cleary who was acting the part of the midwife.

"You must stand and move about, my lady. The baby must come down," said the old woman, her apron twisted in her hands.

Elizabeth nodded, remembering well Violet's birth and the fight to get her to descend. Robert looked above Elizabeth's head to the grey-haired Mrs. Cleary.

"Do you have this in hand?" he asked. His voice was calm, but his eyes were grave.

The elderly woman squared her shoulders and dropped the apron she had wrinkled irreparably. "Yes, my lord. All is under control."

"Good."

Robert stood beside Elizabeth all the while, encouraging her, squeezing her hand, rubbing her back. He never left her side.

Less than an hour later, Elizabeth was on the birthing chair, bent over her stomach and pushing with all her might. With her last push, she cried out so loudly that the maids on the lower floor stopped what they were doing and looked upwards. There was a dreadful moment of silence, then the hearty cry of a healthy babe.

A spontaneous cheer arose amongst the house servants and in the birthing room.

"You have a bonny baby boy, my lady," said Mrs. Cleary as she handed the baby to Elizabeth.

"Oh!" she cried as she looked at his round little face, red and angry at being born. "My son!" Then she wept in exhaustion and relief and more than a little shock.

The midwife arrived just as Elizabeth was delivering the afterbirth. She pronounced both the babe and the countess in good health and commended Mrs. Cleary on a job well done.

~

"What shall we call this little one?" said Lord Asheland softly as he and his wife lay in his bed with their new babe.

"Charles carried me up the stairs," she said.

"What?"

"Jane and I were walking, and my waters broke, and by the time we got here, I was so tired, I didn't think I would make it up the stairs, but then Charles came in like an angel, and picked me up and ran up the stairs, as if I weighed nothing at all."

"I shall have to thank him."

She nodded. "I would like to ask Charles to stand godfather."

"I think that a fine idea," replied Lord Asheland. "What about Bennet Charles?"

"For his name?"

"Yes."

"Bennet Charles Talbot," she said.

"Bennet Talbot. I think that a fine name."

They smiled at the sleeping babe before them.

"You know your sisters will call him Benny," he said.

"Not if I can help it!" she said. "Ben I like, but Benny is a dog's name."

He laughed. "You should try to sleep, Elizabeth. You've had an exhausting day."

"Yes, my lord."

CHAPTER 9

The time after the birth moved quickly and before long, Bennet was being christened, Charles Bingley and John Downing standing as godfathers and Elizabeth's friend Lady Montgomery as godmother. Elizabeth felt a little bad at passing over her sister Mary for her friend, but in truth she was closer to Alice than Mary and thought Mary could be godmother to the next child. She seemed to have a babe every eighteen months.

After being churched, she was still rather melancholy. She thought it was the weather; it had been cold and dark of late, and she was terribly exhausted with the baby. The wet nurse they had hired had contracted an illness and was no longer available, so for the first seven weeks of Bennet's life, Elizabeth was his sole source of food. They had finally found another woman in a nearby village who would arrive tomorrow. Elizabeth was looking forward to the rest. She couldn't remember when she'd felt so tired.

She wandered through the house, her thoughts drifting here and there, until she came to the nursery. She had a keepsake box of sorts for each of her children, filled with the mementos of their first few months of life. Rattles, a lock of hair, a Christening gift or two. She traced her hand over the lid to Robert John's box. He had been a baby just yesterday, but now he was nearly three years old. How had time gone by so quickly?

Alfred Downing and her Uncle Gardiner were Robert John's godfathers, and the dowager Marchioness of Devonshire his godmother. Their housekeeper, Mrs.

Hobbs, had an orphaned niece who had come to live with her aunt while Elizabeth was expecting young Robert. The girl was quite good with a pencil, and after seeing her drawings, Elizabeth asked her to make a few of the christening. The images were tucked inside the memory box, with one framed and hung on the wall. They were remarkably lifelike. Alfred was beyond pleased as he held his godson, and Robert stood watch over it all, the epitome of a proud father.

Violet's christening had been done the same way. Jane and Sylvia Downing were her godmothers and Stephen Carew, her godfather. John Downing, Alfred's son, had teased them about being passed over, but they promised him he would stand godfather to their next child. Elizabeth had wondered if he and Jane might one day make a match of it, but it was not to be. It was just as well. Jane was very happy with Charles and she wouldn't have liked being a marchioness, anyway.

Now there was Bennet. She touched the third box and couldn't help her sigh. He really was a beautiful baby. His eyelashes were already beginning to look long, like his father's, and he was such a sweet boy, if not excessively hungry.

Feeling herself becoming weepy again, she left the nursery, drew on a cloak, and stepped outside for a brisk walk. She would keep to the gardens because of the dark sky, but fresh air would do her a world of good.

She would go to Jane's new home in a few days, and Bennet would go with her. She had not discussed it with Robert yet. She knew he wouldn't like the idea. He was aware of how tired she was and concerned greatly by her moods and continual crying. She told him not to worry about it, she simply couldn't help it. When the sun came back out, and she got a full night's sleep, she would be her old self again. She wasn't unhappy, not truly, just exhausted and a trifle overwhelmed.

After all, three babes in three and a half years, and she not yet two and twenty, would exhaust anyone. Sighing, she pulled her cloak around her and headed to Robert's study. She must talk to him about her trip to Jane's. Putting it off would do her no good.

~

"I simply want to go visit my sister's new house. She wishes to be settled there before the babe is born and I would like to be of assistance. Mary has assisted at Netherfield, I should assist here! I am feeding my baby, so he must come with me. Is that really so terrible?"

He looked at her impassioned eyes and felt the exhaustion coming off her in waves.

"Elizabeth, I am simply trying to take care of you, and our son. I have no objection to you visiting Jane's new home. I think it a fine idea, but you are clearly exhausted. You can hardly stand up! You were only churched last week."

She sighed and slumped her shoulders in defeat.

"Have the wet nurse brought in, don't take everything on yourself, and in a few days, when you are stronger, take Bennet to visit your sister. But please, only two nights away," he said kindly.

"Truly?" she said hopefully, feeling the inexplicable urge to cry.

"Truly. Surely you know I can deny you nothing." She smiled tiredly and he continued, "Just try to be reasonable sometimes! You wear a man out!"

She swatted his arm playfully. "You enjoy it when I wear you out."

His brows quirked up. She was in a much better mood the remainder of the day.

~

A few days later, Bennet and his new wet nurse were inside the carriage as Elizabeth stood beside it saying goodbye to her husband.

"Don't worry, darling, I won't have too much fun without you. Mr. Darcy will be there and we're sure to spend half the time arguing over something or other."

"Mr. Darcy isn't so bad once you know him better," argued the earl.

She huffed.

"You should be easier on him. You are not an easy lady to keep up with."

"I was under the impression some men liked that in a lady."

He smiled. "Luckily for me, it scares away as many as it delights."

She laughed. "I will try to behave, but I make no promises. You said yourself that I have been unpredictable of late."

"Now that the sun has come out you are much improved," he said kindly.

She looked at him warmly and reached up on her toes to give him a kiss. "I shall miss you. I'll return in two days."

"I'll be waiting."

He handed her into the carriage and sent it on its way, watching until it disappeared over the hill.

~

She arrived at the Bingleys' new estate in short order, and immediately went to work helping her sister get organized. They reviewed the servants and discussed with the housekeeper where more were needed in one area and perhaps one or two less in another.

They chose colors for the guest chambers that were being refurnished and discussed new furniture for the main drawing room. The bulk of their time, however, was spent on sorting out the nursery. The repairs to the windows and floor had been made and the new paper was going up when Elizabeth arrived. Charles had kindly ordered some new pieces for the room, and Mrs. Bennet had sent the Bennet family cradle that she had been saving for Jane. She would not allow her husband's horrid cousin to place his homely offspring in her daughters' cradle.

Jane and Elizabeth laughed at their mother's note, but they were both touched by the gift nonetheless. It was fitting that Jane, as the eldest, receive the cradle. After all, when their father died, they would lose their childhood home forever, and Longbourn would no longer be the seat of the Bennet family, for there would no longer be any Bennets once all their sisters had wed.

Elizabeth was feeling better every day, thanks in large part to the sun finally making an appearance and the wet nurse who took over nursing duties at night, allowing her to finally get more than two hours of sleep in a row.

It was good she was in improved spirits, for they were about to be tried by Mr. Darcy, who was helping Charles settle in his new steward and become accustomed to the duties of a landowner. She supposed it was nice of him to help, and he did have an estate or two he was reputed to manage well, but he was terribly irksome.

He was constantly arguing with her, challenging her on all sorts of small details that left her feeling irritated and tired. Every time she saw him, she felt the need to nap afterwards. Why could he not just be pleasant? Did he enjoy their verbal sparring? She certainly did not. She found him proud and disdainful, constantly spouting the most ridiculous opinions she sincerely hoped he didn't hold, but was fairly certain he did. She could not insult Jane's home by arguing with Charles's closest friend, but truly, the man was insufferable. Why Charles was such good friends with him she couldn't fathom. Perhaps he was nicer when not in mixed company. Robert had told her that some men didn't perform well in front of women. She could only hope that was the case, or Mr. Darcy would be awful in every situation, and that would be truly piteous.

Oh, well. She was only there for two days. She could tolerate him for that length of time. She was not without patience, after all.

~

Elizabeth entered the drawing room and heard Charles speaking to Jane.

"It will only be a short while. I'll be home within the fortnight. You know I wouldn't leave you if it weren't absolutely necessary."

"Of course. I understand," Jane said stoically, trying to keep her rapidly building tears from overflowing.

"Pardon me, I didn't mean to interrupt," said Elizabeth.

She turned to leave the room when Charles jumped up from his seat by his wife and stopped her.

"No, Elizabeth, you aren't interrupting. I was just informing Jane that I must go to Town on business. As you know, it is a delicate time."

Elizabeth looked to her sister, her belly distended with her first child, and understood instantly Jane's distress.

"Will you arrive back in time for the birth?" she asked.

"I plan to. Both Jane and the midwife believe there is another month, and I know you can't plan these things, but I will be back within a fortnight, possibly sooner."

"I see."

"I thought perhaps you could stay with her until I return, or she could go with you to Cressingdon," he said hopefully.

"Charles!" cried Jane. "Elizabeth couldn't possibly be away from her children so long, especially for such a reason. You know she and the earl don't like to be parted unless it can't be helped."

Elizabeth wanted to reassure her sister, but it was true. She couldn't think of being away from her children for a fortnight just because Charles suddenly needed to go Town. She and the earl had gone away for a few days on their own last summer after Violet weaned, and it had been glorious, but that was the only time she had left both her children. Baby Bennet couldn't be separated from her and she couldn't ask her husband to give up this time of infancy, which fled by so quickly, for a whim of her brother's.

"Charles, may I ask, what draws you to Town?" asked Elizabeth delicately.

Charles sighed and rubbed the back of his neck. "It is Caroline. Hurst has had enough of her and is refusing to allow her to live with them. I am responsible for her income; I need to settle her into her own establishment and see to her allowance."

"Cannot an agent do that? Or can the Hursts not wait until after the babe is born?" asked Elizabeth.

He looked to Jane. "I doubt they can. But I could ask. Jane, would you rather I go now, before the babe comes, or after?"

Jane looked at her husband and her sister, clearly conflicted. "I think it would be best to go now. Be as quick as you can, and hurry back to meet your son."

He smiled. "Are you sure, dearest? Elizabeth has rightfully made me feel a beast for leaving you at such a time." He glanced to Elizabeth as he spoke and she huffed in mock indignation.

"I did no such thing! But if your own heart convicts you, I will not stand in its way."

He laughed and Jane chucked softly, a hand rubbing her belly.

"Go to Town now. If I am anything like my sister, I will be a weepy mess after the birth and in need of my husband."

"Jane!" cried Elizabeth.

The three of them laughed together.

"You will go stay with your sister?" asked Charles.

"If you insist, but I will be fine here on my own. I have already met the midwife and my maid will be with me. There is much to do to prepare for the babe and I would rather not travel, but if it will make you easier, I will go to Cressingdon."

Charles kissed her hand. "You are truly an angel, Jane, and I do not deserve you. Of course, I will not force difficult travel on you if you would rather not, but I will speak with the housekeeper before I go. I want the entire household to be watching over you."

Jane rolled her eyes and Elizabeth laughed lightly.

"Do not worry, Charles. Jane already has their love and devotion, as only an angelic creature such as she can have."

Jane blushed and looked down, then joined her sister and husband in their laughter.

~

That evening, Jane and Elizabeth were in the nursery examining a selection of baby blankets, while Ben slept in the cradle against the far wall.

"Are you well, Jane? Truly?" asked Elizabeth gently.

"Oh, you know how it is, Lizzy. Everything seems so much more important when one is with child."

"Yes, I do," said Elizabeth with a wan smile. "What troubles you?"

"It is nothing, really. I'm sure I'm being ridiculous. It is just that," she hesitated, "sometimes I wish Charles was more like Robert."

Elizabeth sat back, surprised. "In what way?"

"It is so clear that Robert wants what is best for you. He is so obviously concerned with your welfare and peace of mind. He would never dream of leaving for Town while so close to your lying in."

"No, he wouldn't," agreed Elizabeth quietly.

A slow tear made its way down Jane's smooth cheek and Elizabeth reached out and clasped her hand in hers.

"Jane, do not despair! Charles is simply behaving like every other man of his acquaintance. You must remember that I am not Robert's first wife, and Violet was his fifth child. Five, Jane! He missed four births before he finally decided to see what was going on behind the closed door."

Jane gave her a weary smile and Elizabeth returned it.

"Are you saying that Charles will stand by me by my fifth birth?" Jane asked, only half in jest.

"Possibly. I also think he does not know you want him there. Have you mentioned it to him?" Elizabeth asked gently.

"No," said Jane uncertainly. "But Lizzy, you never asked Robert. He barged in with Violet's birth, unable to bear hearing you in distress and not come to your side. He loves you, Lizzy! Like something from a fairy tale! I thought that was how Charles loved me..." she trailed off and Elizabeth's heart broke a little for her sister.

"Jane, please do not see Charles's willingness to take care of his sister as lack of love for you. He is doing his duty and making every effort to be with you, too. Did he not ask you if you wished for him to stay? If you told him now that you did not want him to go and that he should send an agent in his place, he would stay, would he not? If you asked him to?"

142

"I suppose. Will you think me terribly cowardly if I admit that I don't want to ask him for fear of the answer?"

"Oh, Jane!"

Elizabeth pulled her sister to her and Jane wept quietly on her shoulder. They held each other for some time until Elizabeth felt something bumping against her middle and began to laugh.

"I do believe my niece or nephew wants to be released!"

Jane laughed. "He is a strong kicker, isn't he?"

"Yes. So you think it is a boy?"

"I do not have a feeling, no. I just want to call him something other than 'it.' I would be happy with a boy or girl. There is no entailment to satisfy, and Charles would never enact such a thing, so I am not afraid of a house full of girls."

"I am," said Elizabeth with a smile. "But for completely different reasons."

~

The next afternoon, Jane stood on the front step seeing off Mr. Darcy and Charles in one carriage, and Elizabeth, her son, maid, and wet nurse in the other. It was decided that Charles and Mr. Darcy would stay the night at Cressingdon before leaving for Town the next day. Charles wanted the earl's opinion on what to do about Caroline and Mr. Darcy wished to discuss estate business.

"Darcy?" Charles said as they sat in the carriage.

"Yes, Bingley?"

"Would you think me terribly ridiculous if I wished Jane had asked me to stay?"

Darcy raised a brow in question.

"I know I am ridiculous. You don't need to tell me. It is just that, childbearing is the concern of women. I am utterly lost! I know not what to say to her when she is distressed, or what to do with all of this. And she will never ask anything of me, she is too good, but I wanted her to want me there." He looked at his friend pathetically. "See, I am utterly ridiculous!"

"Charles, you are not ridiculous. It is a difficult time. But don't you think it a little," he hesitated.

"Ridiculous? Stupid? Idiotic?" interjected Charles.

"Bingley," reprimanded Darcy.

"Go ahead." He sighed and leaned back into the squabs.

"I was going to say it is a little immature to expect your pregnant wife to open her heart to you and beg for your presence when you are so eager to run off to Town. She is the one in the more vulnerable position, by far."

"Is that what I did?" He put his hand in his hair and groaned. "I am a horrible husband. And if my first child is born while I am in Town, I will have started out as a horrible father."

"Bingley, stop being so dramatic! You are neither a horrible husband nor a horrible father. Plenty of children are born with their fathers in other countries and they are none the worse for it."

"I suppose so," sighed Charles.

"Bingley," said Darcy with frustrated patience, "please tell me that you actually needed to go to Town and didn't just tell your wife you needed to go to test her affection for you?"

"Of course not!" cried Bingley. "Hurst has put Caroline out and I don't want her living in our house in Town—who knows what she will do to it. Besides that, it would be unseemly. Knowing her, she would hire a carriage and come here on her own, then pretend we had invited her. That is not what Jane needs at this time."

"Did you tell your wife all that?" asked Darcy.

"Some of it," he replied. "I was right. I am a horrible husband! What kind of husband even considers leaving his wife at such a time?"

"Many, I'm afraid, and for much less noble reasons," said Darcy quietly.

"I will talk to Asheland. He will have the name of a good agent I can send in my place, then I will go home to my wife, where I belong."

"That seems wise," said Darcy simply.

When they arrived at Cressingdon, Elizabeth rushed into the house and Robert met her in the vestibule, quickly pulling her to him and kissing her hair.

Bingley and Darcy entered more slowly and stopped when they saw the reunion.

"Asheland would never leave his wife during her lying in," whispered Bingley to Darcy.

"Indeed," Darcy whispered back. *What man would leave Lady Asheland for any reason?*

"Excuse me, gentlemen, I hadn't realized you accompanied my wife," said Lord Asheland apologetically.

"I'm sorry, dear. Mr. Darcy and Charles are on their way to town and Charles wished to speak to you on an important matter. I told them they could break their journey here and continue on tomorrow," said Elizabeth.

"Of course. Did Jane accompany you?" asked the earl.

"No, she is not comfortable traveling at this time," answered Elizabeth.

Lord Asheland's eyebrows shot up, but he said nothing. Charles elbowed Darcy at this perceived proof of his husbandly failure.

"Molly," Elizabeth spoke to the maid taking their things. "Please show Mr. Darcy to the green bedchamber. Mr. Bingley will occupy his usual chamber."

"Yes, my lady." The maid curtsied and waited by the stairs.

"If you'll excuse me, gentlemen, I wish to see my children." She smiled politely and she and Lord Asheland left hand in hand, leaving two envious and confused men behind them, though neither could identify their feelings as such.

~

That night, as Elizabeth lay with her head on her husband's chest, she said, "I could never be happy with a man like Bingley."

"Pardon me?"

"He is a good man, but he could never love me properly, nor I him."

"That is lucky for me, I suppose," said Lord Asheland dryly.

"You know what I mean. He and Jane are so careful with each other. It's a miracle anything gets done!"

"You must account for temperaments, my dear. Jane is not as bold as you, and I am twenty years Bingley's senior. It would be a sorry state indeed if I weren't more knowledgeable than he."

"I suppose so," she agreed reluctantly. "But I still couldn't do it!"

He laughed.

Asheland knew Bingley would learn the way of things. He was a young man still and his marriage was new. Jane would learn to speak up about what was important to her and Charles would learn to rely more on his own initiative. It would take time, but they would both grow into each other.

His wife's voice interrupted his thoughts. "Did you give Charles the name of an agent?"

"Yes, I sent him to Blackwood."

"Good."

"He had already made the decision to return to her."

"What?"

"Bingley. He had already decided to return home tomorrow when we spoke. I just gave him the name of an agent."

"And a bit of advice, I imagine," she added.

"Of course. He is my brother; it is my duty."

"Of course it is. And is it also your duty to advise Mr. Darcy?"

"No, that is just a courtesy."

Elizabeth laughed outright and eventually her husband joined her.

"What did you tell him?" she asked.

"Bingley or Mr. Darcy?"

"Charles, of course."

"I told him that a lady should be able to rely on her husband without having to ask for it, and that since she is doing him the very great honor of bearing his child, the least he could do was be in the county when it arrived."

"Well said, my love. And what was his reaction?"

"As expected. He chastised himself extensively and bemoaned what a horrible husband he was and promised to make it right for his angel, etc."

Elizabeth chuckled. "They really are perfect for each other. Only Jane would be so patient with Charles."

"And inspire such devotion," interjected her husband.

"And only Charles would be gentle enough to make Jane feel at ease."

"Yes, they are well-matched," he agreed.

"Not as well-matched as we are, but a good alliance nonetheless."

CHAPTER 10

Darcy stepped out of the house and turned his face to the newly risen sun, the crisp March air ruffling his hair slightly. Cressingdon was a beautiful estate, well-maintained and prosperous, and a little bigger than Pemberley. He imagined it cleared nearly twelve-thousand a year. Lord Asheland appeared to be a good and fair master. The workers he had seen seemed happy and healthy. None were too thin or bedraggled or had the look of illness about them. Asheland was clearly a generous man. He had offered to loan Darcy a mount for a morning ride before he left for town, just because Darcy had said it was perfect weather for it.

Darcy was just cresting the hill to the east of the estate, admiring the scenery from the back of a borrowed gelding, when he saw a horse and rider come rushing toward him.

"What seems to be the trouble?" called Darcy as the rider approached.

"It's the master! He's taken a fall! I've come to fetch help."

"Where?" Darcy asked urgently.

"To the east half a mile, down by the stream, near the big rocks."

"Go fetch help. I'll go to the earl."

The rider continued on and Darcy headed in the direction he'd specified, quickly finding an outcropping of rocks running along a stream.

"Lord Asheland!" he called loudly.

"Here," came a labored voice from behind the rocks.

Darcy leapt off his horse and scrambled over the stones. He found Lord Asheland on his back, his shirt bloody, a dazed look on his face.

"My lord! What happened?" Darcy asked urgently as he took off his coat and pillowed it under the earl's head.

"Damn pheasant. Startled Goliath," he said with labored breath.

"Are you David in this scenario?" asked Darcy dryly. He had taken off his cravat and was pressing it to the earl's abdomen.

"Very funny, young man. You know it's bad luck to change a horse's name. He was... a gift..."

The earl began to drift off into unconsciousness and Darcy spoke louder.

"Who gave it to you, my lord?"

"Brother... Carew...nephew... named him... big... horse," he breathed.

"Ah, children are always experts at naming horses. If only the horses didn't outlive the name's appeal."

The earl almost chuckled but it sounded more like a wheeze.

Darcy was no physician, but he assumed the earl had at least one broken rib. He'd seen it a few times on the stable hands. There was a large cut that was bleeding on his side. It didn't look too deep, but if it festered, it could be fatal. He'd known men to die from lesser wounds that had become feverish and diseased. Where was the man with the cart? The sooner they got him to the main house, the better.

Finally, after what seemed an age, a cart with several grooms and the earl's valet rolled up. Darcy helped the men get him onto it and they began the painful journey to the house. A rider was sent ahead to alert the countess and when they pulled up to the house, she was waiting on the steps, her face pale and her eyes wide and dark.

"Bring him inside. Gently," Elizabeth ordered. "The physician is on the way."

They carried the now unconscious earl up the stairs on a make-shift stretcher and deposited him in the middle of his bed.

"Porter," she said to his valet, "let's get him out of these riding clothes. Please fetch a clean nightshirt."

"Yes, my lady."

She began removing one of the earl's boots and when Darcy realized what she was doing, he started on the other one. She removed his stockings as well and began on his cravat, which she untied gently and, Darcy couldn't help but notice, with practiced ease.

She left the room only to return a few moments later with a pair of sharp scissors in hand. She began cutting his coat off, first the seam near his side, then the sleeves, until he was free of the restricting garment. His white lawn shirt, half covered in his blood, received the same treatment.

Elizabeth focused on her work with eyes like flint, caring not who watched her and nothing in her mind but a desperate prayer that her husband would survive this ordeal.

Darcy pulled aside a footman and said, "Please find someone to send for Mr. Bingley. He is on the north road on the way to Hatfield Hall. Tell him there's been an accident and to bring Mrs. Bingley here. Lady Asheland will want her sister."

"Yes, sir," said the footman before hurrying down the hall.

"We need more cloths," Elizabeth said to the housekeeper.

"Yes, my lady."

Elizabeth was cleaning the wound on his side, carefully wiping the blood from his abdomen, her entire body humming with a wild energy.

"Porter!"

"Yes, my lady." The valet was by her side instantly.

"I need you to write a letter to Lord Devonshire."

He immediately moved to the writing desk in the corner and removed a pen and ink pot.

"What do you want me to write, Lady Asheland?"

"Write this exactly as I dictate it." She dropped a bloody cloth into a basin and took up another fresh one, dipping it into the clean water and wringing it out before beginning to wipe her husband's face that had become smudged with dirt. "Dear Alfred, You are needed at Cressingdon. Robert was thrown from his horse. Come as soon as you can. Your cousin, Elizabeth." She dipped the cloth and wrung it out again. "Do you have that?"

"Yes, my lady."

"Read it back to me."

Porter recited it exactly as she had said it. She dried her hands and quickly signed it, pressing her husband's seal into the wax.

"Send this immediately. Have Johnny in the stables do it. Tell him to wait for a response."

"Yes, my lady."

Porter left the room quickly to deliver the message and Elizabeth continued tending to her husband, pulling a soft blanket over his now clean body.

Darcy stood at the foot of the bed, watching the proceedings with a horrid sense of helplessness. He would have offered to ride to Lord Devonshire, but he hadn't the slightest idea where the man lived. He thought it might be Yorkshire, but he couldn't be sure. Two of the footmen who had carried the earl upstairs stood near the window, calmly awaiting orders. Darcy was trying to think of something appropriate to say to Lady Asheland when one of the footmen spoke.

"That's the physician's carriage!"

Elizabeth looked up sharply. "Bring him straight here, James."

"Yes, my lady."

A few minutes later, a thin, older man with grey hair and spectacles entered the room.

"Lady Asheland. It is good to see you again, but I wish it were under better circumstances."

"You too, Mr. Oglesby. Did Martin tell you what happened?"

"Yes, he came to fetch me and informed me on the way. The horse was startled by some pheasants who flew up unexpectedly and threw his lordship onto some sharp rocks."

Elizabeth winced at the casual way the man spoke.

"Yes, that is what I was told. There is a cut on his side." She gestured toward the injury.

"I'll examine him now. If you'll excuse us, my lady."

"I'll be staying with my husband," she said plainly.

The physician bristled and pulled his small frame up taller. "That is most irregular, madam!"

"Lord Asheland would want me to stay," she said steadily.

The physician was gearing up for an argument when Mr. Darcy said, "Mr. Oglesby, perhaps time could be better spent examining the earl."

Oglesby looked to the strange man at the end of the bed, then back to Lady Asheland.

"This is Mr. Darcy," she said. "He is a friend of my husband's."

Oglesby nodded and began the examination. "Did you clean the wound, Mr. Darcy? Or was it the earl's man? A fine job!"

"That was Lady Asheland," said Darcy evenly.

The physician did not look pleased at the information and carried on in silence.

"I believe there is some internal bleeding," he said.

152

"Why?" asked Darcy, hoping to circumvent an argument between Lady Asheland and the doctor.

Mr. Oglesby explained his reasoning and his hope that it would resolve on its own.

"How likely is that to happen?" asked Elizabeth.

"I really cannot say, madam. His lordship is strong and in good health, but he is not a young man."

Elizabeth huffed and turned her back in exasperation.

Darcy looked at her and then back at the doctor. "Is there nothing you can do?" he asked.

"There are strategies some surgeons would use, but they are more experiments than anything else. I'm afraid his lordship wouldn't survive them. I can give you a salve for the wound, but otherwise, I'm afraid we must simply wait and see."

Darcy nodded. "I understand. Thank you, doctor."

The doctor nodded and told them to give him laudanum for the pain, then gathered his things and left, promising to look in again that night.

Elizabeth looked blankly at the wall, her hands on her hips.

"Lady Asheland?" came a soft voice from behind her.

She turned to face Mr. Darcy and said, "Forgive me, sir, I had forgotten your presence." She didn't seem to notice the ceaseless tears streaming down her face.

"Understandable, my lady. Is there anything I can do for your relief? A glass of wine? May I get you one?" He spoke softly, as if to an injured child.

She walked to the table next to the fireplace and picked up her husband's brandy decanter. "I think I need something stronger." She poured a half glass of brandy and gestured to Mr. Darcy. "I know it's a bit early, but I can't be bothered to care at the moment."

"Of course, my lady."

He nodded and she poured him a glass. They stood there, looking at the prone form of Lord Asheland on the bed, and drank in silence.

~

Robert regained consciousness an hour later and Elizabeth had the children brought to him, wanting to give him a chance to say goodbye if the worst should happen. She knew how much it had always haunted him that he'd never said goodbye to his children before they died. She sat in the chair by the fire and nursed Ben in silence while Violet sat next to her father and played with a small doll and Robbie regaled him with his latest visit to the farmyard.

The visit exhausted him and Robert fell into a fitful sleep. Elizabeth faithfully applied the salve to his wound, not wanting it to fester, and constantly felt his forehead, watching for a fever. All through the day, till the sun was high in the sky and falling again, she tended to him diligently, pausing only to nurse her son in a nearby chair.

When he awoke again he asked Porter to take a letter for him, and though it took great effort, he wrote to the future Earl of Asheland, advising him on all and sundry, and the six-page letter was sealed and placed in his bureau until his son was old enough to need it. Elizabeth silently prayed that he never would, that his father would be there to teach him, but the garish purple spot on her husband's abdomen was growing larger and darker by the hour, and she felt the hope slowly draining out of her with each of Robert's labored breaths.

"Elizabeth."

"Yes, I'm here," she said. She was seated by his bed, rocking their baby in the shadowy chamber, the fire in the grate and a single candle on the bedside table the only

154

light. She quickly called Porter and gave him her sleeping son, asking that he be returned to the nursery.

"I'm here, my love," she said as she sat on the bed next to him. "What can I do for you?"

"Elizabeth, you remember what I told you? About the will?" She looked at him quizzically. "You remember what I told you, about knowing what to expect?"

"Yes, I remember."

"You know the solicitors, Durham and Brown. Their information is in my desk. A copy of the will is in the third drawer. You remember where I keep the key?"

"Yes," she said breathily. "I remember."

He looked at her with aching tenderness, and then he reached up and touched her cheek lightly with his fingertips. "You are the single greatest gift I've ever received. These years with you have been the happiest of my entire life. You, Elizabeth," he choked and coughed and she was horrified to see blood on the handkerchief, "you are everything to me. You have been the making of me."

"No, Robert, you have been the making of me," she whispered.

He closed his eyes and took a deep breath, fighting for composure.

"I know it is selfish, but I am glad to be going first. I have buried many people I loved, Elizabeth, but burying you would have killed me."

"Oh, Robert," she whispered, clutching his hand to her cheek. "I love you so, my darling." She kissed his hand fervently. "Thank you. Thank you so much."

"For what?" he asked.

"For loving me. For giving me children to love and to remember you by. For choosing this silly girl from the country and making a beautiful life with her," she whispered past the lump in her throat.

"My darling girl, thank *you*. For choosing me, for letting this old man love you," he choked.

"Not old," she said. "You will never be old to me, my love."

He smiled wanly and closed his eyes against the pain. Recognizing the end was coming, she tried to set him at ease.

"Do not worry for us. I will teach young Robert to love the land, just as you do. I will show him every path and tree and stream. I will even take him to that ridiculous fishing spot you like so much."

He tried to laugh, but it sounded more like a wheeze.

"Violet will be well, I promise. She will be beautiful and brilliant and I will guard her with my life, I swear it. And young Bennet." She swallowed a sob and took a shaky breath. "Ben will know his father is a great man, a man to emulate. I will tell him of you. I'll tell them all. They will not forget you; I won't let them!" she declared vehemently.

He squeezed her hand and kept his eyes closed, a single tear falling from beneath his lashes and making its way down his cheek and onto the pillow where it made a dark spot on the white linen.

He was silent for several minutes and Elizabeth feared the worst. Just as she was about to put her hand to his mouth to check for breath, he spoke, so quietly she could barely hear him.

"Promise me, Elizabeth."

"Yes, darling. Anything. Anything at all," she said breathlessly as she kissed his hands.

"Promise me you will love again," he said softly.

"What?" she asked, astounded.

"Promise me you will not be alone forever. You are young, and not built for a solitary life. You must find someone, Lizzy. Promise me." Something inside of him screamed and raged at the words, fighting the idea of his

Elizabeth in the arms of another man, but he knew he must deny his instincts and do what was best for his wife. His precious, perfect, darling wife.

She shook her head in confusion. "What? No! I do not, I cannot, Robert! No!" she cried.

She laid her forehead on his arm where it lay on the bed and sobbed. Horrible, gut-wrenching sobs that tore at his heart until he thought he might break under the weight of her sorrow.

"Shh, shh, my love." He patted her head gently with his free hand.

"Robert, please don't leave me," she whispered into the blankets.

She noticed after a moment that his hand had stopped moving in her hair and he'd fallen silent. Terrified of what she would see, but not willing to hide from the truth, she raised her head slowly and looked at her husband's face. His eyes stared blankly at the ceiling, his body eerily still.

A strangled cry escaped her throat and Porter rushed in, stopping next to his master's bed to stare in horror at the body of the man he had served for the last twenty-five years.

"Oh, my lord," he cried. He dropped to his knees next to the bed and began to pray as Lady Asheland laid her head on her husband's chest and wept until he thought she would break in two.

"Lady Asheland, come, my lady." Porter gently drew her back but she collapsed on the bed next to Robert, unable to bear her own weight in addition to her grief.

"Lizzy?" came Jane's soft voice. She pushed the door open softly, horror-stricken at the sight of her brother so still on the bed and her sister weeping next to him.

"Is he?" Jane asked Porter hesitantly.

The valet nodded solemnly, his eyes downcast.

"Oh, Lizzy!" she rushed to Elizabeth and gathered her in her arms.

"Jane!" cried Elizabeth. "He's gone!" she said in disbelief. "Robert's gone."

"Jane?" Charles called from the door.

Jane looked up to see her husband in the doorway, Mr. Darcy behind him.

"Is Robert?" he asked, unable to finish the question.

Jane nodded. "Porter, could you fetch Lady Asheland's maid?"

He left to collect Watson and a few moments later, the maid was at her lady's side, trying to guide her to her chamber.

Elizabeth took one step off the bed and collapsed to the floor, unable to cease her sobbing. Jane had turned away and was quietly weeping herself, Charles's arm around her shoulder to comfort her. Darcy took in the scene and made a quick decision.

"Come, my lady," he said gently as he knelt in front of Elizabeth. He helped her to her feet, then scooped her into his arms, asking Watson to point him in the right direction. She took him through the sitting room and into Elizabeth's chamber.

"Just put her on the bed, sir."

He set Elizabeth on the counterpane and turned to the maid. "Mr. Bingley and I will be writing letters in the blue parlor should you have need of us."

"Yes, sir."

He left the room and Jane came in shortly after. She and Watson got Elizabeth into a nightshift and under the blankets, her sister settled next to her. Jane leaned against the headboard, Elizabeth's head on her shoulder, her gown soaked through from her sister's tears. Elizabeth finally fell into a fitful sleep and Jane soon followed.

~

Deep in the night, Elizabeth awoke after a horrible dream. She looked to her side to tell her husband of it and allow him to comfort her, but in his place was her sister Jane, her blond hair strewn across the pillows.

She rose from the bed slowly, careful not to wake her sister. She tied a wool robe over her nightshift and slipped her feet into her slippers. She padded to her husband's room and looked through the door. She saw Robert lying in the bed, his valet asleep in the chair a few feet away.

She came closer and looked carefully, hoping against hope he wasn't really dead and that it had all been a horrible nightmare. His skin was cold and smooth, his body already being prepared for burial. Someone had closed his eyes.

Feeling an eerie calm descend on her, she stepped into the hallway. Elizabeth made her way to her husband's study in the dark, her expression blank. Each footman or maid she passed gave her a wide berth, but she paid them no heed. She stepped into the darkened room, lit only by the moonlight shining in the large window behind the mahogany desk.

She rested her hand on the smooth surface and opened the center drawer, pulling out a long, brass key. She lit a lantern and took it to the adjoining room where she set it upon the table beside a large chest. She slid the key into the lock and turned it until it clicked smoothly into place. The doors opened without a sound and she looked at the rifles before her, moonlight gleaming off the metal barrels, lined up neatly in a row on their stands. Steadily, she took the one she was most familiar with, loaded it, locked the chest again, and left the room. She moved quietly through the house, out the side door, and down the grassy slope that led to the stables.

The door creaked loudly as she pushed it open, the horses inside quiet in the late night. She walked down the center row until she came to the large enclosure at the end.

Placing her lantern on the floor by her feet, she raised the rifle to her shoulder and looked at the grey beast before her. He stared at her with large, dark eyes and she stared back coldly, pulling the hammer into place.

"Lady Asheland!" came a voice from her right. She felt a hand on her shoulder and vaguely registered someone trying to remove the gun from her hands.

"May I escort you to the house, my lady?"

She turned slowly and recognized the wizened face of Tom Haskins, the head groom.

Slowly, she released the rifle from her grip and he placed it against the wall behind them. "How can I help you, my lady?" he asked kindly.

The horse whinnied and she turned to the stallion.

"Get rid of it. Shoot it, sell it, give it away. I don't care. But I never want to see that horse again," she said harshly.

She turned swiftly and marched back into the house, her back stiff and her eyes straight ahead, burning with a hate that threatened to consume her.

~

She insisted she go to the funeral. Everyone had protested, from her mother, to her brother Charles, to her husband's family. She stood stubbornly in Cressingdon's grand entrance hall, prepared to leave regardless of their objections. Finally, Alfred approached her quietly and asked if she really believed she should be there.

"He was in the birthing room with me, did you know that?"

Several eyebrows raised and Alfred nodded slowly. "He told me, yes. He said it was the most miraculous thing he had ever beheld," he said softly.

She nodded jerkily, her eyes stinging. "He refused to leave my side, and I refuse to leave his. We are neither of us good at going where we're told."

Alfred nodded, just once, and led her by the elbow to the carriage. He held up a hand when his cousin began to protest. "Robert would have wanted her there."

More than a dozen carriages were in the procession to the church. The Bishop was Robert's second cousin and insisted he perform the ceremony. As the procession passed through the village, men withdrew their hats and ladies bowed their heads as the church bells rang mournfully.

Elizabeth was in the second carriage, her father and Alfred on either side of her, holding her hands. She vaguely noted the villagers' show of respect and told herself to remember to thank them later. As she walked into the church, she saw it was surrounded by early spring blooms, and she remembered how she and Robert had courted in the spring, and the flowers he had sent her, and how he had compared her cheek to a rose petal.

She was grateful for the heavy black veil that concealed her face from the crowd of men who thought she had no right to view her own husband's funeral. The voice of the Bishop echoed through the stone building, the words lost to her. She cared not what he said. She was there to say her own goodbyes.

When it was over, Alfred led her to the front of the church and looked away, giving her what privacy he could. She kissed her fingers, then placed them firmly on the coffin lid.

"Goodbye, my love," she whispered.

She turned slowly and walked away, looking ahead but seeing nothing, past the men bowing deeply, past the stained-glass windows whose light bathed her in an ethereal glow, in an odd reversal of the last time she had walked down a church aisle with Robert at the end of it.

On Equal Ground

CHAPTER 11

"Have you given any thought to what you would like to do?" asked Alfred gently.

He was sitting with Elizabeth in the south parlor a fortnight after the burial. She looked at him with mournful eyes and released a heavy sigh.

"I will meet with the lawyers today. They will tell me what I already know. Robert John should be raised at Cressingdon. It is only right."

"Of course, I'm sure that is what Robert would want," he agreed. "I will be with you at the meeting, unless you prefer otherwise."

"No, I want you there. My Uncle Gardiner will be there as well, and my father, of course," she added. She looked out the window with a vacant expression on her face, one Alfred had become accustomed to recently.

"You know you are welcome to stay with us. We would love to have you and the children. There haven't been little ones about in years. Sylvia thought you might like the change," he suggested.

"Your wife is kind, and I thank you, but I think I want to be alone with my children for now. I will go to Jane in a few days and see her through the birth. She was with me through all of mine, I cannot abandon her when she needs me most."

"Of course. How long will you stay at Hatfield with the Bingleys?"

"I do not know. It will depend on many things, I imagine: how Jane comes through her lying in, the temperament of the baby, how the children tolerate being away."

"How are they faring?" he asked.

She sighed again, brushing her black skirt with a pale hand. "Bennet is well, naturally, though he has been very quiet. I think even he feels the changed atmosphere. Violet still asks for her papa each night. She wants him to read her a story. I have told her that he is gone and won't be coming back, but her mind cannot grasp such an idea. After all, he has always returned in the past." She bit her lips and blinked until she felt more composed.

"And young Robert?" he said quietly.

"He understands, I think. His dog Daisy died last December and he was greatly distressed, but we explained what had happened and had her buried by the lake. He put flowers on her grave and cried over her." She took a deep breath. "He asked if Papa has gone to be with Daisy. I told him that he had, and that afternoon he brought a handful of daffodils he'd picked and asked to put them on Papa's grave."

She sucked in a breath and dabbed at her eyes with her ever-present handkerchief. "I took him, of course." She twisted her skirts in her hand and looked out the window, still unable to comprehend the fact that her husband was gone, and that she was a widow at not yet two and twenty. "I don't know how I will stay here. It is so full of him," she whispered.

Alfred reached out and patted her hand as her shoulders shook silently, her sense of propriety warring with her desire to curl up in the window seat and weep herself into exhaustion.

"I have a suggestion, if I may," said Alfred.

"Of course, cousin. I shall be glad to hear it," she said politely.

"Your birthday is in a fortnight." She nodded, not looking at him. He continued, "Robert had prepared something for you; a surprise of sorts."

She looked at him with interest. "What is it?"

"A cottage at the seaside. He rented it from the end of May until Michaelmas. He knew how tired you had been after the baby…" he trailed off.

"That sounds lovely. We can stay at Hatfield until it is time to depart. Thank you for telling me, Alfred. It is a great relief."

He nodded. "You're welcome, my dear."

"Have you been to the cottage? Where is it situated?"

"Cottage is not really the right word. The house is not large, but it sits on a good deal of land outside Margate. It belongs to a friend of the family. Robert and I stayed there when we were boys."

"I see. It sounds perfectly suitable, and a stay at the seaside sounds just right at the moment."

"John will accompany you and see you are well settled, if that suits you."

"Of course. I shall appreciate the assistance."

"I shall make the arrangements."

"Thank you, Alfred. You have been a tremendous help. I don't know what I would have done without you," she said feelingly.

"I am honored to be of assistance. Robert loved you very much, you know. He was my closest friend as well as my cousin. I can only be grateful for how happy you made him."

She gave him a watery smile.

"And I am somewhat fond of you myself," he added.

She laughed for the first time in over a fortnight.

~

The meeting with the lawyers went as expected. Young Robert would inherit the bulk of his father's land and income, as well as the title. Were he to die without an heir, it would fall to Bennet. Elizabeth was to consider Cressingdon her home until Robbie came into his inheritance.

Violet received a small but profitable estate in Northamptonshire and an impressive dowry. Bennet would inherit the largest of his father's additional estates, a legacy of fifteen thousand pounds, and ownership of Talbot House when his mother died. The children's inheritances would be held in trust until they came of age, or in Violet's case, until she married someone her guardians approved of or reached the age of five and twenty.

Elizabeth was named the children's guardian, as expected, together with Alfred, and in the event of his death, his son John. The money Lord Asheland had settled on Elizabeth was safely invested. In addition, she was to receive a generous allowance, lifetime rights to Talbot House in London and the dower house at Cressingdon, and her choice of one of the estates not intended for their children. It would be hers to do with as she wished.

She also received all the Asheland family jewelry (a small fortune in itself) and Robert trusted her to know what to give to each child. His only request was that his grandmother's pearl necklace be worn by Violet at her coming out ball. His sister had worn it at her ball, as had every other Talbot woman for the last three generations.

To Elizabeth's and her relations' surprise, Robert had left a legacy to be added to the dowries of each of her unmarried sisters. She immediately understood his intentions, for they had spoken frequently of her family, and she knew he had recently made a new will, as he did after the birth of each child. With only three children, and only one daughter to dower, Robert had gifted her unmarried sisters three thousand pounds each. Added to the money he had already put aside for them through Netherfield's income and what her parents had saved, they would have respectable dowries and more options in marriage.

He had also given Charles a valuable collection of rifles, in thanks for his kindness to Elizabeth. Jane received a beautiful necklace with sapphires and diamonds, a Talbot family piece that Robert left with a note for his "dear sister" that brought tears to Jane's eyes when she read it.

Elizabeth thanked the lawyers and her male relations for assisting her, then left them sitting in the library while she attended to the packing. She was taking the children to Hatfield to be with Jane at the end of her confinement, and from there would go to the seaside. She didn't know when she would return to Cressingdon, she only knew she couldn't bear to be there while every room and view reminded her of her absent husband.

~

A fortnight after they arrived at Hatfield, and only two days after Elizabeth's twenty-second birthday, Jane was delivered of a boy, Charles Robert Fitzwilliam Bingley. Mr. Darcy and Mr. Hurst stood as godfathers and Elizabeth as godmother, though she was hard-pressed to remember anything of the ceremony. They had originally intended for Robert to stand godfather. Charles had nervously asked the earl when they were visiting in January, and the younger man had been honored when his new brother agreed. Thankfully, Mr. Hurst had been able to step in.

A day after Jane was churched and the baby christened, Elizabeth and the children traveled to the seaside. She rode in one carriage with Bennet and a selection of books she had no intention of reading, and the second carriage held Robbie and Violet, their nursemaid, the wet nurse, and her lady's maid. Her cousin John rode alongside.

After two and a half long days of travel, they arrived at the cottage. The children were quickly settled in and Elizabeth joined John for a light supper. He would be off to London in the morning.

"How are you, cousin?" he asked.

She sighed. "Is that the first question I will be asked for the rest of my life?" she asked in exasperation.

"It is perfectly reasonable. You have very recently been widowed."

"I know. I simply tire of talking about it." She sighed again and pushed her food around on her plate. "Forgive my pique. I am never at my best after traveling."

"It is forgotten." He looked at her appraisingly, then said, "Are you eating at all?"

She shot him an irritated glance. "Yes! Of course I am eating."

She and John had felt like brother and sister soon after meeting. It was inevitable in a way. Alfred and Robert had been more like brothers than cousins. Similar temperaments and senses of humor made Elizabeth and John fast friends.

"You are looking frightfully thin."

She sighed in vexation. "I am not thin. You last saw me at Christmas when I was roughly the size of a carriage; I only look thin in comparison."

He chuckled. "I give you points for effort, Lizzy, but your collar bones look like razor blades."

She gasped. "And you call yourself my friend!" She had the urge to throw a piece of bread at him but refrained. They were not children, after all.

He chuckled. "You know I am only teasing you. But seriously, cousin, you must eat. For yourself and for the children."

She looked down at her full plate and sighed. "I know. I simply have no appetite."

He moved to the chair nearest her and squeezed her hand where it was lying on the table. "I know it seems impossible now, but it will get better."

"How do you know?" she asked in a small voice.

"It always does."

~

Elizabeth spent the entire summer and the early autumn at the seaside. Lydia joined her in July for Violet's second birthday and they spent the days walking on the shore and taking long slow rides through the neighboring fields. After her husband's accident, Elizabeth insisted Lydia take extra care when riding, and the two of them never went above a canter.

Lydia's high spirits, though dampened after her brother's death, were good for the children, and Elizabeth appreciated the freedom her sister's presence brought. If she needed to steal away for an hour or two alone, her sister would manage in her stead. Lydia was accompanied by her governess, now acting as more of a companion to Kitty since Lydia had been at school the previous year, and she generously began teaching Robbie his letters. Elizabeth supposed she would need to hire a governess soon. She would write to Alfred and ask if he knew of anyone seeking a position.

Mary had become engaged to the eldest Goulding boy in early March, quite to everyone's surprise after her infatuation with his cousin the year before, and they were due to marry in October, just after the first mourning was past. Elizabeth appreciated that they waited, but she was not looking forward to returning to Longbourn and all her family and friends' condolences. She knew they meant well, but every kind word just reminded her that she was a widow now and that her life would never be the same.

~

"Are you going to wear that, Lizzy?" asked Mrs. Bennet.

"Yes," she replied simply.

"You cannot wear black to a wedding!" cried her mother.

Elizabeth looked at her, her expression blank and her eyes cold. "It is expensive material, mama. I had thought that would be enough to satisfy you."

Mrs. Bennet stared at her daughter in frustration, and just as she was about to speak, Mr. Bennet entered the room.

"Are you ready? The carriages are here." He smiled and took Elizabeth's hand and placed it on his arm. "See to Mary, Mrs. Bennet. We don't want to keep Mr. Goulding waiting."

Mrs. Bennet sniffed and shifted like an angry hen, then went upstairs to collect Mary.

Elizabeth whispered a quiet thank you to her father and he squeezed her hand, his eyes full of worry.

~

In deference to the family in mourning, Mary's wedding was simple and small. There was a ceremony in the Longbourn Chapel where Kitty stood up with her sister, followed by a breakfast at the house. Elizabeth generously offered the use of one of the unoccupied family estates in Somerset for their first year of wedded life, so they might become accustomed to each other without the curious eyes of his family on them at Haye Park. Mary's husband would eventually inherit, and it would be good for them to understand the workings of the estate before that day came, but Mr. Goulding senior was in excellent health and a little time on their own sounded perfect to the young couple.

Lydia returned to her seminary after the wedding and Kitty was the only unmarried daughter at home. Elizabeth originally had intended to take her to Town, as she had done for Mary and Jane, but she had spent the spring recovering from childbirth and mourning her husband. Going for the Little Season was out of the question. Poor Kitty would miss her presentation and all its attendant activities. She knew she couldn't change it, but Elizabeth did feel badly for her sister's aborted hopes.

To make up for it, Elizabeth penned a letter to her friend, Lady Montgomery, asking her to assist Kitty in society. She would send Kitty and her companion to stay at Asheland House for a month the following spring. She had no plans to return to Town herself any time soon. Lady Montgomery would sponsor Kitty's court presentation and had kindly agreed to host a coming out dinner, and Kitty would accompany them to various events throughout the Season. Kitty was happy to have a season, Lady Montgomery was glad to be of some assistance to her despondent friend, Mrs. Bennet was thrilled to have another daughter launched properly into society, and Elizabeth was glad to simply be left alone.

~

After Mary's wedding, she and the children returned to Cressingdon. After a fortnight of nightmares, she removed to Hatfield to stay with Jane throughout the festive season. She would try again after Bennet's first birthday.

~

"Welcome home, my lady," said Thompson in his deep voice.

Elizabeth smiled weakly at the butler and entered the house slowly. It looked exactly the same. Shouldn't it be different? She was sure the walls would have turned an ugly gray color and the light wouldn't be as bright and cheerful as it had been before. She was so lost without him—wouldn't his home feel the same?

But even Cressingdon seemed to be surviving without Lord Asheland. She was the only one not going about the daily tasks of life as if nothing had happened. As if the very world had not stopped spinning on its axis.

"It is good to be home, Thompson," she lied. "I'd like dinner in two hours, please."

~

Sometime in mid-February, Elizabeth was dressing for the day when she realized she had just slept through the night—at Cressingdon—without Robert. It was a bittersweet realization and she felt a little weepy, but she went about her day admirably. One night turned into two, then a week, then a fortnight, until finally an entire month had passed without her crying in her sleep or waking in a cold sweat from a dreadful nightmare.

She noticed that it was almost a year to the day after his death. She nearly made a joke about needing a full year to learn to sleep by herself, but she couldn't quite manage it. She knew it would have fallen flat regardless. Her humor was not what it used to be.

She visited his grave every Sunday. Robert John often accompanied her, occasionally Violet and Bennet, too. It was sad, and they often cried, but usually she would sit on the grave with her back to the headstone and talk to her husband. Her children would pile onto her lap and she would tell them stories of their Papa, of how kind he was, how generous, how wise and intelligent and funny. How he had loved her fiercely and them as well. How he had provided so perfectly for all of them and taken such good care of his family.

In April, she celebrated her twenty-third birthday with a trip to Jane's home and a slice of lemon cake, shortly followed by her nephew's first birthday. Young Charles and Bennet were excellent playmates, and Jane and Elizabeth decided to spend the remainder of spring and all of summer at the Margate cottage together. Charles had to oversee the estate, but he would join them in July. She never said she was avoiding her home, but Jane and Charles seemed to understand regardless and did not press her.

The summer was as pleasant as it could be under the circumstances. Lydia joined them once again, together with Kitty, and in the autumn they delivered Lydia to her seminary in Town for the new term and Kitty to the Gardiners where she had been invited to spend the Little Season.

Jane was again increasing and Elizabeth accompanied her to Hatfield for her lying in. She delivered a girl with wispy blonde hair in early October called Jane Elizabeth Cassandra. She was a delightful baby, and by the festive season, the Bingley family was ready to travel and Jane and Charles both insisted they accompany Elizabeth to Cressingdon. It would be her first holiday in the house without Robert and they wanted to be with her.

~

"Welcome home, my lady," said Thompson.

His voice sounded the same as it always had, deep and somber, and Elizabeth took comfort in the familiarity of it.

173

"Thank you, Thompson." She returned his smile, too preoccupied to notice the worry in her servant's eyes.

Elizabeth walked through the halls in a daze. She hadn't spent more than two months at the house since Robert's death and she wasn't quite sure how to go about living there without him. She went into the mistress's study and sat down with an open ledger. She met with the housekeeper and discussed menus. She spoke to the gardener about adding a lavender border to one of the walks.

She was sure it would ache daily, but her son deserved to grow up in the home he would inherit, and her husband's memory ought to be preserved in the place he loved best. It was the least she owed him.

She knew her family would lose patience with her soon. Alfred and Sylvia's letters were becoming more frequent. What were her plans? How were the children? Was she coming to visit soon? They were still her family, they reminded her.

Her mother had grown tired of her mourning a year ago. Mrs. Bennet couldn't understand why Elizabeth hadn't come for a visit, or returned to Town, or taken Kitty for a season as she had promised. Elizabeth merely ignored her mother's letters and wrote to her father, asking him to explain to her mother that she would visit when she was ready, she had not forgotten her family, and Town was not going anywhere—she could visit later.

She knew Mrs. Bennet didn't truly understand her reasoning, but at least her letters insisting Elizabeth do her sisterly duty had ceased. She half wondered if her mother was still writing them and her father simply stole them from the salver. It was like him to deal with problems indirectly—when he dealt with them at all, and he would find his wife's frustration at not receiving a reply amusing.

Elizabeth couldn't decide if the fact that her family never changed was comforting or depressing.

She had been dressing in half mourning for some time, in light grays and lavender, white gowns with black trim, and in three short months, the second anniversary of Robert's death would pass—just in time for the Season. She didn't want to participate, or wear cheerful clothes, or converse with people she merely tolerated, but she couldn't hide at the seaside forever, no matter how much she wanted to. And Kitty would love to accompany her. She could do this; she would.

With a deep breath, she wrote letters to her sisters requesting their company in the spring. Then she asked the dressmaker to attend her. She was in need of a new wardrobe.

Lady Elizabeth Asheland was returning to Town.

PART II

CHAPTER 12

Darcy sat in the corner of the club near a window, reading the broadsheet. He'd just received a letter from Charles stating that they would come to Town in March and stay for two months, possibly longer. He mentioned that his sister Elizabeth would arrive near the same time.

Darcy had not seen Lady Asheland since Bingley's son's christening nearly two years ago. He knew from Charles that she had spent most of her time at the seaside or at Hatfield. She hadn't been to Town since the accident, and after labeling her heartbroken and a shell of her former self, the rumor mill had moved on to more active targets.

He was shaken from his reverie by a familiar voice. He looked to his right and saw a group of several men, including his cousin Colonel Fitzwilliam, in fervent discussion.

"Darcy! How are you, old man?" cried the Colonel.

Darcy stood to shake his cousin's hand and Fitzwilliam quickly led him to the group. Darcy greeted the men he knew and his cousin introduced him to those he didn't.

"Do you know when she will arrive?" asked Wiltshire, a man Darcy had been in school with.

"I heard it was mid-season."

"Will she move much in society?"

Darcy was staring at his brandy glass and mostly ignoring the conversation around him. He didn't know why, but he was feeling very contemplative today.

"No doubt we'll hear soon enough. She'll be on everybody's guest list. Even a countess can't refuse all invitations."

Darcy looked up at this and asked who they were speaking of, unsurprised to hear it was Lady Asheland. He went back to studying his brandy glass, his expression more inscrutable than ever.

"You know her, don't you, Darcy?" asked Colonel Fitzwilliam.

Darcy looked up. "Lady Asheland?"

"Yes."

"Yes, I know her. You are acquainted with her as well, are you not? She knows your parents," Darcy responded.

"Of course, Lord Asheland and father were friendly, but I only met her once or twice at a party. We said nothing beyond simple pleasantries. We thought you might be able to tell us more about her than what color she favors."

He looked at the expectant faces of the men around him and then back to his cousin. "Surely you're not dangling after her!"

"I would hardly call it that, but she is an eligible match, you must admit," reasoned his cousin.

"Come, Darcy, surely you see the benefits of an alliance?" cried Mr. Wiltshire.

Darcy looked at him incredulously, wondering if he was speaking in generalities or of himself specifically.

"Whomever she marries will be as father to the next Earl of Asheland. He'll wield a prodigious amount of influence!" cried Mr. Wiltshire.

"The man Lady Asheland marries or the young earl?" queried Darcy.

"Both!"

"You would seek to attach a fatherless boy to you, to manipulate a child for your own gains?" Darcy asked in disgust.

"I wouldn't call it that, Darcy. We're just being practical," said Wiltshire.

"Curious, I would call it something else," replied Darcy.

"Now, gentlemen, let's be civil about this. Wiltshire, you are speaking of a small boy who has lost his father. Show some decorum, man."

Wiltshire nodded begrudgingly and looked down.

"And Darcy, Lady Asheland is a young, beautiful woman. She obviously must have something to have drawn the earl to her—it's only natural to be curious. She is wealthy, well-positioned, and incredibly well-connected. Surely you're not surprised at our interest?"

"She has lost her husband!" he spat. "A husband, I might add, whom she loved deeply and who loved her in return. She is grieving and the least we can do is show some respect to the earl's memory by not discussing his wife and children like horses at Tattersall's!"

He nodded curtly and walked away, leaving five wide-eyed men behind him.

~

Jane Bingley was a gentle woman. She did not pry into others' lives. She did not insist on having her own way when it would inconvenience someone else—or even when it wouldn't. She was kind to everyone and serene in even the most tempestuous situations. But despite all her complacency, she did not know what to do with her sister.

Elizabeth had always been special in Jane's eyes, a force of nature. Jane had always been a bit in awe of her younger sister. Where she was shy, Elizabeth was bold. Where she was fearful, Elizabeth was brave. When she

179

was at a loss, Elizabeth found a solution. When she smiled, Elizabeth laughed.

Her sister was bright and sunny; living, breathing happiness wrapped up in a wide smile and shining eyes.

Or she had been. Since the death of her husband, Elizabeth had been a shadow of her former self. There had been happy moments, of course, and she had learned to find joy again with her children. She was a wonderful mother and a kind sister and was doing her best to resume her former life, but Jane saw through her bravado. She knew Elizabeth was sleepwalking through life, simply carrying out her obligations without truly engaging in life.

Jane was of the opinion that Elizabeth should remarry. She was too young to remain a widow all her life and her children needed a father. Beyond all of that, Elizabeth was not made for gloom. She had found a measure of happiness since Robert's death, it was true, but Jane knew what her sister was capable of—the devotion, the passion, the deep joy and affection she could give.

Elizabeth needed to share her heart. She was not meant to be alone. Oddly, Jane had often thought that of the two of them, it was she who could be happier alone. Elizabeth had joked that Jane would marry and she would be an old maid, but Jane had silently disagreed. She had always been able to find contentment in her sisters and family, in doing her duty, in a dozen small things in her daily life. Jane would not trade her husband for anything, and she had long suspected that once she loved it would be a permanent sort of thing for her, but had she never met Charles Bingley, she could have been content with her life.

But not Elizabeth. She was constantly looking for more, expecting more, hoping for more. She would never have been happy spending her life at Longbourn with their parents. Hertfordshire was too small to hold someone of Elizabeth's spirit. She needed room to grow and stretch her wings.

Jane had not been surprised at all that a wealthy earl had fallen in love with and offered for her sister. Who would not want such a delightful creature?

Jane couldn't help but feel that it was her responsibility to bring Elizabeth back to herself. She was the closest person to her sister and she knew her best. She also knew what Elizabeth needed, and it wasn't to be alone for the rest of her life, though she was sure her sister would disagree.

~

"You sound like Lady Sylvia," said Elizabeth in exasperation.

She and Jane were seated in her private parlor at Asheland House in town.

"Perhaps if so many people are saying the same thing, you should listen," reasoned Jane.

"You are two happily married women who want to see everyone else happily married. Though I would have thought Sylvia to be more loyal. She seems so devoted to Alfred, I can't imagine her wanting to replace him should he die."

"Don't be morbid. And they have been married more than twenty-five years. She does not have small children to raise," Jane added with a knowing look.

"It really is terrible of you to try to force me into marriage for the sake of the children, Jane."

"No one is forcing you to do anything, Lizzy. But the children do need a father."

"They have a father. I didn't find them growing in the garden and put them in a basket to be displayed inside."

"You know what I mean," said Jane with a shake of her head. Must her sister always be so stubborn?

"I know. You mean that they need a constant gentleman-figure in their lives. They see father regularly, you've seen how he dotes on them, and there is Alfred, too, whom they've always been fond of. For younger men there is John, and even Charles. There are plenty of men in their lives; they will not lack for male attention."

Jane shook her head. "Yes, those men are all available to you and the children and they are wonderful, but it is not the same and you know it."

Elizabeth shook her head and huffed. "Jane," she said in a voice that told her sister she was rapidly losing patience.

"What about you, Lizzy?" asked Jane softly. "Do you not wish for a husband?"

"No, I do not."

"Truly?"

"Truly."

Jane shook her head, bemused. "Do you not wish to share your heart with someone? Does all your devotion not long for an object?"

"I am devoted to my children. I share my heart with you and our sisters and my family. I am content."

Jane continued to look doubtful and Elizabeth elaborated.

"I had a very unusual marriage, Jane. I know that. Robert and I were closer than couples in our circles, or couples anywhere. We shared everything; every thought, every feeling, every desire and idea and dream. We were truly as one. I cannot imagine another such love being granted to me in this lifetime. Nor can I imagine another man such as my husband. After sharing what we did, and living as we lived, I could not accept a cold marriage of convenience, or even a warm one that followed propriety.

"Your husband loves you, Jane, you know what I speak of. Can you imagine lying with a man who only married you because of your money and position? The degradation of it? I am young still; if I were to marry I would likely have more children. Would he stay in the birthing room with me if I asked him? Would I want him there? Would I want to have children with such a man, or allow him to raise Robert's children?"

She shook her head vigorously. "I am under no delusions that there is another Robert in the world, looking to marry an impertinent woman with three children whom he can shower with affection." She laughed wryly. "No Jane, I had the best, and I am simply spoiled for others. It would kill me to have anything less than what I had with Robert, and I do not think that is possible.

"I will not marry again. Please do not ask it of me."

Jane looked at her solemnly with liquid eyes and said, "Of course, Lizzy. I will respect your wishes."

~

"I think it will be Lord Epworth."

"Lord Epworth? What makes you say so?"

"He is her cousin and the heir to the marquess. And you know how much time they've been spending together."

"No more than anyone else. I'll admit it would be a splendid match, but to marry her late husband's godson. It's unseemly!"

"Her husband was old enough to be her father and knew everyone in town. How is she to marry someone unconnected to him?"

"Really, the things you say, Elvira."

"It would be a splendid match! She is already accepted by his family and she's quite pretty. She has proven to be healthy and fecund, and she is fabulously wealthy. What more could be wished for?"

"They *are* rumored to be good friends," she said slowly.

"Exactly."

They tittered behind their fans and moved toward the window. Lady Montgomery stepped away from the plant she had been standing behind and made her way to the door.

"Asheland House," she told the footman as he held open the door to the carriage.

Lady Montgomery swept into the drawing room and sat by her friend who had yet to rise from the chaise.

"Alice! What brings you here today?" Elizabeth asked with a smile.

"Elizabeth, I must speak with you. Privately." She looked sideways at the children playing on the floor nearby.

"Of course," Elizabeth said. "Robbie, Violet, go upstairs with Molly for a little while." She kissed their heads and sent them on their way. "Now, what is all this about?"

"I've just come from Maria Bosworth's."

Elizabeth made a face. "I see you arrived unscathed. I'm surprised you accepted the invitation. You've never liked her."

"That isn't the point!" she said, huffing in frustration. "While there, I overheard Elvira Evans and some woman I can't recall discussing you. And your marital prospects."

"I don't like it, but it's hardly unexpected. We knew there would be talk."

"But did you know they would match you with John Downing and say you were practically engaged?"

"What?" cried Elizabeth. "Me? With John? He's like a brother to me! It would be impossible! What, why," she stuttered.

"Exactly. That is why I rushed over to tell you. We must put a stop to this."

"How will we do that? Surely, if nothing comes of it, the rumors will die down."

"Believe that if you will, but we both know that Lord Epworth is one of the most eligible bachelors in Town and you are now one of the most desirable women. It is a compelling story. I doubt it will die down fast."

"While I must disagree with you on my desirability, I know John is a favorite. But surely the marchioness will correct the rumors."

"Will she?"

"Why wouldn't she?"

"Has it ever occurred to you that Epworth's parents may be in favor of the match?"

Elizabeth spluttered. "What? No! They couldn't—it would be too strange. No, it cannot be."

"I can't know for certain, of course, but we should consider the possibility. You told me yourself the marquess is in excellent health. Their son won't inherit for years."

"But I'm sure they give him an allowance. And the family has another estate. They lived there until Alfred inherited a few years ago. It is a lovely home!"

"Isn't Epworth's younger brother inheriting that estate?" she asked slyly.

"I had forgotten about that," replied Elizabeth. "But that doesn't necessarily mean anything. The marquess is a wealthy man. I know the title holds at least one other property."

"Yes, but though it has rank, it does not have as much money as the Asheland title."

"Really, Alice, how you go on. Alfred may have a tiny bit less in the funds than Robert did, but he is far from poor. They are hardly in need of money!"

"I agree, I just want you to be aware of the possibility. He is well known to you, and he is fond of your children."

"I thought you wanted to quell the rumors, not convince me to marry my cousin."

"I do! If that is what you want. If you want to marry your cousin, I will help you with that instead. Either way, you need to know what is being said about you. You can't hide away forever."

"I went to dinner just last night!" Elizabeth cried indignantly.

"At Robert's aunt's home."

"Still, I was not at home."

"Hmm." Lady Montgomery looked at Elizabeth appraisingly. "So you do not want your cousin, then?"

"No! I most assuredly do not. He is almost like a brother to me. I could never look at him that way."

"Pity. He is a handsome man." They laughed for a moment and she continued, "If that is what you wish, we must dispel the rumors before they harm your reputation and scare off the other suitors."

"What other suitors? I have told you more than once that I am not interested in remarrying."

"Yes, yes, I know, but the *ton* does not. Now, I propose we go to as many parties and balls as possible, where you must talk and dance with as many men as you can, and that should sufficiently muddy the waters so no one is sure *whom* you favor."

"I favor no one!"

"A minor detail." Lady Montgomery waved her hand as if to brush the idea away and sipped her tea. "You can accompany us to dinner at Lord and Lady Marlborough's tomorrow night."

"I already declined the invitation."

"Then write back and say that you have had a change of plans and would love to accept. It will be the perfect opportunity! Will Mr. Downing be there?"

"No, he has gone to Kent for a few days."

"That," she tilted her head toward Elizabeth, "is the sort of detail a betrothed would know."

"Or a sister, or a cousin, or a close friend," replied Elizabeth.

Lady Montgomery sighed. "I should have known you wouldn't make this easy."

~

The dinner at Lady Marlborough's was as expected. Elizabeth was known to the majority of the guests and was quickly introduced to those she hadn't met. Lady Marlborough seemed especially glad to see her, which Elizabeth thought was odd as they had never been particularly friendly, until Lady Marlborough introduced Elizabeth to her younger brother, a man in need of a wife with her own fortune. She smiled tightly and left their company as soon as was polite.

She renewed her acquaintance with Colonel Fitzwilliam, a younger son of Lord Matlock, and they had a pleasant conversation on a variety of topics, but overall the evening was dull and she couldn't wait for it to be over.

Over the next fortnight, Alice dragged her to two more dinner parties, a music recital, and three balls where she insisted Elizabeth dance at least half the dances. She pulled their friend Julia Henley, Countess of Sheffield, into the scheme and between the two of them, Elizabeth was engaged for some sort of silliness nearly every day. She had made something of a friend of Colonel Fitzwilliam, but she knew he needed a wife of independent means, and while she was not repulsed by him, neither was she attracted. She supposed she could grow to care for him if she really wanted to and if he made an effort to endear himself, but she didn't wish it and his thin flirtations would not create the fertile ground necessary for love to grow.

She had known she would be something of a prize on the marriage mart, but she hadn't thought it would be quite this bad. At least her sister Kitty was having a good time. Kitty had been called on lately by a few gentlemen and she was quite pleased with her season in town. Last year, Lady Montgomery had assisted her somewhat, but nothing could quite compare to being introduced as the sister of Lady Asheland by the Lady herself.

Kitty was now twenty and of a mind to marry. She had made a small list of the qualities she was looking for in a man and went about looking for them in the gentlemen she met. Cousin John had suggested it as a joke, and poor Kitty, not understanding the jest, had taken him seriously. Elizabeth tried not to laugh when she read the list, but really it wasn't all bad. Honesty and kindness were certainly admirable traits, and thick hair was always attractive.

To Kitty's dismay, Lydia had joined them in town, but to Kitty's relief, her younger sister did not attend every outing as she was still preparing for her presentation. Mrs. Bennet had held a large party for Lydia when she finished school and turned eighteen the previous June, and it had been considered her official coming out. Now she was in London with her sister, testing the waters as she called it.

Lydia was not interested in marrying for some time yet. Elizabeth had given birth to her first child less than a year after she wed, and Jane almost a year exactly. Even serious Mary, who cared for nothing but her music and her books, was with child within a few months of her wedding. No, Lydia was not eager to be a mother. She enjoyed her nephews and nieces and thought they were perfectly lovely, especially when they were clean. She played with them for a few hours and allowed the nurse to take them away again when they became fussy, but Lydia was no fool.

She knew Elizabeth had made a spectacular match. Jane's was very good as well, and even Mary's was considered good by most standards, but Mary did not have half as many servants as Elizabeth had, and Lydia did not want to find herself in a position of changing nappies or giving baths to wriggling babies.

She was in a perfect position now. Youngest sister to the young widowed countess. She was far from on the shelf, and Elizabeth was happy to have her company and take her to grand parties where she could dance with whomever she wanted and not grow fat with child.

Besides, she knew of the dowry scheme her brother had set in place, and with only herself and Kitty to split Netherfield's income, the longer she waited, the larger her dowry would be. She, the youngest of her sisters, could have the largest dowry of them all. Wasn't it a good joke? Mary had had nearly ten thousand pounds after the bequest from Robert. The Goulding family had been happy when they thought it was nearer six thousand. They were ecstatic when it was increased.

Lydia knew hers had to be somewhere near that now. Could she wait long enough for it to become twelve thousand? She wouldn't want to be an old maid, but certainly twenty-two was a fine age to be married. Jane had been nearly twenty-three when she wed Charles and she was disgustingly happy. Lydia would write to her father and ask how many years she should wait to allow her dowry the necessary time to grow.

CHAPTER 13

Elizabeth and Kitty were sitting in the front parlor when a visitor was announced.

"Mr. Darcy, my lady."

"Show him in, Franklin."

Elizabeth stood and arranged her skirts, wondering what Mr. Darcy was doing here, and failed to notice the flush on her sister's cheeks. The door opened and Thompson was followed in by a tall man with dark hair, a straight nose, and a bright green waistcoat. He was not Mr. Darcy.

"Good day, Lady Asheland, Miss Bennet," said the stranger.

Elizabeth curtsied and tried to cover her surprise.

"Forgive me, sir. I thought you were Mr. Darcy," she said with a smile. She sat on the sofa and gestured for him to sit on the chair opposite.

"I am. Mr. Darcy, that is. We met briefly a week ago, but we didn't speak, so I don't expect you to remember."

He smiled affably and Elizabeth couldn't help but smile back. His manners reminded her a little of her brother Bingley.

"I apologize. Do you know my sister, Catherine Bennet?"

"Yes, we've met on a few occasions." The tips of his ears turned red and he looked at her sister with barely contained excitement.

Glancing at Kitty, Elizabeth saw she was blushing fiercely and her eyes were glued to her lap. Kitty wasn't

190

usually shy in company, so Elizabeth was immediately suspicious.

"I know a Mr. Darcy from Derbyshire. Are you related to him?"

"Yes, we're cousins. Our grandfathers were brothers."

"Ah. Yes, I see a resemblance." Truly, she had seen it the moment he walked into the room. Both were tall and lean with broad shoulders and thick hair. But this Mr. Darcy was all smiles and easy conversation, and his eyes were a warm brown, while the elder Mr. Darcy's were cold and blue.

"Do you live in Derbyshire as well?"

"Yes, I do. I have a small estate not too far from Pemberley. I recently inherited it from my mother's brother. But I grew up in Staffordshire, on my father's estate. He's there now with my mother and younger sisters, but my elder brother is in town."

"Will you be in Town for the season?"

"Yes, I plan to remain until May. Will you spend the summer at Cressingdon?"

"That is the plan, though it is undecided whether Kitty will accompany me. She may prefer to spend the summer at our father's estate in Hertfordshire." Elizabeth smiled encouragingly at her sister and sipped her tea.

"Yes," stammered Kitty, "My plans are not yet fixed. Last summer we stayed at the seaside and it was lovely, but Elizabeth wants to be home this summer."

"There is nowhere like the English countryside in summer, I daresay, though the seaside brings its own joys. Have you travelled much, Miss Bennet?"

"Oh, not too much. I've travelled to my sisters' estates in the north, and I was in school in London, and of course the seaside."

Before she could say more, there was a loud crash followed by the wailing of an injured child. Elizabeth immediately stood.

"If you'll excuse me," she said as she bustled out the door.

She quickly made her way upstairs and found Violet being held by her nurse and a maid picking up flowers strewn across the hall floor.

"She was running from her brother and went right into the table and the vase fell on top of her, my lady," said the nursemaid as she passed over a crying Violet.

"Don't worry, Molly," she said to the nervous girl. "These things happen. Now where is my errant son?"

Robbie shuffled out of the shadows and stood before his mother, his eyes on the carpet.

"Robert John, are you supposed to chase your sister in the house?"

"No."

"Are you allowed to run in the house?"

"No."

"Then why did you?"

He shrugged his shoulders and looked ready to cry.

"Come here, love." She pulled him to her and sat him in her lap, Violet snuggled into her neck and Robbie settled on her other knee where she sat on the floor in the middle of the hall.

"We don't run and chase in the house because that is how we get hurt. Do you see this mark on Violet's head?"

He nodded forlornly.

"We don't want her to get any more of these, so we must do our running outside, do you understand?"

"Yes, mama."

"Now, why don't you two go to the kitchen and ask Mrs. Landers for a biscuit, then Molly can take you outside to play. I'll even ask Aunt Lydia to come and play with you. How does that sound?"

He smiled and agreed and Violet stopped sniffling and peeked out to nod her agreement as well.

Elizabeth dusted herself off and watched them go down the hall with a fond smile. They really were the very best of her and Robert. How they'd managed to have such delightful children, she'd never know, but she was incredibly grateful.

She stopped in the music room where Lydia was practicing and asked her if she would please join the children when she finished, then Elizabeth rejoined Kitty and Mr. Darcy in the parlor. She smiled to herself—it would take time to become accustomed to his name. She had associated the name Darcy with proud and difficult for so long, it would be hard to imagine the name on a man so amiable and charming.

The pair seemed to have stumbled into a stilted conversation, but judging by the smiles and flushed cheeks of both, they were enjoying it. In a moment of mischief, Elizabeth decided to have a little fun and possibly help her sister along if she could.

"Mr. Darcy, we'd be pleased if you'd join us for dinner tomorrow evening, if you have no prior arrangements."

"Oh, that's very kind of you. I am at my leisure, thank you. I'd love to join you."

Elizabeth nodded, Kitty stammered something unintelligible, and he bid them goodbye until tomorrow.

"I think you've made a conquest there," said Elizabeth.

"Do you?" asked Kitty nervously. "He is terribly handsome, isn't he? Do you think he likes me?"

"Why would he not?" Elizabeth smiled kindly at her younger sister. Perhaps she could redirect Jane to matchmake for Kitty and leave her alone. Her sister was at least *interested* in men.

~

Dear Jane,

It would appear that Kitty has an admirer! She was called on today by young Mr. Darcy, not to be confused with stuffy Mr. Darcy. I have invited him for dinner tomorrow evening and you can tell me your opinion of him. He seems like a nice young man. Does Charles know him, by any chance? I would like to know more about him before Kitty becomes too enamoured.

Elizabeth

Dear Lizzy,

Charles has only met young Mr. Darcy on a few occasions, but he said he seems to be a nice enough man and there are no unpleasant stories told about him. He will ask Mr. Darcy—he will of course know more and tell us the truth of it. You really shouldn't call him stuffy, Lizzy. He cannot help his nature. And he has been very kind to us all, including you, though I daresay you don't like to remember that.

Charles forgot we were having dinner with you tomorrow and invited Mr. Darcy here, and of course when I told him, he invited Mr. Darcy to join us at Asheland House. He meant to send a note, but then he forgot. He sends his apologies. I told him you would not be so ungenerous as to deny Mr. Darcy a dinner invitation as he is such a close friend of your brother's and even Robert called him friend. If I am mistaken in your magnanimity, correct me at once so I may notify Mr. Darcy.

Jane

Dear Jane,

194

Don't think I don't know what you are doing. You may be the most angelic of the Bennet sisters, but you are a Bennet sister still, and that must go some way to instilling mischief. Of course Mr. Darcy may have dinner with us. You need not invoke Charles' friendship with him or Robert's memory to induce me to act properly. Mr. Darcy is welcome, he knows that, and I know you do as well, which makes me think there is something else afoot.

I do hope, dear sister, that you are only looking out for Kitty's best interests and not trying your hand at something else. I shall see you tomorrow. Kiss the children for me.

E

~

Elizabeth quickly sent out invitations to both Mr. Darcys, trying not to snigger as she did so. She was unsurprised the next day when they arrived for dinner together. Young Mr. Darcy was all smiles and affability, bowing over her hand, asking after the children, and being very attentive to Kitty who could not stop blushing each time he looked at her.

Old Mr. Darcy, though the title was hardly fitting for a man barely thirty, was as he always was. Quiet, solemn, and slightly offensive, though he did surprise her when he kissed her hand at their greeting, and again when he asked after her well-being with such sincerity she felt herself wishing to confide in him, but she merely said she was well and invited him to sit.

They were a small party, only the Bingleys, Elizabeth, Kitty, and Lydia, the Gardiners, and the two Mr. Darcys. Elizabeth had thought to quickly ask another family to join them so it would appear less like the Mr. Darcys were joining a family dinner, but in the end, she decided against it. After all, she had intended to invite the young Mr. Darcy to a family dinner all along so that she and Kitty might get to know him better. How was Kitty to decide if she should accept his suit if she spent no time with him?

Elizabeth was immensely grateful to her Aunt and Uncle Gardiner for allowing her to get to know Robert before she accepted him. There had been no improprieties and they were rarely ever truly alone, but they had often spoken on their own in a crowded room, or walked apart even when they were with the group. The Gardiners had not wished for her to be uninformed and Elizabeth knew it had been a sound decision. She hoped to emulate something of their discretion with Kitty and Lydia while they were in her care.

Before conversation could truly begin, the Bingleys arrived, quickly followed by the Gardiners with their youngest daughter, who would play with Robbie while the family had dinner.

"Mr. Darcy, I believe you've met my Uncle, Mr. Gardiner. This is his wife, Mrs. Madeleine Gardiner. She hails from Derbyshire as well," said Elizabeth with a smile. "Aunt, Uncle, this is Mr. Darcy of Pemberley in Derbyshire, and his cousin, Mr. Darcy, also of Derbyshire if I remember correctly."

Young Mr. Darcy laughed and said it was true, though he was so close to Staffordshire it almost wasn't Derbyshire. He happily greeted the Gardiners while the older Mr. Darcy looked on with a solemn expression and said nothing, only nodding and resuming his seat. Elizabeth didn't bother trying to draw him out. He was not the Darcy she was most interested in that evening.

By the time dinner was served, Elizabeth was impressed with young Mr. Darcy. He seemed kind and amiable and ready to please. She had always thought Kitty would need a man with a sanguine disposition, preferably one not given to low moods or too many dark thoughts. Kitty was a simple girl at heart, though she could be moody herself sometimes, and occasionally doubtful of her place with the people around her. A cheerful, even-tempered man would be good for her.

But she really must think of something else to call him. Two Mr. Darcys in one room was confusing. As they were walking into the dining room, she said as much to the elder Mr. Darcy, who was escorting her.

"It really is very silly that men are not called by their given names."

"I beg your pardon?" replied Mr. Darcy.

"Do you not find it ridiculous that a family of women are easily distinguished because the younger sisters are all known by their given names, but a family of men are all called the same?"

"Elizabeth, do not tease Mr. Darcy," said Jane from her place behind her.

Elizabeth looked over her shoulder with a smile and Jane merely looked heavenward.

As they sat at the table, Lydia replied that Elizabeth couldn't help it and Charles chuckled and replied, "How would men appear dignified if everyone called them by their given names?"

"Is that what makes them dignified? Well, that is good to know," remarked Elizabeth.

She sat at the head of the table, Mr. Darcy kindly helping her with her chair, and he sat to her right. Next to him was Jane, a small mercy Elizabeth felt equal to delivering, and then Mr. Gardiner and Lydia. On her left was the younger Mr. Darcy, then Kitty, Charles and Mrs. Gardiner. The table was slightly incorrect, but most of the rules of propriety had been followed. She knew Charles should have sat higher than the young Mr. Darcy, but how was she to get to know him if he was all the way down the table? Family parties need not be so formal, or so she told

herself when arranging the seating. She made a concession
by placing Mr. Darcy at the top as his position required,
and she imagined he was the only one who cared about
such things, anyhow.

Of course, had she been privy to Mr. Darcy's thoughts
at the time, she would have felt quite differently.

Young Mr. Darcy laughed along with them and told
Elizabeth, "If it makes it easier to tell us apart, my given
name is Michael."

"Thank you, sir. I don't have much difficulty telling
you apart, though you are quite similar," she shot Mr.
Darcy a smile to her right, "but it will make conversation
easier."

Mr. Darcy inclined his head slightly with a small grin
that looked more like a grimace.

Elizabeth spent the remainder of the meal speaking to
Mr. Michael Darcy and Kitty, with the occasional
comment from Mr. Darcy on her right. Jane and Mr.
Gardiner were having an intelligent discussion on a new
work of poetry recently published. Charles occasionally
made a comment and Mr. Darcy seemed to be listening but
never said much of anything to anyone. Elizabeth
wondered why he even wished to dine in company if he
insisted on being so silent all the time, but her curiosity
would not be assuaged this night.

They forewent the separation of the sexes after dinner
and Kitty entertained on the pianoforte, followed by Lydia.
Elizabeth occasionally sang with them, but declined to
play. She had often played for Robert in the evenings; he
had been very fond of music. He would look at her in such
a way that she could feel herself flushing from her hair
down to her chemise. She hadn't played much since his
death, only a few songs for the children every once in a
while. She supposed she would have to pick it back up
eventually, but since she wasn't in the market for a

husband, there wasn't much need for public exhibition. She could return to music at her leisure.

"Will you be playing for us this evening?"

Elizabeth started and turned to see Mr. Darcy standing beside her.

"Forgive me, Mr. Darcy, I didn't see you. No, I will not be playing this evening."

He nodded and looked at her in such a way that she thought he might have been reading her mind and knew exactly why she didn't want to play. She flushed and his dark eyes moved to look across the room.

"Your sister plays very well."

Elizabeth looked to where Lydia was playing and said, "Thank you. She does not enjoy it much, but her governess insisted she be able to present herself well. She would much rather be doing something active."

"Bingley says she is an avid rider. I hope she hasn't found Town too confining in that respect."

Elizabeth looked at him in surprise. Was he making pleasant conversation with her? And had he and Charles discussed her sisters? "She feels somewhat stifled, of course, but she enjoys dancing and the balls have been a pleasant distraction."

"My sister rides most mornings in Rotten Row, before the fashionable hour. I'm sure she would be pleased for Miss Lydia to join her."

"Thank you. I'll mention it to Lydia. Is your sister enjoying her season?"

"I believe so, though a brother is never a good gauge of these sorts of things." She smiled and he continued. "She would rather be at Pemberley, playing and riding, but society must have its due."

He said the last somewhat bitterly and she looked at him thoughtfully. "Yes, it must. I confess I would also prefer to spend all my time in the country. I miss the long walks and the clean air and the freedom to go where I wish without worrying how fashionable my bonnet is."

He smiled at her tease, looking more approachable than she had ever found him. "I couldn't agree more, though I would not know about the bonnet. I'm afraid they all look the same to me."

She laughed, surprised that Mr. Darcy was capable of making a joke. He looked at her intently for a moment, and she looked back with a question in her eyes.

"Lady Asheland, I would like to introduce my sister to you, if it isn't too great an imposition."

"Oh!" Her eyes widened. "Of course. I should like to meet Miss Darcy. Why don't you bring her for tea? I assume she is already familiar with Jane?"

"Yes, she looks on Charles as another brother."

"I'm glad to hear it, for he is an excellent brother. Shall we say the day after next?"

"I look forward to it."

~

Elizabeth did wonder why Mr. Darcy wanted her to meet his sister, but decided not to consider it too closely. He may want to broaden her social circle or he may desire the connection, he may want his sister to be closer to his friends, and he did spend a considerable amount of time with the Bingleys, according to Jane. Whatever his reasons, she had agreed to the introduction and she would reserve judgment until she had observed more thoroughly.

The Darcys arrived promptly and Elizabeth told the butler she was not home to visitors unless it was Mrs. Bingley. She had decided to meet the Darcys on her own but her sisters would join them later in the visit.

Mr. Darcy performed the introductions and conversation was stilted at first, but eventually flowed more easily. Georgiana was painfully shy and could hardly speak more than two sentences together without flushing and staring at the floor.

"I had the pleasure of meeting your cousin, Mr. Michael Darcy. He is an amiable man," said Elizabeth pleasantly.

"Yes, he has always been kind to me," replied Georgiana.

Seeing no more information was forthcoming, she changed direction. "Are you enjoying your season?"

"Yes, and no. I mean, I have met many people and I enjoy being in Town for the theater and the museums, but, it is very busy."

"It is rather overwhelming, isn't it?" said Elizabeth sympathetically. "I remember my first proper season in town. Well, really, I suppose it was my second. My first season I was staying with my Aunt and Uncle Gardiner on Gracechurch Street, and their idea of a season is much more palatable than the ridiculous pace set in Mayfair."

Georgiana looked at her expectantly and she continued.

"That year I met my husband, and thankfully we were able to spend several months in the country before coming back to Town, but when we did," she looked heavenward and sighed, "everyone was sure to let me know how wrong I was for the title of Lady Asheland and they cared not how little their barbs were appreciated."

"What did you do?" asked Georgiana in a small voice.

"I behaved as I always had, but with a little more dignity, I believe." She laughed at herself. "I had the Talbot family behind me, and a better family I could not have wished for. They cared for me as Robert's wife without requiring more, and my husband made it very plain that he preferred me to be who I was rather than to fashion myself into a version of me that he wouldn't recognize or approve of. Because he was in Parliament, we spent the entire season in Town, and I eventually made friends, some of whom are as dear to me now as sisters.

"It wasn't easy, discerning the insincere from those genuinely interested in friendship, but I had my husband to lean on, and my family to guide me when I was unsure. And now I feel as at ease in Town as I do anywhere else, though I do not love it as much as the country."

Georgiana smiled and Elizabeth returned it, then looked to Mr. Darcy who was staring at her with a light in his eyes she vaguely recognized as interest. He inclined his head toward her and she understood it for the thanks it was.

Elizabeth looked up and saw Kitty and Lydia in the doorway. Elizabeth performed the introductions and soon the three young women were discussing balls and dance partners and strict instructors.

"Thank you, Lady Asheland. You've eased Georgiana's mind a great deal."

Elizabeth turned to face Mr. Darcy. "You have a habit of catching me unawares, Mr. Darcy. I never know you're there until you say something and surprise me. It makes me wonder how many times you've stood nearby without me knowing of your presence."

To her surprise, Mr. Darcy reddened slightly. "Forgive me. I didn't mean to frighten you."

"I'm not frightened, Mr. Darcy," she said steadily.

"Of course not. I begin to think you afraid of nothing."

She flushed and looked away, wondering why his words unsettled her so.

~

Darcy had just had an extraordinary idea. He had long held Lady Asheland as the standard of a good wife and mother and had thought to find a woman like her. Now it occurred to him that with her widowhood and return to society, he could perhaps wed the original instead of a copy.

He had never allowed himself to think of her in that way before. She was, after all, another man's wife. A man he respected and admired. The Asheland marriage had obviously been a happy one and he was not the sort of man to disrupt a healthy union, or even an unhealthy one. But she was now unencumbered and as the men at the club had said, eminently suitable.

She was well-connected, pretty, kind, and healthy enough to bear an heir. More than all of that, he admired her mind and her liveliness. They had had some wonderful debates. He loved watching her engage him in a battle of wits. It was most invigorating and a pleasant change from the fawning insipidity he was generally subjected to.

He'd never seen a woman more dedicated to her children; it was a very favorable quality. She had been incredibly devoted to Lord Asheland. Any fool could see that. Would she be as devoted to her next husband?

For the first time, he thought the devotion of such a woman might be worth having.

~

"Where are you off to so early, Lyddie?" asked Elizabeth when she saw Lydia in the breakfast room the following day.

"I'm going for a ride with Miss Darcy, remember? I mentioned it last night while you were rocking Bennet."

"Of course. I'd forgotten. Rocking a child does have a way of clearing one's mind." She smiled at her sister in her smart riding habit. "I rather like that color on you. Is it the new one?"

"No, it is the one from last September, but it's so pretty I don't want to stop wearing it. I ordered the new one made in the same style and a similar color."

"You may order more than one, you know. For a person who rides as much as you do, it makes sense to have several habits."

"You don't need to spend all your money on me, Lizzy," said Lydia with a cheeky grin. "Besides, I'm saving my pin money for a new mare."

"Are you?"

"Yes. I want to breed her with our brother's stallion. Don't look at me like that, Lizzy! I won't be making the purchase myself! Percy will handle it for me, of course. He's already said he would be happy to assist in any way he can. You know how the Gouldings are about horses."

"Yes. They're almost as wild about them as you are," said Elizabeth with a grin.

"Ha ha, Lizzy!" She planted a kiss on her sister's cheek and walked towards the door. "I'd best go. I don't want to be late!"

Elizabeth shook her head at Lydia's retreating back. Who knew the girl would be so wild about horses? She shuddered when she thought about what would have happened if Robert hadn't given her a horse four years ago. All that energy and passion had to go somewhere. She could only be grateful it was spent on such an innocuous pursuit and not on something embarrassing, like officers, as their mother had done when she was young.

~

After a dinner at the Bingley home with Lady Asheland, Darcy decided his plan was a good one. Lady Asheland was the perfect woman for him. The more he looked at her, the more attracted he felt. He finally admitted to himself that he had never been immune to her,

204

but his knowledge of her marriage had kept him from thinking of her seriously. He had indulged in a little innocent flirtation, but it had all been perfectly harmless. Now that he was allowing his imagination full rein, it dreamt up some lovely scenes, indeed.

They would go to the theatre and have intelligent discussions afterward. They would visit museum exhibits and he wouldn't have to worry about her getting bored and wishing to leave before he had seen fewer than half of the displays. He imagined having breakfast with her: she would read her correspondence while he read the broadsheet. He would share what news she would find interesting with her, and she would laugh over her letters and read him the funny parts. They would smile at each other as they ate and she would always ensure his favorite preserves were on the table.

They would be quite comfortably domestic.

He was sure she would soon be with child. After all, she had given Asheland three children in less than four years of marriage. He pictured her growing round with his child and found that he liked the image very much. He was also quite pleased at the idea of begetting said children. She was a passionate woman. It was clear in the way she defended her children and teased her family. There was fire lurking in her bright eyes, and he knew he would be a very satisfied man when that passion turned to him.

He had been stupid not to think of it before now. A small part of him could admit that he had thought of it, but his decorum had kept him in check. Well, no more!

He did not think she was immune to him. She had flushed when he stood near her on their last meeting. Was that a sign that she was affected by him? He was certainly affected by her. She had been wearing somber clothing, obviously not yet comfortable in the happy colors she had worn before, but she looked remarkably well in lavender, he must say, and her dresses always seemed to be touchable. They were not the frilly, overdone concoctions so many women of his acquaintance wore. How was a man supposed to get close to a woman when she had feathers poking out of her head and stiff lace protruding from every seam?

Lady Asheland was so delightfully approachable, so soft and inviting-looking. He could imagine what it would be like to place his arms around her waist, to feel her soft skin under his hands. Yes, Lady Asheland would make an excellent Mrs. Darcy.

~

A fortnight later, Lydia had ridden nearly every day with Georgiana Darcy and the two had become friends. They had a similar interest in horses and different enough lives that they were each fascinated with the other. Hearing that Georgiana had a dowry of thirty thousand pounds, Lydia wondered how long she would have to wait until her dowry reached the same level, but then decided that marrying at thirty was simply too late.

Mr. Michael Darcy called every other day on Kitty, and they had progressed from blushing and staring at the floor to blushing and staring at each other. The young man's attentions were so marked that Mr. Bingley had taken him aside to ensure his intentions were honorable, and Mr. Darcy had declared that they were as honorable as they could be.

In an effort to promote the match, Elizabeth had invited Michael Darcy to two more family dinners, both of which he attended happily. He was due again that evening for a small musical gathering Elizabeth was hosting. Her former piano instructor had asked her to host a recital of sorts for his two most promising students, a young man on the instrument and a soprano hoping to find her way into an opera company. Elizabeth had agreed immediately and the guest list was small but influential.

The Bingleys, both Mr. Darcys and Miss Darcy, Lord and Lady Sheffield, Lord and Lady Montgomery, two Talbot cousins, and the possibility of Alfred and Sylvia—prized guests due to their high rank and elusive tendencies.

Hosting an elegant party meant wearing an elegant dress, which posed something of a problem for the countess. Elizabeth had only worn bright colors sparingly since the start of the Season—generally when Lady Montgomery was dragging her to some outing or another—and she still felt odd shedding her grays and black trim for pinks and blues. But hosting an event was more important that attending one and she must dress accordingly.

Tonight's dress was a green with blue trim, subdued in nature but still spring-like in style. She had always felt more like herself in light and bright-colored clothes, but she had so long been without them that she felt odd wearing them in company now.

She had always worn what she liked in her private rooms, of course. Nightgowns of pale pink, wrappers of warm red satin. They had been gifts from her husband, or favorites of his, and she felt closest to him in their shared chamber, wearing the clothes he had loved to see her in— and out of.

She had to brace herself for the evening ahead. She was glad it was such a small party. Everyone invited was a friend or at least very familiar to her. This was the best way to ease herself back into her role as hostess.

Thankfully, the evening was a success. The performers were sublime, the guests engaging, and the food delicious. Elizabeth bade her friends goodbye with a cheerfulness she had not felt in some time.

By happenstance, Mr. Darcy was the last guest to leave. Miss Darcy had gone upstairs to spend the night with Lydia, and after saying goodnight to Mr. Michael Darcy, Kitty had skipped happily away to prepare for bed.

So it was that Elizabeth found herself alone in the vestibule with Mr. Darcy as he waited for his carriage to be brought round. She noticed that he smelled slightly of brandy, but only when he stood close to her, and she wondered if that was why she had seen him staring at her the last hour. Unsure what was on his mind, she made general conversation to avoid any potential awkwardness.

When he mentioned the performers that evening, she said, "Yes, I haven't given many of these events. Robert was fond of smaller parties and I have always been so busy with the children that we didn't entertain as much as we might."

He nodded and they fell silent again. She was studying the fringe on her shawl when she felt him step nearer.

"I have been remiss in failing to tell you how enchanting you look tonight," he said, in a soft tone she had never heard from him before.

She flushed.

"Green brings out your eyes," he added.

"Thank you, sir." She took a step back, hoping the carriage would arrive shortly. She was entirely alone with him, having sent the footman to assist clearing the rooms so that everyone might go to bed sooner. How she was regretting that now!

He leaned toward her again, not stepping forward, but simply shifting all of his considerable focus onto her person. His eyes lingered long on her bust and she began to worry over how much he had drunk. She had never seen Mr. Darcy in his cups before, and she had known him some years.

"Is that the carriage I hear?" she asked somewhat desperately.

He turned his head to the door and listened. "I hear nothing."

"Hmm." She turned and paced to the end of the hall, then back, stopping further from Mr. Darcy than she had been.

"Lady Asheland, will you be in Town for the length of the season?"

"It is likely, though my plans are not fixed. Why do you ask?"

"I have come to greatly enjoy your company and I would like to see more of you."

He smiled at her, a seductive smile, and his eyes swept down her frame and back again, lingering on her bosom. She felt her stomach flip in disgust. Was he asking her for a liaison? His look was one of arrogant confidence, as if he had no idea of being refused.

"Mr. Darcy, I do not think that would be wise," she said uneasily, her gaze on the floor.

"Why ever not?" he asked, his tone indignant.

"You know why."

"I assure you, I do not." His back became impossibly rigid as he tried to stand straighter with each statement of offense.

She was becoming exasperated. "I am a widow with three children," she said, believing this explained itself.

"Exactly! A widow!" he exclaimed.

It had always been Mr. Darcy's misfortune that when he most wished to be understood, he gave nearly the opposite impression of the one he intended. He had meant to point out that she was no longer married and now free to entertain gentlemen callers. Elizabeth perceived that he was throwing the earl's death in her face.

She gritted her teeth. "You forget yourself, sir."

"Do I?"

He seemed to have come a little closer, and she could smell the brandy perfectly now. His cheeks were slightly flushed and his eyes a touch glassy, but he still seemed in control of himself. What concerned her was not so much his state of inebriation, but the look in his eyes as he stared at her. Robert had looked at her in a similar manner before they spent the night tumbling in bed.

She stepped back.

He followed.

She would not allow herself to be intimidated and looked him in the eye. "I have given you my answer, Mr. Darcy," she said firmly. She vaguely noted that he hadn't actually asked her a question, but that was a technicality.

"But no explanation!"

She huffed. Really! Did a lady have to explain to a gentleman why she wasn't interested in a liaison? Why would a simple refusal not suffice?

"I owe you no explanation, sir."

He rolled his neck in exasperation. "Of course not. Why should a lady explain herself?" he said sarcastically.

Elizabeth had had enough. "Do you know who I am?" she cried.

"I know exactly who you are, *Lady Asheland*," he said, his face tight with rejection.

He said it with such a strange light in his eyes, and such a tone to his voice that she asked, "What do you mean by that?"

"Your status is based entirely on your marriage. You were not born into it," he replied in a rush. "If Lord Asheland hadn't married you, you would still be living in a backwater in Hertfordshire."

If she hadn't been looking right at him, she would not have believed Mr. Darcy was saying such things to her. Clearly, drink had allowed his true thoughts to exit his mouth.

She flushed with anger. "You are right, I was not born into it." She raised her chin and threw her shoulders back. "I was chosen. Chosen to be the wife and companion of a great man. A man you will never come near equaling. *Chosen* to be the mother of the next Earl of Asheland. *Chosen* to join one of the greatest families in England! Your status is nothing but an accident of birth. What have you done to earn it? Who chose you? No one!"

Eyes blazing, nostrils flaring, hands trembling in rage, she stared at him coldly for a moment, then turned and left the hall without another word.

Darcy stared after her in wide-eyed amazement, suddenly sober. He realized that he'd gone too far, and what was worse, that in the magnificent game he had been playing with her all this time, *she* had not been playing. She had meant every word.

What had he done?

CHAPTER 14

"Good God, Darcy, what possessed you? It does not matter who she *was*. It only matters who she *is*."

"I do not know. I wasn't fully aware of what I was saying until we were arguing. I thought she was flirting with me."

"Apparently, she was not," said Colonel Fitzwilliam dryly.

"We have had so many nice conversations, I was surprised she wouldn't allow me to call on her."

"Conversations or arguments?"

"Stimulating debates."

"Debates?" scoffed the colonel. "Only you would consider debating with a woman a form of courtship."

Darcy dropped his head to his hands and groaned. How was he going to resolve this?

"Now you've made her skittish and ruined it for the rest of us."

"You weren't pursuing her, were you?" Darcy asked, disturbed.

"Not entirely, but if she had shown any interest, I would have. She is a beautiful woman, and lively and clever. A man could do worse."

Darcy stared at his cousin in astonishment. "Did she ever return your interest?"

"Not that I could tell. Either her heart is not easily touched, or she is still pining for her husband," said the colonel. "Either way, I didn't think I'd see much success."

"Her heart can be touched. She can love quite deeply. She was very attached to the earl," Darcy said quietly.

"Aye. And no man will ever live up to him, I wager." He slapped Darcy on the shoulder. "Best move on from that one, my friend."

Darcy thought his cousin may be right, but he feared he was already attached to Lady Asheland. He had become so without reason and entirely against his will; he was in the middle before he knew he had begun. Darcy had long ago acknowledged attraction and general admiration for her. But attachment? That was another thing altogether. Could he un-attach himself? Did he want to?

One thing he was certain of. He did not agree with his cousin about the lady. Perhaps no man would ever live up to Lord Asheland; Darcy himself had looked up to the man. But Elizabeth was a passionate woman and he couldn't believe that she would choose to live the rest of her life alone when she had every opportunity to marry a man of her choosing.

~

Elizabeth took her breakfast in bed and spent the morning in the nursery. She told the butler she was not home to callers that day and didn't come downstairs until she was sure Miss Darcy had been returned home.

She told no one what had happened with Mr. Darcy. His sister was friends with Lydia, his cousin was courting Kitty, and he was her brother Charles' closest friend. What a horrible muddle it was! She couldn't tell them that someone they all trusted and respected had propositioned her in her own home.

No, she would keep this to herself.

Two days after the argument in the vestibule, she returned home from a call to see an arrangement of flowers on the table that had not been there before. There was a note beside them on crisp white paper.

She eyed the card suspiciously and finally picked it up by the edges. There was an elaborate D on the stamp. She broke the seal and read it warily.

Dear Lady Asheland,

Please forgive me for importuning you. I would like the opportunity to apologize in person if you will grant me an audience.

Your servant,
F. Darcy

She wasn't sure what to make of it, but given his connection to the family, she could hardly refuse. She quickly sent a note saying she would receive him in one hour and went upstairs to change.

~

Darcy approached Asheland House with a firm stride and an anxious stomach. He couldn't remember the last time he had been so nervous.

Once the butler had left them alone, he turned to her and said, "Lady Asheland, I must apologize for my behavior two evenings ago. I was churlish and I beg your forgiveness."

He looked at her so solemnly she believed he was telling the truth. But how to reconcile that with the inappropriate man in her vestibule?

"Mr. Darcy, I accept your apology. But I must ask you to refrain from speaking on such subjects to me again."

He seemed disappointed, but nodded and agreed.

After another moment of awkward silence, he asked, "I know I have no right, but would you be so kind as to tell me what your objections were? I'm afraid I am at a loss."

She looked at him in surprise. "Mr. Darcy! Surely you don't expect me to speak of such a thing, in my drawing room in broad daylight, with my children upstairs?"

He looked confused. "My lady?"

She huffed. "I refused your advances. That is all. I have nothing else to say on the matter." She folded her hands primly on her lap and looked toward the window.

Darcy was more confused than ever. He had drunk too much, that he knew, but surely he hadn't done something completely ungentlemanly? He would never forget himself in such a way. And wouldn't he remember it if he had behaved so very badly?

"My lady, I must beg your indulgence. I thought we merely quarreled. Was there anything… more, that I should apologize for?"

She looked bemused for a moment, then seemed to grasp his meaning. "No, Mr. Darcy. Your insults were all of the verbal variety."

He winced.

There was more silence, and now Elizabeth felt that she must be satisfied on another point as well. "I would like to know, sir, why you thought such a request would be welcome?" she asked carefully.

She was equal parts confused and angry, and she hoped there hadn't been something in her manner that had encouraged him. She had been missing Robert dreadfully of late, in the way a wife misses her husband, but she never thought it was obvious to anyone else. Could it be that it was? How humiliating!

Darcy flushed. "I had thought we were friends, and that as such, getting to know one another better would not be unwelcome. Had I known the idea so repulsed you, I would have kept my own counsel."

"Friends! Mr. Darcy, many people are friends without sharing further intimacies!"

"Intimacies?" he repeated quietly, confused by both her choice of words and her vehemence. Finally, he seemed to understand what she was referring to and flushed crimson. "Oh, good God! You thought I was suggesting—that you would... Oh!" he cried.

Elizabeth went completely pale. "You were not?" she asked slowly.

"Madam, I assure you, I would never make such an offer to a respectable lady such as yourself. Or to any lady!" he added hurriedly. He could feel his ears burning and his collar was uncomfortably tight.

"Oh!" Elizabeth stared: at him, at the empty fireplace, at her hands, and back at Mr. Darcy. "So, you were not?" she trailed off.

"No!" he said vehemently. "I was not," he added more calmly. "Why did you think I was?" he asked curiously.

"You said we should *see more* of each other!" she exclaimed, feeling defensive and thrown off kilter. "And you were looking down my dress when you said it!"

She seemed to realize what she had said a moment too late and flushed, dropping her eyes back to the carpet.

"I see," he said gravely. He remembered that part of it. Her gown fit uncommonly well and he had enjoyed watching her all evening. It was only reasonable that she had noticed. "I must apologize, Lady Asheland. While my eyes were drawn to your... while I was looking where I shouldn't, I certainly did not mean to imply anything untoward. My only excuse must be the brandy."

"I see. Please forgive my misapprehension."

She felt a nervous laugh trying to work its way out and fought it valiantly. She had never thought she would be sitting in a drawing room with Mr. Darcy, discussing how he had inappropriately stared at her bosom while insulting her in her entrance hall. A tiny giggle escaped her.

"Forgive me, Mr. Darcy." Another laugh fled from her lips. "I am so sorry. But it is terribly funny!" she said in her own defense.

He began to chortle slowly, his shoulders shaking though he tried to keep a straight face. It eventually evolved into a chuckle, and she found herself wondering how he could manage it without showing his teeth or making more than a polite amount of noise.

She took a deep breath and asked, "If you weren't requesting something illicit, what were you requesting?"

Suddenly, he stopped smiling and straightened his shoulders. "Now that I see the misunderstanding, it is no wonder you denied me so violently. In truth, I was simply asking to call on you."

"To call on me?"

"Yes."

"Oh."

He looked a bit sheepish, and she felt dreadful for having misjudged him.

"Mr. Darcy, I must be honest with you."

He nodded and edged forward in his chair.

"I have no intentions of remarrying." He seemed surprised by this but she continued on. "I had a wonderful marriage with Robert and I do not think it likely to happen again, and it would break my heart to find myself in an unhappy union."

"I see," he said to the floor.

"However," his head shot back up, "I am always in need of a friend, and I am willing to be yours if you would like it." She gave him a soft smile and he eventually returned it.

"I would be glad to be your friend, Lady Asheland," he said sincerely.

"Good. I'm glad." She paused and looked at him mischievously. "And you should be, too! For I am a very loyal friend."

"As am I," he said seriously.

"I expected no less," she replied, all trace of archness gone.

~

Elizabeth was surprised at herself for offering friendship to Mr. Darcy, and equally surprised he had accepted it. She had always thought he disliked her, or tolerated her at best. That he felt an attraction to her was quite shocking and she couldn't remember the last time she had been so surprised.

The biggest shock of all, however, was when she arrived at her sister Jane's home to fetch young Robert. He had been having riding lessons with his Uncle Charles for a few weeks now and Elizabeth had gone to see his latest accomplishments. When she arrived at the small yard, she saw Mr. Darcy walking next to a dappled grey, her son in the saddle.

"That is very good, Robert John. Hold the reins a little tighter. You mustn't let her get away from you."

She stood by the gate, mouth agape, for several minutes before the mare turned and her son saw her, calling out a greeting and asking if she saw what he was doing.

"Yes, dear, I see. You are handling her quite well." She gave him a proud smile, then looked to Mr. Darcy with a quizzical expression.

"I have been helping Bingley with the lessons. I ... thought you knew," he said uneasily.

She paused for a moment, then said, "No, I did not. But that is not unusual. My brother occasionally forgets things. It is of no matter." *What are Jane and Charles up*

218

to now? She smiled tightly and asked how much longer they would be, then told Robbie she would see him on the terrace for tea after he was finished.

Even though she had begged everyone else not to call him that, Elizabeth had slipped into calling her son Robbie. In a way, it was to separate him from her husband. Some had called him Lisle, one of her husband's lesser titles, when he was a baby (Mrs. Bennet always loved to introduce her grandson as Viscount Lisle), but neither she nor Robert had liked it or thought it suited him. She supposed he should be called Asheland now, but she couldn't stand the idea of burdening a tiny boy with such a grandiose title. He would understand his role in the world soon enough. He would go to school where everyone would call him Asheland, and he might even ask his family to do the same. But for now, he was her little boy and she would treat him as such. There was plenty of time to be serious later.

She had made a habit of having tea with her children at least once a week. She didn't hold to the aristocratic idea of allowing hired servants to raise the children. She had always been close to her father and thought she was better for it. She hoped to do the same and more for her own children.

Jane joined her for a time, but then was needed inside when young Charles skinned his knee and wanted his mama. Elizabeth shooed her away and waited patiently for her son. Finally, Mr. Darcy and Robert John climbed the stone steps to join her. Darcy stood with one arm behind his back and young Robert tried to emulate him, his small shoulders stiff and his chin lifted ever so slightly. Elizabeth nearly laughed at seeing her tiny boy imitate a man more than twice his size, and she felt a twinge of sadness that her Robert wasn't the man he was copying.

She smiled brightly to cover her grief and held out her arms for her son. "Come here, darling boy. I want to hear all about your ride."

Young Robert smiled widely and immediately climbed onto the cushion next to her and hugged her tightly before launching into a detailed description of the mare, how to properly tighten the girth, how to hold the reins, how to rub the horse down when the ride was over, and how this particular horse preferred carrots to apples.

"And what is the mare's name?" she asked indulgently.

"Aphrodite! Uncle Charles says it is because she is so beautiful! She is a very pretty horse," he added seriously.

"That she is," replied Elizabeth, in an equally serious tone.

"And her nose is very soft," he whispered.

Elizabeth smiled at him, feeling herself melt a little at each confidence he whispered in her ear. *This* is why she did not want to remarry. Nothing could be better than this sweet joy, and she would not let any man come into her life and dictate how she should raise her and Robert's children.

She poured tea for Mr. Darcy and her son, and Robert solemnly told her he would like his with one lump of sugar. She smiled as she stirred it gently for him, and he very carefully picked up the china and took a sip, trying not to spill any on his riding clothes. Mr. Darcy said nothing and she set a cup of black tea in front of him, though he didn't touch it.

Mr. Darcy watched the scene with a thoughtful expression. His mother had been a good woman, and he could remember having tea with her in her private sitting room, or on a terrace such as they were now, but he did not remember any of the warmth he saw between Elizabeth and young Robert. Lady Anne would kiss his cheek lightly, and receive the same from him, but she had not held him tightly as Elizabeth held her son. Or at least he did not remember it if she had. Watching Robert John lean his head on his mother's bosom, and close his eyes in contentment as she kissed his hair, made him think he had missed out on something rather important, and he suddenly felt futilely jealous of a four-year-old boy. *Stupid man.*

He once again thought he should find an affectionate woman to marry and bear his children. They would surely benefit from it, unknown to him as they were. Of course, the woman before him was an excellent mother and unattached, if only she would think of herself as such. She was determined not to marry, and she had no need for it. If she did not wish it, there was no one who could make her.

Did he have within him what it would take to change her mind? Did he even care to attempt it? Before he had thought it through he knew that he did. Getting Lady Asheland to love him and agree to be his wife would be the hardest thing he had ever done. Such a woman was a prize worth winning and he knew, quite suddenly, that if he could accomplish this feat, it would be the greatest achievement of his life.

Somehow, he knew she would be the making of him.

CHAPTER 15

Darcy went about his campaign to woo the Countess of Asheland as he did everything else: with wholehearted fervency. He called on her frequently. He invited her for a drive in the park, which she declined, and for a picnic with their sisters and her children, which she accepted—though it was so crowded he was barely able to speak to her. He joined the Bingleys for dinner twice when Elizabeth was expected and Jane seated them together. Surprisingly, the Bingleys were his biggest supporters. Without ever talking about it, Charles and Jane seemed to know his wishes and set about helping him in any way they could.

Halfway through the Season, the Bingleys organized an excursion to the gallery. A new exhibition was on display and they were to hold a dinner afterward. Colonel Fitzwilliam, Georgiana, Lydia, Kitty, Mr. Michael Darcy, Mr. Fitzwilliam Darcy, and Lady Asheland were all invited. The group seemed to separate naturally. Colonel Fitzwilliam escorted Georgiana and Lydia, Mr. Michael Darcy offered Kitty his arm, Bingley escorted Jane, and Elizabeth was left with Mr. Darcy.

He offered his arm with a smile and she took it lightly, recognizing a plot when she saw one and not pleased with her sisters. Truthfully, she would have rather walked with Colonel Fitzwilliam. He was more entertaining and seemed to have given up trying to court her interest. But she had agreed to be Mr. Darcy's friend, and she was beginning to think he wasn't wholly bad, despite his tendency to always be more serious than a situation required.

"What do you think of the exhibition?" he asked after they had walked in silence for some time.

"It is lovely, though I confess it all begins to look the same after a while."

"Yes, the artist appears fixed upon one theme," he agreed.

She didn't answer and he followed her gaze to her sister Kitty and his cousin. Their heads were bent close together in front of a large landscape. Her blush was visible even from that distance.

"Do you approve?" he asked quietly.

She looked at him in surprise. "Approve, sir?"

"My cousin and your sister." He nodded in the couple's direction. "They seem to have made a match."

"Yes, they do," she replied softly. "And yes, I do approve, not that it's necessary."

"Is it not?" he asked, brows raised in question.

She furrowed her forehead in thought, a gesture he thought utterly adorable on her pretty face, and replied, "It would be uncomfortable if I did not like him, but I am not her father. She may marry where she wishes."

Darcy raised his brow, wondering if he should challenge her on so false a statement. "Forgive me, my lady, but you are a countess. I know she is not your daughter, but you are the highest ranked person in your family. Surely your opinion matters a very great deal."

She tilted her head and considered him for a moment before replying. "I suppose you are right. But I would never stand in the way of my sister's happiness. She knows that—my entire family does. As long as he is a good and honest man and can support her, I will approve."

"That is generous of you."

She shrugged. "It is easy in this case as young Mr. Darcy is very likeable."

He nodded, thoughtful. "If he is young Mr. Darcy, what does that make me?"

She looked up at him and flushed, then quickly turned her eyes to the floor.

"I believe that is the first time I have bested you in conversation, Lady Asheland," he said, with no small amount of amusement.

She sighed silently and tried to will away her blush with little success. "Enjoy your victory while it lasts, Mr. Darcy. You may not gain another," she said archly.

He laughed. She looked at him in astonishment, wondering if she had ever heard it before. She had seen him smile, and look amused, and smirk, but never truly laugh—shoulders shaking, voice booming, teeth visible laughter. It was discomposing.

And very attractive.

~

After the trip to the gallery, Elizabeth became more guarded. She was careful not to be alone with Mr. Darcy and constantly surrounded herself with sisters and friends to avoid private discourse. She found him utterly vexing and did not wish her composure disturbed further.

After a week of avoiding him, he finally caught her at her sister's house. Jane had gone to see to another guest who had newly arrived, and he cornered her by the window.

"Are you in good health, Lady Asheland?"

"Yes. And yourself, Mr. Darcy?"

"Very well, thank you." He had thought to tease her about calling him old Mr. Darcy, but there was a skittishness in her manner that stopped him. He should tread carefully here, lest the lady bolt.

"Are your sisters here tonight?" he asked.

"Kitty has gone to a musical evening with Lady Montgomery, but Lydia is here. She is talking with your cousin." She gestured to Colonel Fitzwilliam on the other side of the room. He was apparently engaged in a lively conversation with her youngest sister. "Don't worry, Mr. Darcy, Lydia has no desire to be soon married and I'm sure the Colonel is only making polite conversation."

"I wasn't worried," he said, bringing his eyes back to hers. "But perhaps I should be." His mouth quirked as if he were amused. "Every man I have in mind for Georgiana ends up falling in love with one of your sisters."

She looked at him in surprise. Was he making a joke? A funny one?

"Surely Colonel Fitzwilliam is too old for Miss Darcy," she said. It was not their ages she referred to. Colonel Fitzwilliam had the air of a man of the world; Georgiana had a naïve innocence about her.

"Of course. I would never consider it. Even if he weren't too old for her, he shares her guardianship. They have a familial relationship."

"Ah," she tilted her head. "I see. I had no idea you had intended Mr. Bingley for Georgiana."

"Not intended. It was merely an idea. I knew she needed someone kind and gentle, and I trust Bingley." He shrugged.

"He is a good husband," she agreed. *Just as Robert said he would become.* "I must assume the other man you intended for Georgiana is your cousin, Mr. Michael Darcy?"

He nodded. "Again, I had made no arrangements. I had simply thought they may suit. He is kind and Georgiana is not forceful. She would not be able to contend with an overbearing man."

Elizabeth nodded, agreeing with his assessment.

"I am sorry to disrupt your plans, Mr. Darcy. I suppose we Bennet women are simply irresistible," she teased.

He looked at her, her eyes sparkling up at him, her impish mouth tilted up at one corner, her delectable brow raised in challenge and amusement.

"You really don't know, do you?" he asked quietly, his voice thick.

"Know what?" she asked, her expression betraying her confusion.

"How bewitching you are," he stated simply.

She flushed immediately and continued to stare at him, unable to remove her eyes from his. Her mouth opened to speak, but no words emerged and she closed it again with a snap.

After another minute of silent staring, sure that all his desires were on display in his expression, he said, "Have a care, Lady Asheland. It is not fair to make half of London fall in love with you if you never intend to reciprocate."

He bowed and left her with her tumultuous thoughts.

~

The next time Elizabeth saw Mr. Darcy, it was at a large dinner hosted by some old friends of her husband. She went with Lord and Lady Montgomery. Lady Montgomery, Alice as Elizabeth called her, was intent on matching her with every eligible man over twenty-five and under fifty in the place.

Mr. Darcy was present, of course. Somehow, he had escaped Lady Montgomery's machinations and was standing with a group of men across the room. Elizabeth noticed him immediately, though it wasn't hard. He was taller than nearly everyone present and bore the most serious expression in the room. He looked over and met her gaze, a slight smile brightening his countenance as he nodded to her in recognition. She nodded back and returned to her friend.

This continued all evening. He glanced her way when she was escorted into dinner by another man. He sent her small smiles while she sat next to the Viscount Carlton, as if they were sharing a private joke. When the ladies rose to withdraw, he looked at her steadily, then let his eyes rake down her figure and back up, lingering on the necklace that fell to the edge of her satin gown, until finally gifting her with a smile of approval. She flushed and left the table as quickly as possible.

The effrontery of the man. How dare he look at her like that! As if she had dressed for him! He had no right to stare at her so, to smile at her as if they were intimate friends, to look at her as if he knew what she looked like in her shifts. No living man possessed that right.

She would show him his error. The remainder of the night she talked with and smiled at other men, and ignored Darcy completely. He did not exist for her. She knew it would particularly gall him if she flirted with his cousin, so she made Colonel Fitzwilliam her next conquest. She laughed and smiled and teased, and was rewarded with a look of surprise and interest on the colonel's part. Good. She had achieved her objective.

Mr. Darcy knew she was not his to toy with nor look at with knowing smiles. She had much better things to occupy herself with than him. He was the furthest thing from her mind.

~

Darcy had to stop himself from smiling like a fool. Lady Asheland was not immune to him. He had made no secret of his admiration for her and she had not been pleased. This did not surprise him; she was often displeased with him. It was part of her charm. But what

227

did surprise him was her reaction to his appreciation. She had flirted—yes, flirted!—with more than one gentleman after dinner. She had smiled, and teased, and done something with her eyes that made the man she was looking at turn into a blithering idiot. She could bring a man to his knees with those eyes.

And yet, he, Fitzwilliam Darcy, had managed to unsettle her. To make her angry enough to want to seek revenge on him. That she recognized his interest sufficiently to know that flirting with other men would bother him was a good sign in itself. That she cared enough about their friendship—or him—to allow it to bother her was wonderful news.

He would work his way into her affections. If he had to call on her every day for a year and make a thousand blunders, he would do it. He was determined.

~

Elizabeth was going mad. Everywhere she turned, there was Mr. Darcy. Not the man himself, thought he was present enough, but tales of him, mentions in conversation, and suggestions for invitations. She was planning a dinner—invite Mr. Darcy! They would host a picnic at the park—where is Mr. Darcy? Tea at her sister's—who should drop in unexpectedly but Mr. Darcy?

He continued to help Charles with Robert John's riding lessons, and her son was filled with tales about Uncle Charles and Mr. Darcy. How tall they were, what big horses they rode, and how fast they could gallop.

Mr. Darcy also rode with Georgiana and Lydia occasionally, and her youngest sister was filled with nothing but praise for her friend's older brother. He was a very good rider, with a magnificent gelding, and his seat was one of the best she had seen. Elizabeth had stifled a laugh at that comment and looked to her sister to see Jane nearly choking on her tea.

Mr. Darcy had invaded nearly every part of her life! He rode with Lydia, he was instructing her son, he was constantly visiting the Bingleys, and he called with his cousin when he visited Kitty. Would she never be free of the man?

Finally, a week after the Dinner Dilemma, as Elizabeth had come to think of it, she attended a ball hosted by Lady Montgomery. Unsurprisingly, Mr. Darcy was there. She hadn't been in the ballroom above five minutes before he approached her.

"You look very well, Lady Asheland."

"Thank you, Mr. Darcy. Are you well?"

"Quite well."

"And your sister? Is she here this evening?" she asked politely.

"No, Georgiana was tired and remained at home. Are your sisters here?"

"Kitty is here, but Lydia also remained at home."

"I hope she is well."

"Yes, she is merely tired. The Season can be exhausting."

He knew she was deliberately keeping the conversation dull so that he would leave her alone. Or she was trying to frustrate him. Perhaps she was punishing him for his impertinence at their last meeting. Regardless, it would take more than a little dull conversation to deter him.

"May I request a dance, Lady Asheland?" he asked.

She looked startled. "You may."

"Is the first set free?"

She pursed her lips. Her first set was free. She was engaged for the second with her brother Charles, and Mr. Michael Darcy had requested the one after that, but her first was still available.

"Yes, it is."

"Shall we? The music is about to begin." He held out his hand and she took it reluctantly, angry at him for entrapping her.

They danced the first ten minutes in silence, Elizabeth wondering why he aggravated her so, Mr. Darcy wondering how long she would keep it up. It was clear that she was not built for anger. Lord Asheland had been circumspect when it came to speaking of his wife, but he had given Bingley, and by extension Darcy, marital advice upon occasion. The earl had spoken of allowing for different temperaments, and treating one's wife with respect and care. It had set Darcy to thinking.

Elizabeth was of a sanguine temperament. Even with all she had lost, she was still an optimistic woman. She had not allowed her husband's death to rob her life of joy. She was a wonderful mother and a good sister. He imagined she extended the same care to her parents. A woman like that could not stay angry for long. She wasn't made for unhappiness.

Elizabeth was becoming tired. Not from the dance, it wasn't vigorous enough to tire her, but of the cold silence between her and Mr. Darcy. Were they not supposed to be friends? Why was she angry with him, anyhow? Oh, yes, because he had gazed at her inappropriately.

Possessively, Elizabeth. He looked at you as if you were his to do with as he pleased.

This angered her more than the inappropriateness. She had been the recipient of more than one flirtatious look from a man. She was not surprised by a man's appreciation for the female form. What she was surprised by was *Mr. Darcy's* appreciation. He was so staid in every other way. So solemn. So private. And yet he looked at her as if she were a treasure chest he had found the key to.

She could find it in herself to be flattered by his interest, even gratified. He was an attractive man, and an elusive one. But she could not condone his assumption that he had a right to her, as if she were somehow his for the taking.

She released a long breath and Darcy looked at her with concern.

"Are you well, my lady?"

"Yes, I am. Thank you," she replied, still agitated.

They were waiting at the top of the line and had a rare moment of relative privacy.

"Are you angry with me?" he asked quietly.

She looked at him in surprise. She had not expected candor. She looked to the floor and sighed. "Not truly, Mr. Darcy. But I will confess that you confuse me."

"I do?" His eyebrows rose.

"Yes," she said impatiently. "Your behavior is not consistent."

"Isn't it?"

She threw him an irritated look as they began to move down the dance and he smirked. Predictably.

"No, it is not! You say you are my friend, and happy to be, and then you behave in decidedly *un*friendly ways."

"While that is a grave misdeed, I do not think it qualifies as inconsistent."

She stopped herself from retorting in the middle of a crowded ballroom, but her eyes spoke all the words she could not say. He somehow managed to look both boyishly sheepish and confident all at once.

Thankfully, the music ended and Elizabeth saw she was near her friend, Lady Sheffield. She curtsied to her partner and joined her friend. She danced the sets she had promised, then left the ball without saying goodbye to anyone but the hostess.

~

Elizabeth and Kitty were talking in the yellow parlor when the butler announced both Mr. Darcys. Would they receive them here or in the drawing room? Elizabeth said they would see them here, suspecting as she did that Michael Darcy would soon offer for her sister and would then be family. They could meet in the less formal room.

Kitty quickly led Mr. Michael Darcy to a sofa near the window and Elizabeth was left to entertain Mr. Darcy on her own. She was reminded of a similar situation when her sister Jane was being courted by Mr. Bingley. She had been twenty then, with only two children, and most importantly, married. Now she was a widow with three children, Jane was expecting her third child and Mary her second. Where had the time gone?

She rang for tea and invited Mr. Darcy to sit.

"Does your cousin spend the summer with you?" she asked.

He smiled at her, a little too happily she thought, and answered, "He has in the past, but he has no plans to this summer, though he knows he is always welcome at Pemberley. All Darcys are."

"That is generous of you."

"Not particularly. He is family. It is the family seat."

She nodded and the newly arrived tea tray saved her from a longer response.

"Milk or sugar?" she asked.

"Milk, please. No sugar."

She nodded and set about making his cup, adding the milk first, then pouring in the freshly steeped tea. Kitty had done most of the serving this season, but Elizabeth thought she remembered he liked his tea extra milky. She handed it to him and before he had completed his first sip, she had prepared him a plate of little cakes, artfully arranged.

232

He was pleased she had remembered his preference and noted that the cakes with currants were left on the tray. He had never liked them.

"You look very pleased, Mr. Darcy. Shall I assume your tea is well prepared?"

He looked at her arch smile, her teasing brow, the way her eyes sparkled as she watched him, waiting for a response. God, how he loved her!

"You remembered how I take my tea," he said softly.

"Yes," she replied, bemused. "You like it with sugar when you are not having cakes and with milk when you are."

He continued to stare at her and she looked back, puzzled.

"Most people who haven't served me tea in over two years would not remember that."

She sat up a little straighter. "I am not most people, Mr. Darcy."

"No, my lady, you certainly are not."

~

That night, Elizabeth paced her bedchamber. To the window, turn, eight steps to the fireplace, turn. With every swish of her dressing gown about her ankles, her anxiety mounted. What was Mr. Darcy about? She had been very clear with him—she would not remarry. And yet he continued to call and behave in a decidedly suitor-like manner.

The way he had looked at her this afternoon—it sent shivers down her spine to think of it. She knew that look. When she first became engaged to Robert, she had noticed it. The way he smiled when she entered a room, how she could calm him with nothing but a touch from her hand, how a flirtatious glance could bring him to her side in an instant.

He was in her power.

She had known that Robert's happiness rested with her. He was so obviously content in her presence. She could bring him out of a dark mood with a kiss to his cheek, or settle his spirits after a row with his peers with an embrace.

That was what she recognized in Mr. Darcy's expression today—his happiness at merely being with her. As if his day was brighter for having seen her.

And it terrified her.

He should not feel this way! She had told him, in no uncertain terms, that she was not looking for a husband, or a lover, or a man in her life of any kind. She had offered him friendship and he had accepted. He was not supposed to fall in love with her! It would ruin everything.

Though, if she were being honest with herself, she could admit that she felt a tendril of excitement at knowing she had affected such a man. Any woman would feel thus, she told herself. And it had been a very long time since she had been with a man—since she had felt the solidity of broad shoulders beneath her hands, since her face had been held tenderly and kissed with hunger, since she had felt strong hands running over her body, holding her close on a cold night, embracing her with passion.

She was lonely. She could admit that to herself, alone in her room in a dressing gown and nightshift. She missed the companionship she had had with Robert. She missed the intimacy, the tenderness that had been between them. Sometimes she thought her heart might break in two with the weight of missing him.

And yet, for an hour this afternoon, she had not missed him. She had felt seen, as a man sees a woman, and desired, as a man desires a woman. She had blushed under Mr. Darcy's gaze and not out of embarrassment. She had felt heat rushing through her when he touched her, and her

Elizabeth Adams

heart, her wounded, pathetic heart, had stuttered and
stumbled when he kissed her hand upon leaving.
What was she to do with that?

CHAPTER 16

Grief came in unexpected waves. Elizabeth had been doing remarkably well for some time. Months had gone by without her dissolving into a heap of tears and damp handkerchiefs. She had been sleeping through the night with no disruptive nightmares for a year now. She didn't know why she suddenly woke in the night in a cold sweat, reaching for her husband only to realize he wasn't there. It was like the first day after his death all over again, and she spent the next day confined to her rooms, unable to control her weeping and wondering if she would ever be peaceful again.

She had her children, and she felt joy in taking care of them and watching them grow, but she was not happy. She could admit this, despite what her sister and her cousin Sylvia said. She knew she was not happy. But unlike her family, she knew something else: it was unlikely she would ever be happy again. So, given the circumstances, she thought the level of contentment she had achieved was quite impressive.

But some days, even mere contentment was impossible to grasp and she found herself staring into the distance, seeing nothing.

The sleepless nights and difficult days continued for a week and she eventually had to be at home to callers. She couldn't hide away indefinitely without causing talk. Lady Montgomery visited her with little effect on her mood. Charles offered to take her riding and she refused. Jane offered quiet comfort that soothed, but even that was short lived.

Relief came from a surprising quarter. One Wednesday afternoon, a few days after she had stopped weeping ceaselessly but before she felt entirely master of herself, Mr. Darcy called. Not young, cheerful Michael Darcy, but serious, solemn Fitzwilliam Darcy. It was almost past the hour for morning calls and she instructed the butler to admit no one else that day. Darcy sat with her in the blue parlor, her favorite room when she was feeling low, and quietly informed her of the rides her sister had been taking with his, and of the gentlemen that had danced with Georgiana and Lydia at the ball he had escorted them to a few days before.

Quite to her surprise, he chattered on about inconsequential subjects, carrying the conversation and relieving her of the burden of entertaining him. Jane had reminded her a few days before of Mr. Darcy's role in the worst day of her life. She had forgotten his presence on the day of Robert's death, other than a vague recollection of him talking to the doctor. She had been so focused on Robert she had noticed little else. Jane told her of how he wrote letters to the family, and directed the servants, and made sure Charles was brought back with herself so they could be of aid to Elizabeth. Jane also reminded her of her collapse at Robert's bedside and how Mr. Darcy had picked her up, as if she weighed nothing at all, and carried her to her room when she was too stricken to walk.

She had been embarrassed to hear it when Jane mentioned it a few days ago, but now, sitting with him in her favorite parlor on a day when she struggled with even basic social graces, she was grateful for it. Grateful that he had been with her in her darkest hour, and therefore wouldn't have to be told how much she had struggled with letting her husband go. He would understand her grief, and know her sorrow in a way no one else could. She did not have to present a brave face for him, and for that she was immensely thankful.

"Mr. Darcy," she said.

"Yes?"

"Thank you," she said sincerely.

"Whatever for, my lady?"

"For being a good friend," she replied with a soft smile.

"You are very welcome, my lady."

~

The following day, Elizabeth was surprised to find a bouquet of flowers awaiting her when she came down for breakfast. Curiously, she read the accompanying card.

My Dear Lady Asheland,

I hope this morning finds you in good spirits. Should you have any need of companionship, I am at your service. I hope you know I will do anything in my power for your comfort.

Your friend,
Fitzwilliam Darcy

She stared at the note for several minutes before sliding it into her pocket. It was very kind of him to send it, and the flowers. She was relieved he had not chosen to plead his suit when she was vulnerable. Had he pressed her yesterday, she could not honestly say what she would have done. She was so very low she might have made a choice she would regret later. It was gentlemanly of him to refrain.

Dear Mr. Darcy,

*Your kindness is much appreciated, and I thank you
for it. Today I am engaged with Lady Montgomery, but I
will take Robert John and Violet to the park tomorrow
morning, if the weather holds. You are welcome to join us
if you like. I would enjoy your company.*

E. Asheland

~

The next morning, Mr. Darcy was at Elizabeth's door
before breakfast was finished. He could admit to himself
that he was perhaps over-eager, but he could not deny that
he was immensely pleased to have been asked to join
Elizabeth for a walk. The children would be there, of
course, but he was quite fond of Robert John, and he was
sure that Lady Violet would be as delightful as her mother.

The butler showed him into the breakfast room where
Lady Asheland was eating and reading a letter.

"Mr. Darcy! Good morning. Forgive me, sir, I must
have lost sense of the time."

"Not at all, my lady. I am early. Please, do not rush on
my account."

She smiled and invited him to sit. "I must thank you
for the flowers. It was very kind of you."

"You are very welcome." He almost asked if she were
feeling better, but he could see that she was. He shouldn't
mention it. It was probably an awkward topic on the best
of days, though he supposed they would have to talk about
it eventually.

A footman stepped in to say the children were ready
and waiting in the hall with their nurse. Soon, they were
walking down the street, Darcy with Elizabeth on his arm,
the nurse with Robert John and Violet by the hand.

"Does Master Bennet not enjoy the park?" he asked.

"Oh, he enjoys it too much! He runs positively wild and his poor nurse exhausts herself chasing him," she said with a smile. "We always bring a second nurse on outings, but she is away visiting her mother. Molly will bring Bennet to the park this afternoon."

He nodded and watched Robert John and Violet running toward some geese waddling near the lake. Their nurse stayed close behind. It was a perfect day. The sun was shining, the children were happy, and he had a beautiful woman on his arm. There was every reason to be content.

"Mr. Darcy, might I ask you something?" Elizabeth's voice sounded anxious to his ears.

"Of course, my lady."

"How old were you when you got your first pony?"

Of all the things he had expected her to say, that had not been it.

He thought for a moment. "I suppose I was five or six. She was a small pony, very docile. My father gave me a mare when I was bigger. Why do you ask?"

"I have been thinking. Robert John will be five years old soon. His birthday is in June. Charles suggested getting him his own pony. Do you think it is too soon?" She worried her lip and twisted her hands together.

"Ah, I see. No, I do not think it too soon, though you should choose the pony very carefully. Temperament is very important, as is the animal's size."

"Yes, of course," she said quietly.

A few minutes passed as they watched the children play.

"It must be difficult," he said quietly.

"What must be?" she replied, looking up at him.

"Raising such small children. It is good to see them grow and learn, but it is sad to see them leaving other aspects of childhood behind."

"You sound experienced, Mr. Darcy."

"Georgiana. She is twelve years my junior and looks on me more as a father than a brother. Perhaps one day, when she is older and married, we will behave more like siblings, but today..."

"It is difficult to watch her grow up," she said softly.

"Yes."

She smiled and looped her arm through his, pressing her hand into his coat for a moment.

"It is not easy to raise a child, you are right. One is so proud of how they grow and change, and yet sad that they are changing at all. Bennet is so big now. He follows his brother around like a puppy and copies everything he does. He is so eager to be older." She sighed. "It feels like yesterday he was a tiny babe, wanting nothing more than to be held by his mama." She shook her head. "It is strange. I never thought Bennet would be my youngest child. When he was born, I was sure he was third in a long line of Talbot children."

"Yes, it is strange," said Darcy quietly.

She gave him a sad smile and they continued their walk along the lake path.

~

Surprisingly, Elizabeth found that having a male friend such as Mr. Darcy proved advantageous in certain circumstances, especially when she wanted to be left alone by wife-hunting men and matchmaking women. Her cousin John was equally protective, but he was a fun-loving chap and was often off on his own adventures. Darcy always seemed to be nearby, available to converse with when she didn't wish to dance, fetching her a glass of lemonade when she was thirsty, allowing her to be silent when she became overwhelmed. And his glare could send the most stalwart gentleman running in the other direction. It was rather amusing, really.

Quite to her surprise, she found his company more enjoyable the more time she spent with him.

Her walk with Mr. Darcy left Elizabeth more confused than ever. He was being so *pleasant.* So kind, and understanding, and patient with her. What had come over him? He had been haughty and disdainful in the past, always quick to argue with her. Then he had pursued her as if she were a prize to be won—amusing at times, and certainly flattering, but disconcerting nonetheless. But now, he was gentle, and unobtrusive, and discreet. She found that she quite enjoyed his company.

Beyond all of that was her uncomfortable and partially acknowledged attraction to him. He was so very different from her husband. Robert had been playful and loving. He brought out more kindness in her than she had known she possessed. He taught her how to manage their household and deal fairly with servants, how to handle the *ton* without allowing them to change who she was in essentials. More than anything else, she became confident. Under his loving care, she matured from a naive girl to an elegant woman.

She couldn't imagine what she would have been like without his influence—what her family would be like! Her mother would have put them all out at fifteen as she had planned, and in all likelihood, they would have been five single ladies out, for years on end, with no suitors among them. Mary would be pedantic, Jane withdrawn, and Lydia positively wild. Kitty would likely have chosen one of her sisters to emulate and proceeded to follow her everywhere—she had never had many ideas of her own. She could only hope Kitty would have chosen herself or Jane to copy, but it could just as likely have been Mary or Lydia, and then where would they have been?

She knew with certainty that her family's significance and prosperity was due to her husband. She also knew that she would not be the woman she was today without Robert's leadership. His steadfast partnership, his unwavering respect, his perfect decency had been the greatest influence on her young life and she was incredibly grateful to have been the recipient of his love.

Now she simply had to learn to live without him. She had accustomed herself to sleeping alone, making decisions for the children by herself, and managing the household with no one's preferences in mind but her own. The only thing she had yet to adapt to was the lack of a husband—the companionship and closeness of a man she cared for and who cared for her in return.

For a wild moment, she wondered if she should take a lover. Widows did it all the time, and the longer she remained unmarried, the more she understood why. But no, that would never do for her. She would surely become with child and then what would she do? Go away to a hidden cottage until her lying in, endure an agonizing birth with no loved ones about her, and hope she survived it so her children would not be entirely parentless? No, it was too great a risk. She could not do it.

And yet, she found herself noticing things she had not paid attention to in some time. On her walk with Mr. Darcy, she noticed he smelled of leather and soap and something that reminded her of a forest. She recognized that his shoulders were broad and his person lean, and his hands strong with long fingers, like a pianist's, but not as delicate. He was a man, and she was keenly aware of him as such.

She liked having someone *there*—to escort her to the park and to talk to about her children. It had been a relief to discuss Robert John's riding with him. She had talked to Charles, of course; he was a kind brother and they had a close relationship, but it was not the same. Her cousin

John Downing was also a pleasant companion, but he was rarely available, and unfortunately, the speculation of a marriage between them made it nearly impossible for them to spend as much time together as they would like. She quickly thought that one of the benefits of remarrying could be a closer relationship with John, but just as quickly dismissed the idea. One did not marry a man just to spend more time with one's cousin.

~

Feeling as conflicted and lost as she was, it was no surprise Elizabeth found herself in Lady Montgomery's sitting room having a quiet conversation. She had need of a friendly face. They covered a variety of topics as dear friends are wont to do. They spoke of their children, of Alice's husband, of how tedious the season was becoming after so many weeks in town and finally, they spoke of Robert. He had been a friend to Lord Montgomery and their conversations often included some mention of him.

"He was incredibly good to me. I found confidence and a sense of purpose I don't think I would have gained without him. Robert was so kind and generous, and he encouraged me to be so as well. He had a wonderful sense of humor. He could perform the funniest impressions!" She laughed lightly and sighed. "My humor only improved with him. And he gave me respect beyond what I thought I would ever see from a man."

"That is rare indeed," said Alice. "But you know he felt just as lucky to have found you."

"Perhaps," Elizabeth said softly. "If I had never met him, I imagine I would have become a rather vain creature. I was so sure I understood the world around me. I was convinced of my own correctness. He showed me a broader world, and I am better for it. He respected my intelligence, but also saw my limitations. And like the wonderful husband he was, he provided me with opportunities to expand my knowledge, to fill in the gaps in my education. He never mocked me for reading books on science or crops or history. He enjoyed my mind, very much. We would have the most interesting debates. We could speak for hours. And they ended in the most delightful ways," she added quietly and smiled to herself. "Well, that's in the past now."

"Is it?"

She looked at her friend with a question in her eyes. "What do you mean?"

"Surely there are other men you could debate with. There must be one other man in England who enjoys an intelligent woman. I daresay there are several. And you may choose whomever you wish."

"Must we go over this again? I have told you I will not marry again," said Elizabeth impatiently.

"Really, Elizabeth, must you be so tiresome?"

Elizabeth looked at her friend with wide eyes. Alice was never vexed, but she looked very put out now.

"You continue to say you do not want a husband, yet you sit here, lonely and miserable, reminiscing about Asheland as if you are sacrificing yourself on the altar of his memory."

Elizabeth's mouth opened in shock. She stared at her friend, not knowing what to say.

"I am not trying to wound you," said Alice gently, "but Elizabeth, don't you see that you are only hurting yourself with this stubborn insistence to remain alone?"

"I, I cannot," Elizabeth stuttered and took a deep breath. "I will not deny being lonely. We have been friends long enough that you see it without my telling you. But marriage is a very great risk. One that I am not equal to making right now." She looked down and picked at her skirt for a moment.

"I think you are more ready than you think," said Alice softly.

Elizabeth looked at her in surprise and her friend smiled gently, then changed the subject.

~

Lady Montgomery had given Elizabeth much to think on and she spent the next several days wondering if Alice was right. Was she sacrificing herself to a memory? Was she sacrificing herself at all? No amount of pacing in her chambers could answer the question for her, and two rides through the park with her brother Charles did little to clear the cobwebs from her mind.

She finally found herself at Alfred's door. The butler led her into his study and she sat down in front of his desk, ruffled and agitated.

"This is a pleasant surprise," he said. "To what do I owe the honor?"

She took a deep breath, studied the curtains behind his desk, and finally looked at his kind eyes. *Eyes like Robert's.* "Alfred, I am in need of some advice."

"Of course," he said immediately. "How may I be of assistance, my dear?"

"The children," she hesitated, "I am their guardian, as well as yourself."

"Yes?"

"And I know Robert asked you to allow me to raise them as I wish, as we had wished to do, and for you to assist me with finding schools for them, things like that."

"Yes," he said suspiciously.

"What I want to know is, what would happen if I remarried? There is no one," she added in a rush, "no one I am... considering. But I do not want to entertain the idea, I don't want to even think about it, if it..." she trailed off.

246

Elizabeth Adams

"If it would be detrimental to the children," he finished for her.

"Yes," she said in a small voice, hating this conversation.

"Well, as Robert's will dictated, the children are to remain in your care until they come of age or you are unable to care for them. I am to assist where necessary in business matters and when the boys are older, give them a bit of guidance."

"Yes, of course."

"Legally, if you were to remarry, nothing would change regarding Robert's children. They would still be in your care, not your husband's. He would have no power over them or rights as far as money and contracts go."

She nodded, looking relieved.

"However, if you were to reside in the same home as your husband, as I imagine you would, he will necessarily have some influence on the children, regardless of the legalities. If he is a good man, or not very involved, I foresee no problems. Especially once the children go to school. But if he were not a good man," he looked at her significantly, "it would be my duty to intervene. For both you and the children."

"Could I be removed from my husband's home?" she asked.

"It would not be easy, but you are part of a powerful family. They would not want to see harm come to you and would use their combined influence to remove you. The children would be easier, legally speaking. As one of their guardians, a judge could easily grant me sole guardianship."

Elizabeth went pale. Her hands were cold and she felt an icy sensation along her spine.

"Elizabeth, please, don't be alarmed. I am not trying to frighten you. I know how devoted you are to the children. I would never dream of taking them from you.

You know that. I am sure Robert would come back from the grave and thrash me if I even tried it." He smiled but she did not relax. "I only tell you what *could* happen, legally, and what would precipitate it. You have excellent judgment. I am sure any man you choose would be kind and good to the children."

"And if he weren't, I would lose my children, and possibly go through a scandalous separation," she said quietly. "I think I have my answer."

"Now, wait a moment. That is only one possibility. You could meet a kind man and go on to have more children and live quite peacefully. I was not trying to frighten you, Lizzy, truly. I apologize for doing so."

"If I had more children with this potential husband," she continued as if she hadn't heard him, her voice strained, "and he was not a kind man, or mistreated us, or you didn't like him, you could take my children. And I would not be able to leave him with my new children, and thus would be trapped in a horrible situation."

"Really, Elizabeth, that is highly unlikely. Yes, if you were to marry a man who mistreated you, and you had children with him, it would complicate matters, but I need not remind you that you have some very powerful connections. The Asheland title carries much sway, as does Devonshire, and you know I would support you. And don't forget that Robert's mother was an Edgemont and a Cavendish. Lord Sedbury is very fond of you, all the Edgemonts are. If you ever did find yourself in an untenable situation, we could extricate you—with your children. I'm sure of it," he said comfortingly.

She nodded, feeling overwhelmed and frightened. "Thank you, Alfred. You are a good cousin."

He walked around the desk and she rose, trying to hide the trembling of her hands.

He put his hands on her shoulders and asked, "Are you going to be all right, dear?"

"Yes, I will be well." She gave him a false smile and he looked at her doubtfully. "Truly, I will. Any other words of advice?"

"Honestly?" He lifted his brows and gave her a small smile. "If you want to remarry, introduce him to the family before there is a public engagement. Let everyone take his measure. And if you really want to be clever," he said mischievously, "find someone less powerful than yourself."

A startled laugh burst out of her and she felt the tension release her from its grasp.

"That is good advice. Thank you, cousin."

~

Elizabeth had much to think on, and she believed Alfred was correct. She should not marry at all, or marry when she was too old to have children to avoid potential complications, or at least after her children were of age and away from any negative influence. Alternatively, she could marry sooner, but the gentleman would have to be vigorously scrutinized by her family. Robert had had connections to more titles than she could count, and she was sure that she could call on many of them to meet and assess a potential suitor for her.

And truly, she was only thinking of one gentleman, and it was only a thought. Just an idea, really. 'Twas nothing serious.

CHAPTER 17

Mr. Darcy couldn't help but notice the changes in Lady Asheland. She was both more aware of him and more withdrawn. He rightly assumed she had conflicting feelings about being attracted to a man other than Robert Talbot, and he knew he should be patient with her.

When they walked in the park with the children, as they had now done four times, he had noticed her noticing him. She would look at his hands for long moments, or stare at his mouth when he spoke, or sweep her eyes over him when she thought he wasn't looking. She gazed at him with a soft expression in her eyes and carefully listened to his future plans for Pemberley and how he thought to manage a border dispute between tenants. She soothed his fears over Georgiana and told him not to worry over her shyness—the right husband would eventually come along and like his sister just as she was. He found her kind words comforting, and the way she would squeeze his arm where her hand rested was surprisingly calming.

Her power over him was both exhilarating and alarming.

Darcy was fairly sure he was not the only one affected by their blooming friendship. Elizabeth blushed and smiled and he had made her laugh more than once now. Though the first time he heard the musical sound, so close to his ear as she walked with her hand tucked tightly in the crook of his elbow, would remain a great triumph in his mind. The Day Mr. Darcy Made Lady Asheland Laugh.

He found all of this encouraging and believed they were moving in the right direction. But just when he was ready to say something, to ask to call on her, or request to see her over the summer, she would become cold again and behave as if their closeness had never existed.

It was disconcerting.

The season was coming to a close, and Darcy would be returning to Pemberley shortly. He knew Elizabeth would go to Cressingdon, and the Bingley family would go on to Hatfield Hall. They would not return until the following spring. Mrs. Bingley was expecting her third child in early autumn and the family would not want to travel far with an infant; the Bingleys weren't the kind to leave a young babe with a nurse.

Would Lady Asheland visit her sister? He thought she would be there for the lying in. She had been there for the first two children. He supposed he could see Elizabeth there, but he did not want to intrude on his friend's family at such a delicate time. And the idea of using his friend to encounter the lady he was pursuing was distasteful to him. He would much rather meet her by his own means.

He had every reason to believe his cousin Michael would propose to Miss Kitty Bennet before the season was out. Perhaps they would marry this summer? Should that be the case he would surely see her at the wedding. It was probable the ceremony would take place in Hertfordshire, as Bingley's had. He could offer to escort her. Was that too forward? *You want to marry the lady, Darcy. Appearing forward is the least of your problems.*

He was due to have dinner at Asheland House that evening. Lady Asheland had sent him an invitation with nothing on it but a request for his presence at dinner. He did not think it was for a specific occasion, but he dressed with care nonetheless.

He arrived at Asheland House and was quickly shown into the large drawing room where an impromptu celebration was underway.

"Forgive me, Fitz. I wanted to wait until you arrived but we couldn't hold it in!" his cousin called as he rushed to greet him.

"Are congratulations in order?" asked Mr. Darcy.

"Yes! You must congratulate me, for I am the luckiest man in all of England!" said Michael, a wide smile on his face. "I can't believe she accepted me," he said quietly to his cousin.

"Did you honestly think she would refuse you?" Darcy asked.

"I hoped she wouldn't. I've never been so nervous in all my life!"

Darcy clapped his young cousin on the back. "Congratulations, cousin. You've done well for yourself. She is a sweet lady. You'll be very happy."

They smiled and shook hands and then Michael was off, speaking to the other guests so quickly he was nearly incoherent.

"Forgive me for not welcoming you properly, Mr. Darcy," said Lady Asheland.

He turned and saw her standing not a foot from him. "There is no need to apologise, Lady Asheland. I understand it is a joyous occasion."

"Yes, they are very happy." She looked around the room, then back at him. "Do you know everyone here? My Aunt and Uncle Gardiner you've met on more than one occasion, and I believe you know Lord and Lady Montgomery?"

"Yes, we've met."

"Wonderful. Perhaps you might introduce me to your cousin. I assume that is he coming towards the door?"

He looked to the doorway and saw his cousin, Edmund Darcy, Michael's older brother, being led into the

252

room. He escorted Elizabeth to him and performed the introductions.

"It is nice to finally meet you. Your brother has told us so many things about you, I feel as if I know you already," said Elizabeth with a bright smile.

"The pleasure is mine, Lady Asheland. I must thank you for hosting this dinner on such short notice. It is very kind of you."

"Thank you, but it was not a hardship. I am happy to see Kitty so well settled and content. They are a handsome couple, don't you think?" she said as she turned to face the young couple standing together on the other side of the room.

"Yes. I will go congratulate them. Excuse me."

He stepped away and Elizabeth laughed.

"What is so funny, my lady?"

"I seem to have a surfeit of Mr. Darcys in my drawing room," she said with a twinkle in her eyes. She looked around the room and counted, her lips moving but no sound coming out. "There are seven men here, and three of them are Darcys," she said brightly.

He couldn't help but smile back, though he didn't see why it was so amusing to her.

It was impossible for Mr. Darcy not to notice how different she appeared this night. There was something different in her demeanor—an openness that had not been there, a sensuality that she had previously kept hidden but was now released. He couldn't stop staring at her sparkling eyes, her soft skin that seemed to glow with happiness, the way the light reflected off her hair.

"You shouldn't look at me that way, Mr. Darcy," she said, only partially teasing.

"What way?"

"That way! As if you know my innermost thoughts!" When he continued looking at her seriously, she added quietly, "As if we are intimate with each other."

"Ah, but have I not already told you? It is unfair to make men fall in love with you when you mean to remain so elusive."

"I am doing no such thing!" She looked around the room, grateful for all the noise that covered their inappropriate conversation. "Mr. Darcy," she said with great patience, "you seem to fancy yourself infatuated with me. I do not wish to injure you, but you must see that we would not suit!"

"We wouldn't?"

"No!" she cried. "Not in the least!"

"Are you sure of that, my lady?" he said it with such earnestness, his eyes boring into hers. His body was so close she could feel the heat coming from him.

She felt herself waver. "Quite sure," she said weakly.

He smiled. A tiny quirk of the lips that said he did not believe her, but he would allow her the fantasy for a while.

"As you wish, my lady."

~

Kitty's wedding was planned for the twentieth of June. Elizabeth was surprised by the haste—it was the end of May now—but after discovering Kitty and her betrothed in a passionate kiss in the garden, Elizabeth agreed that sooner was probably better. The family let it be known that the couple wanted to go on a wedding tour while the weather was warm, and Kitty wanted her sister Jane to be at her wedding, therefore the ceremony had to be before Mrs. Bingley's lying in.

Kitty asked Lydia to stand up with her and Elizabeth bought them both new gowns as a gift. The sisters did some very rushed shopping for Kitty's wedding clothes, and then they were packing up and traveling to Hertfordshire.

Longbourn was filled with family members. Michael Darcy and his brother Edmund stayed there, as well as their parents and two sisters. Mrs. Bennet was beside herself with excitement. When Jane had married, only Mr. Bingley's limited family had come and they had stayed at Netherfield. The Gouldings lived locally and had hosted their own guests when Mary wed. Elizabeth's marriage had been a larger affair, but only Lord Asheland and his cousin had stayed at Longbourn. And it had been so long ago!

The house had three guest chambers in addition to the girls' rooms. The Darcy family took up all the guest chambers and Michael's two sisters took Mary's former room. Mr. and Mrs. Gardiner stayed in Jane's old room and their children used every available space in the nursery. Miss Darcy had accompanied Lydia and was staying at Longbourn with her. Jane and Elizabeth had each decided they, and their children, would stay with Mary at her home. That left Mr. Fitzwilliam Darcy. He had said he would stay at the inn, but Mrs. Bennet had immediately declared that the inn was nothing to Longbourn and that they still had one chamber free if he would like to stay with his sister and cousins. He accepted, and without realizing it until it was done, he was placed in Elizabeth's former chamber.

Her belongings had been removed long ago, but there were still traces of her in the colors of the wallpaper and linens, and the sampler on the wall. There was a simple painting of the seashore propped on a small shelf with a large shell beside it. He wondered if they were mementos of a childhood holiday.

He lowered himself to the bed carefully, taking in his surroundings with something akin to wonder. Would he succeed in his attempt to win her? He told himself he would; he was determined, and Darcy always succeeded when he put his mind to something. But sometimes, when she rebuffed him for the twelfth time in as many days, his certainty wavered. He had never tried so hard to achieve anything in his life. And what was worse about the situation was that the end result was out of his control. It was not like a jump he was hoping to master or a skill he wanted to acquire. No amount of practice would guarantee his success.

She must simply learn to love him. He prayed that she would, for in his quest to earn her love, he had fallen so deeply under her spell that he wasn't sure he would recover from the loss of her should she decide against him.

~

After the wedding, the family would travel north together. It was a large party including the Bingleys, the Gouldings, Lydia and Mr. and Mrs. Bennet, and the Gardiners.

Everyone was gathering at Cressingdon to celebrate Robert John's fifth birthday. Alfred's wife Sylvia had wanted to bring the family together for some time, and Robbie's birthday was the perfect occasion. It was more than a celebration of his young life, at least to the Talbot family. It was a recognition of the continuation of the Asheland title, and all the authority and prosperity that came with it.

With equal parts trepidation, excitement, and mischief, Elizabeth penned an invitation to Mr. Darcy. Her husband's family would be there in large numbers—what better way to test his motives than to surround him with people who wanted the best for her and her children? He might be a little overwhelmed, but such was her situation. If he could not support that reality, it was best their flirtation go no further.

It is time to make Mr. Darcy as discomfited as he enjoys making me.

~

The plan was to leave for the north the day after the wedding. Mr. Darcy accepted Elizabeth's invitation; he would travel with them until the road split for Cressingdon, when he would go on to Pemberley. He would join them a few days' later in time for the birthday celebration.

Elizabeth had decided to give Robert John a pony for his birthday. Her brother, Percy Goulding, had written to say he had a few small Welsh ponies to choose from—they were very popular with young riders. Elizabeth was unconvinced that a Welsh pony could be small enough for her boy, though Robert John was tall for his age. She thought they should still consider a Shetland. Her brother Percy had cautioned her that Robbie was tall already, and he may become attached to the pony and then be too big for her in only a year or possibly two. Given his temperament, Percy thought an animal Robbie could keep for a longer time would be best. Better to purchase a Shetland for Violet and Bennet—they would be able to keep it longer.

Lydia had been right when she said the Gouldings were ardent horsemen. They had a very successful stud and were becoming better known for it every year. Mary's dowry had allowed them to expand and just last year, they had sold a horse to the Duke of Cumberland, something her mother could not stop boasting about.

Alas, Percy and Mary were quiet people and did not like to leave Hertfordshire often. They found contentment in their home and friends, and to everyone's surprise, Mrs. Bennet and Mary had become quite close. At least twice a week, Mrs. Bennet would take the carriage to Haye Park to spend time with her granddaughter. This trip to Cressingdon was unusual, and Elizabeth understood it for the show of support it was.

Mr. and Mrs. Darcy, Michael's parents, were soon on easy terms with the Bennets, as were their daughters who quickly made friends with the Bennet sisters. They were traveling in the same direction and had decided to drive part of the way together. When Elizabeth heard this, she invited them to Cressingdon for a week to join the birthday celebration. They were family now, after all, and Elizabeth wanted them to know she considered them as such. She had greatly enjoyed joining Robert's family and now viewed them as her own. She hoped her sisters would be able to do the same with their husbands' families. She knew it was preferable to be surrounded by a caring family than to be on one's own all the time.

She thought, with a degree of sadness, that Mr. Darcy might need a lesson in that. He seemed friendly with his Darcy relations, but he also did not seem to know them well. He had not known that his youngest cousin Amelia was coming out next season, or that the eldest brother Edmund was courting a distant cousin on his mother's side. Elizabeth had been told all of this in the space of one afternoon tea. She assumed Mr. Darcy only ever saw the men who did not think to tell him of their family's goings on, or he did not spend much time with them.

He was often with the Bingleys, so he was not friendless, and she had seen him on a number of occasions with his cousin, Colonel Fitzwilliam. It could just be her perception, and she partially hoped it was, but he seemed lonely to her sometimes, as if he didn't trust those around him. Perhaps that was why he kept limited company? Regardless of his reasons, Mr. Darcy seemed somewhat alone in the world. She could certainly understand the sentiment.

Fewer conditions could be designed to stir up more compassion in her.

~

The skies were clear and the roads dry; they made excellent time. Late in the evening on their second day of travel, they pulled into the drive at Cressingdon. The lanterns had been lit in anticipation of their arrival, and the upper servants were awaiting them outside.

Elizabeth couldn't help the smile that spread over her face. She was riding with her sisters—minus Kitty—and they teased her gently about her excitement. The weary travelers piled out of the carriages, nearly a dozen of them lined up along the elegant drive. She took a deep breath of the clean country air. No matter where she went or how long she stayed away, coming back to Cressingdon always felt like coming home.

She searched for her children in the crowds exiting the carriages. Bennet had ridden with the Bingley children and their nurse so he could play with young Charles. Violet had gone with her grandmama, and Robert John was with his Gardiner cousins. Her children quickly found her and wrapped their arms around her skirts. Laughing, the family made their way up the stairs to greet the butler and housekeeper.

It was a well-known fact that the upper servants at Cressingdon adored the Talbot children. Well, perhaps not all the servants, but the housekeeper, Cook, and butler all seemed inordinately pleased to see them. They had been with Robert for many years before he married Elizabeth and they were glad to see the family continuing.

"Welcome home, my lady," said the butler in his calm voice.

"You may smile, Thompson. I know you are trying to suppress it," Elizabeth teased as she removed her gloves.

The butler gave her a small smile in return and she said, "See? You are much more handsome when you smile."

The housekeeper stifled a laugh and Elizabeth fought the urge to embrace her. When she first came to

Cressingdon, eighteen and untried, they had gotten off to a rocky start. Elizabeth had nearly driven the woman mad with questions on how the house was run and what was necessary or not and who was in charge of what. It had been exhausting and the good housekeeper had feared for her job, but they had eventually found their way and over the years had formed a solid respect for each other.

"All is as you requested, my lady. The Gardiners, Bingleys, and Mr. and Mrs. Bennet have their usual rooms. Miss Darcy and Miss Lydia were placed in adjoining chambers—the rose rooms—and Mr. and Mrs. Goulding in the tapestry rooms."

"That sounds ideal, Mrs. Hobbs. Your judgment is excellent, as always. Shall the nursery hold so many children, do you think?" she asked, a smile on her lips.

"We have prepared additional rooms down the hall. We thought the older children could use them, if it suits you, my lady."

"I think it a fine idea, though I will ask my aunt her thoughts on the matter."

Soon enough, everyone was settled. Cressingdon was a large home and between the family and guest wings, there was ample room. Lord and Lady Devonshire would arrive the next day, and each day after that would bring more guests until they celebrated Robert John's birthday at the end of the week.

~

After separating from the traveling party, Darcy arrived at Pemberley hours before he was expected. He bounded up the steps, a smile on his face that greatly confused the servants he passed along the way. He would see Elizabeth in five days. At her home.

He could not be imagining the welcoming looks she had given him recently. She had been quite receptive, he was sure of it. And she had invited him to Cressingdon—the home she had shared with her beloved husband. That must be a sign that she viewed him favorably. She must trust him, at least a little, or she would not have invited him to her son's birthday celebration. Nearly everyone invited was a family member in some degree. His inclusion was a sign of her growing affection for him, it must be.

It could not have come at a better time.

He had some business to attend to at Pemberley, then he would make the journey to Nottinghamshire. He needed to find a gift for young Robert John. Something for Lady Violet would also be nice. He wanted to give the boy a new saddle; he knew Elizabeth was giving him his first pony and a saddle would go perfectly with it. But he had spoken with Bingley and his friend thought someone else in the family planned to give Robert a saddle as a gift, not to mention it was too large a gesture for someone unconnected to the family.

He thought about other things that went along with riding: a new crop, riding boots. He even considered a blanket for the animal. His sister had given him one years ago. She had embroidered his name and the date on one corner and his horse's name on the other. It had been slightly childish—she was only eleven when she gave it to him—but he had liked it and used it regularly. Finally, Darcy thought of the perfect idea. He would ride into Lambton tomorrow.

CHAPTER 18

Cressingdon was magical in summer. The flowers were blooming, the birds singing, and the sun shone brightly across the estate. Elizabeth couldn't have chosen a better day for her son's birthday celebration.

The house was full of friends and family—only three chambers remained unoccupied. She rose before her guests to make sure everything was ready for the party. She met with the housekeeper, the cook, and the butler. She spoke to the groom and was assured Robbie's pony would be clean and brushed and ready for its debut at the appointed time.

After confirming everything was prepared outside and in the house, she went up to the nursery. The nurse assured her that the children's clothes were pressed and ready, and Violet would be sent to her mother before the event to have her hair done by Watson. Elizabeth wanted it curled for the party and had chosen new ribbons for her daughter's hair.

Seeing all was in readiness, she went to the breakfast room. She was just sitting down with her tea when she was informed a carriage was arriving. Elizabeth rose to greet the newcomers—she was expecting the last of her Talbot relations today. She was just descending the stairs in front of the house when the carriage pulled up and, to her surprise, Mr. Darcy stepped out.

"Mr. Darcy! Welcome to Cressingdon. I had not expected you until this afternoon." She extended her hand and he kissed it briefly before rising and smiling brightly.

"I hope it is not an unwelcome surprise?"

"Of course not. Friends are always welcome, whether they are expected or not."

His brows rose at her comment and he couldn't help but smile at her again.

"Come, I'll have someone show you to your room," she said as she turned and walked into the house. "You are only a few rooms away from Miss Darcy."

"Thank you. How is my sister?"

"She seems to be doing quite well. With Lydia, her cousins, the children, and the stables, she has been much occupied," she said with a smile.

"Thank you for allowing her to travel with you. I know she is enjoying being in the company of ladies closer to her age."

"It is no trouble. She is a sweet girl and we have enjoyed having her in our party." She smiled and sent him off with a footman.

~

In the late afternoon, the entire party gathered to celebrate Robert John's fifth birthday. Elizabeth had decided to take advantage of the warm weather, so a sumptuous picnic was arranged beside the lake. There were blankets and cushions to recline on, and a few chairs for the older guests. Tables were set up beneath a large oak tree and covered in food and sweet confections. Cook had made all Robbie's favorites, and everything was presented on colorful linens.

Elizabeth had asked for lanterns to be hung in the trees and ribbons strung along the branches. Games were prepared for the children and croquet for the adults. Robbie squealed with delight when he saw his new pony, brought out by his uncle and wearing a bright blue ribbon.

As a surprise for her son and guests, there was a marionette show put on by a troupe of players, and the children laughed continuously throughout their performance. When the show was over, the performers wandered through the crowd on stilts as they juggled colorful balls. One man twirled a hoop round and round endlessly, and women in bright clothing made paper crowns and flower wreaths for the children. Gossamer wings had been made for Violet and the other young girls present and they ran along the lake, giggling and joyful, like tiny fairies dancing in the sunset.

After the sun had sunk low in the sky, the lanterns were lit and more food was brought out. The youngest children had been taken to bed, but Robert John, as the guest of honor, was allowed to stay up, as well as the older Gardiner children.

Darcy wandered among the revelers, glad to be present for such a memorable event and marveling at Elizabeth's ability to create such a magical day. Now it was full dark, the moon was bright, and nearly everyone was feeling the relaxing effects of the punch. Bingley had escorted an exhausted Jane to bed a quarter of an hour ago, and Darcy was looking for Elizabeth. He had a suspicion her eyes would look especially becoming in the lantern light as it reflected off the lake and he wanted to see if he was right.

Finally, he espied her sitting on a pile of cushions and blankets near the lake's edge. He made his way to her and approached quietly when he saw young Robert John lying on the blanket next to her, his head in his mother's lap, fast asleep.

"May I join you?" he asked quietly.

"Of course." She looked up at him and he smiled as he lowered himself to sit beside her.

"Lovely crown," he said with a teasing smile, nodding towards the spray roses adorning her head.

"Thank you!" She said with a playful grin. "Violet was having one made and wanted me to have one as well." She smiled, and he couldn't help but be impressed at her lack of embarrassment.

She was very becoming, in her gauzy summer gown, her hair piled prettily atop her head, a crooked wreath of flowers perched on her curls.

"I was right, you know."

"About what?" she asked.

"I thought your eyes would look especially bewitching in this light. I'm glad to see I was not mistaken," he said softly.

Her hand stilled where it was stroking her son's hair and her face flushed.

"Are you enjoying the party?" she asked, her voice almost calm.

"Yes. You've done remarkably well. I don't remember when I've had a more pleasant time."

"Thank you. It has been so long since we have been together as a family. Not since..." she trailed off, not allowing her mind to dwell on unhappiness today. "I'm glad you've enjoyed yourself," she added with a smile.

"I think everyone has had a good time. Many are still enjoying themselves," he said with a sly smile and a look over his shoulder.

She smiled and shook her head. Some of her younger cousins had made a little too free with Cressingdon's wine and were now rather lively. Providing no one came to any harm, she saw no reason to intervene. Alfred was near—he would stop anything truly unruly from happening.

One by one the guests returned to the house, some stealing away, others waving at her before they left. She and Darcy sat quietly by the lake, watching the moon reflected in its gentle ripples, staring up at the stars, and saying nothing.

"I should take Robbie inside. It is late," she said quietly.

The servants were beginning to pack up the food and blankets, and only the most determined guests remained.

"Allow me," said Darcy. He gathered up Robbie and gestured for Elizabeth to lead them to the house.

She smiled softly at her sleeping son and began walking along the path. "Thank you, Mr. Darcy. You've saved me some trouble."

"It is no trouble, I assure you, my lady."

"I should thank you again for Robbie's gift. It was very thoughtful of you."

Darcy had given Robbie a set of saddlebags, just the right size, with his initials and the date tooled into the leather on the underside.

"You are welcome. I hope he is able to use them."

"Oh, there is no danger of him not using them!" she said with a happy laugh. "He was so excited to see his pony. I can't believe Percy found one so docile, but I am grateful for it. Robbie will spend the next few days trying to name it, I'm sure."

Darcy chuckled. "I'm sure he will."

They reached the house and she led him up the stairs to the nursery. She opened the door quietly and led him into the dark room. Violet was asleep across the room, and Bennet slept nearby, as did young Jane and Charlie. She pulled back the coverlet and Darcy laid the boy down.

"It's amazing he's still asleep," he whispered in the darkened room.

"Yes, he can sleep through anything," she replied.

She unlaced one shoe while Darcy undid the other, then she gently maneuvered him out of his jacket. Robbie slept through it all. She kissed his forehead and tucked him in, then slipped out of the room and closed the door quietly behind her.

"Thank you, Mr. Darcy," she said.

"Think nothing of it, my lady."

It was a simple statement, and yet she felt herself warming from her head to her toes. She looked to the floor, then back to his face, then to the floor again. She continued to steal glances at him as they descended the stairs, surprised at how peaceful she felt in his presence.

She stepped away at the bottom of the steps and faced him. "Goodnight, Mr. Darcy."

"Goodnight, my lady. Sleep well."

~

The entire party slept well into the morning. Elizabeth entered the breakfast room and found no one but her cousin Alfred and a man she vaguely recognized but couldn't remember the name of.

"Good morning, Elizabeth," said Alfred cheerfully.

"Good morning, Lord Devonshire."

Alfred shook his head—he disliked being called by his title when amongst family. "Did you meet Captain Williamson yesterday? He arrived late with Charles and Mary."

"I believe we met briefly at the party," she said politely. "You're Mary Williamson's son?"

"Yes. You and I are second cousins. My grandfather and Lord Asheland's were brothers."

"I see. I believe you were always at sea when I met your mother. She's very kind."

"Thank you, my lady."

Elizabeth sat and began preparing her tea and the gentlemen joined her.

"Charles, that is, Mary's brother, and Robert were friends," added Alfred.

"Oh?" Elizabeth replied. Robert had been friends with a great deal of people. Since his death, many of them had brought themselves to her notice, hoping she would remember what great friends they had been with her husband. If only they knew how Robert had really felt—he was *friendly* with most people, but *he* only called a select few his friend.

"Yes. He and Mary spent several summers at Cressingdon when they were children," continued Alfred.

Elizabeth looked up, suddenly suspicious of Alfred. She buttered her scone slowly and said flatly, "Did they? How nice. Cressingdon is lovely in summer. I'm sure they enjoyed it."

Captain Williamson shifted in his seat and asked about the arrangements for the coming week. Elizabeth answered and when she had finished eating, she asked Alfred to join her in the rose garden.

"What are you planning, cousin?" she asked as soon as they were far enough from the house not to be overheard.

"Whatever do you mean?"

"Do not dissemble with me, Alfred. You have no talent for it."

She glared at him and he looked back stubbornly. She crossed her arms and he sighed heavily, finally saying, "I thought you might like Captain Williamson."

"You thought I might like him?" she said in confusion. Another look at Alfred's sheepish expression and she understood. "Alfred! You can't be serious!"

She walked quickly away from him and he hurried after her.

"What were you thinking?" she hissed over her shoulder and continued walking, her boots crunching on the gravel.

"You seemed interested in marrying again. He is a fine man, from a good family."

"Yes, this family!" she cried.

"What is so bad about that?" he asked indignantly.

She sighed and pinched the bridge of her nose. "Nothing, cousin, you know that. Please do not misconstrue my words. You know I love this family and am happy to be in it."

They shared an uneasy smile and walked on, more slowly now.

"But do you not think it somewhat... strange... that I would marry into the same family twice?" she asked.

He shrugged. "Possibly, but not necessarily. You need someone you can trust. We have known Captain Williamson his entire life. He is trustworthy and would not treat you unkindly. He would be good to the children. They are his blood, too. It must go some way to engendering affection."

She tilted her head, considering Alfred's words. "Your reasoning is sound, but I cannot help but think it odd to marry my own husband's cousin."

He took her arm and looped it through his, patting her hand affectionately. "You are a young woman. It is only natural that you would want to remarry."

"But that is the point! I don't know that I *do* want to. Remarry, that is. It is all so risky and difficult and there are days when I think it is not worth the trouble."

"And on other days?" he asked gently.

She sighed. "On other days, I think it sounds like a very good plan," she said. *As it did last night*, she thought traitorously.

Alfred chuckled lightly. "I must admit to you a little secret, Elizabeth," he said with amusement. "Many people feel that way about marriage long after the ceremony."

She laughed.

After a few minutes spent walking in silence, Alfred asked carefully, "Is there someone you would consider marrying? A gentleman you... like?"

She sighed again. "There is someone I have... flirted with. But it has not gone beyond that," she added

269

hurriedly. "I have tried to imagine the future, and it is unclear to me."

He gave her a look that told her he thought her silly and she clarified, "When Robert first courted me, my aunt asked me if I could imagine a future with him. Walking, visiting, living a life together. And I could. I could see it all, in my mind, as clear as day. And now, now I cannot see anything! My life stretches before me like some dark sea that I cannot see beneath the surface of. I do not know where I will be, what I will do, or who will be with me when I do it. It is disconcerting."

He squeezed her hand. "I cannot imagine what you have gone through and how you must feel, but I do know what it is to lose someone you love. I do not wish to make you sad, I just want you to know that I understand such loss, and how grief can surprise you." He stopped walking and turned to face her. "If you say you are not ready, I will not press you, and neither will the family. But if you are, we will do what we can to support you."

"Thank you, cousin. That means a great deal to me."

~

Over the next two days, Alfred observed Elizabeth closely. He assumed the man she was *flirting* with was here at the house party. *Half of society is at this house party*. He was a little surprised by what he saw.

Mr. Darcy, showing his cousin every attention— *flirting* with her. Mr. Darcy! And Elizabeth returned his flirtations, much of the time. Her cheeks were frequently flushed and when she sent him shy smiles, the man lit up like a torch. And she *smiled* at him! Clearly, Darcy's attraction was not all on one side. How long had this been going on?

He decided that the length of time did not matter, though he assumed it had begun in Town, probably shortly before Elizabeth came to see him to ask about remarrying. If Darcy wanted to join the Talbot family—and Alfred viewed it as such; after all, Elizabeth was a Talbot now, quite indelibly—he would have to show himself worthy.

He asked his wife what rumors she had heard about Darcy and his family. There was some gossip about his Fitzwilliam cousins, and one gentleman that seemed particularly wild, but nothing too scandalous or out of the ordinary. Financially, Alfred knew he was sound. He would review Elizabeth's settlement to ensure her fortune remained intact. He didn't think Darcy was the kind of man to insert himself into others' concerns, but if he was, Alfred did not doubt his ability to deal with the situation.

The gentlemen had planned a day of fishing. Young Robert John was being taken by his Uncle Bingley and Mr. Gardiner was bringing his two eldest boys. It was the perfect occasion to have a little sport with Mr. Darcy.

"Good morning!" said Alfred jovially to the men gathered outside the house.

Greetings were mumbled back to him, several of the men clearly unused to being outside at this hour. Alfred chuckled to himself and went about his plan.

"Mr. Darcy, have you met everyone here?" he asked as he joined the younger man on the way to the stream.

"I believe so, though I'm sure there are a few I haven't been introduced to yet."

Alfred nodded. He saw his son approaching and called to him. "John, you know Mr. Darcy, don't you?" He gave his son a significant look and John smiled back. "My eldest son, Lord Epworth."

"I believe we met some time ago. A pleasure to see you again," said John affably.

Darcy replied in kind and they spoke of the weather and the fishing. Alfred would greet everyone who came near—and call out to those who didn't—and introduce them to Darcy.

Had he met his youngest son, Lord George Downing? Did he know Stephen Carew, Robert's late sister's husband and nephew of the Earl of Petherton? Was he acquainted with Lord Stanfield? They were cousins, somewhat distant, but the families preferred to maintain the connection. What about Lord Sedbury's son? The older gentleman had remained at the house but his son had grown up with Robert and Alfred and was a very dear friend.

Mr. Cavendish was connected to Robert through the Edgemonts on Robert's mother's side—his maternal grandmother had been a Cavendish. Did he know that? They were not truly related to the Downings, but they were very friendly nonetheless. Lord Fife was on the McClaren side of the family—the grandmother the first Lady Violet had been named for—and had come especially to visit young Robert on his birthday and see his cousin Lord Sedbury.

The introductions continued, and after a dozen such meetings, Darcy's head was spinning. He seldom felt like the lowliest gentleman when in company, but beside this stream in the English countryside, he realized he might very well be the lowest—and the poorest—man here. It was both ridiculously funny and horrifying at the same time. At least Charles Bingley and Captain Williamson were here; they were nearer to him in rank and his income exceeded Bingley's, and he imagined the captain's as well. But they were both well known to everyone there. The captain had always been part of the family and Bingley had married into it—had been the earl's brother—some time ago. Darcy was the outsider here.

He wondered wryly if there was an earldom in England not represented? He knew the Cavendish cousin was closely related to the duke, and he'd been told Lord

Sedbury's wife was the Duke of Cornwall's niece. And, of course, there was the Marquess performing the introductions.

After a moment of gathering his wits, Darcy looked at Lord Devonshire more closely. The gentleman was enjoying this entirely too much. He had heard Elizabeth speak of "Alfred." She had portrayed him as genial and kind, the sort of man who enjoyed a good joke. Darcy was seeing none of that now, unless... he just happened to be looking their way when Lord Devonshire and Mr. Carew exchanged a conspiratorial glance. In an instant, everything fell into place.

They were testing him.

Darcy straightened to his full height and pulled his shoulders back. He enjoyed a challenge, and he had never backed away from one yet. If they wanted to try him, they would find him ready.

It wasn't until he was preparing for bed that night that Darcy realized something. If the family was testing him, Elizabeth must be seriously considering him.

~

Darcy sought out Elizabeth the next day. He wanted to see her, to hear her voice, to compliment her and watch the blush form on her cheeks. He found her in the library after breakfast. Several of her extended family members had left that morning, including his own Darcy cousins, and many of the remaining guests had gone on an excursion. It was the perfect time to seek her out.

He entered the library quietly and closed the door behind him. She was curled up in the window seat, her feet tucked under her and her head resting against the glass. A book lay forgotten by her side.

"Lady Asheland, may I join you?"

"Mr. Darcy!" She jumped up in surprise and smoothed her skirts. "Forgive me, sir, I thought I was alone."

"You were. Forgive me for surprising you."

"Just because it is a surprise does not mean it is unwelcome," she said politely and resumed her seat.

"I had an interesting conversation with your cousin yesterday," he said. He walked to a shelf and examined the books there, his back to her.

"Lord Devonshire?"

"Yes. He seems to be under the impression that I pose some danger to you." He turned to face her. She could not read his expression.

"That is preposterous!"

"I'm glad you think so," he said, moving toward her. "I would never harm you."

"I know," she said so quietly he almost didn't hear her. "Why would Alfred think such a thing?"

"I believe he noticed my attentions, and wanted to let me know you are not alone and unprotected." She flushed and looked away. He continued, "Of course, his warnings were unnecessary. I knew you weren't alone, and I would never think you weak."

She studied the tip of her slipper peeking out from beneath her skirt. *Go on, Lizzy. Don't be a ninny!* "And just what are your intentions, sir?"

He smiled. "They are purely honorable, I assure you."

She looked down in disappointment when he didn't elaborate.

"Lady Asheland, you know how I feel." She looked up and he was before her. He took her hand in his and held it tightly. "I would declare myself this moment if I thought your answer would be favorable."

"You would?"

"Yes, I would."

"What would you say?"

274

He shook his head. "Oh, no, my lady. I shall not debase myself for your entertainment. When you are ready, then we will hold this conversation in earnest."

She pursed her lips in annoyance and squinted her eyes. She hated it when he was right. She was not entitled to demand declarations that she had no intention of responding favorably to. Nonetheless, she had her pride.

"I may never be ready for you, Mr. Darcy," she said haughtily, every inch the wealthy countess.

He looked at her skeptically. "Truly, my lady?"

She looked back at him indignantly. "Truly, sir."

He sighed and looked down, shaking his head in amusement, then looked back at her.

"Believe what you will, Lady Asheland, but you know what they say about the truth."

"What?"

"It shall make you free."

She stared at him in astonishment until he left the room and she was left alone with her unsettling feelings.

~

Elizabeth rode her mare over the lush green grass, filling her lungs with the warm summer air. She skirted her way around the village until she came to the church at the south end. She tied up her horse and went into the churchyard, making her way to the iron gate that separated the Talbots' plots from the rest of the yard.

Robert's grave was the newest one, a row behind his first two wives and their children. She touched a hand to each of the children's headstones, saying a silent prayer, and stood before her husband's grave. She traced the letters of his name and the date he had died, feeling too many emotions to put names to any of them. Finally, she sat down and leaned against the stone.

"Alfred thinks I should remarry. And Sylvia. And Jane. Alice has had her say, as I'm sure you can imagine." There was no reply. She sighed. "Dearest, I wish you were here to advise me—you always knew what to do in difficult situations. I know that is ridiculous. Why would I marry again if you were here?" She plucked at the grass to her side and leaned her head back to look at the sky through the branches of the oak planted just beyond the churchyard wall.

"I think I might be falling in love with Mr. Darcy," she said quietly. "I know you always liked him. You told me not to judge him harshly, that he wasn't at his best in mixed company." She hesitated and twirled a blade of grass between her fingers. "But I think he has found his way in that regard—at least around me. He can be quite charming when he wants to be. And he is a kind man…"

She sighed again and stared at the clouds. "Robert, I am so sorry," she whispered, tears choking her voice. "Can you forgive me for wanting another man? Do I have a faithless heart?" She exhaled heavily, her shoulders falling.

She sat there silently, tears forming tracks down her cheeks. "Do you remember the last thing you said to me? You seemed so earnest, but you were dying! Did you mean it? Do you truly want me to marry and love again? You will not hate me if I do?" she added in a small voice.

She lay her head against the stone and curled her knees beneath her as the sky above darkened. A cloud had moved over the sun and she sat in its shade, remembering her husband's face, the way his arms had felt when they held her, how his lips were smooth against her cheek. She reveled in her memories of him, holding them close and cherishing every bittersweet pang that proved she had not forgotten him.

Finally, after she had lost all sense of time, the sun came out again. She turned her face up and felt its heat on her skin, peace flooding her body.

"All right, my love. I will believe you." She stood slowly and rested her hand on the headstone, looking at it solemnly. "It is time," she whispered.

CHAPTER 19

The change in Elizabeth was obvious to Darcy. She smiled more freely, she laughed more often, and most importantly, she did not pull away from him. He asked her to accompany him on a walk in the gardens; she agreed. He offered to join her on a ride with young Robbie and she welcomed him happily. She began seating him nearer and nearer to her at dinner, until finally, she declared one evening that they would dine informally and allowed her guests to choose their own seats. She gave him a look that summoned him to her side with alarming rapidity, and he spent the meal happily engaged in conversation with his lady love.

The morning after the most delightful dinner of his life, Darcy arose early and prepared for a ride. Just as he was about to leave the stables, he saw Elizabeth walking in.

"Will you ride this morning, my lady?" he asked.

"Yes, I will take Marina out." She seemed to hesitate and he was debating whether he should offer to join her or if it would be wiser to wait for her to invite him when she spoke. "Would you care to join me, Mr. Darcy?"

Her cheeks were flushed and her voice less than confident, but she had invited him and he couldn't help the smile that spread across his face.

"I should like that very much, my lady."

They ambled over the fields—well away from where Lord Asheland's accident occurred—and they were some distance from the house before they spoke.

"I have a request, Mr. Darcy."

"Yes, my lady?"

"Violet has been a little jealous of all the attention Robbie has been getting lately, especially from the guests. I wondered, would you like to take tea with the children and me this afternoon?"

She looked at him with a mischievous smile, as if she knew he could not deny her but neither would he wish to say yes. He would surprise her. "I would be delighted."

She beamed and they rode on in silence for some time.

"Are we still on Cressingdon land?" he asked.

"We've just passed the edge of the estate," she pointed to a row of trees behind them. "This is Mr. Worthington's land. He doesn't mind if I ride here. His sons often ride at Cressingdon as well. He is a good neighbor."

Before he could reply, there was a loud rumble of thunder and the horses had to be calmed. They looked at the sky and saw dark clouds rolling in quickly.

"We won't reach the house before the rain falls. Is there shelter near here?" asked Darcy.

"Yes, less than a mile this way. Follow me," she called over her shoulder.

They hurried to a small hill partially covered with trees. The sky was quickly darkening and the horses were restless. Elizabeth led him into the trees and dismounted, leading her horse as far into the shelter of the dense branches as she could before tying her to a branch.

"There is an old temple through there."

She gestured to her left where he saw a partially crumbled stone structure, overgrown with ivy and hidden by branches. He tied his horse next to hers and they ran to the temple, just as the rain began to fall.

Elizabeth removed her riding hat and shook it out, then patted her hair into place and smoothed the front of her dress.

"We made it just in time," said Mr. Darcy looking out at the steadily falling rain.

"Yes, it is a good thing we were so close."

Several minutes later, Elizabeth said, "May I ask you a question, Mr. Darcy?"

"Of course."

"Why did you follow me out into the rain when we were at Netherfield?"

"When we first met? Four years ago?"

"Yes. Was there another time you chased after me and demanded I return to the house that I do not recall?" she teased.

He grinned sheepishly. "I wish I had a better answer for you, but I'm afraid it is as simple as I thought you were doing something foolhardy and as a gentleman, it was my duty to stop you."

She raised a brow and he could tell she was holding in her laughter. "Do you make a habit of rescuing damsels in distress?" she asked.

He shook his head and looked at his boots, then looked back at her and smiled. "Only very pretty ones, my lady."

She blushed and shook her head. "I hope you have learned the error of your ways," she teased.

He walked towards her slowly, his eyes intent on her. "Yes, you put me in my place quite effortlessly."

She laughed nervously. He was only a yard away. "I should not have lost my temper, but you wouldn't move out of my way!" she cried. He was an arm's length from her now. "You left me no alternative," she said breathily, leaning her head back to look into his eyes. She did not step away.

He was directly in front of her now, his bright eyes burning with a passion she had never seen there before. "You were beautiful."

"Even though I resembled a half-drowned cat?" she jested weakly.

"Beautiful." His voice deepened. "Just as you are today." He reached out and tucked a tendril of hair behind her ear. "I was thoroughly irritated to be attracted to such a stubborn creature."

She almost laughed, the sound sticking in her throat and coming out in a breathy gust. He continued to touch her face, tracing his fingers over her brows, the line of her nose, down her jaw and across her lips.

She watched him, the rain falling in a steady rhythm around them, her heart beating wildly in her chest, her mind whirling with possibilities.

He held her face tenderly, searching her frightened eyes, and whispered, "Let me love you, my lady. Do not push me away." He stroked her cheek. "Your heart is safe with me, I swear it."

She stared at him for a long moment, her heart pounding, and swallowed heavily. Finally, when he thought he would burst from waiting, she pushed up onto her toes and tentatively pressed her lips to his. Slowly, she placed her hands on his shoulders and pulled back to look into his eyes. Why had she ever thought they were a cold shade of blue?

They stared at each other for a moment, breath ragged, then all at once he pulled her to him and crushed his lips against hers. She wrapped her arms around his neck and ran her hands into his hair. He pulled her body into his, so tightly that her feet were off the floor. His hands ran up and down her back, seeking, exploring, and she moaned softly into his ear when he kissed her neck.

She was pure delight—he had never felt so much joy and fervor and fire all at once. His skin felt hot and his mouth wanted to taste every bit of her that she would allow him.

Elizabeth was awash in sensation. She flushed and cooled and flushed again. Every nerve was alive and she nearly cried with elation when he ran his strong hands over her body. She clutched him to her, not wanting him to retreat an inch, and ran her hands over his back, through his hair, down the length of his strong arms. Had anything ever felt so heavenly?

A loud cracking sound startled them both and they looked up to see a branch falling from a nearby tree. They stared at each other, breathing heavily, until Elizabeth looked out and commented that the rain was slowing. His arms were still wrapped around her back and her hands were on his elbows.

"Elizabeth," he said softly.

She turned away from the rain and looked at him, startled. "I believe that is the first time you have ever called me that."

"Do you like it?"

"I do. You may say it again, if you like."

"I do like. Elizabeth," he said deliberately. He smiled and she couldn't help but return it. He stroked the hair at her temple and pushed away a curl that insisted on falling forward. "I have been wanting to do that for a very long time."

"Kiss me or say my name?" she asked impishly.

"Both," he said and kissed her swiftly.

She laughed.

~

Elizabeth hurried to the nursery for tea with the children. She had been talking to her cousin Marianne, Alfred's daughter, who was expecting her second babe. Marianne had a hundred questions for Elizabeth and when those were answered, she wanted to complain about her mother-in-law, the dowager countess.

Marianne had always been a perfectly sweet girl with a pretty face and good prospects. When her uncle died and her father was declared the new heir to the marquess, she went from being a girl with good prospects to one with wildly high expectations overnight. Her dowry was increased and she was declared a great beauty, for the daughter of a marquess would always be more desirable than the niece of one.

Unsurprisingly, Marianne Downing had married the Earl of Rockingham and was in the process of producing an heir for her husband. She desperately hoped this one was a boy, for her last had been a girl and her husband had been dreadfully disappointed. Marianne would never admit it to anyone but Elizabeth, but sometimes she wished her father had never inherited and she had remained merely pretty and moderately dowered, and married a nice gentleman with a simple country estate, or perhaps even a colonel in the regulars.

Elizabeth sympathized, of course, and could understand her cousin's frustration. But she really did need to go to the nursery. Her children were waiting. Marianne offered to go with her, but Elizabeth insisted she should rest. For the sake of the baby, of course.

Finally, she burst into the nursery just as the maid was setting down the tray. The children were dressed in their best clothes and Violet was wearing an old pair of lace gloves Elizabeth had cut down for her. But nothing prepared her for the sight of Mr. Darcy, sitting between Violet and Robbie, his knees nearly up around his chin.

Her hand covered her mouth before a laugh could escape. "Mr. Darcy! There are larger chairs if you would prefer."

"I'm quite comfortable, my lady, thank you."

"Very well."

Elizabeth sat in one of the small chairs around the children's table. She often sat with them there, if only because they were more comfortable that way and she was not so tall that it was difficult for her. But there was a larger table across the room. She was surprised that he had not suggested it.

She poured tea for her children and Mr. Darcy, and let Violet choose her own sugar lump. There was a small argument over the last orange cake, but it was quickly resolved when Elizabeth cut it in half and split it between her sons.

"Master Bennet, I understand you want a dog of your own," said Mr. Darcy.

Bennet blanched in his seat beside his mother and then burrowed his head into her arm.

"Bennet is the shy one in the family," she said with a smile. She gently pried him from her side and asked him, "Do you still want a puppy, Ben?"

He nodded and glanced at Mr. Darcy briefly before diving back into his mother's side.

She kissed the top of his head and lifted him into her lap. "Is that better, love?"

Bennet nodded and from the safety of his mother's lap, was willing to look at Mr. Darcy. He only spoke a few words, generally yes or no, but he was only two-and-a-half. Darcy was inordinately proud of himself when he made the young boy smile.

When tea was over he bowed to the children and kissed Lady Violet's hand and she giggled, giving him a wobbly curtsey. Elizabeth told them she would come to see them before they went to bed and they left the nursery together.

"I wasn't sure you would be here," she said quietly as they walked down the hall.

"I always keep my promises, my lady," he said seriously.

She stopped walking and looked at him appraisingly—at his strong back and broad shoulders, the proud tilt to his chin, the impressive height of him. She sighed.

Yes, he kept his promises.

And now she must keep hers.

~

Once she had made up her mind about something, Elizabeth was quick to act on her decision. She spent the evening examining her feelings and running a hundred possible outcomes through her mind. She was inattentive at dinner and nearly wore a hole in her carpet with her pacing that night. In the end, she knew she must speak to Mr. Darcy. She had resolved her feelings, and now it was time to resolve the details.

Darcy was dressing for the day when he received a note. Elizabeth was requesting he meet her at the summer house on the other side of the lake. Pleased and more than a little curious, he changed into his riding clothes and called for his horse.

The summer house was situated on a gentle rise and secluded on one side. He found it easily enough and tied his horse next to Elizabeth's mare. He stood at the entrance, silently watching her pace back and forth.

"Good morning, Lady Asheland," he said.

She stopped pacing and turned to face him. "Good morning, Mr. Darcy. I think you should call me Elizabeth while we are here."

His brows shot up. "Really?"

"Yes. I thought we could have an earnest conversation."

His eyes brightened in understanding. "Very well, Elizabeth. You have my attention."

She blushed when he said her name. "Mr.

Darcy—"

"Fitzwilliam," he interrupted her.

"I beg your pardon?"

"My name is Fitzwilliam. If I am to call you by your Christian name, you should call me by mine. Elizabeth," he said the last with a warm glance and a half smile and she felt a flock of butterflies take flight in her stomach.

"Very well, Fitzwilliam," she said softly. "You said your intentions are honorable."

He nodded.

"I assume that means marriage?" she asked.

He nodded again. "Are we having that conversation, Elizabeth?"

"Partially," she said softly. It was difficult to concentrate when he looked at her like that. His expression showed his confusion and she clarified. "Before I could in good conscience accept any proposal, or even hear one, I would have to discuss some... details with the gentleman."

"And I am the gentleman in this case?" he said with an amused smile.

"Must you make jokes now?" she cried.

"Forgive me, my dear. You were discussing details. I am listening," he said steadily. His eyes were still full of happiness but she supposed she couldn't fault him for that.

"Yes, details. I have three children, Mr. Darcy. I cannot enter into any marriage without considering it very carefully."

"Of course. You know I am already very fond of Robert John. And Lady Violet is charming. I have not spent much time with Bennet as yet, but I am sure we will get along admirably."

She smiled. "Thank you, that is kind of you to say. I am sure you are right, and I know you are a kind man. My brother Bingley gives me every assurance of your honor and goodness."

I shall have to thank him, thought Darcy to himself.

286

"I'm sure you have seen that I spend a great deal of time with my children?"

He nodded.

"I would not want that to change. I want to continue to care for them as I have done, and any other children that come along. I am trusting your honor and asking you to tell me the truth, Mr. Darcy. Would you interfere in the raising of my children? Or demand any we had together be raised differently?"

He looked at her solemnly, realizing the weight of his answer. "No, I have no intention of interfering with your children, the earl's children, that is. I quite admire the way you are bringing them up. They are delightful and I have often thought you an excellent mother, even when the earl was still alive. I have no desire to change that."

She flushed at his praise. "And what of any children we have together?"

He took a deep breath and walked several steps away and back again. "You know, the day I decided I would not abandon my pursuit of you, it was because of your care for young Robert."

She looked at him in surprise and he continued.

"You had come to collect Robbie from his riding lesson and had not known I would be there. It was shortly after our quarrel."

"I remember," she said softly.

"I thought he was a lucky boy, to have such a mother. I was actually jealous of him, if you can believe it. I wished I had had such a mother. And then I wished it for my children. That they would know the warmth of a mother's affection—of *your* affection. I knew then that I could see no other woman as my wife. I was so in love with every aspect of you—even the ones that had nothing to do with me. I would never be satisfied with anyone else."

Her mouth opened slightly and she stared at him, unable to think of anything to say.

"Elizabeth, if we were blessed with children, I would hope that you would love them as lavishly as you have your other children, and teach me to do so as well. They could only benefit from your attention."

Elizabeth stared at him, feeling an almost overwhelming desire to throw herself into his arms. "Do you mean that?"

"Every word."

She embraced him then, her arms wrapped tightly around his middle and her head on his shoulder. He held her tightly and a relieved sigh escaped her as her body relaxed against his.

"Where would we live?" she asked quietly, her voice muffled by his coat.

He looked to the floor. This was a truly difficult question. "If we were to have a son, he should be raised at Pemberley. He must learn to love the estate," he said softly.

She nodded. She had expected this. "Robert should be raised at Cressingdon—it will be his one day. He should learn to love it." She pulled back to look at him and imagined the sad look of resignation on his face matched the one on hers.

"I will not give you up because we cannot agree on where to live," he said with determination.

"Perhaps we can come to an agreeable solution?" she asked hopefully.

"We needn't spend the entire Season in Town; a few weeks would suffice," he said. "Some years we could even avoid it altogether."

Understanding what he was doing, she said, "I assume you like to be at Pemberley in spring for the planting?"

"Yes, but we could easily spend the summer between here and Derbyshire."

"And it is only forty miles."

"And what is forty miles of good road? Merely half a day's travel."

"Winter is lovely at Cressingdon," she said.

"Pemberley will be covered in snow."

"We could travel before the roads become difficult."

"And we needn't follow the same pattern each year. We may alter our plans if we like," he pulled her closer, excitement building in his chest.

"So I must not give up my children's home?"

"I would never ask it of you."

He took both her hands in his and brought them to his chest. "Are there any other details we need to discuss?" he asked gently.

She looked down for a long moment, then raised her head and said, "No, dearest, that is enough."

He looked at her in surprise and she couldn't help but note how much the expression of heartfelt delight, diffused over his face, became him. "You are very dear to me, Fitzwilliam. How could you not be?" she said softly.

He kissed her then. Gently, tentatively, until she relaxed against him and he wrapped his arms around her, one hand pulling her waist to him, the other on the back of her neck, gently caressing the curls that fell there.

He pulled back and looked at her with heavy-lidded eyes. "Will you marry me now?"

She smiled and he thought his heart would stop while he awaited her answer.

"Yes, Fitzwilliam. I will marry you."

CHAPTER 20

Elizabeth spent the remainder of her day being inattentive to her guests, humming softly to herself, and gazing wistfully out of windows or at whatever piece of furniture was nearest. They had not discussed whom they would tell first or when—they had been too busy with more pleasant pursuits. Thankfully, only close family remained and they did not mind if their hostess was a little less gregarious than usual.

After dinner, Lydia and Georgiana suggested a walk in the gardens and half the party agreed, including Elizabeth and Darcy. They walked arm in arm through the twilight, falling far behind their party and whispering between themselves. She did not want to ruin the evening, but she knew there was something she must speak of.

"Fitzwilliam?"

"Yes, my heart?"

She smiled and felt heat rushing to her cheeks. It would take some time to become accustomed to his terms of endearment.

"There is something we did not discuss."

"Go ahead, my dear," he said kindly. Whatever she wanted to say, it obviously weighed on her heavily.

"I am a widow," she said haltingly. "I loved my husband. It was not a marriage of convenience. I couldn't, I won't be able to," she stuttered and sighed heavily.

"Elizabeth, what are you trying to tell me?"

"There will still be days when I miss him, when I wish he was here to watch our children grow up. I would not want my husband to be angry with me for that," she said in a small voice, her eyes on the path.

Darcy hesitated a moment, wondering how to respond. "Of course. He was a great man. I was proud to know him, and to be called his friend. That you find me worthy, after having been married to such a man, is a very great compliment," he said solemnly.

Elizabeth felt tears pricking at her eyes and she swallowed thickly. "Thank you, Fitzwilliam. I'm happy to see I underestimated your kindness."

"I know how you felt about him. It does not make me love you less. It makes me respect you more. But Elizabeth," he said, stepping in front of her and taking her hands in his, "I want all of you—every corner of your heart. I am too selfish to share you. If you feel sorrow, so be it, but you must share it with me. I want every joy and pain and triumph. I will be as a father to your children and live in your home and welcome your family. But you," he squeezed her hands, "you Elizabeth, *you* must be mine. And mine alone." He looked at her fiercely, blue eyes burning into green. "If you cannot do that, we should have nothing more to do with each other."

She watched him with wide eyes, her breath coming rapidly and her mouth open in surprise. She felt such a wave of fire in her she nearly lost her breath.

"I will be yours, Fitzwilliam. Yours alone," she whispered.

Anything else she might have said was muted by his lips pressing against hers.

~

Though they had discussed many things, it didn't take Darcy long to realize they had missed an important detail: the wedding date. He would like to wed as soon as possible, but he suspected his lady might require more time. And, of course, there were the children to consider. Would he move into Cressingdon? Would the family move to Pemberley? He suspected that no matter how much he might wish for a brief engagement, there was little likelihood of it coming to pass.

Elizabeth was also wondering about the date. How had they not discussed it yesterday? It seemed as if they had spoken of nearly everything else. She would like to wed as soon as possible—she simply saw no reason to delay. She told herself that her need to be near him constantly was not unduly influencing her decision. But the settlement would need to be drawn up and she suspected it would be a complicated business. She also had to have an awkward conversation with her children. Would they even understand what she was telling them? And where would they live? They had agreed to decide the details later, but immediately following the wedding, they would have to sleep somewhere.

Mr. Darcy must want to take her to Pemberley. She had never seen it and while she was not particularly concerned—she did have Cressingdon, after all—it would be nice if she liked her new husband's home.

She knew everyone would ask for more information than she currently had as soon as they knew of the impending wedding, so it was best to seek out Mr. Darcy and decide upon a few matters first. She knew that once her mother found out there was another wedding in the near future, there would be no peace until she walked down the aisle. She was tempted to let them return to Hertfordshire without telling them her news, but they would not be able to travel back for the wedding and would most likely not forgive her for such a slight.

With a deep breath, she went to find her betrothed.

"Mr. Darcy," she said when she found him on the stairs, "I was just coming to look for you."

"And I you, my lady. We have things to discuss."

She wondered how he managed to make such a simple statement sound so utterly appealing.

"Yes, we do. Shall you join me in the parlor?"

She led him to her favorite room, a west-facing parlor she had redone when she first moved to Cressingdon. As soon as they were inside, he grabbed her arm and pulled her to him, trapping her between himself and the wall. She accepted his kiss hungrily, her hands reaching into his hair. She pulled it gently and he groaned in sweet agony.

He finally released her mouth, resting his forehead against hers and doing nothing but reminding himself to breathe until she opened her eyes and looked at him in that way that always made him feel incoherent and a little desperate. He pulled back and straightened his jacket, then tucked a loose tendril of her hair behind her ear. "We should choose a wedding date. Soon," he whispered.

"That might be wise." She stepped away from him and settled into a chair near the window. "When would you like to wed?"

"As soon as possible."

She laughed. "Mr. Darcy, while I certainly appreciate your enthusiasm, we must be realistic. There are letters to write, lawyers to consult, decisions to be made."

"I've already written to my lawyer. As soon as we have chosen a date, I will send letters to my family. What else needs to be done?"

She laughed at his tone and said, "I had no idea you were so efficient. We have been engaged less than two days and already you are planning for the future."

"Elizabeth, I have been planning this in my mind for a very long time. Now I am merely setting those plans into motion."

She felt heat rushing to her cheeks as he gazed at her fervently and began to think he had the right of it. "I must speak to Alfred. He is in charge of my business matters," she said softly, still watching him watch her.

"Of course. Would you like to marry from Cressingdon?"

"I think it appropriate, don't you? It would be inconvenient to travel to London, and it is uncomfortably warm this time of year. I had hoped for a small celebration. What had you imagined?"

"I would also like something small. Only my family and yours, if it suits you."

"I'm afraid my family is rather large, but they may not all make the journey, especially since they have just been here."

He nodded. "Do you think Lord Devonshire could manage the necessary documents in a few weeks?"

"I do not know. I shall ask him. Where would we go following the wedding?"

"We could go to Pemberley. Or even The Lakes, if you like."

"I would love to see Pemberley, and I have never been to The Lakes," she said with excitement. "We had talked of going, but every summer I was with child and the one time I wasn't, Robert's cousin died and we had to travel to Yorkshire instead."

He smiled. This was something he could give her. It was not easy courting a woman like Lady Asheland. What could he give her that she did not have already? He was pleased such a mutually beneficial arrangement had presented itself.

"So it is settled. We will wed from Cressingdon as soon as we may, and travel to The Lakes," he said decisively. "We can break our journey at Pemberley."

"I will ask Jane if the children may go to Hatfield Hall while we are away. I would like to travel there from The Lakes. I promised Jane I would be with her for her lying in."

"Of course. I will speak to Bingley."

She smiled, feeling a sense of disbelief that all had been worked out so quickly and satisfactorily. "I suppose I should go speak to Alfred now."

"I should speak with him as well," he said. "I should ask for your hand and his blessing."

"Alfred is not my father, Fitzwilliam. I am of age—a widow with three children. You do not need to ask anyone's permission but my own."

"Then let us call it his blessing. I believe he would appreciate being asked," he said convincingly.

"Very well," she conceded.

He rose and extended his hand. "Shall I escort you to Lord Devonshire?"

~

Elizabeth sat before Alfred, wondering how to word what she wanted to say. In the end, she decided bluntness was called for and simply said, "I have decided to marry."

"Oh? And who is the lucky gentleman?"

Alfred wasn't nearly as surprised as she thought he would be and she briefly wondered if he somehow knew what she was going to say.

"Mr. Darcy."

He nodded. "Very well. When will you wed?"

"Alfred!" she cried. "Why are you not more surprised?"

He chuckled. "Forgive me, my dear, but you are not as circumspect as you think you are. Mr. Darcy has been obvious in his attentions and it was clear to anyone who knew you that you were not immune to him."

Elizabeth sighed. "Perhaps I shouldn't even make an announcement, since everyone seems to know already."

He laughed again, more loudly this time. "Elizabeth, you are a treasure! What will we do without your humor?"

"You are not losing me, Alfred. We will still spend a great deal of time here, especially in the beginning. Mr. Darcy will not insist we live at Pemberley until I bear a son."

His brows rose. "Are you sure of that? Most men have a great deal of pride in their family seat, especially one such as Pemberley."

"You were friends with Mr. Darcy's father, were you not?" she asked, unwilling to discuss her living arrangements.

"Yes. He was slightly older than I was, but we knew each other at Cambridge. He was a good man, very affable—always generous to the poor."

Elizabeth nodded. "Is Pemberley very beautiful?"

"It is. It is a large estate, nearly the size of Cressingdon. There may even be enough walking paths to satisfy you!"

She laughed with him and then asked if he would arrange her settlement and other business matters. Once she had his agreement, she sought out her sister.

~

While Elizabeth was speaking to her sister, Mr. Darcy was meeting with his. He asked her to join him for a walk in the garden and they strolled arm in arm, Georgiana quietly telling her brother of the plans she was making with Lydia and the ribbons she had purchased for Violet's birthday. He listened to her lilting voice with a smile on his face.

"I have something to tell you, sweetling," he said. "I am to be married."

"You are?" Georgiana gaped at him. "To Lady Asheland?"

"Yes. You like her, do you not?"

"Yes, of course I like her. She has been very kind to me." She looked down and asked quietly. "Where will you live?"

"We thought we would divide our time between here and Pemberley, and of course London. Robert John will inherit the estate, he should live here at least some of the year. Once he goes away to school, we will likely spend more time at Pemberley, though that is some years in the future."

She nodded, her eyes still on the ground.

He stopped walking and turned towards her. "Georgie, are you unhappy about my marriage?" he asked warily.

"No! I know you care for Lady Asheland and it is obvious she cares a great deal for you."

He couldn't help the swell of happiness her words caused. But Georgiana was clearly upset. "What troubles you, dearest?"

"Will I live with Lady Catherine or Lord Matlock?" she asked quietly.

"What? Why would you live with either of them? Georgiana," he tipped her chin up so he could see her face, "do you not wish to live with me any longer?"

She sniffled. "No, of course not. But you will be newly married and Lady Asheland will not wish to share you with a younger sister."

He smiled kindly at her. "Georgie, I am already sharing Lady Asheland with three small children. Surely you do not think you are more troublesome than they are," he teased. She did not look cheered and he looked at her seriously. "You are my blood. Your home is with me."

"Truly?" she asked tremulously.

"Always."

~

Elizabeth sat with Jane in her private parlor and told her sister she had decided to marry Mr. Darcy. He had pursued her for some time, and she felt she could trust him because of their long acquaintance and his friendship with Bingley.

Jane stared at her sister silently for some time, then said, "I don't know what to say! I am shocked! I had no idea that you were warming to Mr. Darcy."

"Truly?"

Jane shook her head. "I had hoped you would, and I occasionally thought you were friendly. There was some flirtation, but you often flirt, so I thought nothing of it."

"I do not flirt!"

Jane shot her a look. "You have always enjoyed a little raillery, Lizzy. It is in your nature. In truth, I was glad to see you teasing again. Your humor has been absent for some time."

"Since Robert's death, you mean. You may say it, Jane. He will not be any more dead if you do."

Jane shook her head. "Lizzy, I am happy for you. But are you certain you feel for Mr. Darcy what you ought? Do you care for him? Truly?"

Elizabeth looked down and traced her fingers over her skirt. "I care for him, Jane. I am well on my way to being in love with him."

"Then I must congratulate you. Mr. Darcy is a good man. You will be very happy together."

Elizabeth smiled and thanked her, then sought out her aunt.

~

Her Aunt Gardiner had a similar reaction when she told her later that day.

"Mr. Darcy? Truly?"

"Oh, dear! If you and Jane do not believe me, how will I tell mama and papa?" she cried in amusement.

Mrs. Gardiner laughed. "I believe you, dear. I was merely surprised. It has been clear Mr. Darcy is in love with you but I thought you would put him off a while longer before you gave in and accepted him."

Elizabeth gasped. "Did you truly think I would do such a thing? I am not the sort of lady to torment a respectable man!"

"No, but you are a lady who has lost a beloved husband and it is not strange to think it might be difficult for you to receive another man in his stead."

Elizabeth sighed. "I loved Robert, truly loved him. But I was so young. A girl, really. As I grew up I loved him more, but I sometimes wonder what it would have been like had we met each other when I was older," she said thoughtfully.

"You will never know. Perhaps it would have been just the same. Or perhaps you would have behaved differently after being out longer in society. Perhaps Asheland would have been lonely and you would have been desperate to get away from Longbourn. It will have to remain a mystery."

Elizabeth nodded. "It is different, with Mr. Darcy. I am full grown now. I do not view the world in the same way as I did when I married Robert. Things feel very… different this time."

"That is only natural. You were eighteen when you married Robert. You are four and twenty now." She looked at Elizabeth sternly. "You must not compare them. They are different men and will each love you differently. Comparing them will only drive you to distraction."

"I know you are correct. I will consider each man in his own right," agreed Elizabeth.

"And regardless of how much you loved Robert, the sad truth is that he is not here, and other gentlemen are. If

Mr. Darcy wants to marry you, and you care for him and believe you could be happy together, do not let silly fears restrain you. You must live life, Elizabeth."

"I couldn't agree with you more."

~

The conversation Elizabeth was dreading the most was with her children. She had no idea what to say to them or how to explain it in a way that they would understand. In the end, she decided to just begin and hope the words would come to her.

She went to the nursery, dismissed Molly, and sat down with Bennet. He was building a tower with blocks and she began building one next to him. She called Robbie and Violet to her and told them she had some important news for them.

"Mama is going to be married." Three blank faces looked back at her and she would have laughed had she not felt so wretched. "Do you remember Mr. Darcy? He took tea with you a few days ago."

Robbie said he remembered, of course, and Violet nodded her head.

"Mr. Darcy and I will be married soon. That means we will go to the church and have a ceremony, and afterward we will live together and be husband and wife."

The children continued playing, a simple, "All right, mama," in Violet's high voice was all she heard from them.

"Will you tie this ribbon on my doll's hair? It came undone." Violet thrust a doll and a yellow ribbon into her hands and she mechanically tied it.

"So Mr. Darcy will live with us. All the time. Sometimes we will live here at Cressingdon, or we may be in Town like we were this spring, or we will stay at Mr.

Darcy's home. It's called Pemberley," she said brightly, smiling at them.

"Pempemley," said Bennet loudly. Then he knocked over his tower of blocks and squealed with glee as they tumbled to the floor.

Elizabeth looked at them with a frown. She didn't know what else to say to explain to them what was happening, and they didn't seem upset. They didn't seem to care at all! She was mildly disappointed—it was a momentous occasion and her children were the most important people in her life. But she recognized that they were too young to realize how much was changing and that it was probably a blessing in disguise. In this way they would not resent Mr. Darcy for stealing their mother's attention or feel that anyone was trying to replace their father as they might have done had they been older.

"After the wedding, I will go on a trip with Mr. Darcy, and you will go to Aunt Jane's house with Molly. Aunt Lydia will be there, and Charlie and Jenny. Aunt Gardiner and the children will be there, too. And maybe even Miss Georgiana."

"Miss Georgie?" asked Violet, suddenly interested.

Violet had taken an instant liking to Georgiana when they met. Lydia called her Georgie and Violet copied her aunt. Georgiana liked it and refused to let anyone correct the child.

"Yes, would you like that?"

Violet nodded her head vigorously and Elizabeth sighed in relief. All would be well.

~

Darcy tied his horse to a branch and entered the churchyard, quickly making his way through the creaking gate to the graves at the back. He stopped in front of Lord Asheland's grave and removed his hat. Darcy was not a superstitious man, but Lord Asheland had been a friend and he thought it only right that he pay his respects.

He took a deep breath and began.

"I do not know what to say." He hesitated. "I am marrying Elizabeth. That is, Lady Asheland," he added quickly. "She is, she is everything I ever wanted," he said quietly. "I see why you were willing to defy society to have her." He looked down and tapped his hat on his leg. "I cannot imagine…leaving her…losing her. That must have been… impossible." He rolled a small rock beneath his boot. "I wanted to tell you that she will be well looked after. She will want for nothing."

He turned his hat in his hands. "Young Robert John is a credit to you. I have no doubt he will grow into a fine man. You would be proud. Lady Violet is as delightful as her mother. Her eyes sparkle when she laughs, just like Elizabeth's," he said with a fond smile. "Bennet is shy, but I believe I understand him." He paused for a minute, thinking on what he should say.

"I am taking Robbie fishing tomorrow. Bennet wanted to come but Elizabeth thought it best that we go on our own. She thinks Robbie admires me," he said with a slight flush. "He is a fine boy. Intelligent, kind. He looks like you." Darcy glanced to the sky, then back at the silent headstone. "I cannot imagine my son being raised by another man. It would be… insupportable." He squared his shoulders. "You have my word that I will be a good father to your children. I will look after them and guide them to the best of my abilities. And I will not insist they forget you. I will ensure Robert John is proud of his heritage. I would never deny him that. You have my word as a gentleman."

He took a deep breath. "One other thing we should discuss." He looked at Robert's name on the headstone. "I know you loved Elizabeth, and she loved you in return. But she is mine now," he said solemnly. He placed his hat on his head and straightened. "I'm glad we understand each other." He bowed slightly and left the churchyard.

CHAPTER 21

Elizabeth peeked out of her room and looked around. All was quiet. There were no footmen about and she could barely see by the moonlight coming through the window at the end of the corridor. She tiptoed away from the apartments where her guests were sleeping and slipped up the back stairwell. Once on the deserted third floor, she quickly rushed across the north wing and paused when she reached the main stairwell, a grand affair that reached four floors. Hearing nothing, she tiptoed across the hall, making sure to stay in the shadows, until she reached the south wing. Nearly all her guests had gone home and the rooms were empty. She slipped down the stairs at the end of the corridor and back onto the second floor, now in the guest wing. Some of these rooms were occupied and she crept along quietly, listening for sounds of movement. All was silent. She counted the doors until she reached the green bedchamber.

"What are you doing, Lizzy?"

She jumped a foot in the air and brought a hand to her chest. "John! You scared me!"

He smirked in the moonlight and stepped closer. "Going on a call?"

She gave him a nasty look. "No. I was merely checking on something."

He raised his brows. "Hm. Is that so? And what are you wearing under your wrapper?"

She gasped and clutched it closer to her. "I beg your pardon!" she cried.

He laughed. "You do not fool me, Lizzy. I can see the hem of your gown." He looked down and she followed his gaze. The ruffled skirt of her morning dress—put on so she might have something to wear the next day—was clearly visible.

She clenched her teeth and exhaled forcibly. "This is my home. I may go where I like."

"Oh, in that case, please allow me to escort you." He gallantly extended his arm and she took it grudgingly. "Tell me, Lizzy, do you often go on nighttime rambles in inappropriate clothes?" he asked as they began walking toward her room.

"That is Lady Asheland to you, *Johnny*," she said haughtily.

Her cousin only laughed as they walked away.

Shortly after they left the corridor, Mr. Darcy poked his head out of the green bedchamber. He could have sworn he'd heard voices.

~

Elizabeth spent the next day thinking of ways to be alone with Mr. Darcy. She wouldn't have thought it would be so difficult. They were both adults, there were no chaperones, and she was a widow living in her own home. But because the wedding was so near, her close family had stayed longer than they had originally planned in order to attend. Thus the Bingleys, Bennets, and Gardiners, her sister Lydia and his sister Georgiana, Lord and Lady Devonshire, their daughter Marianne and her husband, and their sons Lord Epworth (known to Elizabeth as Meddlesome John) and Lord George Downing, were all staying at the house.

She was happy to have them, and the children were certainly enjoying being with their relations, but it did make clandestine meetings more difficult to achieve.

After much deliberation, she realized her error. She had attempted to make her way to Mr. Darcy's room. It was only natural she had run into John. His room was near to Mr. Darcy's, as were his brother and sister's as well as Lydia and Georgiana's adjoined chambers. Elizabeth's own room was out of the question. Not only was it near the rooms her parents and sisters were staying in, but it was also the same room she had shared with Robert. Having a lover in her husband's bedchamber was insupportable— she couldn't think of it.

Finally, she came upon a solution. The third floor was now unoccupied and boasted a great number of comfortable bedchambers. She herself had never stayed in one, but the guests had never complained. In fact, there was one in particular that she had always favored. It was decorated in soft colors that reminded her of spring and had a lovely view of the lake in the distance. It would be the perfect location.

She sent Mr. Darcy a note the next day. In it, she merely listed directions to the room and a time late that evening. She never wondered if he would be offended by her suggestion until she was preparing for bed, then she quickly dismissed the thought. They would be married in less than a month, and he had spent the last weeks stealing kisses whenever he could and looking at her with such naked desire she blushed thinking about it.

She had asked Watson, her maid, to personally prepare the room for use. She then took a gown and some basic supplies for the morning and stored them in the dressing room. She locked the chamber behind her. Only Mrs. Hobbs had another key and the housekeeper had no reason to go there. They would be assured privacy, and then she could spend the night there and ready herself in the morning without having to creep back to her room at the break of dawn.

She was rather proud of herself for her ingenuity.

She slipped a dressing gown over her plain white nightshift—under which was a prettier nightgown in the event she needed to feel more alluring—and stepped into the hall. All was quiet and her cousin John was on the other side of the floor in another wing. She crept along the dark corridor to the back staircase as she had done the night before. Once she was on the third floor, she made her way swiftly to the room she had chosen and unlocked the door. The other benefit of this room, besides its comfort and seclusion, was that the room beneath was her parlor and sure to be empty in the night. Satisfied with her preparations so far, she lit a candle on the far wall and removed her dressing gown. She draped it over the back of a chair and released her hair from its braid. She wondered if she should change her nightgown.

Deciding that she had come this far, what was one step further, she slipped off her linen nightshift and put her dressing gown back on over her silk nightgown. Darcy had complimented her each time she wore green, so she had chosen this nightgown with him in mind. She thought he would like the warm color, and hoped he liked the daring cut even more.

She opened the window for some fresh air. It had been a warm August, but the nights were cool and a breeze wafted into the room.

As she waited for her betrothed, she reflected on how different she felt from what she had expected. She had thought the first time she spent the night with another man would be difficult and uncomfortable, maybe even frightening. But she felt nothing but anticipation. She was a little nervous, of course, but it was a good kind of nervous—the kind of excitement that precedes something momentous.

She supposed she could have waited until the wedding, and while she had a litany of reasons prepared in the unlikely event that she had to defend herself to her family (namely Jane or her Aunt Gardiner), the truth of it was that she simply did not want to wait. She had been alone for two and a half long years, and she wanted to feel the man she loved embracing her in passion. She wanted to feel his heart beating against hers, their heated skin pressed together as they chased their pleasure.

That was the heart of the matter. She loved Mr. Darcy, and she wanted to show him that in the best way she knew how. It was as simple as that.

Her love for him had surprised her in its intensity. She thought she was familiar with the feeling; after all, she had been in love before. But what she felt for Mr. Darcy was so different from what she had felt for Robert that the two were hardly comparable.

She had not loved Robert when she accepted him. Rather, she knew that she *could* love him. He was a dear friend that she knew she could be happy with; she respected and esteemed him. She had felt attraction, and the knowledge that he loved her was very compelling. He had been so wholly devoted to her, to their marriage and their family, that she could not help but be moved by his tenderness and care. By the time they said their vows, she was able to promise to love him with honesty and great joy.

When she accepted Mr. Darcy, she had not loved him completely, though she knew she was vastly approaching the ledge over which there would be no return. She cared for him and enjoyed his company; she respected and liked him. She was attracted to him. She knew that courtship and marriage could do much to strengthen the bond between a man and a woman, and she had expected it to take its natural course over their betrothal; when she said her vows, she would mean them with all her heart.

She could not have been more wrong. She was not growing in respect and love for Mr. Darcy.

She was consumed by it.

Every action, every word, every morning spent riding with him and afternoon taking tea with the children only proved to her that he was the man, in disposition and talents, most suited to her. She could not adequately describe her feelings, but she felt herself so much more grown up than the first time she had loved, so much more aware of what she wanted and the place she wished to occupy in the world. This increased awareness of herself, of her own wishes and desires, changed how she felt about everyone else—especially the men she loved.

She had promised her aunt she would not compare the two men in her life, and she tried not to, but she could not help but note that *she* was not the same eighteen-year-old girl that had fallen in love the first time. If she herself was not the same, how could she expect her experiences to be the same?

What she felt for Robert was brought on by what he had felt for her. Had he never loved her and pursued her, she may never have come to feel more for him than friendship. It did not lessen the love she felt for him, but it did change its composition.

While Mr. Darcy had similarly made his feelings known before she was aware of her own, he had not tenderly ushered her into affection. He had challenged her, angered her, and thoroughly perplexed her until she found herself knee-deep in feelings she could not understand. He had awakened a fire in her she did not know she possessed. His courtship had been so full of missteps, and yet she had seen his heart, in all its many facets, and had come to desire a life with him.

She would not say she loved him any more than she had loved Robert. It felt wrong to even think it, and it wasn't true, anyhow. She simply felt differently.

She could not compare them, not truly. It was like comparing a fish in the stream to a bird in the sky. But oh, how she was flying!

In some ways, her love for Mr. Darcy felt selfish to her—he was something that she wanted and she decided to let herself have him. But she had it on good authority that the gentleman did not mind that he was her gift to herself. He believed wholeheartedly in her goodness, even more than she did. She knew she could be catty and difficult at times. She could be stubborn and contrary. And yet, he continued to love her. She was content to allow him to do so.

She looked up from her reverie when she saw the door open. Quietly, Mr. Darcy stepped into the room and closed the door behind him. She stood from her seat by the window and moved towards him. He took a few more steps into the room and stopped, his expression grave and somehow happy at the same time.

"Elizabeth, I have never seen you more beautiful."

She smiled and stepped closer to him. "So you were not offended by my suggestion to meet here?"

"Not at all! I was coming close to suggesting it myself, but I thought you might be uncomfortable with your family in the house."

"I am not uncomfortable." She smiled and closed the distance between them until she stood immediately before him, daring him to reach out and touch her.

He did not disappoint.

~

Darcy was overwhelmed. From the first time she had told him she cared for him to the moment he opened her note and understood her intentions, he had been going from elation to elation, hopping wildly from one uncontainable joy to another. He had not known he could be so happy. But as his betrothed would say, just because it is unexpected does not mean it is unwelcome. He was so very pleased with her, he sometimes felt ridiculous with it.

She was so very lovely, so teasing and alluring and delightful. She challenged his mind and made him view the world differently than he had before. She brought out greater kindness and compassion in him than anyone ever had, and he felt himself better for being near her.

And when she loved him, Lord, when she loved him! He had never experienced anything like it. Being so close to her, feeling so deeply for her—it had been indescribable.

She had given him a perfect memory, one that he would treasure all his days. He would never forget hearing her say she loved him. He could hear her voice in his mind as he thought about it, picture her face when he untied her dressing gown and slipped it from her shoulders. "I love you, Fitzwilliam," she had said. Simple. Unadorned. With no qualifying statements or flowery words.

He was undone. Her trust, her respect, her love, was the greatest gift he had ever received. He couldn't help but think, as he was drifting off to sleep with his love in his arms, that all the difficulty and pain and doubt had made victory that much sweeter.

She was worth every bit of it. And he would do it all again to earn her love.

~

The next morning, Elizabeth awoke with a lazy smile on her face. She hadn't slept so well in ages. Her body had a certain soreness accompanied by a warm feeling of vitality she had not felt in some time.

Darcy burrowed his nose into the back of her neck and pressed her closer to his body. She smiled when she felt him edge his knees behind hers until they were pressed together from ankle to chin.

How very dearly she loved him! And what a great relief it had been to finally show him.

He had never complained to her, but she thought it might be odd for him, to be at Cressingdon, surrounded by reminders of her first husband and his great and powerful family. He would likely prefer to be at Pemberley, but he stayed because he wanted to be near her. He knew the children felt most comfortable at home and he was kindly allowing them to become accustomed to his presence in a familiar place.

He was a good man. And he would be her husband. She couldn't help the self-satisfied smile that took over her face. How could a country girl from Hertfordshire be so lucky?

~

At breakfast, Elizabeth slathered butter on her bread with a satisfied smile.

"What are you so happy about this morning, Lizzy?" asked Jane as she took a seat near her sister.

She sighed. "You were right, Jane. It feels so very good to love again."

Elizabeth's smile was positively post-coital and Jane flushed in embarrassment.

"Lizzy!" she reprimanded weakly. Then, quietly so the servants couldn't hear her, "It's about time you listened to me."

Elizabeth smiled wickedly. "Had I known your advice was so good I should have followed it sooner."

CHAPTER 22

Though she knew the day would come, Elizabeth was not happy when Darcy told her he must return to Pemberley. The wedding was in a fortnight and he had some estate business to see to before the ceremony. When she pouted prettily over missing him, he tweaked her nose and told her that if she wanted his undivided attention after they were wed, he must accomplish some things before their wedding.

After discussing a somewhat complicated plan for the next few months, it was decided that Elizabeth and the children would go to Pemberley for a visit before the wedding. The children could see the new nursery and Elizabeth could order any changes she wished done before the children moved in. They would return to Cressingdon for the ceremony, and the next day she and Darcy would leave for their wedding trip to The Lakes. The children, Georgiana, and Lydia would travel to Hatfield Hall with the Bingleys. Mr. and Mrs. Darcy would join them there after their trip, in time for Jane's lying in.

If all went according to plan, they would move the children into Pemberley after Jane was recovered. They would likely bring Charlie and possibly young Jenny with them to allow Jane and Charles uninterrupted time with their newest son or daughter. They had yet to decide when they would return to Cressingdon.

The day before Darcy was due to leave, he and Elizabeth took a walk in the garden.

"I was wondering," he said hesitantly.

"Yes?"

"What do you think of my taking Robert John with me tomorrow?"

She looked at him with a blank expression.

"You will follow in three days with Bennet and Violet. He would not be parted from you for long."

She continued to stare at him with wide eyes.

"It would give us an opportunity to get to know one another better. He is already comfortable with my presence. His nurse could come as well." He looked at her hopefully and began to tug on his cuffs when she did not immediately respond.

"You wish to take Robbie with you?" she finally said.

"Yes."

"Tomorrow?"

"Yes."

She took a deep breath and walked ahead a few paces. He wanted to take her child with him. Without her. There was a part of her, in the back of her mind, that knew her hesitation was ridiculous. But the greater part of her was anxiously considering the details. What if Robbie missed her? What if he became upset in a new place without his mama? What if he cried and Darcy did not know what to do with him?

"Elizabeth," said Darcy behind her. He put his hands on her shoulders and turned her to face him. "We are soon to be a family. The children will occasionally be with me when you are not there. We must become accustomed to it eventually," he said reasonably.

She sighed and nodded. "I will ask Robbie if he wishes to go."

~

To Elizabeth's surprise and Darcy's pleasure, Robbie did want to go. He was thrilled with the idea of going

314

somewhere on his own, without his brother or sister, and seeing Pemberley before even his mother saw it. Mr. Darcy had told him much about it and he could not wait to see it for himself.

Elizabeth supervised the packing of his things and insisted Molly, the nurse who had been with them since Robbie's birth, accompany them. Robbie was given strict instructions to be a good boy and not run in the house and to listen to Mr. Darcy and Molly the entire time he would be gone. She told him no fewer than four times that she would be there in three days and not to worry for her.

Robbie was not concerned.

She accompanied her son and betrothed to the carriage early in the morning and kissed them both goodbye, pretending she was happy about her son driving farther and farther away from her. When the carriage disappeared over the hill, she pushed down the pain in her heart and went to meet with Mrs. Hobbs. What she needed was a good distraction.

~

Darcy felt so many emotions he didn't know which to focus on first. He was excited for what he considered his first venture into fatherhood. He was also nervous about the same. What if he made some horrible mistake? He had never spent more than a few minutes with a boy Robbie's age, and he was sure Georgiana, the only small child he had spent considerable time with, was an entirely different creature. She was docile and sweet and shy. Robbie was garrulous and adventurous.

Thankfully, before Darcy had to think of a conversation appropriate to have with a young boy while a nurse and valet listened in, Robbie fell asleep in the carriage. His head fell against Darcy, as if he had slept next to him his entire life, and Darcy felt unexpectedly touched.

When they finally arrived at Pemberley, Robbie had a million questions for Darcy. How large was the house? Who had built it? Had it been there a very long time? Were there any halls he was allowed to run in? Mama had said his pony was being brought to Pemberley along with her mare. When would they arrive? Was he allowed to ride around the lake? Did they have plenty of apples for his pony? His pony preferred apples to carrots, though carrots would do if no apples could be had.

The questions went on and on until Darcy's head was spinning. He wondered why he had ever worried over what they would discuss.

~

The first morning, Darcy gave his charge a tour of the house. He let him run in the Long Gallery if Robbie promised to tell no one and only run there when Darcy was with him. Robbie agreed, of course, and nearly an hour was spent happily running back and forth, waving at the severe expressions on the faces of Darcy ancestors that adorned the walls. Darcy was vastly entertained.

Robbie was confused when the servants called him my lord. Everyone at home called him Robbie or Master Robert. Darcy told him that if he did not like it, he would tell the servants to refer to him as Master Robert. Robbie said that would be better, because he liked his name. Darcy just smiled at his reasoning and said he would inform the butler immediately.

The second day of Robbie's visit, Darcy took him on a tour of the estate. Robbie was especially enamored of the sheep in the north pasture. He tried to name them all, but gave up when the sheep continued to move about and he ended up with three separate sheep named Gertrude. He was then introduced to the animals in the farmyard and after asking very nicely, he was permitted to help feed the chickens and some goats he found particularly amusing. They had goats at Cressingdon, but their goats were white and these were black, something the five-year-old found endlessly fascinating. Who knew goats came in more than one color?

The third day Darcy took him fishing. They took tackle and a hamper filled with food and rode to a stream on the far east side of the estate. They planned to be home well before dinner because Elizabeth, Violet, and Bennet were arriving that afternoon.

They spent the day lounging on the banks of the stream, occasionally chatting, but mostly sitting quietly.

"Uncle Darcy?" asked Robert.

"Yes, Robbie?"

"How did you become my uncle?"

Darcy blinked. "Uh, well, I, uh, I am not your uncle, not truly."

"You are not?"

"No."

"Then why do I call you Uncle Darcy?" asked Robbie, looking perplexed.

"Your cousin Charlie calls me Uncle Darcy. I imagine you got it from him, though I am not truly his uncle either." At Robbie's confused expression, he explained further. "Your Uncle Charles is my very good friend. He is your uncle because he is married to your Aunt Jane, who is your mother's sister." Robbie nodded, as if this were common information. "I am Charlie's godfather and I spend a great deal of time with Bingley, your Uncle Charles, so his children call me uncle."

"But you are not their uncle?"

"No, I haven't been. But I will be their uncle when I marry your mother, who is their aunt."

"If you marry mama, how you can be my uncle? Uncles and mothers are not married to each other."

Darcy could not fault the boy's logic and stared at his fishing line for several minutes without answering.

"Would you like to call me something else?" he asked softly.

"What would I call you?" asked Robbie.

Darcy thought for a moment. Fitzwilliam was rather a mouthful for such a small child, and whatever Robbie called him, Violet and Bennet would likely call him the same. He couldn't imagine two-year-old Bennet being able to say such a word. They could call him Fitz, but he had always hated it. Darcy was what most of his friends called him, but it seemed odd for a child to call their stepfather by his surname. Perhaps uncle wasn't such a bad idea?

"I will be your stepfather in little more than a week," he said awkwardly, his eyes on the stream.

"Shall I call you stepfather?" asked Robbie. His distaste for the name was obvious.

"Or you could call me papa, if you would like," Darcy said quietly.

"Papa," said Robbie, testing out the word. "I should like to have a papa," he said simply.

Darcy looked towards the boy who was smiling at him widely, his toffee-colored eyes bright and gleaming.

"Very well, I will be your papa," he said thickly.

~

Elizabeth sat forward in the carriage, anxiously watching out the window. The house would appear any moment now, she was sure of it. Bennet and Violet were just waking up from their travel-induced nap and they began pointing out the windows and exclaiming about what they saw.

Finally, they pulled up in front of a beautiful stone home and Elizabeth breathed a sigh of relief. She had been prepared to like his home for Darcy's sake, but she was happy she would not have to convince herself of its merits. The butler and housekeeper were outside to greet them, and footmen poured onto the drive to unload their trunks.

Elizabeth looked left and right, and up the steps leading to the main door. There was no sign of her betrothed or her son.

"Pardon me, my lady. The master has not returned from his excursion with the young lord," said the butler.

Elizabeth thanked him for the information and said, "You must be Greaves. Mr. Darcy has told me much about you."

The butler bowed and Elizbaeth silently told herself that she would take it as a personal challenge to make the stiff man smile.

She turned to the housekeeper, who again apologized that no one was there to greet her. She was a cheery looking woman called Mrs. Reynolds and Elizabeth immediately liked her. Elizabeth smiled and told her it was of no great concern; she was sure Mr. Darcy and her son would arrive soon enough. If she could just be shown to the nursery so she could begin settling in the children, she would be appreciative. The housekeeper looked relieved and began to lead her inside.

Before she got halfway up the wide stone steps, Bennet and Violet began giggling behind her. She followed their gazes and saw a dripping wet Mr. Darcy and Robbie walking toward them. Robbie was smiling ear to ear; Darcy was scowling. Elizabeth brought her hand to her mouth to stifle her laugh.

"Have you two gentlemen gone swimming?" she asked playfully.

"Master Robert saw a frog in the stream and tried to catch it," said Darcy flatly.

"Let me guess. He was unsuccessful and you had to wade in and retrieve him?"

"No. He was successful. But his hands were occupied holding the frog, so he couldn't get himself out."

Elizabeth laughed. "And he refused to put her down?"

Darcy nodded grimly and tapped his wet hat on his leg.

"Mama! Look! I named her Georgie!" Robbie had produced a frog from behind his back and was happily showing it to his sister and brother.

"I'm sure Georgiana will appreciate having a namesake. Come inside, dear. Let's get you dry."

Darcy followed her in and she stopped herself from saying she had been talking to her son. Her smile, however, was impossible to stifle.

~

Pemberley was lovely. The paths were long and winding; the gardens were natural but not overgrown. The house was elegant without being ostentatious, and the neighbors were friendly without being obsequious. The local parson was very kind and the servants were efficient.

Elizabeth was exceedingly pleased with her new home.

They spent their days exploring the grounds and attending the children, and their nights sneaking between the master's chambers and her room in the guest wing.

The wedding was only three days away now and they were preparing to return to Cressingdon for the ceremony.

"How long does it take to ride to Cressingdon?" Elizabeth asked one evening.

"From here?" replied Darcy.

"Yes."

"Depending on the rider and mount, half a day, perhaps less. Why do you ask? Are you planning a ride, my love?" he teased.

She smiled and replied, "Would you be upset if we didn't leave?"

"What do you mean?"

"Could we have the wedding here? You have a special license, do you not?"

"Yes, I do," he said, curious.

"Then we may wed from anywhere. Your Darcy relations, and Kitty, are only half a day's drive. They are nearer to here than Cressingdon."

"True."

"Everyone of my family who plans to attend is already at Cressingdon. It wouldn't be difficult for them to come here. I'm sure my mother would love to see it, and obviously Georgiana would be coming home."

He began to look interested as he said, "We could send a rider at first light. He would arrive shortly after breakfast."

She looked at him with excitement in her eyes. "I'll write the letter now."

Elizabeth was halfway through her letter to her family, asking them to travel to Pemberley, when she realized there was a problem. A nearly eight-months pregnant problem.

"Jane," she said despondently.

He looked at her with confusion until he recalled how close his sister-to-be was to her confinement.

"I cannot ask her to make another journey so close to her lying in. She would be utterly miserable, and all for a whim of mine. She has already stayed longer than she planned. *And* she has agreed to take the children while we go to The Lakes. I cannot ask it of her. It would be too selfish of me."

321

"Perhaps it is best if we keep to our original plan," he said delicately.

"Yes, of course. It would be difficult for your staff as well, to suddenly ready the house for more than a dozen visitors and prepare a wedding breakfast. I don't know what I was thinking," she said lightly, trying to cover her embarrassment at making such a foolish suggestion.

She tried to smile, but he could see the disappointment in her features. He moved to sit beside her. "Dearest, it pleases me greatly that you would want to marry at Pemberley."

"It does?" she said in a small voice.

"It does. You wouldn't suggest it if you didn't feel at home here."

Her mouth opened in surprise. After a few minutes of looking at him, she said, "I suppose I do. Sometimes, I think you know me better than I know myself, Fitzwilliam."

~

The return trip to Cressingdon was easily accomplished and before she knew it, Elizabeth was putting on her wedding gown and walking to Cressingdon's small chapel. The chapel was rarely used, but she had thought the small stone structure with its stained-glass windows would be perfect for their ceremony. And of course it had the added inducement of not having her first husband buried outside it.

She wouldn't remember the oft-heard words or the slightly wheezy voice of the vicar. But she knew she would never forget the look on Fitzwilliam's face when she said her vows, or how his voice sounded deep and rich and sure when he slid the ring on her finger, or the satisfied smile that overtook his face when the vicar pronounced them man and wife.

The breakfast was just as forgettable, though she knew it was elegantly prepared. Her mother went on and on about the quality of the food and the expensive wine. Elizabeth noticed none of it. But she distinctly remembered when Fitzwilliam met her eyes across the room and made his way to her, bending to whisper in her ear that they would need to leave soon if they wanted to arrive before nightfall.

She changed into her traveling clothes, kissed her family goodbye, and was assured by Charles that he would watch over her children as if they were his own. Georgiana and Lydia were given strict instructions to assist Jane in any way they could and to keep the children occupied when they wanted someone beyond their nurses. Fitzwilliam generously promised the two Talbot family nurses a sizeable gift for keeping the children as far from Jane as possible. Elizabeth laughed at his methods, then told the nurses something similar after he had walked away. She would rest easier knowing her children were well looked after and her sister was not unduly inconvenienced.

Finally, after a tearful goodbye with Violet and a long hug from Bennet—she refused to allow him to be peeled from her, she insisted he would let go when he was ready—the Darcys boarded the carriage and settled in for the drive to Pemberley.

It felt right somehow, for them to spend their wedding night in their new home. No other place would be as perfect, as momentous.

Elizabeth reached out for Darcy's hand and squeezed it in hers. "Take me home, husband."

EPILOGUE

October 1820

"I think it will be a boy," said Bennet.

"Papa says it will be a girl," said Violet.

"I want a brother!" cried Henry.

"You have three brothers!" retorted Violet.

"I want another brother! Richard wants a brother, too," declared Henry.

"Richard does not. Do you Richard?" She looked at her youngest brother and he looked back at her with wide green eyes, clutching a toy dog to his chest. "See, he does not want a brother," said Violet in her best big-sister voice.

"He did not say that!" cried Bennet indignantly.

"Who did not say what?" came a deep voice from the doorway.

"Papa!" cried Henry. He quickly scrambled up from the floor and wrapped his arms around Darcy's legs.

"Papa," said Violet, looking very put upon, "Bennet says the babe will be a boy, but I told him you said it would be a girl."

Darcy looked alarmed for a moment as four pairs of eyes watched him steadily. "We do not know what the babe will be. But boy or girl, you will be kind to your new brother or sister," he said authoritatively. The children nodded and he reached down to pick up two-year-old Richard. "Would you like to walk around the lake with mama?" he asked.

Richard nodded silently and burrowed his head into his father's neck. Darcy smiled and corralled the children out the door and downstairs to meet their mother.

324

"I can't believe we will have six children!" she said as they ambled around the lake, the children running ahead with their nurse.

"How are you feeling today?" he asked. She had been especially tired of late, more so than she had been with her last two pregnancies, and he wondered if her body was tiring of bearing a child every two years.

"I am tired, but I always am these days." She smiled wanly and put a hand to her protruding belly. "Just a few more weeks now. And Robbie will be home tomorrow. I cannot wait to see him."

"Neither can I," said her husband.

Darcy put a hand to her belly for a moment and felt his babe kick against his palm. He smiled. He would never tire of that sensation. But he was worried for Elizabeth. She looked pale and swollen, and she did not seem to be carrying this babe as easily as she had the others. He would be sure to plan a trip to the seaside after she was churched. Or perhaps they could return to The Lakes. She always loved visiting there.

~

"Fitzwilliam! Where is he? I need him!"

"He will be here soon, Lizzy. He is on the way," soothed Jane.

"Keep breathing, sister," soothed Kitty.

Elizabeth moaned and clutched the bedpost, waiting for her pains to pass. The midwife took her arm and encouraged her to walk. Kitty took her other arm and between the two of them, they led her around the room twice before she was once again panting and nearly doubled over.

"Where is he?" she cried again, tears streaming down her face.

"I am here, my love," came a deep voice from the doorway.

"Fitzwilliam!"

He quickly removed his jacket and waistcoat and passed them to the maid, then moved to stand behind Elizabeth, linking his arms beneath hers and supporting her weight. "There now, my love, I wouldn't miss my daughter's birth."

She squeezed her eyes shut as another pain gripped her. When it had passed, she said, "You are so sure it is not a boy. Just because the last two were sons, does not mean," pant, "this one shall be a daughter."

He brushed her hair from her forehead and walked with her a few steps as the midwife directed. "Poor Violet is outnumbered four to one. She needs a sister."

Elizabeth was breathing more heavily now, her pains coming one after another with little reprieve. He looked to Jane with a quizzical expression, and quietly asked if all was well. Was the babe not early? Jane looked at him solemnly and said he should prepare himself. Darcy paled and swallowed, then nodded and returned his attention to his wife.

"It is nearly time," said the midwife soothingly. "That's it, Mrs. Darcy. You're nearly there. Just a little while longer."

Elizabeth released a high-pitched whine that tapered off into a whimper. Suddenly, she looked up to the midwife with wide eyes.

"Quickly, get her to the birthing chair," commanded the midwife.

Darcy swiftly got her into the chair and stood beside her, his hand grasping Elizabeth's tightly. The midwife began barking orders and before he knew it, Elizabeth was bearing down, red-faced and sweating.

"One more time," said the midwife.

Darcy watched it all anxiously. Even though he had been through this twice before with Elizabeth, nothing quite prepared him for seeing his wife through this ordeal or for meeting his child for the first time. And judging by the grave faces of all around him, he wasn't the only one worried this time.

Elizabeth made a final grunt and slumped back in the chair. The midwife began congratulating her, telling her what a fine job she had done and what a beautiful girl she had delivered. Darcy stared at the baby in awe as the midwife cleaned her with a cloth and wrapped her in a blanket. She passed the babe to a relieved Jane and he watched his daughter go to her aunt, his eyes glued to the newest member of their family.

His attention was brought back to Elizabeth when she cried out.

"It is the afterbirth," said Kitty.

The midwife's hands were on her abdomen, pressing as he remembered her doing after the other births. He watched in horror as Elizabeth's face crumpled in pain and the midwife began to look worried. She pressed his wife's abdomen again, and Elizabeth leaned forward until she was nearly doubled over.

"That's it, Mrs. Darcy. Go on and push," said the midwife soothingly.

Jane, sensing something was wrong, passed the baby to Watson and hurried to Elizabeth's other side.

"Is it?" she asked.

"It is," said the midwife grimly.

She felt Elizabeth's stomach again, and pressed down while turning her hands clockwise. Elizabeth cried out and Darcy took a step forward, though he didn't know what he could do to protect her.

"Wait a moment. Don't push. Just breathe. I must turn her," said the midwife sternly.

Darcy looked around confused. Jane was holding Elizabeth's hand so tightly her knuckles were white. Kitty was watching her sister with wide eyes, her lips forming a silent prayer over and over again.

"What is going on? What do you mean, turn her?" he cried, not wishing to believe what his eyes were telling him was true.

"There is a second babe," said the midwife in clipped tones.

Elizabeth cried out again, panting quickly to prevent herself from pushing. The midwife continued the turning motion with her hands and finally said they needed to get her to her feet.

Darcy snapped into action, shaking off his fear and forcing all his focus onto his wife's care. He stood in front of Elizabeth and hooked his arms beneath hers, raising her to her feet. The midwife said soothing words to Elizabeth and asked her to move this way and that, insensible to his wife's exhaustion.

"Elizabeth," he said quietly.

She looked up with imploring eyes and he gathered his resolve. He could worry later. Right now, his wife needed him to be strong enough for both of them. "You can do this, my heart. You are not alone. I am here with you." She squeezed his hand, unable to speak for panting. "You are the strongest woman I know. If anyone can deliver two babes, it is you," he said confidently.

She nodded weakly but he saw determination in her eyes.

Finally, after several agonizing minutes, Elizabeth was able to whisper that she was desperate to push. Could she please bear down now?

"Now, Mrs. Darcy! Bear down!" cried the midwife.

Elizabeth instantly responded and before anyone knew what happened, there was a great gush and Elizabeth slumped back, Darcy's arms wrapped around her the only thing that kept her from falling to the floor.

"Is she all right?" asked Elizabeth weakly.

The babe had been whisked away to the far side of the room where the midwife was rubbing her with a soft cloth. Jane handed Elizabeth the first baby and she brought her to her breast, cooing at her new daughter.

"Oh! Look at her!" she whispered in exhausted wonder.

"She is beautiful, Lizzy," said Jane. "You did very well."

"You were right," said Elizabeth softly to her husband. "She is a girl."

Suddenly, there was a weak cry from the other side of the room and Elizabeth looked up tearfully. "Is she?" she couldn't finish the question, tears choking her voice.

"Your son is just fine, Mrs. Darcy, though a trifle unhappy at being born," said the midwife.

"My son?"

"A son?" cried Darcy.

"Aye," said the midwife. "'Tis rare. I've only seen it once before myself."

Darcy looked on in shock as she handed him the wrapped bundle and he brought the crying babe to his chest and held him tightly.

"You were right, Elizabeth. He is a boy," he said.

Elizabeth laughed and reached out a hand for her husband.

~

"What shall we call these two?" Elizabeth asked sleepily. She lay in bed, propped up on pillows and in a fresh nightgown, her babies sleeping peacefully next to her.

"I do not know about him, but this young lady should be called after her mother," said Fitzwilliam.

"You want to name her Elizabeth?" she asked, her voice slightly choked.

"Yes. I do."

She smiled and a tear escaped down her cheek. "Very well, she will be Elizabeth. I would like to ask Kitty to be godmother. She was a great help during the birth."

"Elizabeth Catherine," he said.

"Elizabeth Catherine Anne," she added.

He looked at her in surprise. "For my mother?"

She nodded. "It is only fitting, don't you think?"

He gave her a gentle smile and agreed.

"And what about our son?" she asked after a few minutes of quiet.

"We are running out of male relatives to Christen him for."

She chuckled, then pressed a hand to her abdomen and winced.

"I'm sorry, love. I forgot you shouldn't laugh just yet," he said apologetically.

She smiled wanly and took his hand. "I want to name him Fitzwilliam."

"What? Why?"

She almost laughed again but stopped herself. "Because you are his father. And it is quite natural to name a boy after his father." She shook her head in fond amusement.

"But they will call him Fitz. You know they will," he said seriously.

"Then we will call him William before they start. What say you?"

"Fitzwilliam and Elizabeth. The names do go well together," he said with a charming smile.

"Very well together," she said softly.

~

June 1831

"I don't like it," said Darcy as he paced in his study.
"Why not?" asked Elizabeth impatiently.
"She is too young."
"I was two years younger when I wed."
He shot her a glare that she chose to ignore.
"She is not yet twenty!" he cried, moving to lean on the edge of the desk.
"She will be twenty before the wedding." Elizabeth came closer and placed her hand on his arm. "She is determined. And you know how Violet can be. Once she has set her mind to something, there is no stopping her."
He sighed. "But do you really think he is worthy of her?"
"He is your cousin!"
"And I was never fond of his father. I do not like the idea of Violet living under his roof."
Elizabeth sighed. "That will hardly be necessary. We can allow them to stay with us whenever they like. Or she can live at Cressingdon. You know Robbie will deny her nothing. And do not forget she has her own estate. It is small, but very comfortable."
"What about when they are in town?"
She threw up her hands in exasperation. "They may stay with us at Darcy House. Or at Asheland House. I can allow them the run of Talbot House if they want it. It has been vacant for months now."
He looked down at the carpet. "This is an awful summer."
"I know," she said gently. "I do not like it either. Robbie will be one and twenty! I can hardly believe it." She looked out the window and blinked rapidly. "Do you

think he is ready for all that is about to land on his shoulders?"

Darcy put a hand on her back. "He is ready. Do not worry for him. He knows he may call on me or Charles or John if he needs any assistance."

She nodded, swallowing thickly. "And Violet will be well. Do not worry for her. Lord Cross is terribly in love with her. She shall manage him without any trouble. After all, she has been practicing on her brothers all these years."

Darcy snorted. "I know you are right," he finally said. Then, very quietly, "I shall miss her."

Elizabeth rubbed his back and rested her head on his shoulder. "As will I." After some moments, she said lightly, "Lizzy is only ten. And if she is to be believed, she will never marry and leave us."

"Good. She should stay forever," he said gruffly.

Elizabeth laughed. "If you continue to spoil her so, she just may."

~

Violent reined in her gelding when she reached the church and dismounted. She made her way through the churchyard and looked up at the towering oak stretching toward the spire and smiled in the sunlight.

"Hello, father," she said. She placed the wildflowers she had gathered on Robert's grave and touched the cold stone with an open palm. "Sorry I missed your birthday. Robbie promised me that he placed a flower for me."

She sat on the soft grass beside the stone and ran her fingers through the tuft. "I am to be married," she said. "Can you believe that? I will be the next Lady Matlock." She laughed nervously. "Mama says I will do well, but I am a little anxious about it. Lord Matlock is a... difficult man. I can't believe he and papa are cousins! But Cross isn't like his father. Uncle Fitzwilliam assures me that he takes after his mother. I think Uncle's approval has been a relief to papa. He tried not to show how worried he was, but he has never been good at dissembling."

She leaned back against the stone and stretched her legs out in front of her. "Alexander, that is Lord Cross's Christian name, has suggested we travel to the continent for a wedding tour. Mama thinks it would be lovely to go but she worries for my safety, of course. I think papa is terrified but he thinks I will stubbornly insist upon going if he says anything about it." She sighed. "I don't think they realize I've truly grown up."

She looked up through the oak's branches and closed her eyes, letting the sunlight dance across her skin as the leaves rustled in the breeze.

"I will marry from home—from Cressingdon. Pemberley is also home, of course, but Lizzy will marry from there one day. Robert has moved here permanently now. We are all here helping him to settle in. Mama insists he will always have a room at Pemberley, of course, but he thought he should live in his own home. Papa agreed and has helped him learn estate management. I imagine Robert will be good at it—you know how clever he is."

She plucked a blade of grass and tore tiny strips from it. "Poor Mama. I am marrying, Robert has moved, and Bennet is going to Cambridge. Henry and Richard are at Eton. It is only William and Lizzy home now. William ought to go to Eton, but he cannot bear to leave Lizzy. They have always been so close," she said thoughtfully. "I wonder what they will do when they are grown and she marries. Surely he cannot mean to follow her to her new home. Though I would not be terribly surprised if he did such a thing. He is a devoted boy. Mama says he takes after papa in that way." She smiled.

"Don't worry, mama has not forgotten you. I'm sure you've noticed her birthday visits. She says she visits then instead of the anniversary of your death because she would rather remember your life than that awful day."

She sighed, wishing she could remember her father better. All she truly remembered was a warm voice reading her stories. It was a comforting memory so she assumed it was her father, but she wasn't entirely sure. She couldn't even picture his face in her mind—she only knew the portraits painted of him.

"Uncle Alfred insists on telling stories of your childhood adventures nearly every time we see him. He is getting old now, but he promised he will be at my wedding in September. I plan to ask Jenny to stand up with me. I think it sweet that Aunt Jane stood up with mama and her daughter will stand up with me, though Robert says I am being overly sentimental." She huffed and looked heavenward.

"All his friends call him Asheland now. He didn't like it at first, but now he doesn't seem to mind. All *my* friends flirt terribly with him but he doesn't notice. Mama says he is like you in that way. You would laugh heartily to see it. Maria Rippen—Aunt Charlotte's daughter—is half in love with him. It is embarrassing! When he enters the room, she blushes and giggles and acts like a different person altogether. Robert doesn't notice, of course. Mama says men are not as astute about these matters as ladies are."

She heard an approaching rider and looked up. Seeing her brother, she stood and dusted off her skirt.

"I didn't know you were coming, Ben."

"I don't mean to disturb you if you aren't finished," he said hesitantly.

Violet smiled at her younger brother and shook her head. "I'm finished. I was just babbling at the end."

He smiled in that way that made him look like their mother as he approached her. Violet returned his smile, thinking it funny how he wasn't Mr. Darcy's natural son, but of her five brothers, Bennet acted the most like him.

She squeezed his hand. "I'll see you at the house," she said, and left him alone in the churchyard.

~

September 1836

"Why must we go all the way to Yorkshire?" whined Lizzy.

"Uncle Alfred is turning seventy years old! You can hardly expect him to travel to us!" cried Violet. She held up a hat. "Are you sure you want to take this?"

Lizzy snatched the hat from her older sister and placed it in the hatbox out of reach. Though she was nine years younger, Lizzy was nearly three inches taller than her sister, a fact she enjoyed reminding Violet of.

"Girls!" came a familiar voice from the sitting room. They cringed and Elizabeth entered with a dress in her arms. "It is like listening to Kitty and Lydia when they were fighting over ribbons," she said. "I will remind you that you will be sixteen next month, Little Lizzy, and you have two children, Violet!"

"Yes, mama," they chorused with eyes on the carpet.

"Now, we must finish packing before we dress for dinner. Your father insists we leave at first light and you know how he gets if everyone isn't ready when it's time to depart."

Violet shared a sly smile with her sister that Elizabeth pretended not to notice. She shook her head at them and went to check in with her sons.

Henry was completely packed and mortified that his mother would even ask him. He would be twenty in November. He didn't need his mother to ensure he packed properly. She asked him if he had remembered to pack Alfred's gift, and when he admitted he had not (while

335

trying to look proud and failing horribly), she gave him a knowing smile and told him that when he stopped forgetting things, she would stop asking him if he had everything ready.

He reluctantly joined her in a laugh and then decided to accompany her to his younger brothers' rooms. He shouldn't be the only one caught out by their mother.

Richard had, unsurprisingly, forgotten several things, even though his valet was doing most of the packing.

"I thought having a valet would make you more organized, not less," teased Henry.

"It might make me more so if he didn't pack away everything I needed while I still need it. I can't find what I am looking for and I have to dig it out of the trunk and it is all a hopeless mess."

Elizabeth smiled at their conversation. Richard was a perfect combination of herself and Darcy, in looks and personality. He was as fastidious as his father, but impulsive like his mother, and the combination led to some interesting debacles.

She shook her head and entered William's room. Her youngest son was sitting calmly in a chair, reading a book.

"Are you ready, dear?" she asked.

"Yes, mama. My trunks are packed and the stables will have Roman ready in the morning."

She nodded.

Henry came in behind her and exclaimed, "How is it that you are the youngest and yet you are ready first?"

"I am just more clever than you," said William nonchalantly.

Henry smirked and moved toward his brother. William had not yet reached his full height and was terribly thin. His brother Henry was easily five inches taller and a few stones heavier.

William scrambled from his chair and toward the door, preparing to run.

"Boys!" called Elizabeth. "Do I need to call your father?"

"No, mama," they said, hands twitching behind their backs.

She smiled and said she would leave them to their preparations and that she expected to see them on time for dinner that evening and ready to depart at first light the next day.

~

Alfred's birthday celebration was held at his family seat in Yorkshire. The Downing, Talbot, and Stanfield families were there en masse, and a few Cavendishes had made the journey. The Darcy family had become friendly with the Downings over the years and Kitty's husband's parents made the journey, as did Mrs. Bennet. Mr. Bennet was still alive, but he did not think a drive the length of England would be beneficial to a man so old that he had quit counting his age. He did, however, make his grandsons promise to come visit him soon.

Elizabeth was delighted to see everyone. The last time they had gathered like this had been for Violet's wedding five years ago. Now Violet had a three-year-old son and a lovely baby girl. Where had the time gone?

She moved through the drawing room, greeting family and friends, but not seeing the faces she most desired to see. Where were they? They had told her they would leave early and it was not so far that they shouldn't have arrived.

"Are you looking for Robert and Bennet?" asked Jane.

"Yes, you know me too well."

"They are with Charlie at the stables. Lord John has a new stallion they wanted to see."

Elizabeth squeezed her hand. "Thank you, Jane."

She made her way outside and found her sons, Bennet and Robert John, walking up the slope to the house with their cousin Charlie between them. Her heart gave a little lurch and she smiled at how handsome and healthy they looked. She knew it was right that Robert John was at Cressingdon, and right that he should invite Bennet to stay with him, but she missed her boys mightily.

"Mama!" said Bennet happily. He hurried up the slope and stopped in front of her, giving her a very correct bow and kissing her cheek.

"Come here, you darling boy," she cried as she pulled him to her. "Do not stand on ceremony with me."

He laughed and hugged his mother so tightly her feet came off the ground. She pulled back and held his face in her hands. "Are you well, love? Truly?"

"I am well, mama." He placed a hand over hers and looked into her eyes, assuring her he was truly healthy and in good spirits.

In Bennet's second year at Cambridge, he had contracted a horrible fever at the beginning of the holiday. He hadn't noticed how ill he truly was until the carriage was halfway to Pemberley. When he arrived, he was so sick he couldn't walk under his own power. A terrified Darcy and Robert had carried him into the house and Elizabeth had stayed by his bedside, praying and weeping and doing everything in her power to bring his fever down.

The physician had told her to prepare herself for the worst, the apothecary had said there was nothing he could do. Finally, after an eternity of poultices and tinctures and cool cloths applied to burning brows, his fever broke and he came back to her. Darcy later said that Bennet survived through his mother's will alone. She simply would not let him die.

She knew she had been a little anxious for him ever since, but a mother does not easily forget such a thing.

"I will stop fussing now," she said with a smile. "Charlie, you are looking very well!"

"Thank you, Aunt," he said with a sweet smile.

"Do I not look well, mother?" cried Robert playfully. She swatted his arm. "You look like a rascal."

He wrapped his arms around her in a crushing embrace, and just when she thought he would set her down, he spun her in a circle and quickly dropped her on her feet, an enormous smile on his face.

"Robert John Thomas Talbot!"

He laughed in response, as did his brother and cousin. Elizabeth finally joined them and asked the boys to escort her to the house.

~

The next morning, Robert and Darcy were riding, talking of estate matters and their family, when Robert became serious.

"Papa, may I ask you something?"

"Of course, son. You may ask me anything."

"How did you know you loved mama?"

Darcy looked at him with wide eyes. Robert looked back expectantly.

"I cannot fix on the time or the place. I was in the middle before I knew I had begun." He turned to see his son still looking keenly at him. "I had admired your mother as a friend; she was a good wife and mother, and had a lively mind. I had been friends with the earl and greatly respected him.

"When Elizabeth returned to Town after her mourning, we became friends. I had long thought she was the model of what I should look for in a woman, but I had found no one like her." He chuckled to himself. "I was quite foolish when I was younger."

"So you were friends that fell in love?" asked Robert skeptically.

"No. I was her friend and very much enamored of her, but she did not look as kindly on me. And she let me know it!" He laughed at the memory.

"But you won her over?"

"Eventually, yes, though I don't know if that is exactly how it happened. One day, I simply knew that I couldn't live without her. No woman would ever be as precious to me as she was. I was quite besotted," he said with a self-deprecating smile.

Robert grinned. "How long did you court her?"

"Oh, about six months, I think, perhaps a little less. But I had known her for years before that. Remember that I have been friends with Bingley since we were in Cambridge. I had known her through their family since the year eleven."

They rode on in silence, Robert wearing an uncharacteristically pensive expression.

"Is there someone you are thinking of courting?" Darcy asked delicately.

"Perhaps. But," Robert hesitated, "I want to be sure. I would not want to hurt her, or raise her expectations, if it is not right in the end."

"That is honorable."

"But how shall I know it is right if I do not spend time with her? But how can I spend time with her without raising expectations?" He was clearly frustrated.

"That is a valid point. What you need is a mediator."

"A mediator?"

"Yes. Someone who can create situations where you may see each other but where it is not obvious you are courting so you can get to know one another without expectations."

Robert looked thoughtful.

"The Gardiners did it for your parents, and Elizabeth did it for your Aunt Kitty and my cousin Michael."

Robert was mentally categorizing his family members in his mind, deciding who would be most helpful in such a delicate situation. He could not ask Violet. She would think the whole thing hilarious and never let him hear the end of it. He had done the same to her when she was being courted, but he chose not to remember that at the moment.

"May I ask who the lady is?" Darcy asked.

Robert sighed and decided it would be best to be honest. His parents would figure it out soon enough.

"It is Isabel Stanhope."

"Georgie's daughter?" Darcy exclaimed in surprise.

"Do you think it a very bad idea?"

Darcy searched for words for a moment. "I think she is very sweet girl. But I am far from objective—she is my niece."

"Yes, I know. But I have never really thought of her as a cousin. Not because we are not truly related, but she was only a baby when I went away to school, and I rarely saw her when I came home."

"Yes, we often went to Cressingdon on your school holidays," Darcy said thoughtfully. "I can see why you wouldn't think of her as a cousin, but many cousins do marry."

Robert shuddered. "I could never marry Jenny or Arabella or Elinor. They are like sisters to me."

"Yes, well, they were often in the same house with you. You have grown up together. Especially Jane's daughters. We see the Bingleys more than anyone else."

"Even Amelia Goulding is too familiar, though we see them less. She smiles just like mama. That would be odd in certain… situations."

Darcy covered a laugh with a cough and said, "Yes, I certainly see why you wouldn't want that. I wouldn't be able to marry a cousin either. Lady Catherine wished me to marry Anne, but I could never do it. Not for your reasons, but I could never look at her as a man should look at his wife."

"Exactly!" cried Robert. "But I do not know about Isabel. We spent a great deal of time together in Town last Season, and I enjoyed her company, but..."

"You are not sure if you love her or wish to spend your life with her."

"Yes. Thank you for understanding. I know it must be awkward for you."

"Not at all. I am pleased you would come to me with such questions. It is better than going to your Uncle John."

Robert laughed. "I don't even want to imagine what he would say!"

"Perhaps your mother can invite Isabel to spend a month with us. It would not be unusual for my niece to be in my home, and you could visit as well. It would give you an opportunity to become better acquainted with each other. I would not like to see either of you do anything hasty."

Robert nodded. "That sounds a good plan. Thank you, papa."

~

Darcy told Elizabeth about his conversation with Robert, and she quickly invited her niece Isabel, who had arrived that afternoon with her parents, to come home with them after the party. She could stay at Pemberley for a month if Georgiana could spare her.

Isabel accepted the invitation and went to her mother, who then went to Elizabeth. Georgiana told Elizabeth she believed Isabel had developed romantic feelings for Robert, and if he was not interested in her, it would be best for her not to go to Pemberley only to have her hopes dashed. Elizabeth was able to allay her sister's fears and convince her to give the young couple some time, away from the prying eyes of society, to get to know one another better.

What was strange about a niece visiting her uncle and aunt in her mother's childhood home? And what could be more natural than Elizabeth's son visiting her at that same home? There was nothing indecorous and no suspicions would be raised unless the couple was very indiscreet. And, well, then the issue would be decided, wouldn't it?

Georgiana agreed with Elizabeth's logic and prepared to send her daughter to Pemberley.

~

"Lizzy, are you matchmaking?" asked Lydia with a sly smile when she heard of the impending visit.

"I am doing no such thing!" retorted Elizabeth. "I am merely giving them an opportunity to get to know one another."

Lydia nodded. "Of course you are. How magnanimous of you." She took a sip of tea and said, "Just be mindful of my goddaughter. She is a sweet girl. If he throws her over, she might never recover."

"I think you are exaggerating at least a little. She is not a wilting flower."

"No, she is not. But she is young."

"Yes, she is," agreed Elizabeth. "That is part of why I want to give them this time. I would hate for her to make a rash decision in her youth and regret it in a few years."

Lydia made a noise of agreement and took another cake from the plate.

To everyone's surprise, Lydia had married Alfred's younger son, Lord George Downing. She had managed to wait to become engaged until she was nearly four and twenty and her dowry was more than twenty-three thousand pounds. She was very proud of that fact, and that she was the oldest of her sisters to wed.

George had inherited one of his father's smaller estates only thirty miles from Cressingdon; the distance made it easy to see her family whenever they were in Nottinghamshire. She confessed to her sisters on the eve of her wedding that she had always had a fondness for the name George. Elizabeth told her that she hoped her choice of husband was based on more substantial characteristics than his name. An agreeable name would be cold comfort in an unhappy union. Lydia had assured her that she was deliriously happy and could not wait to be wed.

"Perhaps we will come to Pemberley as well," said Lydia with a mischievous smile.

"No, you will not. They need peace and privacy. We will not treat them like a performance on a stage."

"Really, Lizzy, you are becoming tiresome in your old age."

Elizabeth glared at her and Lydia smirked and took another sip of her tea. She squealed in surprise when a small biscuit landed in her cup and splashed tea over her dress. She looked up at her sister with pursed lips.

Elizabeth looked back with an innocent expression.

~

A month later, when they were all settled in at Pemberley, Elizabeth went to find Darcy in his study.

"What brings you to see me, my dear?" he asked with a smile.

She sat on the chair by the fireplace and he came to join her.

"I think Robert is in love," she said quietly, her eyes on the dancing flames.

"Truly?"

"Yes. I have never seen him like this before. He is enamored of your shy, sweet, blue-eyed niece," she said with a sad smile.

"Do you approve of the match?"

"Of course. They are perfect for each other."

Darcy nodded. "The Stanhopes are a good family. Robert is friendly with her brothers. I see no reason to worry."

"He is my son. I shall always worry," she replied.

He laughed. "Come here, Elizabeth." He pulled her arm until she was sitting in his lap, her head leaning against his. "All will be well, my love."

"How do you know?"

"He is a good man and she is a kind woman. But beyond that, they have had excellent examples of loving, respectful unions to follow."

"Is that how you would describe us? As loving and respectful?" she asked playfully.

"Yes. Wouldn't you?"

"I would also say passionate. And devoted. And utterly perfect for each other in every way."

"We are certainly that," he said in hushed tones as he began to nibble on her neck.

"Yes, we certainly are," she breathed.

THE END

On Equal Ground

Elizabeth Adams

ABOUT THE AUTHOR

Elizabeth Adams is a book-loving, tango-dancing, Austen enthusiast. She loves old houses and thinks birthdays should be celebrated with trips—as should most occasions. She can often be found by a sunny window with a cup of hot tea and a book in her hand.

She writes romantic comedy and comedic tragedy in both historic and modern settings.

You can find more information, short stories, and outtakes at EAdamswrites.com

Modern Fiction

Green Card
Ship to Shore

Historical Fiction

The Houseguest
Unwilling
Meryton Vignettes, Tales of Pride and Prejudice
On Equal Ground
The 26th of November